"Michael Eberhardt makes a strong debut in *Body of a Crime*—one that gives his readers memorable characters and an ending that is certain to surprise. It will leave John Grisham looking anxiously over his shoulder."
 —William Heffernan, author of *Winter's Gold*

"Rich and complex, *Body of a Crime* is a high-stakes, high-tension thriller from the first page to the surprising end."
 —Vincent T. Bugliosi,
 author of *And the Sea Will Tell*

"Very compelling. Mr. Eberhardt obviously knows his stuff." —*Washington Times*

"An exciting whodunit and entertaining legal thriller."
 —Robert K. Tanenbaum,
 author of *Reckless Endangerment*

"A ride you will not want to get off."
 —*New York Law Journal*

"No finer courtroom drama to be read anywhere!"
 —Clive Cussler, author of *Flood Tide*

WITNESS FOR THE DEFENSE

Michael C. Eberhardt

AN ONYX BOOK

ONYX
Published by the Penguin Group
Penguin Putnam Inc., 375 Hudson Street,
New York, New York 10014, U.S.A.
Penguin Books Ltd, 27 Wrights Lane,
London W8 5TZ, England
Penguin Books Australia Ltd,
Ringwood, Victoria, Australia
Penguin Books Canada Ltd, 10 Alcorn Avenue,
Toronto, Ontario, Canada M4V 3B2
Penguin Books (N.Z.) Ltd, 182–190 Wairau Road,
Auckland 10, New Zealand

Penguin Books Ltd, Registered Offices:
Harmondsworth, Middlesex, England

First published by Onyx, an imprint of Dutton NAL,
a member of Penguin Putnam Inc.

First Printing, December, 1998
10 9 8 7 6 5 4 3 2 1

PUBLISHER'S NOTE
This is a work of fiction. Names, characters, places, and incidents either are
the product of the author's imagination or are used fictitiously, and any
resemblance to actual persons, living or dead, events, or locales is entirely
coincidental.

ACKNOWLEDGMENTS

I wish to express my sincere appreciation to Don Hanson, Eric Wilinski, John Paine, Avrum Harris, Susan Wilkerson, and The Honorable Kenneth Freeman for their wisdom and technical expertise.

A special thanks to Jennifer Robinson and Edward Stackler for their expert editorial guidance.

A tip of the hat to my son Todd, for helping me ripen this story. His input was invaluable.

Profound and heartfelt appreciation to my agent and friend, Peter Miller. His hard work, advice, and professional guidance will always be appreciated and remembered.

For her keen sense of storytelling and her unwavering faith in both me and my work, a special thank-you to my editor, Michaela Hamilton.

It is the right of a lawyer to undertake the defense of a person accused of a crime, regardless of his personal opinion as to the guilt of the accused; otherwise innocent persons, victims only of suspicious circumstances, might be denied proper defense. Having undertaken such defense, the lawyer is bound, by all fair and honorable means, to present every defense that the law of the land permits, to the end that no person may be deprived of life or liberty, but by due process of law.

—CANON V
Canons of Professional Ethics
of The American Bar Association

Chapter 1

San Francisco in late September should be bottled and sold at Bloomingdale's. The summer fog gives way to crystal-clear autumn air, and blinding sunlight ricochets off the glass high-rises downtown. The damp summer winds suddenly cease, and a balmy warmth envelops the city. Everything is fresh; anything seems possible.

But the San Francisco I know best is one part mahogany-paneled walls and shiny marbled hallways of the city courts, and one part grime and crime encased in the icy steel bars and dirty concrete floors of its jails.

I was sitting in the dank attorney interview room of the courthouse lockup, waiting to question a witness while the officers unloaded the twelve-thirty bus from central jail. I'd been interviewing inmates daily for the last nine years, and had never gotten used to the conditions of the place. The smell of urine was bad enough, but that was nothing compared to the snot-smeared glass between me and my client. And if that failed to turn my stomach, there was the gang logo graffiti written across the inmates' walls—using human excrement as ink.

And I felt tired—dead tired.

The day before, I had joined the ranks of the unmarried men of the world when my divorce to Marlene became final. In California it's called irreconcilable differences. But in our case there was nothing irreconcilable about it. It was that neither of us even tried. We both had all-consuming careers, and the effort it would have taken to save our marriage seemed more than we had in us to expend.

My sleepless night began when the clock struck midnight, making it official. My head swam for most of the night with regrets and recriminations. When I awoke, I found myself reaching for Marlene, more than a year after our separation.

After I showered, I looked in the mirror. The trauma of the divorce had taken its toll. My muscular chest looked like vanilla pudding, my dark hair framed in gray. And if that wasn't enough to make me want to go back to bed and hide, when I stepped on the scale, I weighed in at only one-fifty-nine, down another two pounds.

I tried to focus on the task at hand. In a few minutes, I had to interview Bobby Miles, a potential defense witness, in the Salvador Martinez murder case. Four months earlier, Martinez and one of his buddies were charged with the drive-by shooting of Miguel Flores and his six-year-old sister, Amanda. The two had been shot in their front yard, while Miguel had been walking from the house to his car. Amanda had been hit in the head by several stray shotgun pellets meant for her brother. There was only one witness to the shooting, a twenty-two-year-old buddy of Flores, Jesus Aragon. He had not only identified the car and its license number, but had also been able to convincingly pick both the driver and shooter out of a lineup the following day.

I had received an emergency telephone call from Martinez late the previous afternoon. A fellow inmate, he said, had been present at the shooting; he had seen the whole thing, and would testify to the fact that neither Martinez nor his codefendant was responsible. Oh, sure, I thought. And I'm tired because I slept with Sharon Stone last night.

Normally, I wouldn't waste my time talking to someone a client had primed to lie for him, but this interview wasn't really about trying to help a client. It was about protecting my rear end. This was a special-circumstance murder, one which I knew would be automatically appealed after conviction. When Martinez's guilty verdict went up on appeal, the first thing the appellate court would look for would be attorney incompetence—and the failure to interview a potential defense witness would be number one on their list. As much as I hated the idea, I had to go through the motions and see what this guy had to say. Later, I would inform Martinez that his witness was a liar, and that in my opinion he should take the D.A.'s latest offer.

Finally, one of the jailers opened the steel door. Seconds later, a short, slightly built blond kid came shuffling in. His feet were shackled, forcing him to take mini steps. He sat on the wooden stool facing mine on the other side of the glass partition.

I nodded my thanks to the deputy and sat forward to get a good look at the young man. His head was lowered as he stared at the counter in front of him. I was surprised by his physical appearance. Though I knew he had to be older, he didn't look a day over sixteen. His face was as smooth as a baby's and nearly as pale. His hands were slight and slender, almost artistic. Even his brooding facial expression didn't seem to detract from his overall good looks, a quality that would certainly not be his ally in this hellhole. I would have felt more comfortable attacking some tattooed, slack-jawed rapist than this child.

"Are you Bobby Miles?" I asked.

Without raising his head, he nodded in response.

"Can I call you Bobby?" It was disconcerting to call someone half my age by his last name. But then, I was in a place where all they ever used was last names.

Again, the boy nodded his head. This kid would do great in front of a jury, I thought wryly. Heck of a strong witness.

"Bobby, I represent Salvador Martinez. His trial starts tomorrow, and he informed me you might know something about his case."

"Yeah," the kid said, barely audible.

At least now I knew he could talk. But what was his story? He obviously wasn't one of Martinez's gangbanging buddies.

"Why don't you tell me what you know?" I couldn't lead him. If, by some slim chance, he ever did end up testifying for Martinez, I had to be sure he was telling the truth.

"Where do you want me to start?" he said, lifting his head and looking at me for the first time.

His face was red and puffy and smudged with dirt. His eyes were dark and swollen, like he'd been crying. "What the hell are you doing in this place?" I wanted to ask. But I had long ago learned not to get involved with someone else's client. I could barely manage my own caseload.

"First of all, how old are you?"

"Eighteen last month," he said. He tried to wipe his eyes with his hands, but the chains connected to his waist and feet made it impossible.

"How long have you been in here?"

"I was arrested two days ago for selling some weed to my friends."

"How much?"

"Three ounces."

I shook my head. No big deal, I thought. "And how long have you known my client?"

"I don't," he said. "I've never seen him."

"Then why do you think you can help him?"

"Because I saw it happen," the kid said nervously. "I was there."

I put on a hard skeptical face. "If you were, why didn't you come forward sooner?"

"Because I didn't want to get involved in any gang shit."

"Why do you think the shooting had something to do with gang activity?"

"A car doesn't just pull up in front of a house in that area and start blasting a shotgun unless that's exactly what it is."

I knew the shooting had occurred south of downtown San Francisco in the outer Mission district. The neighborhood used to be mostly Italian and Irish, but since the seventies the influx of Central and South American immigrants had changed the community into a Spanish-speaking cultural enclave. Then came the drug cartels and gangs and the tentacles of the Mexican Mafia, which turned the streets ever more dangerous, and gave rise to the Salvador Martinezes of the world.

"How did you happen to be in the area in the first place?"

"I live a couple blocks over."

"You live there?" He'd caught me off guard. "Where?"

"Well, I don't really live there. I was staying with my grandmother. I live with my parents in San Jose, but they dump me off there almost every weekend while they go off to Reno."

"Why? Aren't you old enough to stay home alone?"

"Oh, I'm old enough," he said, lowering his head. "But they don't trust me."

"What do you mean?"

"I threw a couple of parties."

I remembered what it was like to be his age. "And they got out of hand," I interjected.

"A little."

"Where does your grandmother live?"

"A couple blocks over from the shooting. She's lived there for twenty, thirty years. She says it used to be a pretty nice place. Until . . ."

"Until the gangs took over?"

"Yeah. My grandma says Capp Street used to be one of the quietest streets in the city."

Despite my pessimism, I started to get the feeling this kid might really know something. I even began to feel guilty that I had begun the interview with such a lousy attitude.

"What was the name of the street where the shooting occurred?"

"Minnah," he said confidently.

"And what were you doing on Minnah at the time?"

"Taking a walk."

The kid had me convinced he had a good reason to be in the area. But there was no way he would be walking in that neighborhood after dark.

He must have seen my look of disappointment. "I can't stay in her house every minute," he said. "My grandma is really good to me, but I can only take her for so long. Then I have to go out for a while."

"Isn't that a little dangerous for someone like you?"

"Like me?"

"You know . . . a young white male taking a stroll in one of the most gang-ridden areas in the city?"

"I can handle it," he said, not realizing how much his puffy eyes and the dried-up tear marks betrayed his machismo attitude.

"Do you belong to a gang?"

The kid smiled for the first time. "Are you kidding? All the gangs around there are Latino. No way."

"Then who were you with when you took this walk on Minnah?"

"I was by myself."

"I'm not buying it, Bobby," I said placing my pen on the pad. "I don't think an eighteen-year-old white kid would be out alone in that neighborhood . . . especially after dark."

"Well, I was."

His pouty look hardly convinced me. "Then tell me what happened next?"

"Well, I saw this gray primered Cadillac cruising slowly down the street past me."

"And where were you at the time?"

"Walking toward the house."

"The house where the shots were fired?"

"Yeah, I was about five or six houses down, walking toward it."

"Go ahead."

"This gray car cruises past me, then drives to the end of the block and turns around. It stops in front of a house where this guy is walking out his front door. . . ." Here he stopped for a moment, looking down at his chained hands.

"Then what happened?"

He looked up at me. "All of a sudden I heard what sounded like two shotgun blasts and the car takes off and races past me."

"Two shotgun blasts?"

Bobby hesitated.

"Did you hear my question?" I asked.

"There were two people killed, wasn't there?"

"You tell me."

He lowered his eyes again. "I think I heard two blasts."

"You think, or you know?"

"There were two," he said and shrugged his shoulders. "I wasn't counting."

No, you probably weren't, I thought to myself. Because you weren't there. There were two dead bodies; most people would assume there were two blasts. Except in this case the evidence confirmed there had been only one. The shotgun pellets that hadn't hit the boy had somehow managed to find their way to his sister's face.

"And after the car sped away, did you see if anyone had been hit?"

"All I saw was two bodies lying on the grass."

"And then what did you do?"

"I took off running. I ran to my grandmother's house."

"At either time—when the car cruised slowly past you the first time, or when it sped past you after the shooting—were you able to see who was in it?"

"I remember three black guys. Two in the front and one in the back. The guy that shot them was in the backseat."

"And could you identify any of them if you were to see them again?"

"I don't think so. I wasn't paying much attention until the shooting. Then it all happened so fast I didn't have time."

"But you're sure they were black?"

"Positive."

"And you had never seen any of them before."

"Never."

"Or the car?"

"No."

Sighing deeply, I sat back. "You know what, Bobby?"

"What?" he said, looking at me, a hint of desperation in his eyes.

"You're lying."

"What do you mean, I'm lying? I'm telling you the truth. I saw it. Just because I didn't stick around . . ."

"You didn't stick around," I said wearily, "because you weren't there to begin with."

"But you have to believe me."

"Why?"

"Because it's the truth."

"Then tell me, Bobby, what did the house look like? The one where they were shot?"

Again, the kid hesitated and lowered his head. But this time his hands were formed into fists.

"Tell me anything about the house," I persisted. "The color. Anything."

His voice rose. "I don't remember. But I'm telling you, I was staying just a couple of blocks over."

"And I don't doubt that for a second. What I do doubt is that you were out taking a walk."

"You don't know what I would or wouldn't do."

"No, but if I feel this way, a jury will, too. You'd better tell Martinez to prime you a little better next time."

"What are you talking about?"

"There was only one shotgun blast, Bobby. Not two."

"So?" he whined. "I already told you, I wasn't

counting. I thought there was two, but it all happened so fast; there may have only been one. I can testify there was only one. Anything you want."

"Wouldn't work."

"Please believe me," he said, starting to cry.

"Why?" I leaned closer to the glass partition. "Is it because of what Martinez may do to you if I don't?"

By now tears were running freely down his face. "You don't know what they'll do to me," he whimpered. "Please help me. I'll testify to whatever you want. Just tell me what to say. Attorneys do it all the time."

"Maybe some do. But not this one."

The young man didn't respond. I watched as he began to shake uncontrollably. I knew exactly what was going on here; it wasn't the first time I'd seen it. Most urban California jails have an inmate population of eighty percent minorities, and San Francisco's was no different. When a young white kid is arrested, he's in for quite a shock. For the first time in his life, he's the minority. Sometimes he is the only white in his cell block. Unless he manages to get either the Chicanos, the blacks, or the Asians to take him under their wing, he is fair game for all. Obviously, Martinez's group had been willing to help the kid—and this was their price.

"My client promised to help you if you did him this favor. Am I correct?"

"Listen, man," his voice lowered to a shaky whisper, "they will *kill* me in here."

I didn't know what to say. I felt sorry for him. He might have broken the law, but that shouldn't mean he had to face what this place had in store for him. More than likely, he would survive his ordeal. But I wouldn't be able to convince him of that. Not now. Not when he could become some slimeball's punching bag—or worse yet, wife—as soon as he walked out of the room.

"I'm sorry, Bobby. I wish you could get on the stand and tell the lie of the century." The kid swiveled on his stool, turning away from me. I threw my pen and yellow pad into my briefcase, snapped it shut, and stood up. "But frankly, you're not that good a liar."

Chapter 2

San Francisco County Courthouse is an aging gray stone structure, built in the aftermath of the 1906 earthquake. The elegance of the wood paneling surrounding the long hallways and the magnificence of the carved courtroom doors fail to mask an ever pervasive odor. It is faint, and for years I couldn't identify it. Then one day the light went on. It was the scent of fear. The smell of the human animal being stalked. The benches along the corridor were peppered with the hunted. Eyes wide as they awaited their turn. The same eyes that often looked to me to save them from their hunter, the criminal justice system.

Division Three's spectator section was lined with churchlike pews filled with a mixture of bored reporters, retirees, and the worried family members and friends of the day's featured performers.

Stage whispers and furtive conversations echoed around the room. I slipped inside the gate at the bar, smiled weakly at the bailiff, and sat in one of several wooden chairs on the bench side of the railing. Judge Sherman Kellogg was peering down at me over his wire-rimmed glasses, which were perched precariously on his red bulbous nose. Even though he was presiding over a preliminary hearing in progress, he managed to find the time to acknowledge my presence with a scowl. As he well knew, I was supposed to be there at one-thirty, and it was after two. But knowing Kellogg, he'd probably been late taking the bench anyway. He'd no doubt gulped down several Tanquerays at his favorite watering hole, until his bailiff found him and managed to drag him away.

"You look like hell," Randy Rogers whispered, leaning into me from the seat to my left. Randy was one of the most successful criminal defense attorneys in the county. He was wearing a two-thousand-dollar Armani suit, accented with a red carnation.

"And that's a hell of a good-looking carnation you're wearing today, Mr. Rogers," I said. "I was wearing a nice yellow rose this morning, but I must have lost it in lockup. Just as well. It really didn't go with my jacket anyway." I lowered my voice conspiratorially. "Off the rack, you know."

"Really funny, Dobbs." Randy smirked. "I meant you look like you haven't slept in days."

"Let's just say I've had a better night's sleep."

"Then you should fit right in with Kellogg," he said, nodding toward the judge. "He not only looks half asleep, but he's also slurring his words."

"So what else is new," I said and turned to survey the courtroom. There wasn't a seat to be had in the entire spectator section. Many, including some reporters, were forced to stand in the back of the room.

"Why all the press? They arrest O.J. again?"

"James Chandler's prelim," Randy said, as if that was something I should have already known.

"Chandler?" I really didn't care, but I was trying to take my mind off Bobby Miles and the terrible look of fear in his eyes.

"It's been on TV and in all the papers," Randy said out of the corner of his mouth. "He's the president of Chandler Industries. You must have heard of him. He owns half the damn shopping centers around here."

"Sure," I whispered, not having the foggiest. "What's the charge?"

"Murder. Killed his only child."

"How old?"

"Six months. Can you believe it?"

"You work in this armpit of the world long enough, nothing surprises you," I said.

In front of us, Jerry Lipton, Division Three's deputy D.A., was questioning a patrol cop. He was establishing that the officer found fresh blood in the baby's crib.

"I hope they fry the bastard," Randy muttered.

I chuckled to myself. It always amazed me how most defense attorneys—and I was no exception—prejudged every other attorney's case, yet got very indignant when the press or anyone else did the same thing to one of theirs.

"Well," I said, "it sounds like Mr. Chandler has a lot of explaining to do. . . ."

Suddenly we both stopped talking. Our attention was arrested by a beautiful pair of legs passing directly in front of us on their way to the court clerk.

I slowly surveyed the rest of her. She was small, but not fragile. Slim, yet perfectly shaped. The lighting in the courtroom seemed to center on her to the exclusion of all others, adding golden highlights to her shoulder-length hair. She appeared to be in her late twenties, with a world-disarming smile that she managed to flash for the old goat on the bench.

When she turned to look for a seat, I instantly returned to earth. She was Sarah Harris, the daughter of retired Superior Court Judge Avery Harris. I had the misfortune of being assigned to his courtroom immediately upon being hired by the public defender's office. Avery Harris was arrogant and gave no one, especially the lowly public defenders, any quarter. Always on the attack, he viewed me as nothing more than a minor nuisance the law forced him to tolerate before he could send one of my clients off to prison—whether they deserved it or not. One of the happiest days of my life was when he left the bench.

As Sarah walked to an empty seat several chairs to my right, she gave me a big smile. Before she sat, she paused, waiting for me to return it. I didn't.

Randy nudged me with his elbow. "Who the hell's that?"

"Sarah Harris."

"Of course. I had heard she was a knockout."

"Don't let her looks fool you. After all, she is Judge Harris's daughter."

"I thought she was an investigator for the State Bar," Randy said as he continued to eye her. "I wonder why she's here."

"No idea." I glanced at my watch. It was getting late, and I still had to break the news to Martinez that I wasn't going to use the kid's testimony. I knew he wouldn't be thrilled with my decision, and I wanted to get it over with.

"You in a hurry?" Randy asked.

"I get tired of all this hurry-up-and-wait crap," I said anxiously. "All I have is one lousy arraignment."

"What's the charge?"

"Statutory rape."

"But I thought you were handling most of the death penalty cases for your office."

"Normally," I said. "But I requested this one specifically. Change of pace."

"Why? Stat rapes are a dime a dozen."

"Not when the defendant is a female grade-school teacher accused of having sex with her seventeen-year-old neighbor."

"A female accused of stat rape. . . . Never heard of that before."

"Somehow the boy's father found out and reported it to the cops. The D.A. is asking for fifty thousand bail."

"Well"—Randy smiled—"have to keep those rabid child molesters off the streets."

In front of us, the prelim was winding down.

"We have no affirmative defense," the defense attorney said, after which Kellogg sat up and shook his head violently like he'd been asleep. It was time for him to make a ruling; predictably, he bound Chandler over to Superior Court for trial.

Finally, the day's custody arraignments were escorted into the jury box for their two or three minutes in court. I wasn't surprised when I saw Bobby Miles at the end. He caught my eye and gave me a scared half smile. Seated next to him was my client, Janice Cappell.

"Is that your vicious rapist?" Randy said, nodding toward Cappell. She was a tall young woman with cropped black hair, dressed in a county-issued blue denim dress.

"That's her."

Kellogg pounded his gavel, waiting for silence while most of the reporters filed out of the courtroom.

"If you're in a big hurry," I said to Randy, "you can forget it." I nodded toward Harris. "Five bucks Blondie gets priority."

"Are you done with your little gab session?" Kellogg barked, scowling at me. "If you are, maybe we can all get out of here on time."

Randy jumped to his feet. "I'm ready, Your Honor."

"In a moment, Mr. Rogers." Kellogg looked at Sarah. "How about you, Counselor?"

She stood and scanned the courtroom behind her, then turned back to Kellogg. "Thank you," she said politely. "I'm Sarah Harris, and I'm appearing on behalf of Peter Jessup. I would appreciate the court placing his matter on second call. Mr. Jessup is out of custody, and I am expecting him at any moment."

"Isn't he the attorney who embezzled his client's funds?" Kellogg asked.

Now, there's an impartial judge for you, I thought. But I had come to expect no less from Kellogg.

"I believe what the court is referring to are only charges. My client will be entering a not-guilty plea."

That was the Sarah Harris I remembered. Like her father, she didn't appear to give anyone an inch. I had to admit though, her overly confident attitude served her well in court: She gave every appearance of being a good lawyer.

"Of course," Kellogg oozed. "Well, you just let us know when your client arrives."

I stood, but pointedly ignoring me, Kellogg turned to Randy.

"And what brings you to my humble little court-room?" he asked.

Typical Kellogg. A big-name lawyer and his two-thousand-dollar suit got instant respect.

"The Tomlinson arraignment and bail motion," Randy answered.

"No bail, huh," the judge grunted. "Mr. Lipton, are you prepared for Mr. Rogers's bail motion?"

"Your Honor," the D.A. replied as he lifted his pants over his expanding belly, "the Tomlinson matter has been specially assigned to another member of our office, Mr. Kroft. If your clerk will call him, I know he strongly opposes bail."

Lipton glanced at me. "However, I am ready on Mr. Dobbs's case," he said, like I was an after-thought. "And I believe he is also requesting a bail reduction."

"Just one moment," Kellogg said to Lipton and then turned back to Randy. "I apologize for you having to wait, Mr. Rogers. But I'll make sure Mr. Kroft is up here momentarily. In the meantime, we will handle Mr. Dobbs's case."

I stepped forward, trying my best not to smile. Randy wasn't as high on Kellogg's pecking order as he might have hoped. If he'd been some out-of-town powerhouse, Kellogg would have had the A.D.A. up there in a matter of seconds.

"Before we set a prelim date, Mr. Dobbs," Kellogg said, turning to give my client the once-over, "you also want to be heard as to bail?"

Normally, Kellogg would be gawking at someone half as good-looking as my client. But with her lack of sleep, wrinkled denim dress, and unkempt hair, she didn't get more than his parting glance.

"I would," I said.

Kellogg waved at me to proceed.

"Your Honor, Miss Cappell has been a resident of San Francisco County for over fifteen years. She has been employed as a grade school teacher for six of those years and has had no prior contact with the criminal justice system. I am requesting she be released on her own recognizance."

"And how do you feel about that?" Kellogg asked Lipton, but not before he smiled at Sarah, again.

"We would strongly oppose the defendant being released OR," Lipton said, glancing over his shoulder to see whom Kellogg was smiling at. "She lives next door to the victim, and we are afraid she might try to continue her aberrant behavior."

"Aberrant behavior!" I said, more than a little

too loudly. "My client is being charged with statutory rape. In the realm of things, I would hardly characterize such behavior, even if she is guilty, as aberrant."

"Your Honor," Lipton continued, "our investigation is ongoing. We have information that the listed victim may not be the only one."

It was absurd. He was implying that my grade school teacher was some kind of *serial statutory rapist*. I couldn't believe it. And the sound of Randy chuckling behind me sure didn't help. I tried to gather my thoughts.

"If Mr. Lipton has other victims," I said, glaring at the stocky D.A., "then tell him to file additional charges. Otherwise, he should be instructed to limit his argument to the charges before the court and not baseless rumors."

Lipton didn't miss a beat. "All we are asking for is fifty thousand, which is exactly what the bail schedule calls for. If we do file additional counts, Mr. Dobbs can rest assured we will be requesting additional bail."

I looked up at Kellogg, hoping to see that he shared my opinion. Unfortunately, he was still staring at Sarah. I was sure he hadn't heard a thing either one of us had been saying. Clenching my teeth, I moved a few steps to my right to block his view.

Oblivious to what was really happening, Lipton went on. "Additionally, since Miss Cappell is a school teacher and is therefore around minors on a daily basis, I would request that as a condition of bail, the court restrain the defendant from teaching until this matter is resolved."

I slammed the palm of my hand on the counsel table. "That's ridiculous. This court cannot take away my client's ability to earn a living!"

Kellogg sat forward and propped his elbows on the bench. His eyes were darting back and forth between me and Lipton. If my hand slap had done nothing lese, at least it got his attention.

I took a deep breath. "Your Honor," I continued, a bit apologetically, "my client has been a teacher for over six years. To take that away from her would be disastrous. She is as ideal a candidate for an OR release as I have ever seen."

"But rape is a serious charge, Mr. Dobbs, and if you have nothing more to add, I will have to go along with Mr. Lipton's request."

"Rape!" I shouted. "What are you talking about? The charge isn't rape. Read the complaint and you'll see it's statutory rape. Maybe if you would take the time to read the penal code, you'd see that means the minor consented."

Kellogg's mouth dropped. He sat motionless, paralyzed, glaring at me. Then his attention was drawn to the few reporters who still remained in the front row, their pens poised. I looked over at the bailiff, who was waiting for the judge to just say the word. It was the OK Corral, and I was outgunned. Kellogg's face turned a bright red. Except for the creaking of the bailiff's leather holster, the courtroom was totally silent. Then Kellogg bellowed, "I'll see you and Mr. Lipton in my chambers."

I had no idea what he had in store for me. But as I followed Lipton from the courtroom, I shot a parting glance at my client. She had a look of total disbelief. I knew she had to be wondering who in the hell was the nut-case she had for a lawyer.

Kellogg slumped in his maroon wing back chair and took a deep breath. Like his courtroom, Kellogg's chamber was old and musty. The smell of wood, damp and on the verge of rotting, filled the air. Rows and rows of dusty law books lined the mahogany shelves behind his prodigious desk, which served as a natural barrier between the two of us. I was sitting, with Lipton to my left, on the edge of my chair.

"I hope you are not inferring, Mr. Dobbs, that I don't know what I am doing."

The judge wasn't slurring his words anymore. Amazing what a little adrenaline will do.

"Your Honor, I'm sorry if I may have said anything out of order. But not only is my client's freedom at stake, but the D.A. is asking you to take away her livelihood. And I don't think that should be taken lightly."

"Correct me if I'm wrong, counselor," Kellogg said and I grimaced. Judges only call you "counselor" if you're losing an argument. "You basically said I was unfit—in front of a filled courtroom."

Does the truth hurt your feelings? I wanted to say. But I knew the old soft-shoe might be the better approach. "I apologize, but I just want to make sure you understood what the charges are."

Before I had even finished, I knew I was dead. Bad choice of words. I watched as Kellogg's face turned an unnatural shade of red.

"What I mean is—"

"Mr. Dobbs!" Kellogg bellowed. "This isn't the first time you've practiced in my court. Have you ever known me not to pay attention to each and every matter brought before me?"

I didn't know what to say.

"Well?" Kellogg leaned forward. His face was within a foot of mine. I could smell the gin on his awful breath.

Out of the corner of my eye, I noticed a smile playing at the corner of Lipton's mouth. And that, I think, is what finally did it. The blood rushed to my face, and my heart began pounding so hard I thought it was going to explode right through my shirt.

"If you're not going to answer me," Kellogg said, "I'm prepared to rule exactly as I have already stated."

"I don't think so." The calmness in my voice surprised me.

"What?"

"Are you feeling all right?" I asked, too sweetly.

"What the hell does how I *feel* have to do with anything?"

"Well, it's just that I thought I smelled something like cough medicine on your breath. And I noticed during the preliminary hearing that you were having a difficult time staying awake. Maybe you're taking some kind of cold medication, and it's making you a little sleepy?"

Kellogg looked at his bailiff, who was standing in front of the closed door. Both were speechless.

"I totally understand how that could affect your ability to pay attention," I continued.

Lipton sneered. "That's chicken shit," he mouthed, out of the judge's view. But Kellogg wouldn't have noticed, anyway. You could almost see the wheels turning in that pickled brain of his. I felt bad, but I was tired of letting him get away with his drunken rulings day after day.

"I wouldn't go any further," the judge finally said.

"You're right," I said confidently. I saw an opening and I wasn't going to back down. "I believe we should all go back, and I will state my position in open court."

"About what?"

"Just that I feel you're in no position to rule. I believe, considering your current condition, it would be best if you disqualified yourself and sent us next door." I wasn't really very good at bluffing, but I knew that if he disqualified himself, he would have to do it in front of the several members of the press, who were hopefully still seated in the front row.

Kellogg took a deep breath and leaned back in his chair. He then slowly turned and stared blankly out the window. He was either too upset or too embarrassed to look either of us in the eye. "Let me ask you, Mr. Lipton," he finally said as he massaged his forehead with his hand. "Do you have any indication that this Cappell woman has ever done anything out of line to one of her pupils?"

"Well, n-no," Lipton stuttered.

Kellogg nodded, considering it.

"I believe what Dobbs is doing here amounts to blackmail," Lipton interjected.

"I resent that," I said. "If I feel a judge is suffering from some physical malady, such as the ingestion of too much medication and it interferes with his ability to make a sound judgment, then I have a duty to bring that to his attention."

For a moment everyone was silent. I stared at Lipton, who was shaking his head in disbelief. He knew I wouldn't have a problem establishing Kellogg's sobriety, or the lack thereof, at a formal hearing.

"Come on, Richard," I continued. "We're talking about a young woman who may have had consensual sex with a seventeen-year-old boy, who is probably bragging to his friends about it this very second."

Kellogg was still staring out the window.

"How about ten thousand bail and no restraining orders?" I asked Lipton.

Suddenly, Kellogg was completely out of the loop. The D.A. Lipton and I would work this out between the two of us. Thinking about it, $10,000 was a good deal. I didn't want to press for the OR. Reduced bail would be a victory. My client's mother was already at the bondsman prepared to bail her out at $50,000.

"I guess that will work," Lipton said grudgingly. "But I won't forget this, Dobbs."

"Your Honor," I said, "we have both agreed that ten thousand would be fair."

Kellogg had the look of someone who had just been defeated.

"Fine," he said, buttoning his robe, "let's go take care of it."

I stood to leave when it occurred to me.

"Before we do," I said, "there is one other matter I would like to bring to the court's attention."

I was pushing it now.

"What is it?" Kellogg sighed.

"There is a young man in custody. He is seated next to my client at the end of the jury box."

"What about him?" Kellogg asked.

"His name is Bobby Miles."

"He's Shelby's client," Lipton said, referring to another public defender.

"He probably is," I said. "And I expect Mr. Shelby to be out there any minute, but in the meantime I would like for the court to consider an OR for him."

"What are you talking about?" Lipton said. "He's charged with possession for sale. In addition, if you look at his rap sheet, he has three outstanding traffic warrants. No way. He's a bad risk for OR."

"Three traffic warrants?" I knew that any outstanding warrant was the kiss of death when you were trying to get someone out on their own recognizance. Especially in Kellogg's court.

"Mr. Dobbs," Kellogg said, "I wouldn't go any further than you already have."

"But, Your Honor—"

"You know better than that," Kellogg barked. "I will not let you argue bail for someone else's client."

He was right. I was treading on thin ice. But even though there was nothing I could do for Miles in court, I planned to talk to Martinez later and make sure he understood that he and his buddies better leave the kid alone.

"Do you want to pursue this matter any further?" Kellogg said. His expression convinced me that I better not.

"No, Your Honor," I said and walked out the door.

Chapter 3

It had to be one of the longest days of my life. Not only was I almost tossed in jail, but I'd received a death threat to boot. When I informed Martinez that I wouldn't use Bobby Miles's perjured testimony, he went after me like a mad dog. I was thankful for the wall of glass between us.

There was only one cure for the way I felt. The Gavel, for a quick platter of hot wings before I put me and my tired body to bed. Stopping at The Gavel on the way home had been part of my daily routine during my law school days. Back then money had been, to say the least, a little sparse. Every evening after class, I would hit The Gavel for happy hour and buy just one beer. That beer, which I'd sip slowly, entitled me to all the free hot wings and mini carved beef sandwiches I could eat.

For years a large man named Jake Horgan ran the place. His face was like the map of Ireland and his liquor-laced veins added a substantial road-network to the chart. Jake would treat everyone to tales of the days when the two premier defense attorneys named Jake Ehrlich and Vincent Hamilton had the criminal justice system by the throat. Those were the stories that stuck with me through the years, and were as much a part of the place as the familiar dingy wood floor and the peeling vinyl on the red booths.

I had promised myself I would stick to wings and a club soda, then be on my way. However, the confrontation with Kellogg, and later with Martinez, must have bothered me more than I'd thought. Or at least, that's what I rationalized as I contemplated whether or not I should order something stronger to calm my nerves. But if a childhood with a drunken father taught me anything it was that "just one" would usually lead to others. And the last thing I needed was to begin jury selection with a hangover.

Across the horseshoe-shaped bar Sarah Harris was engaged in conversation with one of the newer D.A. recruits. After several minutes, she gave the attorney a platonic-looking hug, then turned in my direction. I lowered my eyes and played with the beads of sweat forming on my glass.

"Hunter." A second later. "Hunter Dobbs."

"Hi," I said, looking up, feigning surprise.

"Don't you remember me?"

She had me cornered, so for the first time that day, I took the easy way out. I played dumb.

"Weren't you in Kellogg's court?" I asked.

"No. I mean, yes," she said, "but that's not what I meant. You really don't remember me, do you?"

"Did you go to Hastings?"

"Yes," she said, "but I'm afraid it would have been quite a while after you did."

"I'm sure of that," I said. I had a good eight or nine years on her—at least.

"I'm Sarah Harris. You know, Judge Harris's daughter."

"Of course," I said. "It's been a while."

"By the way you looked at me in court, I was afraid I'd done something wrong."

It was the perfect time to tell her how I felt about her father. But I decided changing the subject would be best.

"So how is the judge?"

"We both live in Ukiah, now," she said cheerfully.

"Really."

"He got a great deal on a big piece of land right off the Russian River. He's fat and happy, growing Christmas trees."

"Christmas trees? No kidding. I never thought he'd be able to stay away from the law for a minute."

"Oh, he still manages to take a case here and there. Mostly wills, trusts, stuff like that."

"I'm happy for him," I lied, and gulped the rest of my drink. I shook the cubes in the glass and placed it on the bar, wondering how I was going to leave without being rude.

"You're still with the public defender's office, I see."

"Probably die there," I said in mock resignation.

"You don't sound very enthusiastic."

"I'm not having one of my better days."

"You're not letting that tussle with Kellogg get you down?"

I lifted an eyebrow. "Not one of my prouder moments," I conceded. "I'm afraid I've been appearing in front of that old drunk just a little too long."

She leaned into me as if she were afraid someone would hear. "You shouldn't say that so loud."

The scent of her perfume flooded my senses.

"Don't worry. I'm not saying anything I didn't say to his face."

"You didn't—" she said, when suddenly someone grabbed my arm. I spun around and saw my boss, Steve Ogden, standing next to me.

In his early fifties, Ogden was short and stocky like a tree trunk.

"We have to talk," he said.

"Can it wait? It's late and I've got a trial starting in the morning."

He leaned forward and looked past me at Sarah. "Steve Ogden," he said, extending his hand.

"Sarah Harris."

"You're not Judge Harris's daughter?" he said, holding on to her hand.

"Ever since I can remember."

They both laughed, and I started to stand, but Ogden pushed me back down onto my stool.

"We just need a few minutes," he said to Sarah. "Can I get you something?"

She smiled and turned to the bartender, who was waiting to take Ogden's order. "A Coke would be fine."

When Ogden ordered himself a martini, I realized how upset he was. I'd never known him to drink anything stronger than a glass of wine—and then only when someone was being toasted.

"So what's wrong?" I asked.

"Your attitude," he began. Like me, Ogden didn't believe in pulling punches.

"If you're referring to what happened in Kellogg's courtroom—"

"That will do for a start."

"It wasn't any big deal," I said. "And you know Kellogg. He was so ripped he'll forget what happened by morning."

Ogden's face turned grim. "You shouldn't be blackmailing judges to get them to rule in your favor."

Although some hedging was definitely in order, I went on the attack. "I didn't do anything of the kind. Kellogg was intoxicated. All I did was make sure it didn't affect his decision."

Ogden looked to Sarah for help, but she turned to me with a sympathetic smile instead. She surprised me. Knowing she was a judge's daughter, I'd have thought she would have sided with Ogden.

"You know, Dobbs," he continued, "you're not the only attorney working for me. I have over a hundred others who have to appear in that court and you have made them all *persona non grata*."

I felt myself getting riled up all over again. And Sarah Harris listening wasn't helping my mood any. "How long do we have to let that drunk administer justice like he's some kind of Bob Barker? Last time we talked about this, you promised me you would try and do something about him. Hell, you have enough pull. You're the head deputy for the whole damn county."

Ogden didn't respond. He knew I was right.

I waved a hand. "I'm sorry. Maybe I should have been a little more subtle, but he deserved it."

"No, what a judge deserves is respect," he said flatly.

"Not Kellogg." Just as flatly.

He slowly stirred his drink with his olive-bearing toothpick. "There's going to be an investigation."

That threw me off track. "What do you mean an investigation?"

"The matter has been referred to the state bar and the D.A.'s office is nosing around, too."

"Well, I feel sorry for Kellogg, but someone had to stand up to him."

"You don't understand," Ogden said. "They're investigating you."

"Me! There is no way Kellogg has the balls to make such a big deal of it. He's too afraid. He knows he takes the bench half in the bag every afternoon."

"Kellogg's not the problem," Ogden said quietly. "You're being accused of suborning perjury."

"Suborning perjury!" By now half the bar was looking at us. "What are you talking about?"

"Your murder trial, the one that's supposed to start tomorrow?"

"Yeah?"

"A young man in lockup says you asked him to lie on the stand for your client, Sal Martinez."

I was too nonplused to be angry. "There's no way would I ever do that, and you know it."

Ogden shrugged uncomfortably. "Sorry. The D.A. interviewed him, and the state bar has been contacted."

"This young man you're talking about—is his name Bobby Miles?"

"The same one you tried to get out OR," Ogden said. "Now, why in the hell would you have done something like that?"

I knew exactly what the D.A.'s office was thinking. That I tried to bribe Miles into testifying falsely for Martinez by promising him I would get him out on his own recognizance.

"He's lying. He's just some kid who's scared to death," I said. "Martinez is the one who asked me to interview him in the first place. He told me the kid saw someone else shoot the two victims. After I asked Miles a few questions, I knew he was lying. I told both of them that there was no way I would use perjured testimony."

"Well . . ." Ogden said, hesitating, "that's not what the young man is saying."

I shook my head. "And you're telling me the D.A. is going to believe a scared kid over me?" I slammed my open hand on the bar top. "Aren't they going to even ask for my side?"

Ogden's answer was subdued. "You'll get your turn."

"I want to talk to the D.A. now," I said. "Which one is it?"

I felt Sarah rest her hand on mine. "I don't think you're in the right frame of mind to talk to anyone, Hunter."

"Ms. Harris is right," Ogden said. "Let things cool off for a while. I'm sure they will want to talk to you before they complete their investigation."

"And how long will that take?"

"If the state bar is involved, you can count on a minimum of two or three months," Sarah interjected.

I pulled my hand away and shook my head again. "This is all so damn ridiculous."

"I'm going to have to reassign your cases," Ogden said meekly.

That hit me like a thunderbolt. "But why?"

Ogden stood up from his stool and placed his hand on my shoulder. "I'm sorry, Hunter. But until this matter is resolved, I have no choice but to place you on suspension."

Chapter 4

It had been years since I'd been in rural Northern California. While driving, I considered my situation. As soon as Ogden left, I'd wanted to march into the D.A.'s office and explain what had really happened. Luckily, Sarah reminded me that "spilling their guts" was exactly what most suspects did when they were accused of a crime. Having been a defense attorney for almost ten years, I knew she was right. The prisons were filled with people who thought they could talk their way out of an arrest. Half the time, if they had kept their mouths shut, the prosecution wouldn't have had enough to file a case, let alone manage a conviction.

Also as Martinez's attorney, I was over the proverbial barrel. Anything he said was privileged and couldn't be divulged. I saw that aspect of my job in an entirely new light. It didn't seem right that he could accuse me of a crime, and I wouldn't be able to repeat what was said between us. How could I defend myself? The system had me by the throat.

Someone who knew the intricacies of this kind of problem had to be in my corner. Luckily, Sarah had been right there and offered immediately to help. That was why I was driving up to Ukiah. She had as much experience as anyone dealing with a state bar investigation. She had once been one of them, and I was sure she wouldn't hesitate to use that to her advantage.

The only down side to Sarah was that she was Avery Harris's daughter. For most of my career the mere sound of his name had nettled me. I could only hope I'd be able to keep my contact with him to a minimum.

Traffic was light on Highway 101 as I drove north from Healdsburg where the road undulated over the rolling hills of Sonoma County. As I neared Hopland, truckloads of Mexican pickers were parked along the side of the highway getting ready for the grape harvest. Here and there a winery appeared on a hillside like a medieval monastic retreat.

Entering Ukiah, I found Sarah's office in a two-story brick building across the street from the courthouse. Ten minutes late, I checked with the receptionist—an elderly lady with Coke-bottle glasses. With a warm smile, she informed me Sarah would be available in a moment.

The reception room was a mixture of aged brick walls and dark woods highlighted with a woman's touch—colorful paintings, plants, and earth-tone furniture. Its small size amplified the electronic chatter of the telephones, business machines, and conversations of the employees busily working on the other side of the counter. A few minutes passed before Sarah walked into view. She handed a document to an assistant, then laid her hand on a typist's shoulder, clicking off a list of to-do's. She seemed in control of everything and everybody around her. The receptionist said something to her and Sarah disappeared. Seconds later the door opened.

"I hope you had a safe trip." Sarah extended her hand. She was dressed in a dark blue pinstriped suit, and white silk blouse accented with a red chiffon scarf. I looked down at my own attire: worn Levi's and a yellow pullover. I'd have to remember to wear snappier threads next time.

"All these people work for you?" I said, following her into the inner office.

Sarah chuckled. "Does that surprise you?"

"Of course not," I said, even though I was dumbfounded that someone only three years out of law school could be so successful.

Sarah motioned for me to be seated in one of two client chairs in front of her desk. "I've been lucky."

"I don't think so," I said. "I was watching and you give every appearance of being in total control."

She seemed pleased, but remained businesslike. "Enough about me," she said. "You have a problem and let's see what I can do to help."

It felt strange going through the lawyer routine from the other side of the desk. "Where would you like me to begin?"

She opened the side drawer of her desk and fished out a new yellow legal pad. "How about the conversation you had with . . ."

"Miles," I volunteered. "Bobby Miles."

"Thank you." She wrote his name on the pad. "Now tell me what happened."

For more than an hour we dissected everything said during my interview of Miles and another half hour about my conference in Kellogg's chambers. I was tired and glad we were about finished when she asked, "Now, tell me about Sal Martinez."

I sighed deeply and gave her a "you've got to be kidding" look.

She angled her head. "Unless I know everything, I won't be able to help."

I slowly nodded while massaging my forehead. "I understand."

"First of all, who is he?"

"One of the meanest and slimiest gangbangers I've ever had the misfortune of representing." I slumped in my chair. "I can't understand why he's so determined to take his loser of a case to trial. From the outset, the D.A.'s offer had been two concurrent first-degree murders without special circumstances; if he and his buddy accepted, they would be sentenced to twenty-five years to life, which meant they would stand a good chance of seeing the outside before either of them died of old age. That sure beat the alternative: having the starring role in an upcoming execution. I kept trying to pound the risks of trial into his head, but he'd never budge. 'A life sentence is as good as being dead,' was always his response."

"Why did you feel Martinez was forcing Miles to lie?" she asked.

"It didn't take me long to figure it out." I then went on to tell Sarah what had happened when I confronted Martinez in the attorney interview room.

* * *

When I walked in, he had been lying on a wooden bench on the other side of the wire-mesh window which separated us. His hands were folded behind his head like it was a sunny day and he was sunbathing on the beach.

I opened my briefcase and spread his file on the counter. He didn't move a muscle, not even a twitch; nothing to acknowledge my presence.

"You alive, Martinez?"

His lips were the only thing that moved. "Trial starting tomorrow?"

"Looks like it."

Martinez muttered something unintelligible in Spanish, closed his eyes again, and turned his head away as if to tell me to leave. After my confrontation with Kellogg, I wasn't in the mood to put up with his arrogance. I threw his file back in my briefcase and snapped it shut. With the sound, his eyes opened and he sat up.

"Did you talk to that kid?" he asked. "Tell me what he had to say."

"He's lying."

Martinez leaned into the glass. A tattoo of a spider and cobweb behind his left ear was barely noticeable under his dark greasy hair. "That's your opinion."

"Maybe so, but I'm not going to put him on the stand if he's not telling the truth."

"But he is."

"Tell me exactly what it took, Martinez. Did you tell him you wouldn't hurt him, kill him, or what . . . ?"

His face shut down completely. "I don't know what the hell you're talking about."

"Bullshit. That kid is scared to death."

"Is that what he told you?"

"He didn't have to. I know what goes on in there, and believe me, so does the D.A. If that kid ever takes the stand, they'll rip him apart."

Martinez began to pick at the dirt underneath his fingernails. Suddenly, he jerked his head up and glared at me. "Man, you're a real piece of work."

"Sure am," I shot back. "And I've had it with your stupid games."

"Shit, man, you're my lawyer. You're supposed to look out for me."

"That's why I'm not calling any of your lying buddies to the stand."

"You will if I tell you to."

I merely laughed.

"You're an asshole, Dobbs." Martinez then paused as if he was actually trying to control his anger. "You know I'll be convicted without him," he said in a lower tone.

"That's why you better take the gift the D.A.'s been offering."

"I ain't copping no plea, man." Martinez glared at me, putting on a show of disgust. "All I know is any good lawyer can win this."

"Well then, I guess I'm just not good enough, because in my opinion, you're going down in flames."

"Then, I want another lawyer."

"Sorry," I said with a dismissive shrug. "You don't get to pick and choose public defenders."

His eyes blazed with venom. "Man, why don't you get the hell out of here?"

"Fine by me."

As I rose slowly to leave, he stiffened. "You better hope they convict me." He clenched the edge of the counter with both of his chubby hands. "Because you're the first one I'm coming after when I get out of here."

I forced myself to suppress a smile. If he ever did get out, he'd be encased in a six-foot wooden box. "Is that supposed to scare me?"

He was standing now. We were face-to-face with only a half wall and glass between us. "It better, asshole."

This time I did smile. His pitiful life was in my hands and he decided the best way to make sure he didn't end up in the electric chair was to threaten me—his lawyer.

"You'll get a fair trial. But that's all you're getting."

His face turned beet red and he jumped onto the counter and started viciously kicking the glass partition. Leaning against the metal door, waiting to be let out, I couldn't help but wonder how far he'd go.

"You're going to ruin your new white tennies."

Martinez kicked the glass several more times and it began to crack. Luckily, the wire mesh kept it in place. I began to get concerned. It was like watching a deranged animal. He began to pull on the cracked glass, piece by piece. In a matter of seconds the glass was covered with his blood.

"I'll kill you," he yelled just as the door behind him burst open. Three deputies rushed in. It wouldn't have surprised me if they'd been waiting outside to see how badly Martinez would injure himself.

Sarah's mouth was open.

"The last time I saw him," I concluded, "three deputies grabbed him by the hair and threw him head first onto the concrete floor. Blood gushed from his mouth and nose."

Sarah looked shocked. "How badly was he injured?"

"Later on, Howard Millings, one of the deputies, told me he was fine. All he needed was a couple of stitches."

Sarah shook her head and made a few more notes.

"Enough business for now," she said and looked at her watch. "How about something to eat?"

After the long drive and interview, I was beat and not in the mood for a leisurely lunch. But she had been nice enough to spend most of the morning with me, so I acceded.

"Where to?"

"I'll meet you at my father's place," she said, pushing past me to tell the receptionist her plan. "I'm sure the two of you are anxious to see one another again."

"You're right," I mumbled to myself as I followed her out the door. "I can't wait."

Chapter 5

Located twenty miles north of Ukiah, Judge Avery Harris's farm was acres upon acres of Christmas trees in various stages of growth. A gravel road led to a large two-story house perched on top of a grassy knoll, with a smaller one-story cottage next to it.

I knocked on the screen door of the house, but received no answer. While walking to the smaller dwelling, I saw the flash of something shiny reflected from the middle of a field. I tried to make out what it was—and it happened again. Then, off to its right—another flash. I had no idea what was causing it. Probably some old pie tins to keep the birds away? But birds couldn't harm a pine tree. At least, I didn't think so. I wasn't exactly up on pine tree lore.

At the side of the main house was a late-model Blazer parked under a corrugated-steel shelter. To its right was a black '56 Chevy two-door. I hadn't seen one up close since I'd sold my red one over ten years ago. I looked through the open passenger window. The interior was a mess, cotton stuffing bulging out of the seats, dirty clothes and loose trash strewn about the floor. It was obvious someone had been living in it. Even with the doors closed, there was a hint of a funky smell.

From the rear of the property came the sound of running water. I made my way to a stream and found an old wooden bench with a fishing pole resting against it. I hadn't touched a pole in years. To be more exact, I'd handled one only once, when I was eight years old. My father, for the first and last time, had taken me fishing on a similar stream. After he baited and threw in both our lines, we sat on an old log for about an hour without a nibble. Then, without saying a word, he reeled in. Storming off to his car, he told me to get inside. While driving back to our house, the only thing he said was that there were no fish in that crappy little stream, and that waiting around was a waste of his valuable time. Once back at the house, he spent the remainder of that Sunday drinking his daily case of beer while flipping from one football game to another. So much for quality time with Dad.

"Hunter," a familiar voice yelled. Sarah hurried toward me, wearing a pair of tight-fitting Levi's with a white pullover sweater and tennis shoes. "I'm sorry," she said, half out of breath, "I decided to stop at my apartment to change into something more comfortable."

"Don't apologize. I haven't been here that long myself."

"So how do you like the place?" she said, waving her hand to show off the tall redwoods surrounding the property.

I knew she wanted me to say how the magnificent beauty of the place impressed me. But she had no idea I was raised in a very similar setting—memories of which continued to haunt me.

"I haven't seen this much green since the last time I went to Golden Gate Park," I said, uninspired.

Her smile faded somewhat, but her enthusiasm was still present in her voice. "Sometimes I have to force myself not to take all of this for granted."

I smiled and nodded my head.

She quickly glanced around the property, shielding her eyes from the afternoon sun. "Have you seen my father?"

"Not yet," I said. "And I don't think he's in the house. I knocked on the door. . . ."

"He must be trimming trees," she said and reached for me. "Let's go find him."

Hand in hand, Sarah led me off into the field in the same direction the reflections had come from. The smell of Christmas morning surrounded us as we walked through hundreds of small pine trees. "Be careful of your clothes," she said. "The branches have sap on them."

As we pushed our way through, the mystery of the flashes was solved. Up ahead, I could see an arm swinging a long metal object repeatedly at the ground.

"Dad?" Sarah yelled.

"Right here," a deep voice responded. A voice I'd never forget.

"Someone would like to say hello," she said and led me over to the next row of trees.

Judge Avery Harris had the same unsmiling mouth and arrogant look in his eyes. Farm life had changed him a little physically. His five-foot-ten frame wasn't burdened with the large belly that used to hang over his belt. His face had more color, and the salt-and-pepper beard that seemed an affectation with his black robe somehow fit his redefined role.

"Good to see you, Judge Harris. You're looking well."

Without responding, he turned away, sizing up the next tree.

At least he didn't kiss me on my cheek. "I never knew Christmas trees were trimmed with a knife," I said, just to say something.

He wiped the long blade on his dirty overalls. "It's a machete, son."

"But I thought they had machines to do that."

"Nope," he said and whacked his way around the tree in a matter of seconds. Small branches flew everywhere.

"How many times a year do you have to do this?"

Always a man of few words. "Once, maybe twice," he said.

"But there must be thousands. . . . Do you have to do all of them yourself?"

"Not with his bad heart," Sarah said and glared at her father. "Where's Jared?"

"A few rows over," he said and moved on to the next tree.

"Who's Jared?" I asked.

"He was in my father's platoon in Vietnam," she said. "He's been helping trim trees the last few weeks."

"Is that his Chevy I saw up at the house?"

"That's what he usually lives out of," Sarah said, frowning at the thought. "But since he's been working here, Dad's letting him stay in the guest house."

The judge stopped measuring the next tree. "Sarah tells me you managed to get yourself into a bit of trouble."

I should have known better. It didn't take him long to get to the point. In his mind just the accusation made me guilty. "I believe I'm innocent until proven otherwise."

The old man laughed. "I believe we've had this kind of discussion before."

His attempt at humor caught me off guard. In all the years I'd known him, he'd never directed even the hint of a smile at me.

"Well, I hope it's not too serious," he continued, glancing at his daughter. His show of concern had to be for her benefit.

"Just a misunderstanding that I'll be able to straighten out," I said.

His face turned stony again. "Like hell you will!"

"What?" I said, unsure of what he'd meant.

"You've never been very good at keeping your feelings to yourself, Dobbs." He lifted the blade of his machete and jammed it into the dirt. "You let Sarah handle it. She knows what she's doing."

Sarah smiled at my bewildered look, then turned to her father. "Hunter's staying for lunch. How about you?"

The judge shrugged. It had to be painfully obvious to Sarah that there was no love lost between us. "Give me a few more minutes," he said and turned to attack his next victim.

As Sarah and I walked back to the house we heard the sound of sirens coming from the main road.

"Wonder what that's all about?" she said and stepped up her pace.

By the time we reached the driveway, she got her answer. A black-and-white patrol car swerved off the highway and raced directly at us.

"That looks like the lieutenant."

"Who?" I asked, trying to catch up.

The car slid to a stop, too close for comfort, and Sarah grimaced. "One of our county's finest."

I waved my hand in front of my face, trying to clear the cloud of dust which had been kicked up. A tall, middle-aged man, with brown hair and mustache, jumped out from the passenger's side and marched toward Sarah. The driver, a short muscular cop, was close behind.

"Miss Harris," the lieutenant said as he adjusted his brown herringbone coat so that it squared with his loud blue and green tie. "Where's Jared Reineer?"

"With my father."

"Where exactly?" the uniformed cop said and pulled his revolver from his holster.

"Wait just a minute!" Sarah snapped.

The lieutenant gave the young cop a disgusted look. "Jamison, holster that weapon and call for backup."

"Lieutenant," Sarah said, "what's this all about?"

"We're here to arrest him."

I had to toss in my two cents. "Do you have a warrant?"

"And who in the hell are you?"

"Hunter Dobbs."

The lieutenant started laughing. "It's been a while, Dobbs," he said. "I thought you were with the P.D.'s office. Aren't you supposed to be helping put the scum of San Francisco back on the streets?"

Finally I realized who he was. I should have recognized him sooner. It was the mustache that fooled me. At least six years had passed since I'd last seen him. William McBean had been a homicide detective for the San Francisco Police Department. He'd disappeared—right after I proved he'd beaten a confession out of one of my clients.

I wasn't about to back down from this gorilla. With my phoniest smile, I said, "And are you still making sure the innocent get convicted?"

Scowling, McBean turned back to Sarah, who appeared confused. "Are you going to tell us where Reineer is or will I have to tear this place apart to find him?"

I stepped forward to help, but Sarah firmly placed her hand against my chest.

"Who do you think you are?" she said to McBean.

"Someone doing his job."

"And I'm sure your job doesn't include harassing innocent people." Sarah stepped right up to his face. "Now, if you have official business on my father's property, then you had better make sure it is transacted according to the letter of the law."

McBean was momentarily taken aback by the young beauty challenging him.

"Unless you have a warrant," she continued, "I suggest you leave this property immediately."

She had to be irritating the hell out of him. His bullying tactics weren't working. I was mightily impressed.

McBean pulled a document from his coat pocket. "Here's the arrest warrant," he said, handing Sarah a stapled document. "The second page is a search warrant for the guest house and a black 1956 Chevrolet, California license number JYT 076."

After reading what McBean had given her, Sarah turned to me with a pensive look. "It says the charges are kidnapping and child molestation."

"That's correct," McBean said. "The victim is a ten-year-old named Danny Barton. I wanted the D.A. to file attempted murder, but unless we get additional information, that will have to do."

Sarah handed the document back to the detective. "I'd say it's enough."

"You better believe it," Jamison chirped. "Kidnapping carries a life sentence. Now we won't have to worry about seeing that derelict's sorry ass hanging around this county anymore."

McBean shook his head at the rookie cop's remark. "What about backup?"

"Be here any minute," Jamison replied.

I heard rustling from the treeline at the edge of the field.

"What the hell's going on here?" Avery Harris shouted as he emerged from the trees with a scraggly, middle-aged man following closely behind. Both were carrying machetes.

McBean and Jamison drew their guns. "Freeze," the lieutenant yelled.

The judge continued to walk straight ahead. "I will do nothing of the sort."

The two cops pushed the judge aside and charged the other man. With a confused look, the man raised the machete over his head.

"Drop it, Reineer, or I'll blow your head off!" McBean yelled. Both he and Jamison stood with their revolvers pointed directly at the man's face.

Sarah rushed to intervene. "Do what the lieutenant says, Jared. Please, put it down."

The man held his free hand out to the judge. He wanted an explanation.

"They have a warrant for your arrest," Sarah said without taking her eyes off him.

"Kidnapping and child molest," Jamison yelled as the gun shook violently in his hand.

The man glanced over his shoulder like he was thinking about making a run for it. He had retreated several steps when I heard the firing pins on both guns click back.

"Jared!" the judge shouted. "Put the damn thing down!"

The man's gaze bounced back and forth between the two cops, then settled on the judge. Finally, the machete fell to his side. Jamison rushed him while McBean kicked the machete out of reach. In a matter of seconds, his arms were yanked behind his back and handcuffed.

"He's not resisting," the judge said when Jamison dragged him toward the black-and-white.

Jared let out a scream.

"You don't have to hurt him!" Sarah yelled, but both cops ignored her and roughly ushered Jared into the patrol car, slamming his head against the top of the door as they threw him inside.

McBean walked over to Sarah with a satisfied grin. "Now we're going to take him down to the station. And that," he said, pointing to a tow truck driving up the driveway, "is going to hook up the black sedan. Several deputies should be here any second to search the guest house. Are there any questions?"

"I want to talk to my client," Sarah said.

"We're booking him, and then I need to see whether he wants to talk to us first."

"I can tell you now," she said with authority, "I don't want him talking to you. At least not until I've discussed it with him first."

"I understand, Miss Harris."

"I'll bet," she said.

McBean grinned like the cat who just ate the family parakeet. "I'll be in touch." As the two cops turned back to their car, they noticed that the judge's head was inside the driver's side door. He was saying something to Jared.

"Get the hell out of there," Jamison yelled.

As the two sheriffs rushed forward, the judge turned to them. "Mr. Reineer is exercising his right to remain silent."

Jamison grabbed the judge by the arm and pulled him. Suddenly, a second patrol car turned off the highway and sped up the driveway, stopping next to McBean, who said something to the driver while pointing at the guest house.

"What did you say to Jared?" Sarah asked her father.

"Nothing much." He grinned. "Just made him promise he would keep his mouth shut until you had a chance to talk to him."

"I hope he understood."

"He did," the judge said. "But you better get down there and make sure they don't talk him out of it."

Sarah turned to walk to her car, then stopped as if she had just remembered something. "I'm sorry, Hunter. Is it all right if I call you tomorrow?"

I quickly stepped aside to get out of the way of McBean's car as it headed toward the highway with Jared. As it passed, McBean gave me a face-wide grin from the passenger seat. That was when it hit me. Sarah hadn't done enough criminal work to handle a snake like McBean. She had no idea what he was capable of. But I did.

"No way," I said. "I'm going with you."

Chapter 6

Sarah turned her gold Lexus onto what used to be old Highway 101 as we entered downtown Ukiah. The largest town in the county is a mix of the old and the new. Fast-food joints and modern gas-station-convenience stores share frontage with sun-faded lapboard housing dating back to the turn of the century.

Along the sidewalks in the business district, old-timers in overalls linger amongst younger, long-sleeved businessmen. Here and there are a smattering of 1960s hippies who escaped Haight-Ashbury when San Francisco no longer wanted them. Their ponytailed hair and beards now graying, they are an accepted part of the community mix.

We pulled up in front of the Mendocino County sheriff's station, a small three-story redbrick building with filigreed wooden fringe surrounding the roof line. What I saw next, I wasn't expecting.

It had been scarcely more than an hour since Jared was arrested, and already dozens of reporters were at the station's entrance, jockeying for the best position. The kidnapping of a young boy wouldn't make a three-inch story in the metro section of the *San Francisco Chronicle*. But in a small community, where a traffic stop is a newsworthy event, Jared's arrest would be tomorrow's front-page headline.

Sarah had changed into a tight-fitting suit with a soft leather bag slung over her shoulder. She pushed her way to the main door, and I followed close behind. Except for its smaller size, the station wasn't much different from the many I'd frequented throughout San Francisco County. Within its institutional brick walls was the same deep-soaked stench of piss and body odor that buckets of disinfectant couldn't wash away.

Sarah and I both knew that McBean was likely inside trying to trick anything he could out of Jared. Once he was booked and fingerprinted, McBean would settle Jared into the interrogation room. He'd offer a cup of coffee and a cigarette and start sympathizing. Then McBean or one of the other sly coppers would tell him that they were just there to "clear up a few things."

The sergeant at the front was fumbling through his paperwork, looking bored out of his skull. He was a red-faced mongrel with a graying mustache that had overgrown his mouth. As he drank coffee from a Styrofoam cup, the droplets that remained on his hairy upper lip fell on the paper below.

Sarah let her heels click heavily on the tiled floor to let him know she was coming. He looked up as she approached.

"I'm here to see Jared Reineer," she said with the faintest of smiles. "I'm his lawyer."

"He's busy right now."

"But McBean is expecting me. . . ."

"You'll have to wait." He lowered his head back to his paperwork. "I'm sure he'll be busy for some time."

"I don't care," she started to say when a voice from behind cut her off.

"Hey, Fillmore," McBean called out, "is there some kind of problem?"

Sarah quickly jumped on the lieutenant. "I want to see my client."

"Counselor, I'll be the one to decide when you can talk to him."

Sarah threw her arms in the air in a display of disgust.

"Sorry, sweetheart," he said. "The law is clear. Unless Reineer asks to speak to you, I can proceed with my questioning. And that's exactly what I intend to do."

Sarah stepped toward the arrogant veteran. The hard look in her eyes made him stand up straighter. I was sure it was the "sweetheart" remark that did it. "And you better make sure you advise him of that."

McBean grinned. "I have."

Sarah took a deep breath. She was up against someone who had heard it all before. I was tempted to jump into the fray, but unfortunately, McBean was right. The attorney doesn't decide whether or not their client can be interviewed; the client does. The cops know that and use it to their advantage as soon as they get the suspect alone.

"I'm sure he doesn't understand," Sarah said. "My

father told me he has received monthly aid from the military for some kind of mental disability."

"He and a million other druggies the damn liberals are letting milk the system," McBean spat back. "That doesn't mean squat to me."

I couldn't keep silent any longer. "You know, McBean, what any of us think really doesn't matter. What if he does have some kind of mental disorder and you won't let him talk to his attorney?"

"Dobbs, you're the last person I need to spout the law to me. I asked him if he wanted to talk to an attorney, and he said no. That's all I need. I don't care if an army of you ambulance chasers show up."

"I wouldn't be so sure of that."

"Tell it to someone who cares."

"I think the judge who eventually hears this case might," I said, "and if he doesn't, I'm sure the jury will."

He looked over at Fillmore, who shrugged. I suspected McBean was weakening.

"A retired Superior Court judge informed you back at the farm that Mr. Reineer was exercising his right to remain silent."

McBean shrugged. "So he changed his mind."

"A jury won't buy that. Especially when they find out your propensity for coercing confessions out of perfectly innocent people."

I regretted the remark as it came out of my mouth.

McBean let go of the door and stepped quickly toward me. "You'll always be a jerk, Dobbs."

Sarah grabbed my arm and stepped between us.

We all stood silently looking at each other. The distant moan of an inmate broke the silence.

"I believe if he's interrogated without my permission it will only create problems for you later," Sarah finally said.

McBean started to say something, but she cut him off. "By interviewing him now, you run the risk of not being able to use what he tells you. If that's the case, then what do you have to gain? Just let me talk to him first."

McBean sneered. "So you can tell him what to say."

Sarah took a deep breath. It was obvious to both of us that we were getting nowhere trying to bully him. "I would never do that," she said in a soft, polite tone.

McBean, surprised by Sarah's change in demeanor, looked over at Fillmore again. The sergeant's head was lowered as he scribbled something on a form in front of him. Knowing McBean, he didn't want to make it look like the young attorney had gotten the best of him.

"Look," Sarah persisted, "you and Mr. Dobbs have obviously had your past differences, but I hope that won't influence a decision you may regret later. If after I talk to my client, I believe his best option is to speak to you, even if what he says amounts to a confession, then I'll recommend it. Doesn't that happen all the time? A suspect confesses in exchange for a reasonable disposition. Maybe I can help you put a big red bow on this case. What do you have to lose?"

McBean sighed and gave me one last look of disgust. "All right," he said and opened the door. "I'll give the two of you twenty minutes."

McBean escorted us down a poorly lit hallway to a small alcove. Two uniformed cops were sprawled out on swivel chairs behind an old beat-up desk, sipping coffee and laughing it up. Both eyeballed Sarah as we neared them, their tongues all but lolling out of their heads.

"I'll need a copy of the police report," Sarah said to McBean.

"Hold on to your skirt, Counselor. You'll get one in due time."

Sarah glared at him. "I understand," she said. "But I can't recommend anything unless I'm familiar with the evidence."

McBean knew he had nothing to lose because the D.A. would give her a copy before court anyway. Besides, he was probably hoping Sarah would get Jared to confess in time for the evening newscast.

"All right." McBean pulled a several-page document from the desk drawer and handed it to Sarah as we walked down the hall to where Jared was being held. With a heavy brass key he unlocked the large steel door and swung it open. "Just make sure you tell him the D.A. will make it worth his while."

Sarah and I were stunned by the sight of Jared huddled in the corner of the cold cell. Dressed in jail-house blues, he was shaking uncontrollably while sitting in a pool of his own piss. His head was cradled between his knees.

McBean grinned from ear to ear. "Never touched him," he said and slammed the door shut.

Sarah walked straight to Jared. "Are you all right?" she asked, placing her hand gently on his shoulder.

Jared didn't respond. Instead he covered his head with his arms, trying to shield himself from the forces that were converging on him. For the first time that day, I could tell that Sarah was shaken.

"Why don't we see what they have?" I said, pointing to the police report she was holding.

Sarah sat on the edge of an old makeshift bed and began to read the report. I couldn't help but notice the contrast between her pristine skirt and the dirty mattress. While she seemed unaffected by it, I wanted to sit anywhere but on that germ-infested thing. But after surveying the cell and seeing that the only other seat was a stainless-steel toilet caked with dried urine, I reluctantly sat next to her. The steel frame moaned with the added weight.

Sarah handed me each page once she'd finished with it. After giving me the last one, she studied Jared, who hadn't budged.

"I don't see why they think they have enough to even arrest him," I volunteered.

Sarah gave me a quizzical look as if she didn't comprehend my optimism. "You don't?"

"Not really. The victim couldn't pick him out of the six-pack." I'd read that six photos were shown to the boy the day after he was attacked. One of them was Jared.

"But even without a positive identification, they

have a strong case. They have a description of his car. . . . But," she said and hesitated as if in deep thought, "it's the candy they found inside the car that really nails him."

"Come on," I said. "There has to be a hundred cars in this county that fit the vague description the boy gave."

Sarah gave me a look as if to say, Think about it. "Not with a package of the boy's gummy bears on the front seat."

I shook my head. I wasn't buying it. It was too pat.

"All I'm saying is we better see what kind of offer the D.A. will make him," she said.

"No way."

"Why?"

"Because I know something you don't."

Sarah had no idea what I was getting at. "Are you going to tell me?"

"The package of gummy bears."

"What about it?"

"Only that I don't remember seeing it there."

"I don't understand," she said. "When could you have possibly seen Jared's car?"

"While waiting for you at the farm, I happened to look inside. And I sure didn't see any package of candy in the middle of the front seat."

Sarah gave me a perplexed stare. "You're sure?"

"Hey, it's not often you get to see a '56 Chevrolet. So I took a look. There was a bunch of junk in it, but nothing on the front seat. I'm positive."

Sarah grimaced as she shifted her weight, causing the old bed to squeak. "You think someone planted it?"

"With McBean, anything's possible."

Sarah was having a hard time accepting the notion that the police would manufacture evidence. "You've been watching too much TV," she remarked. "They wouldn't do something like that."

"It's rare," I said. "But it does happen. And that's not only experience talking, but someone who has had McBean on the opposite side before."

Sarah dropped her head and silently stared at the report in her lap. I knew she was overwhelmed by what I was saying and the responsibility she was about to take on. A case always looks its bleakest when you read the police report for the first time. The worst thing she could do was form any opinion until she fully investigated and understood all the facts.

"Play the devil's advocate," I said. "Don't believe anything that is written in that report, whether it helps or hurts your client. Make sure you check everything out yourself." I waved my hand at Jared. "And that includes anything he tells you," I whispered. "That is, if you ever get him to talk."

Sarah placed her hand on his arm. "Jared," she said in a motherly tone, "you have to talk to me."

He raised his head so only his eyes were exposed. They were dark and swollen and fixed on me. "Who . . . who's that?" he said in a cowering tone.

"Hunter Dobbs," she said. "Remember he was at the farm? He's a criminal defense attorney from San Francisco."

Jared looked quickly around as if it were the first

time he realized he was locked up. "Where's my necklace?"

"Necklace?" she asked, unsure of what he meant.

Jared's eyes were bigger than saucers. "My leather necklace," he stammered. "I want it back."

If it wasn't so sad, it would be almost comical. He had just been arrested for a very serious crime, facing the possibility of life in prison, yet all he cared about was some damn necklace.

"I'll see what I can do." Sarah's voice was soft and understanding. "For now, I have to talk to you about what happened."

"Nothing happened, so get my necklace back."

Sarah's confused expression lingered.

"They normally won't allow you to keep any personal belongings once you've been booked," I said, trying to help her out.

"But it's part of me," he said and jumped to his feet. "I'm nothing without it. You have to get it back." Jared grabbed Sarah's arm and yanked her toward the cell door. "Go get it!"

Sarah tried to pull away. "You're hurting me."

He grabbed her by the shoulders and shook her like a rag doll. "Why won't you help me get it back?"

I'd had enough. I gripped Jared just under the chin and forced him onto the bed. "Calm down," I muttered fiercely into his ear.

As Sarah straightened her suit, I eyed her and circled my index finger to the side of my head. I was beginning to question how they could have allowed such a nutcase to live with them.

"I know you're afraid," Sarah said patiently, "but you have to talk to me."

Jared glared at her. "Not until I get my necklace back."

"Miss Harris will get your necklace back," I said, sure there was no way that would ever happen. But if a white lie helped to get him to calm down and talk to us, it would be worth it.

Jared raised his head and gave Sarah an urgent look. "Can you?"

"Only if you'll help me."

"But I didn't do anything," he said.

Sarah reached for the report, which during the scuffle had fallen to the floor, and handed him a copy of Danny Barton, the victim's, photo. "Have you ever seen this boy before?"

"Never," he said without the slightest hesitation.

"Then can you explain how a package of his gummy bears could have been found in your car?"

Jared's eyes darted around the small room before they settled back on Sarah. "Gummy what . . . ?"

"Gummy bears," Sarah repeated. "It's candy."

Jared briskly shook his head. "No way. They're lying if they say there was candy in my car."

"Are you sure?"

"I'd know what's in my own car, wouldn't I?"

"Do you know anything about the attack on the boy?"

Jared's shoulders visibly slumped. He was tired of her questions.

"Everyone does," he finally mumbled. "It's been in all the papers."

Sarah searched his face. "You're sure you don't

know anything about the attack other than what you've either read or heard?"

"Positive," Jared said and his expression abruptly changed back to one of desperation. "Tell them I'll agree to talk if they'll give me my necklace back."

"No," Sarah said. "Promise me you won't talk to anyone unless I say it's all right."

He lowered his head, shaking it slowly.

"Promise," she repeated.

"Okay," he finally said.

I heard the rattling of keys in the hallway. I knocked on the cell door and waited for Sarah as McBean swung the door open. She gave me a half-smile as she passed. I knew what she had to be thinking. She had never handled a case close to this serious and I was sure she had her doubts. Child molestation was one of the most difficult cases a criminal defense attorney could be faced with. Taking on an experienced district attorney, a slick investigating officer, and combine that with a sympathetic victim, you have a mixture that would create anxiety in even the most seasoned trial attorney. And as Sarah would be the first to admit, she fell far short of that.

Chapter 7

Sarah asked me to find her father, who she thought would be trimming trees. She was on the telephone with the D.A. in San Francisco, to find out when they wanted to meet and discuss Bobby Miles's baseless allegations. We were hopeful that once they'd heard my side, they would realize all they had was the word of a young, petrified kid, and they would fold.

I stepped out onto the broad expanse of the verandah into the cool evening air. Gleaming white wooden columns rose all around me to the second floor above. A waist-high lattice wall connected each to define the porch. I glanced at a porcelain tea set sitting on a wicker coffee table next to an old wooden swing. I felt like a character in a Tennessee Williams play.

"Hunter," a man's voice called. Judge Harris was standing in the middle of the stream in hip-length rubber boots, whipping a long fishing rod over his head. After one last graceful thrust, the line fell gently on top of the slow-moving water.

He motioned me forward with a nod of his head.

"Catch anything?" I yelled, trying to be friendly.

Except for the modish boots, he was dressed the same as when we'd left earlier that afternoon.

"Where's Jared?" he asked as he slowly walked through the shallow water, reeling in his line.

"Still in custody."

The judge stopped short of the water's edge, dipped his hand into the water and pulled out a long shiny chain. On the end, three large fish struggled for oxygen. They appeared too big to have come from such a small stream, but what did I know?

"What happened?" he asked as he trudged his way up the rocky bank, trying to balance his fishing rod with his heavy catch.

Jared was Sarah's client, and she was the one who should break the news. I changed the subject.

"Those are real beauties."

The judge handed me the cold, wet chain. "Take them," he said. The weight surprised me, and the twisting fish fell from my grasp to the dirt.

"Hold 'em up," the judge barked as he steadied himself with one hand on a large redwood and stepped out of his boots. "Don't want any sharp rocks cutting into that sweet meat."

"Sorry." I pulled the silver-hued monsters off the ground.

"Let's go clean them," he said and walked past me, up to the house.

"But they're not dead."

"So?" he said as he waited for me at the back door of the house. "Haven't you ever cleaned a damn fish before?"

"Of course," I lied. It was if my manhood had been attacked.

He opened the door with a lingering smile. "Good, I'll let *you* do it."

"Are you sure?" I said, hoping Sarah would walk in and rescue me.

The judge could tell I was out of my element. "I was joking," he chuckled as he grabbed the chain and threw it into the sink.

Silently, he rinsed each fish, then tossed them, one by one, on a big wooden board where, with a cleaver big enough to decapitate Godzilla, he whacked off each head. Pausing only long enough to change blades, he ran a knife down their soft white underbellies and extracted masses of bloody guts.

Knowing I'd never be able to look at a tuna sandwich the same way again, I slithered to a large bay window off the dining area. I looked out at the trees silhouetted by the setting sun.

"Have you seen Sarah?" the judge asked as he wiped his fish-scaly hands with a blood-soaked towel.

"Must still be on the phone." Next to where I was standing, an old grandfather clock caught my eye. It was getting late, and I was eager to begin my long drive back.

He opened the refrigerator door. "How about a beer?"

A beer? That was the missing ingredient to another banner day. Alcohol, a crooked cop, a judge who enjoyed taking a bite out of my ass every chance he got.

I nodded in the direction of my car. "Better not . . . I have to get going."

"Nonsense," Sarah said from behind me. Her cheeks flushed, her eyes darkened, she looked drawn from the grueling day.

The judge handed me a cold bottle anyway. "You're not going anywhere until you have something to eat."

I noticed several fish scales attached to the amber bottle as we walked into the living room. With my back to him, I removed the sticky debris with my fingers. "I really do have to get back, Judge," I said.

"Damn it, Dobbs! I haven't been in a courtroom for years. If you call me Judge one more time . . ."

Sarah smiled and plopped onto the sofa. "I believe he wants to be called Avery."

Easier said than done.

"Sorry," I said and turned to Sarah. "Did you set up a meeting with the D.A.'s office?"

"We're meeting with Michael Patterson on Thursday."

Patterson was an assistant to the San Francisco District Attorney. I knew him from Department G, where I had been assigned for four years. A Rhodes scholar from an ivy league law school, Patterson may have been one of the most intelligent attorneys I had defended against, but he lacked the most important attribute of a good trial attorney— street smarts. We had tried at least eight trials against one another, and he lost every one.

"He must have called in every marker he had to get assigned to my case," I remarked.

"What did he have to say?" Avery asked Sarah.

"He wouldn't discuss any specifics."

Typical Patterson, I thought. I'd be kept in the dark until he had enough time to prepare his witnesses. I knew from experience he wouldn't divulge more than he had to unless the press asked the questions. "We'll probably have to read about it in the papers."

"I don't think so." Sarah reached for the glass of white wine her father was handing her. "He'll try to keep it quiet. He knows how easy it would be for him to end up with egg on his face."

Avery walked to the fireplace and threw in a couple of small logs. "Is someone going to tell me what happened to Jared?"

I blew air from my mouth at just the thought of it.

Sarah made a point of glaring at me before she went on to tell her father that as soon as she informed McBean that her client was invoking his right to be silent, he immediately took Jared into court to be arraigned. Sarah entered a not-guilty plea and the preliminary hearing was set for the following Wednesday. Everything seemed to be going smoothly, until the judge denied her request to order the sheriff to return Jared's necklace. When the judge refused, Jared fell to his knees and pounded the floor with his fists while yelling obscenities at the judge. Four deputies had to tie his hands behind his back while pushing Jared's face into the courtoom's cold wooden floor. The elderly judge mumbled something about contempt as he repeatedly pounded his gavel. Everyone else in the courtroom stood openmouthed.

"Do you have any idea why he is so attached to that necklace?" Sarah asked her father.

He was staring blankly into the fire. "I don't have the foggiest."

Sarah leaned her head back against the cushions and closed her eyes. "Probably the only thing he owns that means anything to him," she mumbled. "Sentimental value or something."

"I'm not so sure he understands what's happening to him," I interjected.

"Don't underestimate Jared," Avery said. "He's no dummy."

"I'm not worried about his intelligence. It's his emotional stability that concerns me."

"Neither one of you should pay much attention to how someone reacts when they're behind bars," Avery barked. "How would you act if you were arrested for a bunch of trumped-up charges?"

I could tell Avery was upset and was trying to rationalize his ex-army buddy's bizarre actions. "You're probably right," I said, though still thinking his behavior was odd.

"So what proof does that idiot McBean think he has?" the judge asked.

Sarah lifted her head from the cushion. "The police report indicates they have a pretty strong case."

"But the prosecution does have a few problems," I volunteered.

Avery's look was strained. The newspaper's reporting of the details had been sketchy at best. He was anxious to find out what the evidence was, and he didn't like having to pry it out of us. "Like what, exactly?"

Sarah brushed several stray strands of hair from her face. I could tell she was having a difficult time even thinking about the terrible things that had happened to the ten-year-old. Especially when her father's friend was the one being accused of perpetrating them.

"The boy had just left Sav-on drugstore when he was jumped by someone and thrown into a car," I said.

"That someone," the judge interrupted. "Did the boy give an accurate description?"

"It was too dark to get a good look," I said. "He couldn't even pick him out of a six-pack."

Sarah slowly shook her head. "But the general description fits Jared."

I gave her a look as if she should know better. "That vague description fits half the men in this county."

"What description?"

"Nothing much, really," I said. "Only that it was a man who had a full beard and he was wearing a baseball cap."

"I see," the judge said, contemplating the possibilities.

I continued. "The man threw the boy into his car. Then, as they drive out of town, he slugged the boy in the face, knocking him out cold. By the time the kid regained consciousness, they were somewhere in the mountains."

"Does the boy know where, exactly?"

"Also too dark," I said.

Avery rested his hand on the mantel and nervously thumped his fingers. "Then what happened?"

"When the car finally came to a stop, the man dragged the boy to a spot where he eventually ripped his clothes off."

Sarah rose and slowly walked in front of the fire and stood with her back to the flames, warming herself. "Can you imagine what must have been going through that poor boy's mind?" she said. "He must have been scared to death."

"I'm sure he was," I said. "But he sounds like he's a pretty spunky kid."

"What makes you say that?" the judge asked.

"Because as he's lying in the dirt, naked, with the man straddling him, he lets the man have it," I said. "He kicked the pervert square in the groin. When the man doubled up in pain, the boy escaped deep into the forest."

"He's lucky to be alive," Sarah said. "I'm sure whoever attacked the boy wasn't planning on letting him live to tell about it."

The judge angled his head, musing over what we just told him. "What that boy went through is gut-wrenching, but so far I haven't heard anything that implicates Jared."

"That's because the real problem," Sarah said and gave me a look as if to say she knew I had an explanation for what she was about to say, "is the boy purchased a package of candy while he was at Sav-on."

"Don't tell me," Avery interrupted.

Sarah nodded as if she knew her father had figured it out. "The cops found a package of the same kind of candy on the front seat of Jared's car."

Avery sat on the sofa, thinking. "That sure doesn't help."

"But Hunter believes he has an explanation."

Since she brought it up. "Not an explanation really," I said and told him how I had looked inside the car when I arrived earlier in the day.

Avery's face brightened. He'd been on the bench twice as long as I'd been an attorney. He knew what some cops were capable of.

"Hunter's right, Sarah. A good attorney should never accept anything at face value."

For an instant Sarah was off balance. "And I don't," she said defensively. "But cops planting evidence is almost impossible to prove."

I nodded my head in agreement. She was definitely right about that. And knowing McBean, he'd likely done a very good job of covering his tracks.

"Look at the mess they made," Sarah said as she tiptoed among piles of loose clothing, magazines, and books strewn across the floor. We were in the guest house that McBean's posse had ransacked earlier. It was after ten and the only source of light was a red Lava lamp set on a nightstand.

We'd just finished dinner. Avery had hardly said another word, and Sarah hadn't said much more. The day's events had them both rattled. My original plan was that as soon as Sarah and I discussed how much money she would need to represent me,

I would be on my way home. But that was before the two beers I guzzled to wash down the fish. Sarah could tell I was tired, and she persuaded me to stay in Jared's room for the night. I didn't put up much of a fight.

Sarah righted an old lamp on the dresser. "This should work." The bulb flickered several times, and she reached to the side of the dresser to see if the plug was loose.

"There." She pushed it securely into the wall. Nothing. She shook the lamp a couple of times and tweaked the bulb with her finger before she gave up.

"It must be the bulb," I said and looked to see if there was anything else we could turn on.

Sarah gestured at a closed door behind me. "Try the bathroom."

Picking my way through the mess on the floor, I felt around for the switch and flipped it on. The bathroom wasn't much bigger than a phone booth. The white porcelain in the sink and bathtub were yellow with age or lack of cleaning; I wasn't sure which.

"Open it farther," she said.

The old hinges creaked as I pushed on the door until it banged against the toilet. It was open wide enough for the light to illuminate most of the room.

"I'm sorry, Hunter." Sarah was standing with her hands on her hips, surveying the damage. McBean's buddies had tossed the joint, all right. The drawers of the old rickety furniture were open, their spilled contents lying beneath them. Some magazines and books lay haphazardly on the dresser and table tops, but most were scattered about the floor. "Why don't you just sleep in the extra bedroom inside the main house?"

"Don't worry about it," I said and bent down to pick up a few of the books. I idly thumbed through them when one title caught my eye.

It was a small pamphlet with the title *The Dark Side* in bold red print. The pages were brown with age and appeared to deal with the power of black magic. "Looks like Jared was into reading some pretty heavy stuff."

Sarah bent over to pick up several similar titles while I picked up a small paperback by my foot. "This sure looks out of place," I said. It was an old Catholic catechism.

Our eyes met.

"What the hell is he doing with all this stuff?" I asked.

"No idea," she sighed.

Whatever remained in our way, I pushed aside with my feet. The beer was taking its toll. I considered using the bathroom, but if I closed the door, it would have left her in the dark. And I wasn't about to leave it open and take a leak in front of her.

"This is ridiculous." Sarah kicked a pair of dirty Levi's into a corner next to the bed. It was unkempt, the sheets stained with God only knew what.

All I wanted was to get the bed made so Sarah could leave. "Don't worry about it. A couple fresh sheets should do the trick."

I reached down and ripped off the old ones with one quick pull. We both stared at the naked mattress; it was dirtier than the sheets. Sarah scrunched her face. "Are you sure?"

Little did she know she was talking to someone who, except for three years of marriage, had been a bachelor since he graduated high school. Although the sight of what we were standing over did almost make me gag.

I eyed the bathroom again. If I didn't take a piss soon, the mattress wouldn't be the only thing that was soiled.

"We still have to talk about how we are going to deal with Patterson," she said as she tucked the bottom sheet under the mattress.

"Tonight?"

Sarah threw the top sheet in the air and it fell gently to the mattress. "We seemed to have gotten a little sidetracked this afternoon."

"I know. We still have to discuss your fees."

"My fees," she said. "I've already figured that out."

Staring at her blankly, I finished tucking in my side. I sat on the edge of the newly made bed, anxious to find out what she meant, when a pain, like a dull knife, pierced my side. I considered running outside and making a beeline for the nearest tree.

"Let me explain," she continued. "Even if the D.A. decides not to file charges, the state bar won't give up so easy. And they are slow. We could be looking at three to four months before they complete their investigation."

"Well, if you're worried I can't pay . . ."

"That's not what I'm saying," she interrupted. "What I mean is . . . you are going to have a lot of free time on your hands."

"Looks that way."

"So, I'm going to make sure you have something to do," she said brightly like we were about to have some fun.

"What did you have in mind?"

Sarah placed her hand gently on mine. With her touch I felt goose bumps forming all over me. I quickly looked away, hoping she hadn't noticed. "My father wants to make sure Jared receives a good defense." Her voice was unsteady, and I was sure she felt the charge, too. "So, I was thinking," she said, still a little shaky, "why don't you stay here and help me represent him?"

She'd caught me off guard. "I don't know," I mumbled.

"It's perfect." Her voice was smooth again, in persuasive lawyer mode. "I'll represent you in exchange for your help with Jared. A little quid pro quo."

The squeeze of her hand on mine was distracting me. Gently, as if I hadn't even noticed, I extracted it. "I'm not sure," I said. "After all, I do live two hours from here. Plus, I don't know anything about how the courts up here operate."

"Hunter, I've never handled a case even remotely as serious as Jared's." Her baby blues were pleading for me to say yes. "But with your help it would be a walk in the park."

"What about your father?"

"The pressure of a trial . . . with his heart . . . No way."

I reached to help her off the bed.

"Plus, he's too close to Jared," she added.

It did make a lot of sense. I'd handled dozens of similar cases. Even though I had been making a lot of noise about McBean planting evidence, it would likely be impossible to prove. I'd need to take some time investigating, ruling out the possibility that the cops framed Jared, then working out a satisfactory plea bargain. Actually, I would be getting the better end of the stick. Needing my limited savings to live on, I wasn't sure I could afford Sarah anyway.

"Are you sure this is what you want?"

Sarah nodded. "I'd really appreciate it."

The tingly feeling was back. I turned to look out the window. The moon was just beginning to show over the ridge of redwoods to the north.

"Dad will clean this place tomorrow," she said. "You'll see. It won't be so bad."

The mention of her father doing something for me woke me up. I understood why the two of them had been so friendly, insisting I stay for dinner and boozing me up. She'd do anything for her father. And he needed me.

"I get it. . . ." I began, but stopped myself. What was I thinking? I needed her help more than she did mine. I had no room to complain.

"Let's give it a try," I said.

"Great, we'll start tomorrow." Sarah gave me a quick peck on the cheek. A twinkle appeared in her eye. "Now I have to leave before my bladder explodes," she said and rushed out the front door.

Chapter 8

The San Francisco County District Attorney's Office had an eerie coldness about it. I felt like a stranger sitting in front of Michael Patterson's desk, flanked by Sarah and Steve Ogden. This time I wasn't fishing for some poor slob who'd had his sorry butt hauled in for something he deserved. This time I wasn't one of two adversaries doing their traditional dance around the court's maypole. This time it was my ass on the line, and I didn't like the feeling.

We had been waiting for Sergeant Musgrave, the investigating officer assigned to my case.

Ogden sat very still, his hands folded in his lap. Except for how the allegations reflected on the integrity of the public defender's office, I figured he didn't give a damn what happened to me. Otherwise, he wouldn't have put me on immediate suspension.

Patterson, on the other hand, fidgeted in his chair as he contemplated his next move.

During our long drive, Sarah and I had agonized over how much I should say to him. Like most defense attorneys, we were aware that anything I said could be twisted. But we were also aware I had nothing to hide.

"Let's get started without him," the D.A. finally said. His voice had a smoker's gravelly sound to it. "Miss Harris has informed me you are willing to discuss the allegations that Bobby Miles and Salvador Martinez have lodged against you."

"If that's what it takes."

Patterson slowly thumbed through the open file on his desk, exposing the yellow tobacco stains from his three-pack-a-day habit.

"These are very serious charges," he said, as if he were reading them for the first time.

"All lies," I responded.

With a raised eyebrow Patterson fixed his gaze on me. "I better advise you of your rights."

"Come on, Mike." I looked at Ogden for help, but he was adjusting the shoelaces on his newly polished wingtips.

"Is that really necessary?" Sarah asked. "I thought this was just an informal meeting."

"It is," he said. "But you both know it's required." Patterson probably thought I'd come in cowering, begging for his understanding. But that was his fault—just as marching into his office thinking the matter would be informally resolved was mine. We both should have known better. He pulled a card from his top pocket. "You have the right—"

I grabbed the card from his hand and signed at the bottom. "I've heard it a thousand times," I said and flipped the card at him. It whizzed past his head and fell harmlessly to the floor.

Patterson's face hardened, as did mine. Sarah scooted forward in her chair to say something but I waved her off.

"I signed it," I said, "so let's get going."

After making a show of taking a deep breath, Patterson leaned to his side, picking up the card. "Are you ready to begin, Mr. Dobbs?"

"As long as it's tape-recorded."

Patterson opened his top drawer and pulled out a small cassette recorder, set it on top of his desk and pushed the record button. He then explained the preliminaries, including who was present and the subject matter of the interview. "And you understand that you do not have to talk to me?"

I just looked at him.

"We understand," Sarah answered.

"Good."

The next half hour Patterson spent reading Miles's and Martinez's statements.

"And that's a bunch of bull," I said as soon as he finished.

Patterson didn't hesitate. "Then what's your version?"

"You know I can't tell you what was discussed."

"What Mr. Dobbs means," Sarah explained, "is that he cannot divulge any of his conversation with Mr. Martinez."

Patterson looked at Ogden. "I believe," Ogden said, "there is the problem of attorney-client privilege."

Patterson closed the folder and sat back in his big leather chair, rubbing his chin, pondering the dilemma. "I may have a solution," he eventually said, like the thought had just occurred to him. "What about a lie detector?"

"Polygraph!" I vaulted from my chair. "You've got to be kidding."

Ogden held up his hand. "Maybe it isn't such a bad idea."

I looked at him in amazement. Had this all been rehearsed? "If you'd personally handled a case in the last dozen years, you wouldn't say anything that stupid."

Ogden sat expressionless, his eyes glued to mine.

Patterson's voice went cold. "I've done my best to be nice to you and—"

"That's more bull." I paused, to take a deep breath, trying to calm myself. But it didn't do any good. "Anyone with half a brain knows Martinez put that kid up to it," I said, pointing a finger at him. "But that thought hasn't occurred to you, has it, Mike? This is personal. I kicked your ass every time you came up against me, and this is your way to get even."

Patterson rose to his feet. "I resent that!"

Sarah gave me a shove toward the door. "What are you doing?" she whispered between clenched teeth. "If you don't cooperate, he'll file charges."

I shook my head. "Taking a polygraph isn't cooperating." I turned to look at Patterson. "No one passes the *police* polygraph."

Patterson was planted again in his chair. "That's not true."

"Oh, really?" I said. "I'll tell you exactly what

will happen. I'll take the polygraph and immediately be informed I flunked it. Then your examiners will tell me how they want me to retake it. But this time they're going to help me pass it. But in order to do that, they have to know what it was I originally deceived them about. Then once I open up a little, they start grilling me, the whole time trying to get me to confess."

Patterson scoffed, but he didn't look too convincing. "That's ridiculous."

"I have more than a dozen taped polygraph interviews in the desk in my office to prove it." I turned to Ogden. "Assuming I still have a desk, that is."

Ogden looked at Sarah for help, but I pushed my way past her and stood in front of Patterson. "If I won't allow one of my clients to be polygraphed, I'm sure in hell not going to subject myself to one."

"Are you going to let me finish?" Patterson said, nodding his head for me to sit back down.

As I slowly took my seat, I glanced at Ogden. Again I had this peculiar sensation that this had been choreographed by the two of them. I couldn't believe how spineless he was. How could I have worked for him all these years?

"I mentioned the polygraph in light of your fear about breaching a confidential communication. It's the only way we can resolve this matter."

I didn't think for a second that Patterson wanted to help, but I wanted to hear everything, to make some sense out of what was happening. "Go on."

Patterson's gaze settled on the top of his desk, as if he was embarrassed by what he was about to say. "I promise if you pass the polygraph, I will close the file and you can get back to work."

The room was silent while everyone absorbed what he was saying. "And," he said in an assuring tone, "I will forward the results to the state bar so they'll get off your back."

"And?" I said.

Patterson smiled. "And the examiner will not ask you any further questions if you fail to pass it."

"What do we have to lose?" Sarah whispered.

I sat motionless, staring at Patterson. "Do you want to tell her what I have to lose, or do you want me to?"

Patterson looked over at Ogden and shook his head. Their little ploy wasn't working.

"Why don't we quit playing games?" I said. "You want me to enter into an agreement that if I pass the test, that will be the end of it, right?"

"That's correct."

"What happens if I don't pass?"

Patterson squirmed in his chair. His face said it all.

"I'll tell you what," I said to Sarah. "They want a stipulation that if the machine shows I'm deceptive, they can use it in court against me."

Sarah stiffened, caught off guard. "There isn't a court in this state that would allow the results of a polygraph exam into evidence," she protested.

"Normally you'd be right," I said, scowling at Patterson. "But there's this game the San Francisco D.A.'s office has been playing for a few years now. Do you want to tell her about it, Mike?"

Patterson shrugged. "It's authorized by statute."

Sarah folded her arms across her chest. "What is?"

"Evidence code section 351.1 permits the results of a polygraph to be admitted into evidence as long as the parties stipulate to it," I explained.

Sarah's voice was cold. "Who would ever agree to that?"

"Anyone whom the D.A. convinces that it's the only way they can resolve the matter short of filing charges. Either you agree to it or they arrest you and get as high a bail as possible."

Patterson shrugged again. "It's entirely their choice."

"It's blackmail is what it is," Sarah said, louder than anyone expected. "Are you telling me that's what you want Hunter to agree to?"

Patterson nodded. "That's correct."

"You want us to agree to that, knowing how unreliable the polygraph is?"

"My office doesn't feel it's unreliable."

"Well, I do," Sarah exclaimed, then paused to lower her voice. "What you're suggesting is totally unacceptable."

"Wait a minute," I said and turned to Ogden. I was going to see once and for all whose side he was on. "What do you think?"

He shifted nervously, looking at Patterson. He finally met my gaze. "Under the circumstances, I really don't feel the polygraph would be in your best interest."

Thank God. I knew we'd had our problems in the past and I wasn't the easiest guy to get along with, but I'd always given him my best and I was thankful to see he felt some loyalty to me.

The D.A. sat back into his big leather chair. "Then you're declining my offer?"

There was stone silence. Patterson's eyes and mine were locked, waiting to see who would be the first to blink.

"Not really," I finally said. Sarah and Ogden both jerked their heads at each other and then at me.

"What are you saying?" Sarah snapped.

"I'll take a polygraph."

Patterson leaned forward in anticipation. "And if you fail, you'll stipulate the results can be used in court?"

"Sure."

Sarah gave Patterson a look like, He's such a jokester. "I need to talk to Mr. Dobbs in private," she said.

"No need," I said and propped my elbows on Patterson's desk. Our faces were only a foot apart as I went on. "As long as the polygraph examiner is not on the county's payroll."

"A private examiner?"

"Exactly."

Patterson stared at me as if he was considering it, but I was sure he wasn't.

"You see, Mike, I have nothing to hide. I'm telling the truth, and I'm ready to prove it."

Patterson's face turned cold. "You know our office will only allow a police examiner."

"Well, then," I said, "do what you have to because I'm not going to let one of your examiners get their hands on me."

Patterson reached for his telephone. "And you're

not willing to discuss what was said between you and either that boy or Martinez?"

I knew what all this was leading up to, and I was going to put in my last two cents before it happened. "You know as well as I do it doesn't matter if I discuss each and every detail of my conversation with that boy and Martinez. You aren't going to believe a damn thing I say anyway. So why don't we top screwing around here? This interview is over with as of this second." I grabbed his recorder and punched the off button.

Patterson immediately flipped on his intercom. "Send the detectives in."

We both sat glaring at each other.

"Aren't you being a little premature?" Ogden said when the door burst open and two plain-clothes detectives stood just inside the doorway. Their coats were open—holstered guns exposed—just in case I had any ideas.

"Hunter Dobbs," Patterson said, "you are under arrest for subornation of perjury." He then waved his two thugs toward me. "Take Mr. Dobbs into custody."

Chapter 9

I can't count how many times I'd been in a municipal court lockup, but it was the first time I had ever been on the other side of the glass. As I waited for Sarah, my forehead was slick with beads of sweat, yet my hands and feet were cold as ice. I'd always tried to appreciate the anxiety my client experienced during an initial interview, but only at that moment did I fully understand how being handcuffed and shackled, with a guard watching your every move, could make someone feel so impotent, so utterly helpless.

Subornation of perjury. Christ. That's first-year law school stuff. That was something we were taught they used to do in the twenties and thirties during the reign of Al Capone. I remembered some of the stories told around The Gavel about the days of the labor wars down on the docks and the crackdown on the city's crime bosses. A few flamboyant defense lawyers would have off-the-shelf eyewitnesses at their fingertips who would prove their client was on the East Coast at any given moment of any given day.

But that was folklore, and this was the era of

post-Watergate ethics and the strict compliance with a lawyer's ethical duties. Today, even the sloppiest and most crooked lawyer didn't finagle testimony. But a slimeball and a scared juvey had me by the short ones. I was facing not only sure disbarment, but serious jail time.

Thankfully, the detectives brought me straight to an interview room while I awaited my appearance in court. I had the impression they didn't like their jobs at that particular moment, but that was probably just my way of rationalizing my predicament. I thought the absurdity of the charges would be obvious to all—but clearly I was wrong or I wouldn't have been there.

"You won't believe it," Sarah said, closing the door. She looked disheveled, her hands trembling as she placed my file on the counter. I was sure it hadn't occurred to her that she would run into such a buzzsaw. She looked around at the filth and stench we found ourselves in. It wasn't bucolic Ukiah.

"Remember when I told you about the glass partition Martinez shattered?"

At this mention, she looked uneasy. "Is this the room?"

I looked up and down at the glass between us. "One good thing came of it."

Sarah gave me a puzzled look.

"New glass."

After a pained smile, she got straight to why she was there. "You are going to be arraigned in Kellogg's court."

I thought for sure she had to be joking. "No way."

"Do you want me to paper him?" she asked, referring to the filing of a motion under 170.6 of the penal code that allows a defendant to disqualify a judge.

"I'm not sure we should." I paused to think it through. "We can only do that once. I'd rather wait."

"But after what you said to him, there is no way he's going to be fair."

It was time to break the news. "He's not the only judge I've ever had a problem with. I'd rather save my 170.6 for trial. That's when the judge can make a real difference. All Kellogg can do is schedule the preliminary hearing."

"But what if he sets it in his court."

"Can't," I said, pointing to the front page of the complaint. "My case number ends on an even number. Only odd-numbered prelims are heard in his court."

Sarah smiled for the first time that day. "That was sure a stroke of luck." Her face just as quickly turned serious again. "But what about bail? You can't leave that up to Kellogg."

"I really don't think that will be a problem," I said. "Not even Patterson would oppose an OR."

"I hope you're right." Sarah's eyes shifted to my hands, wrapped in chains, folded on the counter in front of me.

"Looks like I blew it," I said.

"What do you mean?"

"If I would have kissed Patterson's feet," I said,

shaking my head at the thought of it, "you and I would be having lunch about now."

Her gloomy look didn't change. "It wouldn't have made any difference. After you left, he explained a few things."

"Like what?"

"That he honestly doesn't feel Bobby Miles is lying."

I snorted. "Patterson wouldn't recognize the truth if God stamped it on his forehead," I said. "If he could, he'd still be in the courtroom instead of pushing paperwork."

Sarah's voice became flat. "He'll be the trial deputy on this one."

"That's because no one else believes in what he's up to," I said weakly, knowing full well I was dreaming. The D.A.'s were likely lined up, each begging to take a shot at me.

"Hunter," she said in a somber tone, "there is no way Martinez could have forced Miles to lie."

This startled me. "Of course he could have."

"It's going to be tough to prove." Sarah pulled several documents from her briefcase. "Here's their records. They were never together in lockup. They were never even close enough to shout to one another."

I slammed my hand on the counter. "I don't give a damn what their records show. Someone told that kid what to say, and it sure wasn't me!"

She closed the folder. "They're asking for fifty thousand bail."

"That's just great," I said, throwing my hands in the air. "I don't have that kind of money. I just finished paying off all the damn lawyer bills from my divorce."

The door opened behind me. It was Kellogg's bailiff. "The judge wants this handled before lunch."

Because he's in a hurry to down several martinis to celebrate my demise, I wanted to say, but I'd said enough for one day.

"People versus Hunter K. Dobbs," Cindy, Judge Kellogg's perky young clerk, called out. My head throbbed from nerves. I feigned a lack of concern as I stood in the jury box, my hands and feet shackled. Sarah was next to me, nervously tapping her pen on the counter.

Patterson was standing behind the counsel table next to his cohort, Jerry Lipton. Several court clerks from the other courts were leaning against the wall on the other side of the room. Next to them stood several D.A.s and fellow P.D.s, waiting to see what Kellogg would do. I glanced at the spectator section: thankfully, I didn't see any reporters.

But who was I kidding? The press would be all over this like the proverbial cheap suit. I would likely end up on page one of the metro section. Someone—one of Patterson's minions, maybe—would slip a word to one of his favorite media contacts. Or maybe Kellogg would do it himself; he was never above getting his mug in the papers. Especially as a crusading jurist, trying to save the image of the bench and bar from a horrible breach. Some good reporter could get two weeks' worth of column material out of a P.D. getting tossed into the can for conjuring up tailored testimony.

Kellogg appeared bored as he stacked and un-stacked the files in front of him. I could tell he was playing for time, heightening the suspense. Revenge is sweet, unless you happen to be the target. Then it just plain sucks.

Sarah was the first to speak. "The defendant is ready."

Kellogg looked down at Patterson. "Read the charges."

"The defendant will waive formal reading," Sarah interjected.

"That's your prerogative, Counselor. But I would like to hear them." Kellogg turned to me. "You may be seated, Mr. Dobbs."

Kellogg wanted to give the appearance that he was being fair and harbored no ill will. Then, when Patterson asked for bail, he'd ream me—and get to blame it on the D.A.

Patterson read the complaint slowly, enunciating every word. It seemed to take an eternity. Everything seemed to be in slow motion.

When he finished, Patterson faced me. "Hunter K. Dobbs," he said, "to the charges as read, what is your plea?"

"Not guilty," I said without the slightest hesitation.

"Now, Your Honor," Sarah said to Kellogg, who was already leaning back in his chair, expecting what would happen next, "we would like to be heard as to bail."

As if swatting a pesky fly, Kellogg waved at Sarah to proceed.

"I know the court is aware Mr. Dobbs has been a practicing attorney in this county and a respected member of the legal community for nearly ten years."

Kellogg glared at Sarah. "I don't need to hear about his family tree. Just tell me why bail of $50,000 should not be increased."

"Because the charges are totally false, and anyone who has worked as closely with Mr. Dobbs as this court and the District Attorney has knows it."

"Counselor—" Kellogg said, and Sarah cut him off.

"These allegations are based on the word of two inmates, and each has an obvious motive to lie—"

"Your Honor," Patterson said.

"If you would allow me to finish," Sarah scolded the D.A., then turned back to Kellogg. "One of the two informants is accused of murder and has a serious criminal history since he was thirteen years old. To place such a high bail on such weak allegations would be a travesty."

"Are you finished?" Patterson said to Sarah, but Kellogg felt it was his turn.

"Your personal opinions are not relevant here," the judge said. "These are very grave charges."

"But that doesn't make them any more truthful," Sarah shot back.

Kellogg slapped his hand on the bench. "You don't appear to have any more respect for this court than your client does."

Sarah paused, taking a deep breath as she glanced at my pale face. Slowly, she turned back to the judge. "I apologize if the court feels I am being disrespectful, because that has never been my intention. It's just I feel strongly that—"

"I don't want to hear anything more from you," Kellogg said, and turned to the D.A. "What's your position?"

"What I've been trying to say," Patterson said, "is that my office has reconsidered, and we do not oppose an OR release for Mr. Dobbs."

Kellogg lurched forward in his chair. "Well, I do," he bellowed. "Mr. Dobbs is accused of breaching a trust he is sworn to uphold. And for purposes of bail, I have to assume that the charges as read are true and have a basis in fact."

"No one realizes that more than Mr. Patterson," Sarah interrupted. "If he feels they do not justify bail, then I believe the court has to consider that."

"And I have," Kellogg said. "Because of Mr. Patterson's position I will not increase bail at this time, but I will not lower it either. Bail will remain set at $50,000."

And that's what you get for telling a judge he's a drunk.

"Payback's a bitch," Howard Millings said as he pressed my inked thumb onto a small card alongside the prints of my other fingers. I was in a small room in the police department, completing the booking process. It was an ordeal everyone who has been arrested for a felony must go through. Howard had asked specially to book me. He was waiting for me in lockup when I left the courtroom.

Howard and I became friends right after I hired

on with the P.D.'s office. My first assignment in Superior Court was in Sarah's father's courtroom where Howard was the bailiff. Harris didn't treat him much better than those of us who appeared in front of him. Like myself, Howard was an avid Forty-niners fan. That is, until they let Joe Montana go. Howard, like many of the Montana faithful, changed alliances and rooted for Kansas City. Since Montana had retired, Howard had changed back to the Niners. I was a fan, but Howard was one of the faithful. A lifer.

He was also a walking history book. A cop for over thirty years, he had the inside scoop on just about everyone and everything. He knew where all the skeletons were buried among the city's elite. Who was banging whom and how much they enjoyed it.

Howard waved my booking card in the air so my fingerprints would dry faster. "I never thought Kellogg would be so petty," I said.

"I hear you as much as called him a sloppy drunk in front of the whole courtroom."

"That's not entirely correct."

"If I know Kellogg," he chuckled, "I'm sure that's the way he saw it."

Howard placed the card into an envelope with my name in bold type on the front. "So who's going to spring you?"

"Damned if I know." I'd been wondering the same thing myself. Sarah promised she would make sure it was taken care of, but when you're in jail, cut off from the world, you quickly realize the only person you can count on is yourself.

"Do you need to make some telephone calls?"

I didn't want to. I was too embarrassed to call anyone.

"You better," Howard persisted. "Once I drop you off at the main jail, you'll be fair game."

"Cavity search?" I asked, cringing at the thought.

"Yep, the whole ball of wax."

Howard placed the telephone in front of me. "Start calling."

The first person that came to mind was my mother's brother, who had raised me since I was ten. But Joe Calabrese was not just an uncle—he was my best friend—the father I never really had. I loved him dearly.

I reached for the phone, then hesitated. I couldn't do it. This would break his heart. His life revolved around his "successful attorney nephew." He was in his mid-sixties and retired in Palo Alto. He'd help me, all right, but I wasn't sure I could handle breaking the news to him.

As I held onto the phone, it rang. I almost jumped out of my skin. Howard laughed as he picked it up and plopped his feet on the large metal green desk. "Yeah, he's here."

What now? It was probably his sergeant asking him what we were still doing in the booking room.

"No shit, Judge Harris," he said and grunted. "Well, you better hurry up, I can't keep him here much longer."

Howard slammed down the receiver and shook his head. "I thought you and Judge Harris never got along."

"What are you talking about?"

"That was the bail bondsman. He's writing a bond for fifty grand right now."

Thank God, I thought. "But what was that about Judge Harris?"

"He's the one springing you."

"No, he must have meant his daughter," I said. "She's my attorney."

"No shit! Sarah's your attorney?"

"Do you remember her?"

"Remember?" he said and howled like a wolf. "How could anyone ever forget that face—that luscious body. What a package."

I smiled. Same old horny Howard.

"You and her wouldn't be . . . ?" he said and rapidly pumped his fat overweight pelvis in the chair. It wasn't a pretty sight.

"Please," I said, holding my hand in front of my eyes. "Our relationship is strictly business."

"Right," he said and laughed, until he noticed I wasn't. He then swiveled in my direction and, with a serious expression, said, "I just thought that maybe you and her . . ." Howard's face began to redden. It had been quite a while since the two of us had had a talk like this.

"I know you better than that. You weren't thinking, you were hoping."

Howard stared into the distance as if he was trying to remember. "I never knew you kept in touch with her."

"I haven't."

"I can remember you and Judge Harris used to really go at it," he said, smiling at the thought.

"Seems to be ingrained in my nature."

"Hey, don't kick yourself around the block for what you said to Kellogg. He's a drunk and everyone knows it. I can't believe no one has stood up to him before."

"Because look where it gets you."

"This is nothing more than a pimple on the tip of your nose," he said. "I respect you for what you did. I'm sure those punks are lying, and it wouldn't surprise me if the D.A. doesn't know it, too."

"They are lying."

"Don't have to convince me. I was there when that idiot Martinez tried to claw his way through the glass. Remember?"

"How could I forget?"

"Matter of fact, you better call me as a witness."

"About what?"

"Hell, there's no doubt in my mind that the reason Martinez was so pissed was because you wouldn't do whatever it was he wanted."

"You're not going to be well thought of if you testify for a defense attorney."

"Who gives a shit? You're getting a raw deal and everyone knows it."

"I'm glad to hear someone believes in me."

Howard placed a pen in his mouth and immediately withdrew it, like he was smoking a cigarette. "Are you going to tell me what Judge Harris is doing bailing you out?"

"Sort of puzzles me, too," I said.

"See much of him?"

"Until just a few days ago, I hadn't seen him since he retired."

"Yeah," Howard said as he casually placed his

feet, one at a time, back on the desk. His shirt was stretched so tight that the buttons on his huge gut were about to pop. "I haven't seen or heard from the old fart since he was booted off the bench."

"You mean since he retired?"

"Call it what you want. But I'm sure he was forced off."

An alarm went off. "I never knew that."

His voice fell to a whisper. "Not many do. It was kept pretty hush-hush."

"What was?"

He saw how curious I was and straightened in his seat. "Nah, I'm probably talking out of school."

"Come on," I said. "Don't clam up on me now."

He thought for a moment to find the right words. "It was just rumor, mind you." Howard glanced over his shoulder to make sure no one was listening. "But it had something to do with a child."

"His own?"

"Got me. All I know is he resigned because of it." He was whispering again. "And he got divorced about the same time."

I was as close to speechless as I'd ever been. "You'd think I would have heard something."

"Hell, we both know the guy was hard to get along with," Howard said, shaking his head. "But, I never imagined he'd be into little kids."

"Do you know the details?"

"Only that he'd worked out some kind of deal with the D.A. His early retirement was part of it."

"He just doesn't seem the type."

Howard gave me a blank look. Then his eyes narrowed. "None of them ever do."

My thoughts were revolving so fast I almost forgot where I was. Some of what Howard was saying rang true. I had been transferred from his court a year before the judge left. He was in his late-fifties at the time and in the middle of his term.

The phone rang again, and Howard grabbed it.

"Good," was all he said and hung up. "The bondsman's out front. You're free to go."

Chapter 10

A home should be like a new pair of soft flannel pajamas that you get into on a cold winter's night, warm and comfortable. But my house hadn't felt that way for years. Not because it wasn't nice enough. A three-bedroom Cape Cod, it was located on Telegraph Hill, one of the oldest and most prestigious neighborhoods in San Francisco, with a fantastic view of the city and bay below. But when we separated, I wanted Marlene to take whatever furniture she wanted. Whatever remained was sold. I didn't want anything left that reminded me of her. I should have sold the house, too. Its feeling of warmth and comfort was gone, and I was sure it would never return.

"This is interesting." Sarah was standing in the open doorway, musing over what I referred to as a fully furnished house. All she could see was a black leather love seat and matching recliner sitting in front of a twenty-five-inch TV with videotapes strewn haphazardly on the floor.

Ignoring her lack of appreciation for my ascetic simplicity, I walked into the kitchen, where a pervasive odor was painfully evident. Under a sink full of dirty dishes was trash that had been rotting for nearly a week.

"Little ripe," I said. I held the trash bag far from my nose as I rushed past her on my way to the garage.

When I returned, Sarah was at the kitchen sink up to her elbows in soapy water. I grabbed the air freshener and sprayed it throughout the kitchen. But it only made the smell worse. A sour rotting odor mixed with sweet pine, like a garbage dump in the High Sierras, surrounding us.

"Don't worry about the dishes," I said, hoping she'd ignore me.

"You're going to be gone for at least another week," she said. "I'll take care of these while you get your things."

We'd already decided that it would be best if I continued to stay in her father's guest house. We were going to need a lot of time together to prepare for my prelim. And, for a while at least, I had nothing to do in San Francisco.

"Sorry it took so long to get you bailed out," Sarah said as I packed just about everything I owned, which wasn't much.

"They were just about to make me bend over and spread my cheeks," I joked and immediately regretted it. I was talking like she was one of my bowling buddies.

When I returned to the living room with a suitcase and overnight bag, Sarah was standing in front of the fireplace holding a picture of Marlene. The photo had been taken the month before we separated.

"You still love her, don't you?"

I was taken aback by the question. She may just have been trying to be friendly, but her timing was wrong.

"If it's all right with you, I'd rather not talk about it."

Sarah replaced the picture. "It's obvious you do."

"And what makes you so sure?"

"It's not often someone keeps a framed photo of their ex on the mantel."

I didn't want to talk about it. With all that had gone on that day the last thing I wanted to do was discuss my past marital problems. It was still painful just to think about.

I shrugged my shoulders instead, hoping that would end it.

"Damn it, Hunter. Something's bothering you."

She was right about that. And it had nothing to do with Marlene. I was still upset over what Millings had told me earlier about why her father had been forced to resign. Could it be just a coincidence that he had a history of child molests and Danny Barton's attacker matched his description as well as Jared's? That question kept gnawing at me. But I wasn't sure it was the right time to get into it.

"With everything that's happened today I feel a little rattled," I said.

Sarah stepped toward the window and looked out at the lights of the city below. "You think my father put up the bail to make sure you were available to help me with Jared's case."

"I wish it were that simple."

"It is simple," she said with a raised voice. "He bailed you out because he cares for you and thinks you're getting a raw deal."

"Your father may grow Christmas trees," I said, "but he's sure as hell not Santa Claus."

It was a sour joke that I regretted the minute it left my mouth.

Sarah stood glaring at me. It was becoming evident we couldn't work together as long as I suspected her father. I had to clear the air.

"I heard something in jail," I started. "And unless I know the truth, I'm not sure we can continue to help one another."

She stepped closer. "What are you talking about?"

I hesitated, then took a deep breath and blurted it out. "Was your father forced to resign from the bench because of an incident involving a young boy?"

Sarah looked surprised, but not shocked. "Secondhand jailhouse gossip," was all she said.

I stepped closer. "Are you saying it's not true?"

"That is none of your damn business."

"How could it be none of my business when your father not only resembles the man who kidnapped the Barton boy but, might I remind you, also had access to Jared's car?"

Sarah stomped back to the window and made a show of turning her head away from me. "Don't say anything else," she said.

"I need answers, Sarah."

She marched toward me while folding her arms across her chest like she was about to scold me. "You wanted your privacy when I asked about

Marlene," she said.. "I respected yours. Now you'll have to respect mine."

"Your questions were merely personal," I said. "Mine go to the heart of Jared's case."

Her face turned red. I knew it was time to regroup.

"I'm sorry, Sarah," I said. "The last thing I want to do is hurt you, but you must see my point."

Her eyes seemed to brighten, and I could see a calm came over her. "Think about it, Hunter. If my father was somehow implicated, do you think for a second he would have bailed you out? If he had anything to do with the attack on Danny Barton, why would he want you to help me with Jared's case? My father knows you don't like him. Why would he help set you free only to save the fall guy? He knows you'd expose him without hesitation."

Sarah stopped for a moment as if she were thinking it through.

"Look," she said softly, "I've believed in you from the very beginning. I know your life has been upside down ever since that day in Kellogg's court. I know you would never have asked anyone to commit perjury. Now I need you to believe in me. And that includes my father."

She was right. If Judge Harris was involved, the best thing for him would be to let his daughter handle Jared's case alone. At least that way he could maintain some control.

"I'll try," I said and picked up the bags to leave.

Chapter 11

Reporters, cameramen, and their crews shouted, shoved, and pushed one another as they positioned themselves between a white police van and the courthouse's side entrance. Without warning, the van's side door burst open and several uniformed officers jumped out, followed by Jared, who, with his hands and feet shackled, fell to the ground. Before the media realized what had happened, the officers formed a protective cocoon around their bounty. Then, like a pig hanging from a roasting rod, they swiftly carried Jared into the building.

As soon as the door slammed shut, all but a few of the frustrated scribes ran to the courthouse steps, where a mob of curious onlookers and demonstrators were noisily milling about.

"What a circus," Sarah complained as we picked our way through a group of locals standing in the parking lot. They were upset about not being some of the chosen few selected to be allowed inside.

I nodded to the top of the courthouse steps, where several of the reporters had already spotted us and were watching our every move. "It's even worse up there."

Sarah sighed and ironed her skirt with the palm of her hand. She was dressed in a light brown tweed suit and beige silk blouse buttoned tightly to her neck. She looked as though she was preparing for her first on-camera interview, but I had other intentions.

"Well," I said, picking up the pace, "put your head down and hang on tight."

"Child molesters!" someone yelled, and the crowd closed in front of us. As Sarah held onto the back of my coat, I lowered my shoulder and plowed up the steps.

A young woman grabbed Sarah by the hair. "You're no better than that scum you represent."

"Let go of me!" Sarah swung her briefcase at the woman's arm, knocking it free.

When we finally reached a pair of huge, carved oak doors, mikes, some attached to the ends of long poles, were pushed in our faces. Two sets of kliegs went on, and a man with a camera resting on his huge belly pushed himself between us and the entrance.

"Are both of you going to represent Jared Reineer?" he said and shoved a microphone with a big number 9 on it at me. Before I could answer, the jostling of the crowd caused the mike to slam against my lips. A warm, salty liquid trickled from the corner of my mouth.

I grabbed the mike and threw it at the fat man's feet. Then, like a fullback in front of the goal line, I plunged past him through the heavy doors as Sarah pushed from behind.

Once inside, I was surprised to see, that except

for three uniformed officers, McBean, and a tall, muscular, middle-aged man, the courthouse lobby was empty.

"Thanks for the help," I growled. The three stooges were too busy snickering at the sight of a bloodied defense attorney to respond.

McBean was relishing the moment, too. "What's wrong, Dobbs?" He smirked. "Little rough out there?"

Their attention shifted to Sarah as she adjusted her skirt and jacket. "They're all crazy," she said to McBean.

"Just concerned citizens, ma'am."

"More like an angry mob," I fired back and wiped my chin with my bare hand. "Can someone help me here?"

Sarah pulled a handkerchief from her purse. "How did that happen?"

"Some of his so-called concerned citizens." As Sarah wiped my chin, I placed my tongue against the front inside of my mouth. I could feel the tear caused by my lip being sandwiched between the mike and my teeth. But at least the bleeding had seemed to stop.

Sarah spun on McBean. "Next time we want protection!"

"Whatever you say, Counselor," McBean said in a sarcastic tone. As he slowly stepped aside for us to enter the courtroom, the tall man next to him slid into the spot vacated by the lieutenant.

Sarah looked up at the man's face. Her chin was even with his belt buckle. "Excuse me, sir."

The giant didn't budge.

Sarah turned to me as though I was supposed to do something.

I took a deep breath. "Would you please get out of her way?"

"Screw the bitch."

I wasn't sure what to do. He obviously needed a lesson in manners, but I didn't like the thought of being the one to give it. I turned to McBean instead. "If you want us to tell the judge that you and this foul-mouthed idiot wouldn't let us pass, then keep it up."

The man stepped around Sarah toward me. "Who's an idiot?" he bellowed in a deep, throaty, reverberating-off-the-walls voice.

"All right, all right." McBean held his hand against the man's chest. "Mr. Cosgrove, would you mind waiting for me over there?" he said, pointing at a wooden bench at the other end of the hallway.

The man's eyes darted back and forth between me and Sarah as he brushed past us. "Your client killed my little boy," he said. "You tell that piece of shit that I'm going to make sure he doesn't get away with it."

"What's he talking about?" I mouthed to McBean.

"Mr. Cosgrove lives a few miles outside Boonville. His son disappeared, and he thinks Reineer is responsible."

Typical. Anything unexplained that had happened in the county in the last dozen years, Jared would be blamed for.

"Does he have any proof?" Sarah asked.

"We're working on it," McBean said and walked

to the three cops who'd been waiting for the word to let the public in.

When we entered the courtroom, I paused to take in its grandeur. The high ceilings and wood-paneled walls dwarfed the rows upon rows of wooden pews, all darkened black with age. The stately room was a striking contrast to the modern and sometimes sterile houses of justice I was used to.

On the other side of the hand-carved railing which separated the gallery from the participants was a short man in his mid-to-late-thirties, watching as we walked to the counsel table. Each step echoed throughout the room.

"Ms. Harris," the man said and extended his hand to Sarah. I could see a gold watch chain dangling from the vest pocket of his black, hand-tailored suit.

Sarah had clued me in about the head district attorney of Mendocino County. He had a reputation for a big mouth and an ego to match. After eight years as a lower-level prosecutor, J. J. Bragg had been elected district attorney. His father, Raymond Bragg, the third-generation owner of Camelot Winery, was one of the most successful farmers in the state. While most of the other vineyards were owned and operated by generations of offspring who worked the family farm for the pride and fulfillment it gave them, Raymond Bragg was different. Over a hundred years of family tradition meant nothing. To him Camelot's success only meant money. Bundles of it. Enough to ensure that his only son, J.J., could climb as high on the political ladder as either of them wanted.

"My son was born to be governor," Ray would joke with his golf buddies. "No matter how much it costs me."

As I continued my slow walk down the aisle, I was more in awe of my surroundings than meeting the rising star of Northern California politics. It was easy to imagine Clarence Darrow sitting behind the heavy oak counsel table, dressed in an old tattered suit. I could see him cross-examining the prosecution's main witness while chomping on his saliva-drenched stogie—its long ash threatening to fall in his lap.

"This is Mr. Hunter Dobbs," Sarah said. I extended my hand, but Bragg was busy fluffing the bright red hankie in the breast pocket of his suit. "He will be assisting me," she added.

"That's what I understand." Bragg looked at me for the first time. "Lieutenant McBean tells me he's worked with you in the past."

"We've had the pleasure," I said curtly. I withdrew my empty hand and placed my briefcase on the counsel table and opened it.

The D.A. smiled, flashing his perfect white teeth. "He tells me you were with the P.D.'s office." It was Bragg's way of letting me know McBean had informed him of my problem.

"I still am. No matter what the good lieutenant has told you, I'm on temporary leave."

"Then I hope you enjoy your temporary stay in our beautiful county."

Sarah nodded toward the front of the courthouse. "That mob outside doesn't make a very good impression."

"Mob?" he scoffed, and then noticed my puffy bottom lip. "You didn't have a problem out there, did you?"

"Problem?" I scratched the caked blood from the corner of my mouth. "Nothing that three or four stitches won't help solve."

"Who's responsible for that?" Bragg said, with about as much sincerity as a candidate playing a voter the day before an election.

And I wasn't buying any of it.

"Forget it." I pulled the police report from my briefcase. "Why don't we discuss what you have planned for this prelim?"

"Like the names of the witnesses you intend to call," Sarah said.

Bragg gave us a curious "you should know better" look. "Why, just Lieutenant McBean," he said.

"What about the boy?" Sarah asked anxiously. "Surely you will be putting him on the stand."

"This will be a Prop 115 prelim," the D.A. said matter-of-factly.

Sarah stiffened. I knew what she was thinking. In a prop 115 prelim, the arresting officer testifies to the hearsay statements of the victim and any other witnesses he may have interviewed. That meant she might not be able to examine the young boy before the trial.

"Could we discuss that decision with the deputy who is assigned to the case?" she asked.

"Why, you have been," he said with an incredulous tone. "I'll be handling both the prelim and the trial. If it goes that far."

"But—" Sarah said and he cut her off.

"We consider child molestation and kidnapping to be very serious offenses in this county."

"I'm not aware of any county in this state that doesn't," I shot back. "We just never thought the head district attorney would be the trial attorney."

A small smile appeared at the corner of his lips. "Well, I am." The smile quickly faded. "And as far as this preliminary hearing is concerned, I'm not going to force that poor child to relive the events of that night unless he absolutely has to."

"But normally," I persisted, "when allegations have little, if any, corroboration, the victim testifies at the prelim."

He shook his head in disgust. "Maybe where you come from, but in this county we protect our victims."

"Come on, Bragg," I said. "You're not in front of the cameras now. Save your champion of the public's welfare speech for them."

Sarah raised an eyebrow at my combativeness. She knew it was time to regroup. She had to make Bragg understand that he had as much to gain by the boy's testimony as we did. "I can only advise my client to accept or reject whatever offer you're making if I know exactly what that boy has to say."

"See, there you go. The only person who benefits is your client."

"Not really," she said in a reasonable tone. "It may also help you see the weaknesses in your case."

"This case doesn't have any weaknesses."

With her hands on her hips, Sarah looked at him like he had to be kidding. "The victim can't even give an accurate description of the car or his attacker," she said. "I'd call that pretty weak."

Bragg reached for a folder on the counsel table and placed it under his arm. "And what about the candy wrapper?"

"I'll tell you what I think about that wrapper," Sarah said, but I interrupted her with a shaking of my head. If the D.A. wasn't going to allow us to hear what the boy had to say, I didn't see why she should alert him that we suspected his investigating officer had planted the key evidence.

Bragg pulled his chair away from the table. "Are you ready to begin?"

As long as McBean would be Bragg's only witness, I knew we had nothing to gain by going through with the prelim. McBean's testimony would consist of only what was contained in the police report. And we knew that by heart.

"No way," I said.

Bragg jumped out of his chair. "Well, I'm telling you now, I'll be objecting to a continuance. And knowing Judge Willamont like I do, I'm sure he'll agree. Child molestation has statutory priority."

I was sick of the pious show-off. "Don't spout the law to us," I said. "If the boy's not going to testify, then we'll be waiving the preliminary hearing."

That got him.

"What?"

"We don't want to put your investigating officer through the trauma of cross-examination," I said sweetly.

"Is that so?" Bragg withdrew a one-page document from the folder he'd been holding under his arm and handed it to Sarah. "You may want to review this before you and your friend make any hasty decisions."

Bragg grinned, with his arms crossed in front of his chest, while Sarah and I read the summary of an analysis of the Gummy Bear wrapper for fingerprints—indicating that Danny Barton's fingerprints had been on the candy wrapper found in Jared's car.

"That should about do it, wouldn't you say?" Bragg's eyes narrowed as if he were about to say something we'd better pay attention to. "However, in order to keep that poor young boy off the stand at trial, I'm offering a plea to ten years in state prison."

"I don't think so," I said dismissively. I knew full well that if Sarah couldn't dispute the report or prove that somehow McBean had finagled it, her chances of success would be next to impossible. But I also knew that ten years for a first offense was as good as no offer at all.

Ignoring me, Bragg turned to Sarah. "What's it going to be, Miss Harris?"

Sarah mused over the report for a moment longer. It obviously bothered her. "How long have you known about these results?"

"Not long."

"It doesn't look that way to me," she snapped, and I smiled. She had the moxie of a hardened veteran. "This report is dated over three days ago.

Don't you feel the day of the prelim is a little late to be springing this on me?"

Bragg's hands dropped to his side. "If you think I've done something wrong, I suggest you take it up with the judge. Otherwise, I'm informing the clerk I'm ready to begin the preliminary hearing."

Sarah looked up at me as if she wanted my input. "Waive it," I mouthed.

Without hesitating, she turned back to Bragg. "I'll be waiving the prelim."

"What about my offer?"

Sarah placed the document inside Jared's file. "Doesn't thrill me."

"Well, I can't do any better," he said flatly. "Why don't you see what your client has to say?"

"By law I have to," she said and abruptly walked away. Halfway down the aisle, she stopped and turned to Bragg. "But you can bet the only meaningful discussion I'll have with Mr. Reineer will be convincing him to waive the prelim."

Chapter 12

"In a molestation case, if the victim doesn't testify, a prelim is next to useless."

Sarah and I were discussing why it was best that we waived the hearing. It was after eleven and we were sitting at a diner called Harvey's Eatery off the main highway.

My uncle, Joe Calabrese, had been a trucker most of his life, delivering produce up and down the northern coast of California. Like most truckers, he thought he was a real connoisseur. He'd always boast there wasn't a better meal served anywhere in the good old "U.S. of A." than the mom-and-pop operations that dotted the coastal highways.

I'd persuaded Sarah to stop and give the place a try.

I was inspecting a water-stained spoon on the counter in front of me. We'd only had ten minutes to explain to Jared what we had in mind. He readily agreed with us once he understood that waiving the prelim wouldn't delay the start of the trial.

According to Sarah, Jared had been a drifter for most of his life, wandering aimlessly from place to place, relying on handouts to stay alive. I would have thought a place like the Mendocino County Jail, which provided three meals a day, would be welcome. But Jared was still very upset about being incarcerated. He wouldn't eat. He looked like he'd lost ten pounds in less than a week.

The waitress emerged from the kitchen, wiping her hands on her dirty apron as she walked toward us. She withdrew a pencil and pad from her breast pocket, ready to take our order.

"What'll it be?" she said, snapping her gum.

I was planning on my monthly allotment of fat and cholesterol—the trucker special—eggs, country-fried potatoes, sausage, and pancakes. But after a good look at the grill and the deep fryer, which hadn't been cleaned since probably the last time my uncle ate here, I ordered a doughnut instead. Sarah did the same.

"Wouldn't it have been worth going through with the prelim?" she asked. "We could have asked Mc-Bean that if the boy was wearing gloves, then how could his fingerprints be on the candy wrapper?"

"Why alert him? Let him think he's getting away with something. Otherwise, he'll get nervous and do his best to cover it up. Plus," I said, "we don't know if the boy was wearing his gloves the whole time. Maybe he took them off."

Sarah nodded. "If we could just get Danny alone, he could tell us whether or not he ever took them off."

Except for the waitress barking out an order, there was total silence as she considered it.

"We also have to start broadening the rest of our investigation," I said.

"Like what?"

"Well, if Jared didn't do it, who did? We have to find out if there is anyone around here who has a prior history of molestations. And that will take some time."

"Not as long as you may think," she said, smirking. "This isn't San Francisco, you know. Everybody in this county knows his neighbor's business."

"What about a stranger to the area?"

"Someone would have noticed him. I can guarantee it."

Just then a heavy-set, middle-aged man, dressed in a plaid shirt and black suspenders, belched at the end of the counter. He then leered at Sarah and took a big chomp out of his doughnut, which he immediately washed down with one gulp of coffee. A real attractive sight like that would bring Sarah right over.

She chuckled. "That's your uncle twenty years ago."

"Nah," I deadpanned. "He never wore suspenders."

Sarah glanced at the man again.

"He reminds me," she said as we watched him dump a handful of change on the counter. "What do you make of that man from Boonville who was with McBean at the courthouse?"

I frowned at the memory of the big redneck. "Just a grieving father who feels he has to blame someone."

Sarah nervously ran her finger around the rim of

her mug. "I wonder if he has any proof," she said quietly.

"I don't see how. By the looks of him, his son probably took off on his own."

I began to dunk the doughnut that was thrown in front of me, when I caught Sarah running her finger along the top of hers and then licking it.

"I only like the chocolate," she said, by way of explanation. Her gaze settled on the front of my shirt. "At least I don't need a bib," she jabbed, referring to the coffee spatter on my breast pocket.

I looked at it and shook my head. "No wonder everyone around here wears overalls."

Sarah tried to smile, but something was bothering her. "I find it hard to believe it's just a coincidence that the day after Danny is attacked that boy from Boonville disappears."

That *was* hard to believe. "Are you sure. The very next day?"

"Positive. The attack on Danny and the boy's disappearance were front-page news at the time," she said. "But it wasn't even hinted there could be a connection."

"There probably isn't. But we have a couple of days before we have to go to San Francisco for my prelim. Let's check it out."

"Do you even know where Boonville is?" she asked.

"Don't have the foggiest."

She nodded in the direction to the rear of us. "It's a half hour toward the coast."

Sarah dipped the tip of her napkin into her water glass and wiped a syrup stain from her laminated menu. "What if the two are connected?" she muttered.

"If they were, we would have heard about it by now." I paused to consider. "Relax," I finally said. "The boy's father is just grasping at straws."

"But if they are connected, that would mean whoever kidnapped Danny may be a murderer."

"You're not beginning to doubt Jared, are you?" I asked.

"Of course not," she said. "It's just that suddenly this case has far greater implications than I ever imagined. Once that Cosgrove fellow tells the press what he suspects, all hell will break loose."

I knew what Sarah was driving at. The Boonville boy's disappearance would be the cause célèbre that was sure to make Jared's case a higher-stakes trial than it already was. His prosecution would be the only chance to get the man who many believed was responsible for the Cosgrove boy's disappearance.

"The D.A. will have to prove an awfully strong connection between the two before a judge will ever allow it in."

Sarah made a face, like she didn't want to tell me what she was about to say.

"Why don't you tell me what's really bothering you?" I said.

She took a deep breath and slowly let it out. "I think I'm in way over my head. I don't have enough criminal-law experience to properly defend someone charged with child molestation. I've handled maybe three or four criminal cases in my life and that's only because, like your case, they also dealt with attorney discipline."

"Who do you think you're kidding? I've seen you in court. Jared's lucky to have you."

"But I've never handled anything remotely close to a criminal case like Jared's," she said and hesitated. "If you hadn't been there today, I would have been lost."

Even though Sarah was having a hard time saying it, I had a good idea of what she was driving at. Our current arrangement didn't make much sense for either of us. I had my specialty, she had hers. She felt uncomfortable being the lead attorney on such a notorious case, and it seemed strange for me to be her assistant.

"Do you want me to take over?"

Sarah crinkled her eyes as she picked at the rest of her doughnut. She was embarrassed by what was happening. "I can't ask you to do that."

I wanted to tell her that that was exactly what was bugging her and to quit hemming and hawing around. But just admitting her anxiety was tough enough. She didn't need me to rub salt in the wound.

"Look," I said, "consider it done. You'll represent me and I'll take over full responsibility for Jared's case."

Sarah looked me straight in the eye. "Are you sure?"

All that anxiety, and I had the power to make it vanish. "Actually, I figure I'm getting the better of it."

She gave me a puzzled look.

"You have an S.O.B. like me for a client. I only have Jared to deal with."

Sarah nudged me with an elbow and we both took a deliberate sip of our coffee while pondering what had just happened. Then suddenly she dipped her napkin into her water again—she'd found a stain on my menu, too.

"For chrissake," I sniped and grabbed my menu back. I was embarrassed I'd ever picked such a filthy place. "Let's go."

I placed a five-dollar bill on the counter and the waitress snapped it up. "Keep the change," I said, but she was already on her way back to the kitchen.

Sarah rose from her stool and I did the same. As we walked to the door, she looked out the dirty plate-glass window which fronted the building. "It looks like it's turned cold out there." She grimaced and we stepped outside. A chilling breeze stirred the branches of the pine trees surrounding the diner.

"I wish I wouldn't have left my coat in the car," she remarked. As we pushed against the wind, her silk blouse clung like cellophane to her chest. She was right about one thing. It was definitely cold out.

"First thing tomorrow the two of us are going to Boonville and interview that boy's father."

"Sorry, but I have to be in San Francisco for the Jessup prelim," she said, and snuggled into me, burying her head deep into my chest.

I was amazed at the warm glow that radiated throughout my body. It seemed so natural having Sarah that close to me. I had been wrong about her. She wasn't at all like her father. And was I thankful for it. But my newfound feelings had to be tamed. Our relationship had to remain professional.

"Isn't Jessup the attorney who's accused of embezzling his client's trust account?" I said, trying to take my mind off what I was really thinking.

"The same one I appeared for in Kellogg's court," she said.

"What's going to happen to him?"

"Three years formal probation and restitution."

"And the state bar?"

"License suspension for two years with a probationary tail."

I opened the driver's door. "Is that what I have to look forward to?"

"Nah," she said. "Your case is much more serious. You'll get the guillotine for sure."

Chapter 13

It was late afternoon by the time I arrived at the jail to tell Jared I'd be taking over as his attorney. I'd waited for more than fifteen minutes when the jailer informed me someone was with him. I didn't know who and he wouldn't say. The first person that came to mind was McBean. I knew he was a snake, but not even McBean would be dumb enough to interview Jared without his attorney's permission. I was about to insist the jailer tell me who was in there when the buzzer on the door to lockup sounded. The door opened and Avery walked out toward me.

The thin, middle-aged jailer tossed a clipboard on the counter. "Sign in, and don't forget to put down your bar number."

"Where's Sarah?" Avery asked, approaching me.

"As far as I know she's at her office." The jailer angled his head like he was trying to hear what we were saying. I signed the sheet and slid the clipboard across the counter. "She wants me to be lead counsel. I'm here to see what Jared thinks."

Avery seemed stunned by the news.

"Sort of a trade-off," I said. "I'll be responsible for Jared's case in exchange for her handling mine."

Slowly a smile appeared on his face. "Jared's case should be right up your alley."

"And with the suspension and all, it's not like I'm real busy right now."

This was followed by an uncomfortable silence. Avery didn't like talking about the charges pending against me. I had the feeling he thought there might be some truth to them. But I had to remember that he'd been a prosecutor before he was appointed judge. To him, the term "presumed innocent" was a technicality our liberal-minded forefathers—a bunch of longhaired rebels—had invented for their own advantage.

"I hope you left him in a good mood," I said, breaking the silence. "Because what I'm going to tell him won't make his day."

"You're wrong," he said. "Jared knows Sarah doesn't do much criminal. He will be relieved to hear you'll be in charge."

Realizing he'd no idea what I was referring to, I told him how they were trying to connect his former captain to the missing Boonville boy.

"What evidence could they possibly have that implicates Jared?"

"Whatever it is, they're keeping it to themselves. I'm driving to Boonville tomorrow to see what I can find out."

Concern masked his face.

"I'm sure there's nothing to it. But I don't trust McBean. He knows his case is weak, and he'll do anything to make it appear Jared has something to do with it. If he ever does, I want to make sure it's not a product of his imagination," I said.

He nodded. "Like the Gummy Bears."

Avery then arched his back like it was bothering him.

"You're getting a little old to be playing kung fu, day in and day out, on poor defenseless trees." As soon as I said it, I wished I hadn't. I didn't know him well enough for such a personal remark. "I mean, whipping that big machete around all day would make even a teenager sore."

Avery placed his hand on my shoulder as he walked toward the exit. "Don't be so damned intimidated by me, Hunter. It's been years since I was on the bench. Relax, would you?" He patted me once on the back and walked out the door.

Jared was leaning back against the wall. We were in an interview room no bigger than a closet. I'd just informed him I'd be taking over.

"Fine with me," he said. "Avery says you're one of the best."

I paused for a moment. First Avery treats me like an old friend and now I hear he complimented me. I was dumbfounded.

"Let's just say I'm not lacking for experience."

Jared looked around like he was afraid someone else might be listening. "Actually, I'm relieved. I wasn't really sure Sarah could handle it."

"You'd be surprised." I knew I was. "She's a very good attorney."

"I'm sure," he said. "But I'm still here and they don't have shit."

It was a defendant's typical attitude when an attorney substitutes in on a case. They blame their past attorney for being in their current predicament and believe the new one will be able to set matters straight.

I wanted to make sure he understood. "Just because I'm your attorney from here on out doesn't mean the charges will miraculously disappear."

He scowled. "Maybe not, but I have the feeling you're a whole lot more familiar than Sarah is about what the cops will do to get a conviction."

Especially McBean, I wanted to say, but that was a long story and I only had about ten minutes left. I still had to discuss the missing boy.

Jared leaned closer, his lips nearly touching the glass that separated us. "Except for that candy wrapper, they don't have shit, do they?"

"How about the boy's description of you and your car?"

"Too vague. It'll never hold up," he said with an air of confidence. "They'll need a hell of a lot more than that."

"They're working on it. McBean's trying to connect you to a similar kidnapping right now."

Jared lightly stroked his salt-and-pepper beard. "That will never happen."

"What makes you so sure?"

"Because I didn't do anything. Not to the Barton kid or anyone else."

I angled my head to help eliminate the glare off the glass. I wanted to watch Jared closely to see what his reaction would be to my next question.

"Do you know anything about a boy who disappeared just west of here?"

Jared sighed. "Is that what they think?" he said, shaking his head. "Just like that Unabomber fella, I'll end up getting blamed for everything before they're done with me."

"Maybe," I said, "but you haven't answered my question."

His look became more intense. "You're wrong. That's exactly what I'm doing."

"The missing boy is close to Danny Barton's age," I said. "They'll do everything they can to connect the two."

"Including planting more evidence." Jared raised his voice. "Because that's what it will take before they'll ever get enough probable cause to arrest me for another trumped-up charge."

His remark took me by surprise. How did he know what that term even meant? "Probable cause?"

"Do you think I'm just some ignorant transient?"

Before I had a chance to answer, something occurred to me. Something that none of us had ever addressed before. "Why do you think McBean picked you out of all the people in this county to plant that candy wrapper on?" I asked.

He assumed the conspiratorial look of a wise old hippie. "That's simple," he said. "I was a thorn in the cops' side."

"But why?"

"I don't fit in around here. They were constantly hassling me, hoping I'd leave."

"McBean would?"

"No, the patrol types."

Jared went on to explain that when he'd first come to town, he'd lived out of his car. Whenever he'd park it somewhere to sleep, the cops would roust him.

"They'd bug me every time they saw me," he added. A look of sincere gratitude crossed his face. "Thank God, I ran into Avery when I did. I didn't even have enough money for gas."

"Why? Couldn't you find any work?"

"If my freedom is going to depend on you," he said, "you should get to know me better."

I gave him a puzzled look.

"I'm a bum," he added matter-of-factly. "Working on Avery's damn tree farm is the first time I've worked in one place for more than a few days."

"But why?"

"Post Vietnam syndrome. Can't handle the mainstream."

"Then you have been diagnosed with a mental problem?"

"Yeah, but don't worry," he said and smiled. "I may be a little off center, but that doesn't mean I molested some kid."

"More than one," I said, mostly to myself.

Jared's interest was piqued. "So that's it," he said as if he'd figured something out. "McBean thinks I'm responsible for that Boonville kid's disappearance."

I'd never mentioned where the boy was from. How in the hell did he know? "Boonville?" I said.

"Don't look so worried, Counselor. It's been in all the papers."

"Of course," I said, relieved.

Jared rolled his eyes upward and slowly closed them. After a few seconds, he lurched forward. "I have to get out of here," he said. "And I'm sure all this bullshit about that missing boy won't help."

The jailer opened the door and informed me that our time was up.

"Hunter," Jared whispered, "I'm entitled to a speedy trial. They don't have shit. What I need from you most is to get the trial started as soon as possible."

I bobbed my head in agreement. The sooner that happened, the less time McBean would have to fake something else. "I'll do what I can."

"Thanks."

I watched as the jailer led Jared down the hall. He wasn't the same bewildered and scared Haight-Ashbury reject I'd met just a few days before. He seemed more at ease, confident he'd be found not guilty. At times overly confident. But I had enough experience to know—the innocent normally were.

Chapter 14

On a narrow two-lane highway winding through miles of old-growth redwoods, the drive from the Harris ranch to Boonville took a little more than a half hour. After reading old newspaper clippings at the library, I had found out little about Gary Cosgrove's disappearance other than he was last seen walking home on September 26, 1998, the day after the attack on Danny Barton. By the following evening, when no one had heard from the boy, his father had put up a ten-thousand-dollar reward for any information leading to his son's whereabouts—dead or alive.

On the outskirts of Boonville, I approached a large, corrugated-steel building overgrown by weeds and shrubbery. Directly above the solid steel-door entrance, COSGROVE AUTOMOTIVE was spray painted in red. I pulled onto a gravel driveway that separated the automotive shop from a small stucco house hidden behind a huge stray redwood. An old wooden plank with the words WORMS FOR SALE in faded black letters was tacked to the center of the tree.

Parking on the side of the driveway closest to

the shop, I noticed a man on the porch next door, rocking back and forth in a weathered wooden chair. He was watching my every move.

"How are you?" I called out. Except for his heels lifting with each roll, the man didn't move a muscle. I waved at him anyway, then walked to the metal building to find Otto Cosgrove.

The front door was padlocked shut. After pounding several times, I gave up and walked to the rear of the building. Except for several dying cars hidden amongst the weeds, it was deserted, too. I decided to see if the man on the porch could be any help.

"You sell worms here?" I asked, pointing to the sign as I plodded over the thick gravel driveway.

Without a break in his slow rock, the frail old man, heavily wrinkled by age, tilted his head and peered over his wire-rimmed glasses. "You sure don't look like a fisherman." He smacked his lips and nodded toward the sign. "I'll bet you never even fished with a worm before."

"As a matter of fact, you're right," I said and placed my foot up on the wooden stoop like I was about to shoot the bull with an old friend. "But I'll bet there's nothing better."

He slid his bony frame to the edge of the chair. "Buck-fifty a dozen."

"Don't get up. I'm afraid I don't have time right now."

"Figured as much."

I gestured at the shop next door. "I'm trying to locate a man named Otto Cosgrove."

He sat back, rocking again. "Gotta make time. You young folks are always in such a damn hurry."

"You're probably right," I said and made my way up the steps. "But as much as I would like to be doing something else, it's important I talk to him as soon as possible."

"Sure you don't want no worms?"

"Sorry, not today."

The old man scowled for a second, then rested his head on the back of his chair and closed his eyes. He looked like some old codger in the backwoods of Arkansas, napping while his bloodhound was out chasing rabbits.

"Do you know where I might find him?" I asked before he nodded off.

His eyes remained closed. "Car problems?"

"Nothing like that," I said and walked closer. The creaking of the old wooden boards announced I was now on the porch, standing within a few feet of him. "I'm investigating the disappearance of his son."

Except for his eyes opening slightly, he acted like he didn't hear me.

"The boy's name is Gary," I said.

"If you're an investigator, you should know Otto ain't got but one child."

"Then you know him?"

"There ain't too many in these parts I don't."

"Do you know anything about what may have happened to the boy?"

Confusion, followed by concern, crossed the old man's face. "Nah, talked enough. If you don't want no worms, I'm a very busy man."

"Look," I pushed, "I'll bet there also isn't much that goes on around here that you don't know about."

The old man grinned, exposing his naked gums. "Likely not."

"Including what may have happened to Gary Cosgrove."

He reached for a cigarette behind his ear and snapped off its brown filter. "There's really not much to tell," he said, and struck a wooden match on the side of his chair. He lit the cigarette and we both watched the plume of smoke drift past my face. "The boy was last seen getting into a red truck."

I was relieved it wasn't Jared's old black Chevy.

"Things like that just don't happen around here," he continued, while slowly shaking his head. "How could someone hurt such a sweet, innocent child?"

"I know what you mean."

I paused before my next question. The one I'd hoped would for sure clear Jared. "Did anyone get a good look at the driver of the truck?"

The old man shook his head. "A couple school chums that he'd been shooting marbles with were the only ones who saw anything. When they was done, Gary got in the truck. But it was too far away for them to see who was driving."

"Too bad."

"Even if they'd been closer, they wouldn't have been able to see much," he added. "The front and backseat windows were heavily tinted."

"But," I said, puzzled by what the old guy was

saying, "I thought you said it was a truck. They don't have backseat windows."

"Those passenger trucks do."

Was the old coot senile? "Passenger trucks?"

"Hell, you mean to tell me you ain't never seen one of them Blazers before?" He scratched his near-bald head. "Or maybe it was a Bronco?"

"Are you saying it may have been a red Blazer or Bronco?"

The old man shrugged and took a long drag off his cigarette. "One or the other," he said and spat a piece of tobacco by my foot. "And I'll bet that pervert they arrested in Ukiah has one just like it."

"No," I mumbled to myself. But I knew Judge Harris did.

"Come on," he said and pushed himself up with a cane that had been resting against the side of the chair. "If you promise you won't drive too fast, I'll take you to Otto's house."

I extended my hand. "My name is Hunter Dobbs."

The old man jerked his head and looked me sternly in the face. His lower lip began to quiver. "You're no cop."

"No . . . I'm a lawyer."

His eyes narrowed. "You made me think you were a detective." His voice raised with each word. "You're that damn faggot's lawyer, aren't you?"

"If you mean Jared Reineer," I said, withdrawing my empty hand, "I am his attorney."

"You tricked me. No wonder everyone hates you damn lawyers."

It was obvious that any chance he'd take me to

Cosgrove's house was history. "I'm sorry if you misunderstood," I said, backing down the steps.

"I didn't misunderstand nothing. Now get the hell off my property!"

"I really don't believe my client had anything to do with the boy's disappearance."

"Is that so?" He tossed what was left of his cigarette at my head. He opened the screen door and reached inside. With catlike quickness, he lifted a double-barreled shotgun and pointed it directly at my face.

"What are you doing?" I yelled.

He was holding the butt of the rifle so tightly that the whites of his knuckles showed through his liver-spotted skin. "You're worse than the dirt you represent!"

"All right, all right." I slowly backed toward my car as he pulled the rifle tighter to his face. He looked like a sharpshooter ready to yell "Pull." My skull his clay pigeon.

"And leave my son alone."

"Your son?"

His voice cracked. "And Gary's my grandson."

The old man was obviously hurting. And that's what made him so dangerous.

"I really am sorry," I said.

"Bull shit! All you really care about is that your faggot client gets off. Matter of fact," he said, squinting over the butt of the rifle, "I think I'll do my part to make sure that doesn't happen and blow your ass off right where you stand."

I tried to stay calm. At least I wanted it to look that way. "A lot of people know I came here," I lied.

"So what?" He nodded in the direction of the front door. "You shouldn't have tried to break in."

"From out here?"

"That's what it will look like by the time I'm done."

"Come on, don't be crazy."

"Crazy! Crazy! That was my grandson your client killed."

"Everyone has the right to be defended—" I said, but the last thing he needed was a civics lesson.

"Animals don't," he screamed. "Anyone who'd do that to that young a boy is an animal, and that's exactly how they or anyone who tries to protect them should be treated."

His arms were trembling, the barrel of the rifle shaking violently. I thought about making a run for it, but where would I go? My car was still twenty yards behind me.

It was ominously quiet. A car hadn't passed since I'd arrived. Even the birds were mute. I could feel my heart pounding. I hoped the old man was just trying to scare me: At that he'd already succeeded.

"I know how you must feel, but shooting me won't help. If I don't represent him, someone else will. . . . What are you going to do, shoot us all?"

As he continued to look down the barrel of the rifle, his expression changed from one of rage to that of sadness. He dabbed his eye with the edge of his shoulder and slowly lowered the rifle to his waist. His face was smeared with dirt and tears.

"Get the hell out of here," he said with a choked whimper.

Without a second thought I ran to my car. When

I reached for the driver's door, the old man shouted, "You better hope you don't get him off. Because if you do, I can guarantee Otto won't be so easy on either you or your damn client."

Chapter 15

We were in Division Six of the Municipal Court for the County of San Francisco awaiting the start of my preliminary hearing. As far as we knew, Patterson would be calling only one witness. Bobby Miles was scheduled to take the stand and testify that I promised if he'd falsely testify for Martinez, I would make sure he didn't spend another night in jail.

I was sitting at the counsel table behind a wood sign etched with the word DEFENDANT. I had sat on this side of the counsel table thousands of times, but never been positioned in the seat farthest from the jury—the one always reserved for the defendant. I felt like a stranger in my own home. Welcome only because I was the day's main course. Michael Patterson was hungry for what he loosely referred to as justice. But from where I was positioned, it had all the earmarks of revenge. Revenge not only against me, but all defense attorneys who, in his paranoid little mind, were causing the failure of the criminal justice system. What separated a typical prosecutor from a defense attorney was their belief that the greatest injustice that could ever occur in a courtroom was that a guilty person be set free. To the likes of Patterson, a few "innocents" who ended up behind bars was a small price to pay for the assurance that all the guilty were convicted.

Patterson was standing, waiting for the judge to instruct him to begin. To my immediate left, Sarah was poised with pen in hand. My vision of her as a truck-stop goddess had faded. We were, I was determined, going to remain on the safe ground of attorney and client.

Seated in the first row of the gallery were four young Hispanics with clean-shaven heads. Some of Martinez's buddies, no doubt. Three were dressed in white dress shirts with their collars buttoned tightly to the neck. The fourth, who was carrying about thirty extra pounds of chiseled muscle, was wearing a clean white tank top. He needed the extra bulk for the fanciful artwork, which, except for his face, covered every exposed area of his body. Serpents breathing fire, cobwebs, spiders, girls' names and gang logos, all linked together from his wrists to the base of his jaw.

"Call Bobby Miles to the stand," Patterson announced, and the short, skinny kid I remembered from lockup was escorted into the courtroom. He had the same pitiful look. After he was sworn and seated, he glanced around nervously, unsure of what was going to happen next.

Patterson helped the young man adjust the mike and then began. Question after question, he patiently led Bobby through everything I supposedly said to him.

"He promised he'd get me out of jail," Bobby said, concluding his direct testimony.

Judge Paul Brown, a diminutive black man in his early sixties, peered down at Sarah. With his long, spidery hands, he waved her forward to start her cross.

As Sarah approached, Bobby looked at Patterson for guidance. But the D.A. was busy arranging his file, gloating over what I'm sure he thought was an excellent job of questioning.

"Bobby," Sarah began in a soft, congenial tone, "why do you think Mr. Dobbs picked you out of all the other inmates?"

He quickly glanced at me for a reaction. I was reclining in my chair, trying to appear confident, hoping it would somehow rattle the kid. "I don't know," he replied meekly.

"And if you had never seen Mr. Dobbs before, why did you agree to talk to him?"

"I thought he was my public defender." He looked up at the judge. "I hadn't talked to anyone since I'd been arrested."

"Does that include Sal Martinez?"

Miles scrunched his face and gave Sarah a bewildered look. "I don't know what you mean."

"You do know Salvador Martinez, don't you?"

"No, ma'am."

"I see." Sarah walked to the counsel table and rummaged through several documents. Bobby was squirming in his chair, adjusting himself from one cheek to the other.

"Mr. Miles, how old are you?" she asked and

walked back to the witness stand while reading what she'd been looking for.

Bobby acted like he hadn't heard the question. Or, maybe it was just that no one had ever called him "mister" before.

"How old are you?" she repeated.

"Eighteen."

"How many times have you been in custody?"

"Never, ma'am."

"You're scared, aren't you?"

"I'm a little nervous," he said, still fidgeting. "I never had to testify before."

"What I mean is," Sarah said, as she placed her hand on the witness box, "you were afraid of the other inmates when you were first taken into custody."

"A bit."

"You had a lot of problems with them, isn't that correct?"

He feigned a smile. "They like picking on the new fish."

"Did they threaten you?"

The boy didn't answer. He shrugged his shoulders instead.

"They stole your shoes, didn't they?"

Bobby's eyes lowered to the floor. He appeared visibly shaken just thinking about it.

"Answer me, Bobby," she pushed. "They stole your shoes, didn't they?"

The young man slowly raised his head and nodded. "They took my food, too."

"And you would have done anything to get them to stop?"

"What do you mean by anything?"

"You needed protection," she said with a sense of urgency. "You were afraid they would physically harm you, and you needed someone to protect you. Isn't that correct?"

"No one can protect you." He waved his hand at the back door. "In lockup, you're on your own."

"And the population in lockup is segregated into certain ethnic groups, isn't it?"

With a flustered look, he asked, "Ethnic?"

"Browns, blacks, Asians, and whites, etc."

"If you're asking if they hang out together," he said, "I guess some of that goes on."

"You guess?" she said incredulously. "You are white, aren't you?"

"Yes."

"And in county jail whites are the minority, aren't they?"

"There is less of us," he said and lowered his voice. "There's hardly any my age."

Sarah paused. She was doing a good job of leading the kid. "Sometimes you are the only white in a particular cell?"

"It happens."

"And when it does, you're the first person the others pick on?"

The boy could see where Sarah was heading, but he was either too scared or not smart enough to avoid it. That was the one thing I believed was on my side. Sooner or later, Bobby would crack. But it wasn't likely to happen until he was out from underneath Martinez's control.

"Well?" Sarah pushed.

"Yes," he said, sighing deeply. "They know they can get away with it because it's just me against all of them."

"And your only hope of not being harmed is if one of the non-white groups helps you?"

"Sometimes."

"Like the Hispanics?"

"Sometimes," he said again.

"But you have to pay something for that kind of protection, don't you?"

Bobby's eyes darted back and forth between Patterson, Sarah, and myself. "Pay?" he finally said, as if he didn't understand. But it was obvious to all he was stalling.

"I'm referring to money, food, shoes, drugs, cigarettes, or articles of personal clothing."

"Except for the food, which they can have, I really don't have anything to give them."

Sarah clasped her hands at her waist, her expression pained. "What about sexual favors?"

There was an uncomfortable silence. Bobby gazed at the ceiling. Tears began to well in his eyes.

"Bobby," Sarah said in a gentler tone, "were you sexually assaulted?"

He lowered his eyes. They were red and puffy. I could see tears glistening as they ran down his cheeks. "At first I was."

"And that was because if you didn't let them have their way, you knew they'd really hurt or maybe even kill you?"

Bobby nodded.

"Is that a yes, Mr. Miles?" the judge asked.

"Yes, sir," Bobby said, and Brown motioned at Sarah to continue.

Sarah paused again as she walked to the podium. "You said at first you were sexually assaulted?"

Barely audible. "That's correct."

Sarah hesitated for a moment like she didn't get it. "When did these sexual assaults stop?"

"After the second or third day."

"Why?"

Bobby shrugged his shoulders. "I don't know for sure."

"Correct me if I am wrong," Sarah said as she stepped in front of the witness box, "you don't appear to have any physical signs of having been beaten."

"I haven't been lately," he conceded.

"Can you explain why?"

"Not really."

"You can't explain how all of a sudden you stopped having any problems?"

Bobby gave Sarah a perfunctory smile. "Just lucky, I guess."

"Luck?" Sarah scoffed. "Or is it because someone is protecting you?"

His face went blank, and he glanced at the group of Hispanics seated behind Patterson.

Sarah grabbed the railing that surrounded the witness box and leaned into Bobby. "Isn't it a fact that you are no longer being beaten or sexually assaulted because Salvador Martinez promised you he would make sure no further harm came to you as long as you agreed to falsely testify for him?"

"No way."

"And because Mr. Dobbs told you he wouldn't use your false testimony," Sarah said, raising her voice, "Salvador Martinez forced you to make these false accusations against him?"

"I keep telling you, I don't know who Salvador Martinez is."

"So you say," Sarah remarked and paused to underscore the point.

Patterson slowly stood. "Your Honor, I fail to see the relevance of this line of questioning."

"I imagine," Brown said, "Ms. Harris is trying to establish that maybe Mr. Martinez, rather than Mr. Dobbs, planted a seed in your witness's head."

"Then, Your Honor, may I be heard?" Patterson asked, as if he was being inconvenienced.

"I've not stopped you so far." The judge leaned back in his chair, only the top of his head visible.

"I believe we are getting into discovery here, which as the court is aware is not allowed at a preliminary hearing under Proposition 115."

"I'm aware of Prop 115, Counsel," Brown rasped. "And I feel all of this is relevant. I'm overruling your objection."

"But I have information," Patterson said, rising while waving a several-page computer printout, "that at no time since Mr. Miles's arrest has he been housed with Mr. Martinez, or, for that matter, been within a hundred feet of him. There is no way Mr. Martinez could have promised him anything."

"Sounds like Mr. Patterson should call himself as a witness," Sarah remarked. "But unless he does, he should not be allowed to state what did or didn't happen."

"And I will produce this and a lot of other information at trial," Patterson said, ignoring Sarah.

"That's it!" Brown slammed his gavel on the bench.

Sarah was taken aback by the power and strength of the frail judge's voice. She looked over at Patterson, who had been on the wrong side of Brown's fury before.

"Even if Mr. Miles didn't come in contact with Mr. Martinez himself," the judge said, eyeing the four in the front row, "it is within the realm of possibility that one of Mr. Martinez's acquaintances could have."

The D.A. turned to see what the judge was looking at and slowly sat back down.

"You may proceed, Ms. Harris," Brown said.

"Bobby," she said gently and walked closer to the young man, "did any of Salvador Martinez's friends approach you in lockup and ask you to lie for Mr. Martinez?"

Bobby hesitated, and his eyes shifted again to the four young men whose stares were fixed on him. He looked at me, and his shoulders began to heave. "I can't answer any more questions."

Sarah reached to the side of the bench and pulled several tissues from a box that was there for just this sort of occasion. She handed them to Bobby.

"I don't feel good," he said.

"Would you like a break?" Brown asked.

"I don't feel good," Bobby repeated, like a child trying to get out of going to school on the day of a big exam.

"All right, let's take a break," the judge said,

standing to exit the bench. "Court is adjourned until after lunch. In the meantime, I want to see both counsel in chambers, along with Mr. Dobbs."

"Mr. Patterson, I hope you have additional witnesses." The D.A. was sitting in one of two brown Naugahyde chairs across from the judge's desk. Sarah and I were in the matching sofa to his left.

"Subornation of perjury normally doesn't have many witnesses. We have to rely on the testimony of the person to whom the request for false testimony was made."

"In other words, you don't have anything to corroborate that young man's testimony?"

Patterson took a moment to search for the right words. "I didn't say that," he said. Both Sarah and I sat forward, not knowing what additional evidence he could be referring to.

"Well," Brown said with the palm of his hand out, waiting for the D.A. to elaborate.

Patterson leaned back in his chair, relaxed. "I anticipate calling Judge Kellogg as a prosecution witness."

"What?" I screamed.

Brown pounded his fist on the desk. "Mr. Dobbs," he growled, "I'm allowing you in my chambers as a courtesy. Now sit still and keep your mouth shut."

Knowing my propensity for flying off the handle, Sarah pulled on my sleeve before I could say anything further.

"Your Honor," she began, "we were not informed there would be any other witnesses, let alone a member of the judiciary. All the discovery we've been given is based solely on the statements of the young Bobby Miles."

"Let me see if I can clear this up for everyone," Patterson said, as if we were all idiots. "I issued a subpoena *duces tecum* on the municipal court for a copy of the transcript of the arraignment of a Miss Janice Cappell. Part of which, I might add, was argued in Judge Kellogg's chambers."

"Come on, Mr. Patterson," Brown said in an annoyed tone. "Who is this Janice Cappell, and what does she have to do with this case?"

Patterson looked at me and snickered. I had a good idea what he was up to. "You see, Judge," he continued, turning back to Brown, "Mr. Dobbs was the attorney of record for Miss Cappell who, on the day in question, was being arraigned on a statutory rape charge."

"A female charged with statutory rape. How unusual," the judge remarked.

"And," Patterson said, "an accurate reading of the transcript should convince anyone that Mr. Dobbs coerced Judge Kellogg into lowering her bail."

"That's a lie," I said and stopped. I made a point of not looking at Brown, who I was sure was within an eyelash of booting me out.

"What's even more interesting," Patterson continued, "after Judge Kellogg agreed to lower Miss Cappell's bail, Mr. Dobbs then tried also to coerce the judge into lowering the bail on Bobby Miles. Who, as the court is aware, wasn't even his client."

Sarah gave me a "what the hell did you do that

for?" look. That was a minor detail I'd failed to mention.

Brown turned to Sarah for a response.

"Your Honor, I seem to be in the same position you are. I don't know what any of this is about."

"All right," Brown said and glanced at the clock on the wall behind me. "Mr. Patterson, I want you to make a copy of that transcript and give it to Ms. Harris to review over the lunch hour. I expect all of you to be ready to proceed at one-thirty."

"I'll be ready," the D.A. said, smiling.

"And," Brown said, "I want you to bring the Bobby Miles file with you when we resume."

"May I inquire as to why?" Patterson asked.

"You may and you have," the judge said. "I'll see the three of you at one-thirty."

Chapter 16

The Greenhouse is a crowded Italian café located two blocks from the courthouse. Sitting across from Sarah, I watched the lunch crowd scurry for an open booth while she carefully read the transcript Patterson had given her. She had barely said a word since we left Brown's chambers. I knew exactly what she was feeling. Betrayed by a client who had withheld incriminating information. She had been blindsided and I was to blame.

"I make a pretty lousy client."

She didn't flinch.

I scooted my chair forward. "Talk to me."

Sarah slowly lifted her head and peered over the top of her reading glasses. "What could you have been thinking when you asked Kellogg to lower bail on someone else's client?"

"I felt sorry for the kid."

She deliberately removed her glasses and placed them in her purse, making a point of snapping it shut. "I hope you don't think for a moment Brown will buy that."

"Brown is one hell of a judge, but this is just a preliminary hearing. You know as well as I do that he'll rubber stamp me up to superior court for trial, no matter how weak Patterson's case is."

Sarah angled her head. "Brown *was* on our side. He wasn't buying Miles's story. But with this," she said, pushing the transcript at me, "you'll be lucky if he doesn't increase bail."

"And if that should happen," I replied, trying to make light of the moment, "my guardian angel will have to rescue me again."

Her face darkened. "Don't count on it. The way I feel about you right now, I'd let you rot."

Her severe remark hung there for a moment. She wasn't joking. I felt she was beginning to doubt me, too.

"Look," I said, "I know I screwed up."

Sarah's face turned the same shade of red as the rose in the center of the table. "It's more than that, Hunter. It's your attitude. You act like there's nothing to worry about. Not only is your freedom at stake, your career is hanging by a thread. What's in this transcript may be all that not only Judge Brown but eventually a jury may need."

I found myself smiling. Not about my lack of concern, she was wrong about that. She had no idea how worried I really was. It was the fire in her eyes when she wanted to prove a point that amused me.

Sarah threw her hands in the air. "You think this is one big joke."

"Oh, I do?" I said, picking up the volume. "You don't know me well enough to know how or what I feel."

She lowered her eyes and ran her finger around

the rim of her water glass. Two old ladies, who'd been conducting business over lunch at the table next to us, frowned at me for raising my voice.

I slumped in my chair. "Miles won't hold up."

"Well, he's doing a pretty good job of it so far."

"That's only because he's still under the control of Martinez and his goons."

"What makes you think that's going to change?"

"He won't be in that lockup forever," I said, and noticed the waitress hovering within a few feet of our table, waiting for our order. "The kid was involved in a penny-ante drug deal. If he had been in a court other than Kellogg's, he would have been released on his own recognizance by now."

The thought seemed to intrigue Sarah. "You think when he's arraigned in superior court, the judge may cut him loose?"

"I'm counting on it."

She took a deep breath. "I'm not so sure."

Sarah then turned to the waitress and ordered a Caesar salad. I did the same.

I then excused myself to go to the restroom, but not because I really had to. Sarah's doubts had me concerned and I needed some time alone. It had all seemed so simple, but I obviously didn't have the right perspective. This time I was inside the fishbowl looking out. I was likely being too subjective, and that was why it was so important that I listen to her. I might not agree, but I understood her objectivity was what I needed most.

Standing at the urinal, I heard the door open behind me, followed by several footsteps walking in my direction. With an empty urinal next to me, I thought nothing of it until I felt someone's warm breath on my neck. Before I could react, I was grabbed by the back of my head and my face was slammed into the wall. My flattened nose felt like a steel spike had been driven into it.

"What do you want?" I screamed.

"Shut your mouth, SA," a voice said.

Before I had a chance to put myself back in my pants, someone pushed his knee into the small of my back. The hand I was holding myself with was jammed into the cold, wet porcelain. I couldn't move.

"What are you doing?" I tried to yell. But it came out garbled, unintelligible.

"Man, you better keep it down," a second voice from farther behind me said.

I was having difficulty breathing. For all I knew, one of the two was about to put a knife to my throat and slice me from ear to ear. Yet all I could think about was how my hand and dick were crammed up against the side of the germ-infested urinal—the part the water doesn't touch.

"Let me go," I said.

The hands on the back of my head pushed harder. "Listen, SA," the second voice said. "You tell that bitch of yours to lay off our homeboy."

"Who are you?"

"None of your business," the first voice said. His mouth was touching my ear. He then gripped my hair tighter, pulled my head back, and pushed it forward again into the wall. Dazed, I could barely make out the splatter of blood in front of me.

"Now . . . are you paying attention?"

There was nothing I could do other than to listen to what the thugs had to say. If they were friends of Martinez, I knew what they were capable of.

"Yes, yes, I'm listening."

"Leave our homie alone."

"But I could end up in jail."

"Be patient, ese." The pressure to my head lessened.

"I don't understand."

"Damn it, attorney, you don't have to," the second voice shouted. I cringed, expecting my face to be bounced off the wall again. "Just do what we say, and before your case ever gets to trial that kid will disappear."

"How can I be sure?"

"Because I'm a fortune-teller." The second voice was doing most of the talking now.

"Are you going to hurt him?"

"Your ass is on the line, and all you worry about is what we might do to some drug pusher," he said, and they both laughed. "We won't have to do shit to him. He's so damn scared he'll run like a rabbit as soon as he's cut loose."

My face was hurting so badly, I couldn't respond.

"And if you don't do what we say, there's no telling what will happen. Including," the first voice said, and I felt something cold and sharp against my throat, "what we'll do to that pretty little bitch of yours. Get my drift, SA?"

I'd no intention of letting these small-time punks dictate my future conduct. But I also knew it wasn't the best time to argue. "I'll do whatever you want."

"Good," he said, and the pressure against my lower back stopped. I quickly zipped up.

"If you turn around before we walk out the door," the first voice said, gripping my hair tighter for emphasis, "you're history."

"All right," I said, and he let go.

Before the door closed, I became light-headed and my knees buckled. I found myself on the floor with my head inside the urinal, blood running freely down my cheek and into the drain. I crawled to the sink and pulled myself up to rinse the blood from my face.

My first thought was to call the police. But what would I tell them? They would look upon anything I said with suspicion, thinking I was lying and faking a swollen nose to bolster my position in court. And I wouldn't blame them. What had just happened didn't make any sense. I had no idea what those hoods were up to. Why would they want me to prolong my case? How could it possibly benefit them?

Just as I began to wonder what could possibly happen next, the door burst open. Panicked, fearful they had returned, I quickly glanced around the room for something to protect myself with when someone grabbed my shoulder from behind. Cocking my arm, I spun around and saw Sarah with both her hands cupping her face. Her eyes were darting back and forth between me and the mural of my blood above the urinal.

Chapter 17

"I understand why I should terminate my cross of Miles," Sarah said. "But why stipulate to the admission of the transcript into evidence? Let's force Patterson to call Kellogg to the stand."

We were waiting for Judge Brown to take the bench. I'd finally convinced Sarah not to call the police, and now I was asking her to do something both of us could later regret.

"It isn't worth it."

"Are you sure?"

"No, but since I'm not contesting the fact that I asked Kellogg to OR the kid, what do we have to gain? There's no denying any of it. It's in the damn transcript. Besides," I said, getting to the real reason, "I don't want to give Kellogg the satisfaction of testifying against me."

"Is this the Hunter Dobbs that never gives an inch to anyone?"

"Maybe you're having a positive influence on me, after all," I said, half smiling.

Sarah didn't seem to hear me. She was busy looking to the rear of the courtroom. "It looks like they're gone," she said, referring to the four Hispanics.

I touched my nose which—fortunately—didn't look half as bad as it felt. "I wouldn't doubt if two of them were the restroom bandits."

Sarah grimaced. "I still think we should inform the police."

"Maybe you're right," I said, not wanting a chance like this to pass. "After all, they said they'd take care of my bitch attorney if I didn't cooperate. They didn't say they'd do anything to me."

"There you go again, joking," she said. Hearing the edge in her voice, Patterson glanced at us. It was killing him not to know what we were so busy talking about.

"Actually, I'm not really worried about those hoods as much as you might think, because I intend on doing exactly what they asked."

"I'm not so sure that's wise."

"Stalling may be best, but for a different reason than they had in mind. The more this case ages, the better chance we have that Miles will end up telling the truth."

"But we don't have to wait. A jury won't believe him anyway."

"That's not what you were saying back at the café."

"I was trying to make a point," she said. "You didn't seem to be taking any of this seriously."

"Well, you convinced me. Between the kid's and Kellogg's testimony, we'll have an uphill battle. And that's not even taking the attorney factor into account."

"Attorney factor?"

"As far as the public is concerned, all attorneys

are crooks. Especially defense attorneys. Hell," I said, "they think we suborn perjury all the time. They'll be thankful one of us finally got caught."

"Do you really think so?"

"You bet. I'll be guilty before the trial even starts. Don't you think Patterson knows that? Why else do you think he's so damn cocky? If he had a chance at the jury right now, he's sure I'd be convicted."

Sarah was silent.

"That's why stalling makes so much sense. Sooner or later that kid is going to be released, and when that happens," I said as I saw Judge Brown in the back hallway say something to his bailiff, "he will either run—in which case he won't be testifying at the trial—or he won't be under Martinez's control. And if the latter should ever happen, I think the kid will eventually tell the truth."

"You are expecting an awful lot from an eighteen-year-old drug dealer."

"He's really not such a bad kid."

"And that's the kind of thinking that got you in this predicament in the first place," she said, and the judge entered the courtroom.

"Before we continue with your cross of Mr. Miles," Brown began, "have you had enough time to review a copy of the transcript, Ms. Harris?"

"One minute." Sarah turned to me. "Are you sure?"

I wasn't. But I didn't much like the alternative. "Let's go as planned."

"The defense will stipulate that the transcript may be used in lieu of Judge Kellogg's testimony."

Brown narrowed his eyes as they became fixed on Sarah.

"For preliminary hearing purposes only," she explained. "However, if this matter should ever proceed to trial, I'd expect Mr. Patterson to make sure Judge Kellogg is available."

Brown looked at Patterson. "Do you agree with that stipulation?"

I knew Patterson didn't know what to make of it. But he wasn't about to let the opportunity pass. "Of course," he responded.

"So ordered," Brown said. "Ms. Harris, you may now continue with your cross of Mr. Miles."

"No further questions," Sarah announced and sat down.

Patterson jerked his head toward us as the words came out of Sarah's mouth. He scrunched his face and looked at the judge, who appeared even more mystified.

"Well then," Brown said, sitting forward. "Do you have any re-direct, Mr. Patterson?"

"Ah . . . no, Your Honor." His eyes were glued to Sarah, trying to make sense of it. "No questions. The witness may be excused."

Caught off guard, the bailiff jumped out of his chair and rushed to the witness stand to escort Bobby back to lockup.

"Leave him where he is," Brown said, holding his hand up for the bailiff to stop. He then turned to the still stunned D.A. "Do you have any further witnesses?"

"None."

"Any affirmative defense?" Brown asked Sarah.

"No, Your Honor."

"Then I have no other choice," Brown said, and I stood. I knew the routine by heart. The defendant stands while the judge orders him to superior court for trial.

"Mr. Dobbs," he said and took an audible breath. "I believe for purposes of the preliminary hearing there is reason to believe that a crime was committed and that you have likely committed it. Therefore, I am binding you over to superior court for trial. Your arraignment will be on October 24, 1998 in Department A. Bail to remain."

As soon as Brown concluded, the D.A. started to walk away. "Mr. Patterson," the judge said, "earlier I asked you to bring Mr. Miles's file."

Bobby was still sitting in the witness stand. He didn't have a clue as to why he was still in court. Neither did the rest of us.

Patterson pulled a file from his briefcase. "I have it."

"Then please tell me why this young man is still in custody."

"I guess," Patterson began, like he was stating the obvious, "because he's unable to post bail."

"Brilliant," the judge scowled. "Why don't you explain to me why his bail is set at fifty thousand?"

"Judge Kellogg set the bail."

"Only after your office requested that amount, am I correct?"

Patterson thumbed through the file. "It would appear that way."

"Why does the District Attorney's office feel an eighteen-year-old who, at worst case, sold a couple of marijuana cigarettes to a friend, warrants such high bail?"

"I really don't know," he said. "I'm not familiar with this case."

"Well, you should be," Brown barked. "He's your primary witness in the case against Mr. Dobbs, isn't he? You should be completely familiar with it."

Patterson stood dumbfounded.

"You are aware what the defense is, aren't you?"

"I know what they would like us to believe," Patterson scoffed.

"Well, what if there's just a smidgen of truth to the proposition that someone like Mr. Martinez or one of his friends put this young man up to framing Mr. Dobbs?"

"That's up to the defense to prove."

"On the contrary, sir, your office has the responsibility to seek the truth, am I correct?"

"With all due respect, I feel this court is going beyond the—"

"I don't care what you feel," Brown growled and turned to Bobby. "How long have you been in custody?"

"Almost two weeks."

"I'm surprised at your office, Mr. Patterson. I have seen cases like Mr. Miles's reduced and sent out for diversion. Six months' worth of counseling and his case would be dismissed."

The D.A.'s teeth were clenched, he was so angry. "As I already informed the court, I'm not that familiar with his case."

"Well, I know enough about it," Brown said, turning to his clerk. "The defendant in case number

MA118799 is released on his own recognizance."
The judge turned to the smiling young man. "Mr.
Miles, you should be out of custody within the
next twenty-four hours. Be sure you make all your
future court appearances. Do you understand?"

"Yes, sir."

The judge walked from the bench, but before he
left the room, he gave me a parting glance. I had a
good idea what he was up to. With Bobby out of
custody, he would be free of Martinez's control.
The judge wanted to make sure I was playing on a
level field.

Chapter 18

Sarah and I hurried up the long walk to the Bartons' yellow Victorian house. A late October wind gusted around us. As I leaned into the punishing gale, I couldn't help noticing how the ailing structure was sorely in need of repair. The doorway was heavily framed, topped by an elegantly carved wooden header. Like the rest of the house, though, its veneer was thinned by age and the elements of the rough northern coastal seasons.

We had to try to interview Danny before Jared's trial began. Hopefully McBean hadn't told either him or his mother not to talk to us.

A small cowbell attached to the inside front-door knob announced our presence. As we stepped in, a loud creak from the wooden floor groaned from our combined weight. The inside of the house was much smaller than it appeared from the street. It was built for smaller people during a simpler, yet more elegant time.

A middle-aged woman dressed in a flowered print dress eyed us from a position behind a glass display case filled with lime-green dishware. Her smile was warm and real. "May I help you?" she asked.

As we slowly made our way forward, we looked
for any sign of the boy. What at one time must have
been the living room was now filled with rows of
tables stacked with used clothing. Here and there
small pieces of furniture, priced as antiques, served
as resting places for ladies' hats of all sizes, colors,
and eras.

Sarah was the first to speak. "Is this the Barton
residence?"

A light shade of red flickered across the woman's face. I had the feeling she was embarrassed
her living room was being used to house discarded
clothing reeking of mothballs. "The second floor
is," she said, waving her hand at the stairs located
off the front doorway.

"Is Danny here?" Sarah asked.

"Why, yes . . ." she stammered. "Who are you?"

"This is Hunter Dobbs, and my name is Sarah
Harris. Are you his mother?"

The woman glanced over her shoulder out a
small window behind her. "What's this all about?"

I stepped closer. "We represent Mr. Jared Reineer."

"Jared Reineer," she said, and her face abruptly
tightened. "Lieutenant McBean never told me anyone else would want to talk to Danny." Her right
hand, which was resting on the counter, began to
tremble.

"We were wondering if that would be possible,"
Sarah asked.

The trembling became more noticeable. "Are you
supposed to?"

"That's entirely up to you," I said, knowing full

well we shouldn't talk to a minor without a parent's permission. "We only want to ask him a few questions."

She nervously looked around the room, as if searching for someone to tell her what to do.

"We understand how traumatic it must have been for the two of you," Sarah said, and placed her hand on top of Mrs. Barton's. "We aren't here to upset him. And we have no objection to your being present."

"I don't know." She turned and looked out the window again. I followed her gaze through the sheer white curtains and saw a young boy out back cramming a rumpled cardboard box into one of several trash cans.

She noticed me watching. "I guess it would be all right," she said. "I'll get him."

"Don't trouble yourself." I nodded at Sarah to follow me. "It looks like he could use some help with those boxes."

Before the mother could say anything, I was out the side door, with Sarah trailing close behind. Since it was cold and windy out, I was hoping that would be reason enough for the mother to stay inside. I wanted to talk to the boy without her.

I extended my hand. "Danny Barton?"

Eyeing Sarah, who had her hands buried deep in her coat pockets, the boy reached for my hand.

"Do I know you?"

"We're lawyers."

"Really?" he said, and turned to push a crushed box into one of the trash cans. "My dad wanted to be one."

I already knew his parents were separated. "Where is he?" I asked, trying to make the kid feel more at ease talking to us.

He waved to his mother as she watched us through the window. "I don't know and I don't care. We don't need him."

I liked the kid already. We both seemed to have something in common—we hated our fathers.

"It looks like you and your mother are doing just fine," Sarah said in an understanding tone.

Danny picked up a box and placed it in front of him to jump on and crush like the other one he'd shoved into the can.

"Can I show you a trick?" I said, reaching for the box. "I used to work at a supermarket when I was in high school. I had to throw away hundreds of boxes a week."

The boy eyed me as if I was intruding on his space.

I placed a corner of the box against the center of my chest while firmly gripping its sides—one in each hand. "Each corner is like a heavy crease in a piece of paper," I said. "If you pull in the opposite direction, on each side of the crease, it will tear evenly with very little effort."

The boy tilted his head, studying me. I could tell he wasn't buying it.

I then pulled, and the box ripped neatly down the corner. I quickly did the same to the remaining three corners and folded what was left of the box and handed it to the boy. "Now it will take up a lot less room in the trash can."

Danny smiled for the first time. The splash of freckles across his nose and cheeks was a sharp contrast to the rest of his face, white from the chilling wind. "How did you do that?"

"Just pull away from your body, and the crease on each corner will give way."

The boy watched as I ripped apart another one and placed it inside the trash can.

Without saying anything further, Danny picked up the last box and easily ripped each of the box's four corners.

"Beats the heck out of having to jump on it," I said.

Danny tossed the box into the can. "Sure does."

I knew I had him. I was his buddy now. If his mother would just stay away long enough, I was sure he would tell me everything.

"My name is Hunter Dobbs." I turned to Sarah to introduce her, but the boy cut me off.

"Hunter's sure a funny name for a lawyer."

The boy laughed and Sarah snickered. I knew what she was thinking. All that effort with the boxes to loosen him up, and all I had had to do was tell the kid my name.

She extended her hand to the boy. "I'm Sarah."

"Danny Barton," he said, politely shaking her hand. He then turned back to me. "I'm sorry. I didn't mean to laugh."

"Don't worry about it," Sarah said and plunged her hand back into her pocket. "It really is a funny name."

We were there to talk to the boy, not play with him. "Are the two of you done?" I asked.

The two smiled conspiratorially at one another. Before they had a chance to take another shot at me, I continued. "We'd like to ask you about the night you were attacked."

"I get it," Danny said. "You must represent the guy who kidnapped me."

It was so cold, Sarah was shaking, almost convulsing. I'd have laughed at the sight of her, and the dampness under her shiny red nose, but I wasn't much better off.

"We know how upsetting all this has to be to you," she said.

"I'm not upset."

"That's good," Sarah said, and the boy glanced at the window. His mother was no longer watching.

"My mom was really upset, though."

"I'm sure," Sarah said. "You're her little boy."

Danny twisted his face. She had blown it with the "little boy" remark.

Sarah tried to regroup. "I'm sure you're a big help to your mother," she said.

Danny turned to me. "How many years is he going to be in jail?"

"If you mean my client," I said, "he hasn't been convicted yet."

"Isn't he going to cop a plea?"

"What?" I was more surprised by the source than the question itself. Where do kids pick up this stuff?

"Lieutenant McBean said he has enough evidence to bury him forever. I figure he doesn't have much choice."

"That's the lieutenant's opinion."

It was time to get to the primary reason we wanted to talk to him: the candy wrapper found in the car with his fingerprints all over it.

"The report says you were eating some Gummy Bears before the attack."

The boy shook his head vigorously. "Never had a chance."

"But you did have some with you at the time?"

"Yeah, I just bought 'em."

"This is very important, Danny." I held my breath. "Did you ever take your gloves off that night?"

The boy screwed up his face and squinted one eye, thinking. "You know," he said, but stopped to watch a black-and-white race up the dirt drive directly at us. It was McBean. I was sure that meant the end of our interview. But I had a couple of seconds before he reached us.

"Danny?" I pushed. "The gloves? Did you take them off?"

It was too late.

McBean was shouting as he sped toward us, "Leave that kid alone!"

The car skidded to a stop next to us, pelting our legs with loose pebbles. Then the door flew open, almost hitting Danny.

"Watch out!" I yelled.

McBean grabbed Danny by the arm and dragged him toward the house. "The two of you wait right there," he shouted as they approached the back door—where Mrs. Barton was waiting.

"What a genuine jerk," I said to Sarah. She was

rubbing her bare legs. They were spotted with red marks.

"Why is he so upset?"

"It's obvious he doesn't want us talking to the boy. If we could have had just one more minute alone, we may have found out why." I reached for her hand. "Let's get out of here."

"But he asked us to wait."

"He can keep us away from his victim. But I'll be damned if I'm going to take any of his abuse."

"Hey, Dobbs!" McBean started running toward us while Danny and his mother watched from the open doorway. "I want the two of you to stay away from him."

He stopped next to us, half out of breath.

"Are you going to apologize?" I said, waving my hand at Sarah's legs. A trickle of blood was running down the front of her left shin.

"About what?" He turned to see what I was talking about. Sarah was standing with her hands on her hips.

"Sorry, ma'am," he said, tipping an imaginary hat. He then spun on me. "I want you out of here."

I'd had enough of the Wyatt Earp act. "When I damn well feel like it."

"Is that right?" he said, walking to within a couple of feet of me. "You're trespassing."

"I wasn't until you got here."

"The mother said we could talk to him," Sarah said.

"She changed her mind."

"I'll bet."

A gust of wind took McBean by surprise, and his hair was blown about. Holding it in place with his right hand, he took one more step toward me. His face was within inches of mine. "The lady wants you off her property."

I turned my head away. Even with the strong wind, I could smell the stale cigarette smoke and coffee on his breath.

"We have the right to interview witnesses," Sarah said.

McBean glanced at her and sighed. "Are the two of you going to leave, or do I have to call for backup?"

"Backup? For trespassing?"

He didn't respond. We just stared at each other, waiting to see who would be the first to flinch.

"What are you hiding, McBean?"

His eyes remained slits. "Are you going to leave?"

I looked to Sarah, who nodded for me to get going. I shook my head, upset that we had come so close to finding out what had really happened that night. But none of this was news to me. Even though the cops aren't suppose to instruct their witnesses not to talk to the defense, the witnesses very seldom did. Funny how it always seemed to work that way. Must have been just a coincidence.

"We'll leave," I said. "But before we do, I want to give you something."

"What?"

I put my right hand in my pocket and watched McBean's jerk to the butt of his revolver. I slowly withdrew a roll of Certs breath mints and flipped one into the air. He caught it, reflexively.

"You need that, McBean, because your damn breath stinks worse than your case does."

Chapter 19

It was late afternoon when I pulled in front of the guest house. I sat in the car for a moment, admiring the orange glow of sun slipping behind the mountains. It was my thirty-sixth birthday and I was looking forward to a nice warm bath and a chance to relax in front of the tube all night.

When I reached the guest house door, I saw a note tacked to it. It was from Sarah.

Emergency! Must see immediately. Come to main house.

Before I could even knock on the house's front door, it was opened and Sarah appeared with a sad look.

"What's wrong?"

The door opened wider and Avery came into view, his expression as glum as Sarah's.

"Is somebody going to tell me what's going on?"

Avery stepped aside. There my Uncle Joe was, sitting in his wheelchair with a face-wide grin.

"Happy birthday!" the three shouted in unison.

Blood rushed to my cheeks. It was a birthday

party—mine. I couldn't remember the last time I'd been so touched.

"Are you going to stand out there all night?" Avery asked as Uncle Joe opened his arms and I rushed to him for a hug. It had been more than a year since we'd seen one another.

When we finally separated, I had another surprise—Avery wrapped his arms around me and gave me the same kind of strong affectionate hug that Joe used to give me before his hips gave way to arthritis.

"Quit hogging the guest of honor." Sarah nudged her way between the two of us and gave me a quick peck on the cheek, hugging me. "Are you surprised?" she asked, oblivious to the rush that her touch gave me.

"I really am," was all I managed to say as we parted, and walked into the living room. Sarah and I sat on the sofa, and Avery stationed my uncle and his wheelchair in front of us.

Joe tilted his head and looked up at the bottom of Avery's beard. "These are good people," he said.

I was sure Joe knew that Avery was the judge I had constantly complained about during my first few years with the P.D.'s office.

Not wanting to get into it with the judge standing next to him, I changed the subject. "You're sure looking good."

"Maybe you know how I look if you see me now and then," he said in his familiar broken English. Joe had always sounded as if he was auditioning for a movie part, but I knew Joseph Calabrese was the real thing. A retired truck driver, he'd spent the better part of his life as a high-ranking official for the Teamsters. Jimmy Hoffa was not only his boss but a good friend. His house was peppered with pictures of the two of them, Joe usually to the side of Hoffa, as the head of the Teamsters made one of his many speeches to the faithful.

Once, when I asked him why he started driving a truck again, Joe told me, "Because Jimmy's at the bottom of the ocean sleeping with the fishes." But I knew better. Hoffa didn't disappear until 1975; Joe moved to California right after my parents' funeral in 1972. He came out here to raise me, leaving his job and friends behind.

"I've been pretty busy," I said.

As usual, Joe knew when I was lying. "You never too busy for family." He gave Sarah the once-over. "Maybe I not so old I can't see why."

Sarah blushed. She didn't know there wasn't a thought that ever entered my uncle's head he wouldn't say out loud.

"Why you don't tell me you move here? I call for weeks, but you never home."

I looked at Sarah, and then to Avery, who was busy pouring everyone a glass of burgundy. I'd no idea if either had said anything to Joe about my arrest.

"I'm preparing for a trial."

Sarah picked up on my uneasiness. "It'll be starting next week," she added. "It's been in all the papers."

Joe gazed at me. There was no fooling the old Sicilian. "You work for the County of San Francisco. . . . Why you have trial way up here?"

It was no use, I had to tell him. With Sarah and Avery's help, I explained the charges pending against me.

Joe studied Avery, who was handing him a glass of wine. "You big-time judge. Why you can't help my boy?"

Avery shook his head. "It doesn't work that way. A jury will have to decide."

That was the last thing Joe wanted to hear. He'd lived half his life in Detroit and Chicago during the years when there wasn't a government official who didn't have his hand out for a bribe.

"No jury," Joe said. "Ever since Jimmy get caught paying them off, they not worth anything."

I smiled. I'd forgotten how much I loved his distorted sense of reality.

He scowled at me. "This no laughing matter." Joe leaned toward me. "I still got lots of friends. . . . You want me see what I can do?"

"Thanks," I said and rose to hug him. "Let me take care of this one. I'll be fine."

He gently pushed me away. "You don't do very good job so far," he said, and then a hint of a smile appeared. "You smart boy though. So I give you chance."

Sarah, who hadn't said a word during Joe's godfather act, gave me a look as if she thought he was just trying to be funny. Little did she know how serious he was. She rose and placed her hand on Joe's thick shoulder. "I'll start dinner."

"Remember, al dente," Joe called out.

I winced—pasta for dinner. Joe refused to eat spaghetti unless the sauce was made from an old

Sicilian recipe—tomatoes, Italian spices simmered all day with beef and lamb ribs, with several pigs' feet thrown in for added flavor.

"I remember," Sarah said and kissed him on the cheek. "Al dente."

Joe's smooth olive face flushed. "You let her get away," he said and nodded to the space Sarah had vacated, "and you'll answer to me."

I winked at Avery. "Whatever you say, Uncle Joe." I walked into the kitchen, leaving Avery to listen to Joe's war stories about the days the Teamsters ruled the land—or thought they did.

Sarah was at the sink, filling a pot full of water, when I walked to the side of her and placed my arm around her shoulder. "I don't know how to thank you," I said, gently squeezing her. She turned to me and like metal drawn to a magnet, her deep blue eyes met mine. There was an awkward pause—as we waited to see what the other would do next. My resolve to stay on neutral ground was quickly melting away.

I gently pulled her into me for a kiss. Our lips touched and just as I was about to draw her into my mouth, we jerked apart. From behind came a purposeful cough—it was Avery.

"I just wanted to check on the sauce," he said, seemingly more embarrassed than we were. He stirred the pot once. Before he left, he placed his finger over his lips as if to say he wanted to tell me a secret. "I didn't cook the pigs' feet," he whispered. "Do you think he'll notice?"

I had to chuckle. I should have known Joe would have made Avery cook his favorite recipe.

"Nah, I haven't put pigs' feet in for years."

"Phew," Avery said. He left the kitchen, shouting at Joe to see if he wanted another glass of wine.

Sarah nodded at her father as he walked away. "You know, this was his idea. He's had it planned for weeks."

I stared blankly into the middle distance, thinking. I was having a difficult time believing he'd do that for me.

"He really is fond of you. And, like your uncle," she said, gesturing to the living room, where we could hear Joe's booming voice, "underneath that rough exterior is a heart of gold."

Joe had been my guiding light for most of my life. His presence had made me realize something I should have been aware of long ago. Avery Harris and his daughter, Sarah, really were good people.

"I can see that now," I said.

Chapter 20

The Sav-on drugstore was located at the end of a long line of redbrick buildings, dwarfed by large redwoods to the rear. I'd wasted the last couple of hours sitting in my car, waiting to interview Carol Sealy, the cashier who'd sold Danny Barton the candy. The Gummy Bear wrapper had become the focus of my investigation. It was the one piece of evidence that directly connected Jared to the boy. And, it was crunch time. The trial was about to start and I hadn't come up with anything to prove that either McBean or one of his men could have planted it.

Even though nothing about Jared's case seemed to be falling into place, Sarah had been more successful with mine. Our plan to stall *my* trial had worked. She'd been able to put it off for a couple of months using Jared's trial as an excuse.

I was just about to nod off when a loud hacking sound startled me. A thin, gray-haired woman with her hands cupped in front of her face was trying to light a cigarette against a persistent late-afternoon breeze.

She didn't budge when I jumped out of the car and rushed up to her.

"These damn safety lighters," she complained.

"Having a problem?" I searched my pockets for matches that I knew weren't there.

"They make them this way to protect the kids, but hell, us old folks have the damnedest time. My skin's so thin, I'm afraid I'll cut myself every time I try to light the damn thing."

"I wish I could help."

"Could if you had a match."

"Sorry."

She furiously ran her thumb on the rough metal wheel until a flame appeared. She lit the cigarette and inhaled deeply. "I haven't seen you around here before," she wheezed through a cloud of smoke.

"I'm from San Francisco."

"Who around here isn't?"

The thick haze of carcinogens attacked my face. I moved to one side so the wind wouldn't hit me head-on. "Could I talk to you?"

"About what?"

"The boy who was attacked last month."

"I've already talked to you cops."

"I'm not a cop."

"Then you must be a reporter," she said, patting her windblown hair. "I don't want to talk to any reporters."

I hesitated, expecting the worst. "I'm not a reporter, ma'am. I'm an attorney."

"A lawyer?" She scowled. "I definitely won't talk to you."

"It's very important," I said with a sense of urgency. "I represent the man accused of attacking the boy."

"How can you do that?"

"Ma'am?"

"I just don't understand how you people can live with yourselves." She threw her half-finished cigarette on the ground and stamped it out. Interviewing witnesses can be really charming sometimes.

"I just want to understand better what happened that night."

"Yeah, and you'll twist and turn everything I say just to get the guilty S.O.B. off. . . . I watch TV."

It was obvious I wouldn't get anywhere asking her to talk to me for either Jared's or my sake, so I used the old standby. I'd take advantage of her natural sympathy for the young victim.

"Do you really want to put that boy through the trauma of having to testify?"

She looked at me sharply. "That's not up to me."

"In a way it is." I explained. "If no one will tell me what they know, then how will I ever know what the truth is?"

"The truth is your client is guilty or they wouldn't have arrested him."

I knew she wouldn't talk to me for sure if I tried to debate that point—so I didn't. "If I'm convinced my client is guilty, then the young man won't have to testify."

"How's that?"

"If what's stated in the police report is correct, I'll recommend he plead guilty."

"Well, I can tell you that whatever that lieutenant put in the report is the truth."

"You mean McBean."

The old woman nodded, and her eyes narrowed as if she'd finally realized what I'd been saying. "Are you telling me the only way that boy won't be forced to relive that horrible night is if your client pleads guilty?"

"That's correct."

She angled her head, thinking about it. She then withdrew another cigarette from the pack she kept in the breast pocket of her pink uniform. "Make it quick," she said and held out the pack to me. "Like one?"

"Nah, just gave it up," I lied. "It wasn't easy."

"Ah, these things won't hurt you," she said between hacks. "These are Carltons, son. Only one-tenth of a gram of nicotine per smoke. Hell, a whole pack of these aren't as bad as just one of those Marlboro cigarettes most of the kids smoke these days."

"Is that so?"

I waited as she lit it, inhaled, and held the smoke inside her for several seconds like she was smoking a joint.

"Do you recall the night the boy was attacked?"

"You know," she said, holding the cigarette in front of her face, studying it, "my father smoked Camels since he was twelve. Lived to be ninety-five. All this surgeon general stuff is a crock."

The woman started coughing again. This time she couldn't seem to stop. She bent slightly at the waist, holding her cigarette in one hand and a hankie up to her face in the other.

I didn't want her to die on me right here. At least

not until I had a chance to see what she knew. "Can I help?" I said. But before I could finish she placed the hankie over her mouth and spat God knows what into it. She straightened herself and looked at her burning cigarette, then took another drag.

"Don't know what causes that," she said, shaking her head. "Must be a lot of pollen in the air."

"That time of year," I supplied lamely.

"I remember the night it happened," she said, once she had caught her breath.

Slowly, so as not to alarm her, I took out a small notebook. "How about what the boy was wearing?"

"I don't remember the exact color of his clothes, if that's what you mean."

"No, ma'am," I said, scribbling while she was talking. "But do you recall if he was wearing a coat and gloves?"

"Of course I do," she said. "He was wearing a large overcoat. Does it say in that report what color it was?"

I could have cared less what the color of the coat was.

"The report describes the coat pretty well. . . . I need to know more about the gloves."

"What's there to say?" She glanced over her shoulder. I could tell she had to get back inside.

"Was he wearing them in the store?"

"As a matter of fact, he was."

"Are you positive?"

"I know what I saw," she said. "The little darling had quite a time when I handed him the change. With those gloves he could hardly hold onto the coins. And that magazine," she said and laughed.

"Magazine?"

"Right before he paid for the candy I saw him looking at a magazine."

"Did you notice if he was wearing his gloves at that time?"

"Sure was," she said. "And it was what was so funny."

Too busy writing, I didn't say anything.

"He was holding it upside down." She chuckled.

Ignoring the humor, I asked her again, "He was wearing the gloves while he was reading the magazine?"

"I doubt if he was reading it if it was upside down," she scoffed, obviously miffed that I didn't so much as smile at what she thought was so funny.

"Was he?"

"Yes, but I don't know why you think it's so important. He was wearing those gloves from the time he walked in until the time he walked out."

I wanted to kiss the old bat. But between her hacking and the smoke that enveloped her, I decided just to thank her instead. "I really do appreciate your time."

She flipped her cigarette butt on the sidewalk. "I have to get back."

"I understand."

"By the way," she said, backing up toward the door, "tell Lieutenant McBean he still owes me for that package of candy I gave him."

"What package?"

"When he interviewed me, I gave him a package of those Gummy Bears," she said. "You know, the same kind I sold to the boy."

"McBean kept it?"

"Sure did," she said. "And he never did pay for the damn things."

I was fighting hard to hide a triumphant smile. "When did this happen?"

"The day after the attack. McBean and some uniformed officer were waiting to talk to me as soon as I came on duty."

"Any idea what he did with them?"

"Damned if I know," she said and the automatic door opened. "I'm going to call that S.O.B.'s boss, though, if he doesn't get back here and pay for them."

"How much?" I asked, pulling some loose change from my pocket.

"Buck fifty plus tax."

"Will a dollar sixty-five do?" I said, handing it to her.

"I didn't mean for you to have to."

"That's all right," I said. "I'll be seeing McBean soon."

"Make sure he pays you back."

"Oh, he'll pay, all right. You can count on that."

Chapter 21

"All rise," Billy Danks, a solemn elderly clerk, bellowed as Judge Priest, dressed in a freshly pressed black robe, rushed up the wooden steps to take the bench. "The State of California versus Jared Reineer, Judge Mary Jane Priest presiding."

Normally, I don't get a queasy feeling in the pit of my stomach when a trial is about to begin, but Jared's was different. It wasn't because I was unfamiliar with the court, the players, or the seriousness of the charges. I had enough experience not to let any of that bother me. Rather, it was because of my strong belief in his innocence. As far as I was concerned, Danny Barton wasn't the only victim in this trial. Jared Reineer had been locked up because of the act of a crooked cop. It was my responsibility to expose Lieutenant William McBean and return to Jared the freedom he, like everyone else, held so dear. A responsibility I didn't take lightly.

To my right, Jared, dressed in one of Avery's gray suits, turned to me with a strained look. Minus the beard, he was a sharp contrast to the wild-eyed paranoiac who, just a couple of months ago, had bawled like a baby as he lay in a pool of his own urine. He appeared the opposite of what I was sure Bragg would try to portray. On the other side of him, Sarah managed a stiff half-smile when our eyes met. She was wearing what she described as her jury suit—a classic gray wool with a snug, fitted jacket and skirt. It was just tight enough for the men to take notice, but not so tight that it would alienate any of the women jurors.

Sitting in the front row directly behind Jared, with his familiar stoic expression, was Avery. The sixty-five-year-old was tan and trim. A powerful man both in manner and appearance.

Jury voir dire had taken the better part of a week. The most difficult task when selecting a jury in a high-profile case is to find twelve individuals who, after having been bombarded with pre-trial publicity, can still maintain an open mind. Since the moment Jared was arrested, the media had, without exception, slanted every report in favor of the prosecution. According to them, Bragg had all the evidence and the trial was nothing more than a waste of the county's valuable time and resources.

However, Bragg and I knew differently. The only certainty was that the final outcome was uncertain. I'd won more than my share of cases that I shouldn't have and vice versa. I was sure the same held true for Bragg. There was never a guarantee of what twelve people might do. It was a crapshoot under the best of circumstances.

Bragg, who was to the left of McBean, fidgeted nervously in his chair. If he should lose what his faithful believed was a certain victory, he could kiss any chance of becoming the next governor good-bye. His wealth and connections wouldn't help him then. The pressure was on.

"I will remind the gallery that they are to be silent throughout these proceedings," Judge Priest said, peering down from her lofty perch. She was tall and thin, yet broad shouldered like a swimmer. In her mid-forties, she wore little makeup, making her pale green eyes even lighter—more masculine. The book on Priest was that she was fair to both sides no matter what the consequence. She was exactly what was needed to preside over the most notorious case to be tried in Mendocino County since anyone could remember.

"Consider yourselves my guests," she concluded, "and as such, I can have any one or all of you removed at any time."

There was a general shifting as everyone glanced around to see if there was someone in particular she might be referring to. Within seconds everyone settled, and the judge nodded to Bragg to begin his opening statement.

The head district attorney was dressed in a new black suit, crisp white shirt, and a red-and-blue-striped tie. Sighing deeply, Bragg arranged the several documents that were spread out on the table in front of him. He knew all eyes would be focused on him—everyone anxious to hear what he intended on proving—and he was milking the moment for all it was worth.

Once the papers had been finally arranged in a neat stack, he gently picked them up and tapped them on the table. Then, with the stack in one hand, he paused momentarily and slowly rose to his feet. The only sound was a slight screech of the wooden chair as he pushed it away.

Looking at the floor with a somber expression, he walked between the bench and counsel table. "Thank you, Your Honor," he said, and bowed slightly at the waist. After a brief pause, he swiveled on one foot toward the jury. Placing his hand on his chin, he fixed his gaze on the documents he was holding in front of him.

I had to turn from the jury to hide a smile. The guy was putting on quite a show, and like everyone else, I couldn't wait to see what he was going to do next.

"I don't need these notes," Bragg said and tossed the papers on top of the counsel table. Most, however, fell harmlessly to the floor.

"Why?" he said loudly. He paused as he walked closer to the jurors. "Very simple, really. You see, ladies and gentlemen, I know the facts of this case by heart. But before we get to that, my name is J. J. Bragg, district attorney for the County of Mendocino. In this case, I represent the people of the state of California. You see," he continued, picking up the tempo, "when someone has committed a crime in this county, it is not only my duty, but my moral obligation to make sure that person is brought to justice."

He quickly turned around, and after one long step, pointed his finger directly at Jared's startled face. "And that is why we are here," he cried.

The jurors' eyes shifted to Jared.

"That," Bragg said in a more suppressed tone,

while shaking his head in disgust, "is the defendant, Mr. Jared Reineer."

The D.A. dropped his outstretched hand and surveyed the jury as he continued to shake his head. "A truly despicable man."

While the jury focused on Bragg again, I sneaked a look at Jared to see how he was holding up. I had warned him something like this might happen. The D.A. was egging him on, hoping he could elicit some kind of violent response in front of the jury. But Jared had his hands clasped in front of him while looking straight ahead. He appeared calm and in control. As a matter of fact, I saw a smile playing at the corner of his mouth. It was his way of telling me he was fine.

Bragg looked to the heavens and threw his hands in the air. "Dear Lord, Danny is just a child," he beseeched. "But his childlike innocence was stolen from him the night of September twenty-fifth in that dark forest. It was taken from him by that animal," he shouted, pointing at Jared again.

With his head bowed, Bragg walked to the jury box and placed his hands on the railing. His eyes slowly shifted from one juror to another. "I will prove that Jared Reineer kidnapped and beat a ten-year-old boy named Danny Barton. And, if not for the grace of God, he would have had his way sexually with that poor innocent child as well."

Bragg pulled a red handkerchief from his coat pocket and removed his wire-rim glasses, which he wiped clean. "By the time I'm finished with Jared Reineer, everyone in this courtroom, everyone in this county, everyone in the world, will know what Jared Reineer is." Bragg lowered his voice to a whisper. "He's a molester of children, pure and simple . . . or God help us, maybe even worse."

Bragg put his glasses back on and focused on Jared. Then with the suddenness of a rattlesnake, he thrust his arm at Jared again. "But this wasn't the first time, was it, Mr. Reineer? Maybe for Danny Barton. But not for you. No, sir, you've done it before." Bragg was shouting now. "How many times? Two? Three? A dozen? A hundred? And I'll bet Danny was lucky not only because he escaped, but because he is alive today. How many of your victims aren't?"

An opening statement is nothing more than an outline of what each party intends on proving. However, I knew it wasn't unusual for the D.A. to throw in a little argument—punctuated by emotion. When they do, I normally don't object because I'll try to get away with the same. But Bragg's opening was going beyond that. Even though I wasn't positive, he had to be referring to the disappearance of the Boonville boy, which had nothing to do with Jared's trial.

I looked up at Priest, who was about to nod off. She had probably heard Bragg make similar speeches. But I hadn't and I'd had enough.

"Objection, sidebar!" I said, jumping to my feet.

Priest extended an open hand to a spot next to her. "Will counsel please approach sidebar?" she ordered like it was her idea. I was already there by the time she'd finished.

The judge rolled her eyes. "Is this the first time you've heard one of Bragg's openings?"

"And hopefully the last."

We both waited while Bragg, with his shoulders slumped, making sure everyone in the courtroom knew he felt my interruption was unwarranted, slowly approached.

"Go ahead," Priest said once Bragg was in position, "state your grounds."

"I feel I have allowed counsel a lot of liberty by not objecting until now," I began. "But I believe Mr. Bragg has gone way beyond the bounds of an opening statement. He is not only arguing his case, but now he is referring to matters that have no relevancy to this trial whatsoever." I lowered my voice to a near whisper. "He is telling the jury my client is responsible for other crimes."

"Is that true, Mr. Bragg?"

Bragg taunted me with a quick, bitter smile. "The law is clear that I can mention in my opening statement anything I intend on proving. Including similar crimes."

Priest shook her head impatiently. "What other crimes?"

"He's referring to the disappearance of a boy named Gary Cosgrove."

The judge looked to Bragg for a response, and the D.A. nodded his head. "Counsel for the defense is correct," Bragg said, as if there were a dozen other defense attorneys up there.

I glanced at Sarah, who gave me a subtle smile while slowly shaking her head. She probably thought I was about to lose it.

"What proof do you have that my client had anything to do with that boy's disappearance?"

"I'll prove a connection."

My hands dropped to my sides out of frustration. I felt my heart sink. What did Bragg know? Had he found out something that connected Jared to the Boonville boy?

"Even if, for the sake of argument," I said to Priest in a strained voice, "he can prove a connection, what possible relevancy does it have in this trial?"

"Modus operandi," Bragg said matter-of-factly.

"And which, under 352 of the evidence code," I responded, "I'll object to as highly prejudicial and will cause an undue consumption of this court's time."

Seemingly unimpressed, Bragg flipped the back of his hand in my direction. "The circumstances behind that boy's disappearance are highly prejudicial because you know a jury will believe he killed the boy. Object all you want."

I brought him back down to earth quickly. "What circumstances are you talking about?"

Bragg's eyes narrowed.

"Well?" I demanded.

"We're still working on it."

"Just as I thought." I turned to Priest. "At this moment I believe the issue is whether or not Mr. Bragg can mention that my client is responsible for other crimes. I am putting this court on notice that before the district attorney should be allowed to make such inflammatory statements, you first have to rule on their admissibility."

"So, you should have requested a hearing," Bragg interrupted.

"How?" I said. "I didn't have any idea you intended on introducing any of this."

Priest slammed her open hand on the counter. The sound created a much louder noise than she had intended. The bailiff stiffened.

"Mr. Bragg, you have been practicing long enough to know that before you can mention such damaging collateral evidence in your opening statement, you should make sure the defense has been provided with any and all information concerning it."

There was a lumbering silence. Bragg gazed at the floor, pondering his next move.

"And if there is an objection, an evidentiary hearing would be in order before you could even breathe a word of it to the jury."

"Then, let's have a hearing."

With that, the corner of Priest's mouth twitched as she glanced around the packed courtroom. I knew what she was thinking. Everyone was expecting the opening statements to be made today. It had been front-page news and the subject of talk shows as far away as San Francisco. There was no way she would disappoint them.

"Counsel," she said, "you should have known that anything close to something this prejudicial would be objected to."

"But—" Bragg said and the judge cut him off.

"Mr. Dobbs, are you objecting to any and all references being made to the disappearance of a young boy from Boonville?"

"His name is Gary Cosgrove," I said respectfully. "And yes, I am objecting for the reasons previously stated."

"Sustained." Priest turned to Bragg. "You will finish your opening without any further reference to what may or may not have happened to anybody other than the victim listed in this case."

"But that could be a major part of my case."

"Then you should have thought about that before you tried to blindside the defense."

"I wasn't."

Priest glared at the prosecutor. "I'm not buying any of it. You tried to get away with something, and Mr. Dobbs called you out."

Bragg opened his mouth and started to say something, but thought better of it.

"Now, either you continue according to my guideline, or I'll tell the jury you have concluded your opening."

Without saying anything further, Bragg strutted back to the jury box, grinning as if he had won the argument. The man should have been an actor.

"Ladies and gentlemen," he said, launching right back into his opening, "Danny Barton will testify that he left his mother's old Victorian house after spending most of that Saturday helping her around the store. His reward was the five dollars she'd given him to buy whatever he wanted."

The corners of Bragg's eyes crinkled with empathy.

"Five dollars was a fortune to Danny. And that night, he knew exactly what to do with it. You see, the following day was his mother's birthday. He was going to buy her a bottle of perfume at Sav-on.

"When Danny left for Sav-on that evening, neither he nor his mother could have known that a man in an old, dented sedan had been waiting for more than an hour in the parking lot of the new strip mall where the drug store was located."

Bragg looked pointedly at Jared and shook his head in disgust, then he began to pace in front of the jury.

"Danny was sad when he learned that five dollars wasn't enough to buy even the cheapest bottle of perfume. So instead he bought a package of Gummy Bears and left Sav-on for home. But as Danny Barton rushed around the corner of the building, he ran smack into someone. Looking up, Danny saw looming over him a large man wearing a baseball cap and a long green army overcoat. Danny was momentarily paralyzed. He didn't know what to do. The man grabbed Danny by the arm and dragged him into the passenger seat of his car. The man jumped in and threw the car into gear and it sped away. The old car turned onto Danny's block and picked up speed as it passed his mother's big Victorian house."

Bragg paused as he surveyed the faces of the jurors.

"Danny will tell you he screamed for his mother as he looked out at the porch light that she had left on for him. And that was the last thing he saw before the man turned and with a clenched fist struck Danny on the side of the face.

"When Danny regained consciousness, he found himself on the floorboard, bouncing around like a rag doll. They were on a dirt road somewhere. When the car finally came to a stop and the man climbed out, Danny looked out to see where the man was, but all he could see was the silhouettes of large pine trees.

"Suddenly, Danny heard the gruff sound of the man cursing. Turning quickly, he saw the man trying unsuccessfully to get his key to open the passenger's side door lock. Danny knew he had to do something. Leaning back, he started kicking furiously at the window. The man cursed again as he finally pulled the door open, reached inside and yanked the boy out of the car by one ankle. The back of Danny's head thumped onto the cold, wet ground outside.

"Danny tried to see what was happening, but it was dark. He could barely make out the shadowy figure as it grabbed the collar of his coat and began dragging him through the forest, winding quickly through the trees as if he had been there many times before.

"Finally, in a small clearing, the man let go. Danny slumped to the ground and covered his face with his arms, crying. The man kicked Danny in the ribcage. Gasping for air, the boy screamed for help, but the sounds seemed to disappear in the dark dense fog.

"The man laughed as he knelt over Danny, ripping the boy's coat open, exposing his yellow T-shirt and blue jeans. He then grabbed at Danny's pants, popping the metal button and zipper in a single motion. Inch by inch, he relentlessly pulled the jeans over the boy's shoes, leaving the child shuddering with cold and fear and shame.

"He then turned Danny over and lifted his long coat. When the man grabbed the boy's briefs, Danny kicked back, catching his attacker squarely in the groin. The man slid off to Danny's side, growling in agony. By the time he managed to reach for Danny, the boy was already running through the forest as fast as he could.

"Danny eventually hid behind a large redwood, exhausted. It was dark and deathly quiet; all he could hear was his own gasping. He tried to stay as still as possible, listening. He had run far enough into the forest, he thought, that the man could never find him.

"But then, from somewhere through the trees, he heard the car start. Danny held his breath until seconds later the glare of the car's headlights shone directly on the large tree that shielded the boy. Just as he was sure he'd have to make a run for it, the car turned and drove slowly away."

Bragg took a deep breath and slowly let it out before he concluded. "As I said, ladies and gentlemen, but for the grace of God, Danny lived through that ordeal and escaped from the depraved animal who kidnapped him." The head D.A. then lunged in front of Jared and pointed his finger at him again. "I will prove that that animal is none other than the person sitting right here in front of you. That loathsome, despicable man is Mr. Jared Reineer."

Bragg straightened himself and gave the jury a semi-bow, then strutted back to his seat. I had to admit, he put on one hell of a show. I felt like clapping.

"Mr. Dobbs," Priest said, "will you be making an opening?"

I didn't have to think twice. Sarah and I had discussed it at length. If I did make an opening statement, I would have to outline for the jury the evidence I intended on producing. The problem was, I didn't know. I didn't know if Danny would still be unable to positively identify either Jared or his car. I didn't know if or how I was going to be able to prove McBean planted the Gummy Bears. I didn't know if Bragg would figure out a way to connect the disappearance of the Boonville boy to Jared. And I didn't know whether or not to call Jared to the stand.

Too much depended upon what the prosecution did.

"Your Honor, the defense wishes to reserve its right to make an opening statement."

"Then this court will be adjourned until ten tomorrow. Mr. Bragg, please be sure you and your first witness are ready to proceed at that time."

All smiles, Bragg quickly rose to his feet again. "You can rest assured, the people of the state of California and our first witness, Danny Barton, will be more than ready."

Jared was fired up after Bragg's ferocious attack. His eyes darted from one blank wall to the other, never once settling on mine. I'd patiently listened, understanding perfectly well how disturbing it must have been. If the D.A.'s finger had been in my face all afternoon, I'd have likely bitten it off.

We were alone in the attorney interview room, where Jared was changing out of his civilian trial clothes. "Someday Bragg will regret what he did to me in there," he said, balancing on one leg and then the other as he stepped out of his dress pants.

My eyes widened. If I didn't know him better—wasn't convinced he was afraid of his own shadow—I would have thought he was making some kind of threat. "What did you say?"

Jared thought for a moment. "I mean, when we win this thing, his political career will be history. No matter how much money he or his old man has."

"I'm surprised you know so much about him."

"You should always know as much about the enemy as you possibly can." He unbuttoned his white dress shirt. "Isn't that what good trial attorneys do?"

"I just didn't know you had access to the history of Bragg's family life," I said casually.

"It's well chronicled. Do you think I can't read?"

"Not with all the books I found strewn across the guest house floor," I remarked.

Jared's face went stone cold. "What do you mean, strewn across the floor?"

I knew as soon as the words left my mouth, I shouldn't have mentioned anything about his personal property. It was the one thing guaranteed to set him off. "Let's just say that when the cops search a place, they normally don't tidy up afterward."

Jared was frozen in place. "But you said they didn't wreck any of it."

"They didn't," I said. "Sarah boxed everything and stored it someplace safe."

Jared placed his hands on the counter and leaned

into me. Except for his boxer shorts, he was totally naked. "Everything?"

I was tired. It had been a long day, and I anticipated an even longer one tomorrow. "I'm not sure," I said impatiently. "I know there were a lot of clothes and books."

"And my necklace?"

"Come on, Jared," I said, sighing. "We've been over this before. As far as I know, it's still in the property room along with the rest of the stuff they took from your person the day you were arrested."

He looked at me long and hard. "What do you mean as far as you know? . . . Aren't you sure?"

"Yes, yes . . . you'll get it back when you're released."

His eyes dropped and his face turned sad. "I'm sorry, Hunter, but I've had that necklace most of my life, and it means a heck of a lot to me."

"I understand."

I hesitated. I needed to figure out the best way to approach him about the real reason I needed to talk—Avery's Blazer. Because of what Bragg had said in his opening, it was obvious that he was going to try to connect Jared to the disappearance of Gary Cosgrove. I knew Bragg could be bluffing, but I had to be prepared for the worst. I had to find out exactly what Jared knew.

"Do you recall driving Avery's Blazer a day or two before you were arrested?"

"Why do you ask?"

"Some old man told me one was used to kidnap that missing boy."

Jared slowly stepped into his blue denim trousers

and gave me a look as if he thought I was joking. "Do they think I'm the only person in the state of California who has access to a red Blazer?"

"That's what Bragg was talking about in his opening when he told the jury you'd done something similar to another boy."

"I remember," he said and lifted an eyebrow. "That's when you were a little slow pulling the trigger."

It didn't take a genius to realize he was criticizing me. I knew I should have objected a bit sooner, but I didn't need a tree trimmer to remind me. "What did you just say?"

"I just thought," he said as he sat across from me, "that you let that pompous idiot carry on longer than you should have about something that has nothing to do with my case."

I let the remark pass. But not before I took a deep breath and made a show of blowing it out. "There are a couple of witnesses who saw the kid driven off in a red Blazer, and he hasn't been seen or heard from since."

"Did anyone see who the driver was?"

"Not as far as I know. But they seem pretty confident they'll be able to prove it was you."

Jared's eyes never wavered. "They're wrong. I told you weeks ago that I don't know anything about that missing kid."

Jared leaned back and plopped his bare feet on the counter. "How can they think I kidnapped some kid in a red Blazer the day after I supposedly kidnapped a different kid in my black Chevy?"

"I know it's tenuous," I said. "But they must

know you had access to Avery's Blazer about that time."

"Access only," he said and sat forward. "I never drove there. I don't know where the place even is." He then tilted his head. "As a matter of fact, I forgot the name of the damn place."

"Boonville."

No sooner did the name come out of my mouth when our eyes locked on each other's. "That sounds like a damn place you'd find in a Disney movie," Jared said and we both smiled.

"Our problem is," I said, "this is McBean's *fantasy* we're dealing with, not Walt Disney's—and we both know what that means."

Chapter 22

Everyone watched as Danny Barton followed the bailiff down the center aisle on his way to the witness stand. He was dressed in clothes that looked to be straight off the rack from his mother's secondhand store. The sleeves of his faded blue blazer were so long they hid everything but his fingertips. With every step his pant cuffs were pinned between the heels of his shoes and the floor. A wide paisley tie covered most of his thin chest.

When Danny neared the front of the witness stand, he turned to the clerk, who was busy rummaging through the top of his desk. With his right hand in the air, the boy surveyed the courtroom while he patiently waited to be administered the oath. When his eyes eventually found Jared, they came to an immediate halt and a glint of concern crossed his young face.

I didn't know what to make of it. Danny had never been able to positively identify Jared. Not from photographs, or any of the two live lineups that were held for him the day after Jared was arrested.

So why the trancelike stare?

Finally, the clerk found whatever it was he was looking for and interrupted the anxious moment. "Do you solemnly swear . . ." he began. The boy, as if a hypnotist had snapped his fingers, blinked once and turned back to the old man with his hand still above his head.

I breathed a sigh of relief and glanced at Sarah, who was clearly as puzzled as I was. "What the hell was that all about?" I mouthed as I heard Danny, who was now in the witness chair, accidentally bump the mike with his hand.

"You may begin," Priest said, nodding at the D.A.

Danny looked immediately at Bragg. The boy knew what would happen next. I was sure they had spent many hours rehearsing the moment.

Bragg began by asking a few foundational questions to help put the boy at ease. However, it didn't take long for everyone to realize that the D.A. was wasting his time. Sitting straight, the ten-year-old would pause briefly to consider each question before answering it with an air of certainty. Amusement intermittently flickered across the judge's face. The jury seemed captivated. Danny Barton was in control.

Bragg finally asked about the night the boy was attacked. "Why were you out so late?"

"It wasn't that late," Danny said indignantly. "I'm old enough."

Bragg faced away from the witness stand and smiled at the jury. "I'm sure you are."

"And, I'd been working all day," he added. It was obvious the boy knew Bragg was poking fun at him.

Danny looked at his mother as though he had done something wrong. She was sitting in the front row behind the prosecution table, dwarfed by the scowling Otto Cosgrove, seated to her right. After she nodded, he turned back to Bragg.

"My mother's birthday was the next day. I had to buy her a present."

"That's nice," Bragg oozed like he was talking to a two-year-old. "What did you have in mind?"

"She needed perfume."

"And is that what you bought her?"

"No," he said sadly. "I didn't have enough money."

"How much did you have?"

The young boy lifted his head and gave his mother a quick smile. "I made five dollars that day," he said proudly. "I sure thought that would be enough for a bottle of perfume."

"Everything is just so expensive nowadays."

The boy grimaced. "Sure is."

"So what did you end up buying her?"

Danny paused. There was something about Bragg's question that bothered the boy. His air of confidence was gone.

"What did you buy her?" Bragg repeated.

Danny slowly hung his head and stared blankly at the floor. "Nothing."

Bragg rushed to Danny's side and placed his hand on the boy's shoulder to soothe him. Danny shrugged it away and gave the D.A. a look saying "stop doing that."

I laughed inwardly when Bragg stepped back,

startled by the boy's reaction. It was obvious to all he'd embarrassed the ten-year-old.

"So everything was too expensive?"

"Not everything. But I wanted to buy her perfume."

Bragg paused to underscore the importance of his next question. "So you left the store without buying anything?" he said, knowing perfectly well the boy hadn't.

The smile returned to Danny's face. "I bought some Gummy Bears."

"Really?" Bragg said as if he had heard it for the first time. "What are Gummy Bears?"

"Chewy candy."

Bragg placed his hand on his chin, considering it. "What kind of a package was this chewy candy in?"

"That clear plastic kind of stuff," he said and hesitated. "I forget exactly what you call it."

"Cellophane," Bragg said, helping him out.

"Yeah, that's it." Danny looked at McBean. "Told you I'd forget that word."

There was laughter in the gallery and smiles from most of the jurors. If they'd thought Danny's answers had been spontaneous, they didn't anymore.

Bragg waited for the courtroom to settle. The Gummy Bears were the foundation of the prosecution's case. He didn't want anyone to miss what would come next.

"Danny," he finally said, "tell us what happened after you left the store with the Gummy Bears."

For over an hour, with most of the jurors sitting on the edge of their seats, Danny explained everything that had occurred after he left Sav-on. Little detail was spared. Bragg glossed over the fact that, except for a beard and a baseball cap, Danny couldn't give an accurate description of his attacker.

"What happened to the Gummy Bears?" Bragg asked.

"I was holding them when he grabbed me."

"Were you still holding them when you escaped?"

"They were gone. I must have dropped them somewhere."

"Like maybe when you were inside the car?" Bragg asked.

I jumped to my feet so quickly I almost knocked my chair over. "Objection. Calls for speculation."

Priest nodded. "Sustained," she said, and with a flick of her hand waved at the D.A. to proceed.

Bragg faced the jury and walked slowly toward them with a concerned look. "The car that the man used," he said and placed his hands on the jury railing, "would you describe it?"

Danny angled his head. "It was pretty big."

"How about the color?"

"Black."

McBean handed the D.A. several photographs. "Danny," he said and placed the photos on the counter in front of the boy. "I'm showing you what has been marked for identification as People's One through Four. Would you please look at each and tell us if you have ever seen the car that is in these photographs?"

I edged forward in my chair as Danny eagerly picked up the photos, glanced at each, and placed them back on the counter.

"Yes," he said.

Sarah gave me a quizzical look. We both knew he'd never been able to positively identify Jared's car.

Bragg stepped aside so the jury could not only hear but see Danny answer his next question. "When have you seen that car before?"

There was an eerie quiet throughout the courtroom. Danny hesitated, and a concerned look replaced his boyish grin. For the first time the carefree boy seemed to grasp the importance of what he was about to say. His eyes jumped from Bragg to Jared, and then settled on Bragg. "It's the car the man who attacked me was driving."

There was a general stirring in the gallery which Priest put to an immediate halt with one smash of her gavel. The D.A. paced in front of his star witness until calm was restored. He then swiveled on one foot to look up at Priest. "Your Honor," he said with a grin, "the people of the State of California have no further questions of this witness."

"Mr. Dobbs?" Priest said.

I was puzzled by more than Danny's identification of Jared's car. What concerned me most was that the boy's gloves were never mentioned. The crafty D.A. knew the boy's mother said Danny had left the house wearing them. And I was sure he knew my main contention would be Danny's fingerprints couldn't be on the wrapper because he had been wearing gloves. What was Bragg up to?

Then it occurred to me. I was being ambushed. Bragg wanted me to ask the question. That way it would look like Danny hadn't been spoon-fed the answer. That had to mean Bragg knew the boy would say he wasn't wearing them the whole time. As much as I didn't want to, I had to stay away from that area. Bragg had me boxed in.

"Mr. Dobbs," Priest pushed, "are you ready?"

I slowly approached the witness stand, trying to take my mind off the gloves. "Hello, Danny," I said in a lighthearted tone.

Danny was intelligent, forthright, and most of all likeable. I had to be careful. Attacking him would surely alienate the jury. But I had to at least prove that his identification of Jared's car had always been shaky, at best.

"Hi," he said with a quick, edgy smile. I was sure Bragg had warned him to be wary of me. Hopefully, though, the boy would remember our friendly talk back at his house.

"Regarding this car," I said, pointing to the photos, "do you know what kind it is?"

"Oh, sure," he said, enthusiastically. "It's a 1956 Chevrolet coupe."

I could tell by how quickly he answered that either McBean or Bragg had informed him. I had to find out what else they may have planted in his young fertile mind.

"That's a pretty old car."

"To me it is," he joked, but didn't smile until he heard laughter from the gallery.

"So you've seen one before?"

A warm smile covered his young face. "Sure have."

"Where?"

His mother gave him a soft, reassuring smile while nodding that it was all right for him to answer. "A couple times my dad took me to Cruise Night at A&W Root Beer," he said in a somber tone.

"Really." I tried to mask my disappointment. "There were probably lots of old cars there?" I remarked while pondering how I was going to attack his identification now that everyone knew the prosecution hadn't helped him.

"There sure was," he said all lit up. "My favorite is a 1958 Corvette."

"Mine, too," I said.

Bragg grimaced and wrote something on his yellow pad. He was probably making a note to himself that all the time he'd spent trying to get the boy to be afraid of me had been wasted. But I realized something that had never occurred to Bragg. It wouldn't be in Danny Barton's nature to dislike anyone for too long.

I decided to take advantage of that trait and lead him into a corner that neither he nor Bragg could escape from.

"You indicated earlier that it was dark in the forest that night?"

The boy hesitated a moment. The change of direction momentarily caught him off balance. "Awfully dark. I could barely see a thing."

"It was so dark you couldn't get a good look at the man?"

"That's right."

"So dark you probably couldn't get a very good look at his car either?"

"You're right," he said and bobbed his head to confirm it.

I walked away and exhaled the deep breath I'd

been holding. I was sure everyone in the court-room could see the smile I was desperately trying to hide.

"But, Mr. Dobbs," Danny called out, "it wasn't that dark back at the lot where he first grabbed me."

I walked back to the witness stand, doing my best to appear unaffected by his shot to my gut. "But didn't you say it was dark there, too?"

"Sort of," he said. "But not as dark as it was out in those trees."

"Now, Danny." I said it a bit too tersely. I stopped to inwardly call a time-out. I had to make sure I didn't lose my patience.

Jared and Sarah had a look of concern on their faces. Behind them, Avery, with a slight smile, slowly nodded his head. It was his way of telling me I was doing fine.

"Tell me," I asked, walking closer, "were there any lights on in that lot?"

"I don't remember seeing any."

"Yet you're saying there was enough light to be able to see the car?"

"I'm saying," he replied in an impatient tone, "that there was more light than in the forest."

It appeared as if Danny was becoming tired and frustrated. It was my fault. I was so afraid of what he might say, I was pussyfooting around too much. I had to get to the point.

"When you ran into him, wasn't he standing in front of the car?"

Danny thought for a moment. "Within a couple feet of it."

"And you already testified that except for the

baseball cap and beard, you didn't get a good look at his face either before or after he grabbed you because of the darkness. Is that correct?"

"That's right."

I was finally there and the boy didn't have a clue where I was headed. Bragg did, though; he continued to scribble on his pad, but now he was frowning. I could almost hear him gritting his teeth.

"If there wasn't enough light for you to see the man's face and he was standing right in front of you, how were you able to get a good look at his car?"

Danny began to shift nervously in his chair. With a furrowed brow he looked to Bragg for help. The D.A. started to rise, but reconsidered it. He knew any interruption now would look as if he was trying to hide something from the jury.

"Look," Danny said, "I didn't say there wasn't enough light to see his face."

"You didn't?" I asked in a cynical tone.

"I just didn't get a real good look at him." Danny lowered his voice as if he didn't want the whole courtroom to hear what he was about to admit. "Because I was scared when he grabbed me."

The boy was on the verge of tears. I wasn't sure if it was because he was recalling the attack or because he was forced to admit he was frightened at the time.

"When you ran into the man, he really startled you, didn't he?"

"I guess."

"Because you didn't know what he wanted?"

"And he just seemed to come out of nowhere."

"When he grabbed you, you were more concerned with what he wanted than with the kind of car he was driving?"

"I didn't even know it was there until he threw me into it."

"Everything was happening so fast. Wasn't it, Danny? You never did get a good look at that car. Isn't that correct?"

The boy took a deep breath. "You're probably right," he said, exhaling. "I just remember it was there."

I took a position to the side of the boy, facing the same direction he was. I wanted to see McBean's face when the boy answered my next line of questioning.

"Did you ever tell Lieutenant McBean that the man drove you away in a 1956 Chevrolet?"

"Not really."

"As a matter of fact, you didn't have to tell him because he told you."

Danny looked at McBean and then at Bragg, who had finally stopped his scribbling and raised his head. He was watching the boy closely as he bit on the end of his pen.

"Danny?" I coaxed.

"He didn't say that exactly."

"Did he say anything like that?"

"It was like . . ." the boy said, and stopped to straighten himself in the chair as he looked at McBean.

"Do you understand my question?"

Danny nodded his head. "I knew it was a 1956 Chevy as soon as he showed me the pictures."

I grabbed one of the photographs and waved it in the air. "You never did tell Lieutenant McBean that the man who attacked you was driving the car that is shown in these photographs."

"No, sir."

"And you never said the car was a 1956 Chevrolet?"

"I thought it had to be because he said the car in the photographs belonged to the guy who attacked me."

"Now I understand."

Every head in the room—including those of the jury—was turned toward the prosecution table. Bragg and McBean were doing their best to look unconcerned.

"Just so there isn't any confusion," I said. "Am I correct that you never described for either the lieutenant or Mr. Bragg the car that was used?"

"Except for it being big and black, I couldn't describe anything else about it."

I paused for the jury to digest the importance of what Danny said. It had gone better than I'd hoped.

As I walked back to my seat, ready to tell Priest I was finished, I saw a relaxed look on Jared's face. It gave me an idea. What I was thinking was risky, but I'd been lucky so far and I wanted to end my cross on a dramatic note. One that the jurors wouldn't forget and would haunt them during their deliberations.

"Danny," I said, turning back to him, "what you remember most about the man is that he had a beard and a baseball cap, is that right?"

"Like I said, it was pretty dark."

And you also said you were scared to death, I wanted to remind him. But the jury didn't need to hear that again.

"Do you think if you saw that man again, you'd be able to recognize him?"

The boy tightened his lips and twisted his face. "Maybe."

I slowly walked in front of Jared, who was sitting less than fifteen feet from the witness stand, and casually pointed to him. "You see this man sitting next to this nice lady?"

"Do you mean the man sitting next to Miss Harris?" Danny said and smiled at Sarah.

I was surprised he remembered her name. "Yes, Danny," I said and took a deep breath. "Would you please tell us if you have ever seen that man before?"

Danny looked at Jared long and hard. And then, just like before, he seemed to lose focus. I thought about withdrawing the question, but it was too late.

"You mean, do I think the man sitting next to Miss Harris looks like the man who attacked me?"

I cringed. "That's right."

"Nope," Danny replied. "Not really."

There was a loud stirring throughout the courtroom. A few reporters ran out to call in the news, their cell phones in hand. I finally exhaled on the way back to my seat. Priest was standing, slamming her gavel onto the old hardwood bench. I was about to announce I had no further questions when I noticed Danny's eyes still hadn't budged off Jared.

The courtroom silenced when the boy slowly rose from his chair and pointed at Jared. "Mr. Dobbs?" Danny said. "He sure looks like the man."

I spun around. "But I thought you just said—" I blurted.

Danny gave me a withering look. "Not your client," he said. "But the man sitting behind him sure looks like the guy."

There was a collective gasp as every eye in the courtroom suddenly shifted and settled on Sarah's father, Judge Avery Harris.

Chapter 23

A severe storm out of the Gulf of Alaska centered directly over the northern coast. Ukiah was just beginning to feel the brunt of its high winds and heavy rain. The handle of the heavy metal door ripped from my hand as a strong gust blew it open. With my hair whipping my eyes, I peeked around the open doorway to make sure I'd escaped the horde of reporters who'd been waiting for me outside the courtroom. Seeing no one, I made a dash for my car.

As soon as Danny pointed to him, Avery walked out of the courtroom with most of the reporters in hot pursuit. After several minutes of sitting through Bragg's attempt at rehabilitating the boy, Sarah excused herself to check on her father.

On redirect Bragg had Danny explain what there was about Avery Harris that caused him to say he resembled the attacker. The door finally opened for Bragg when he got the boy to admit it was mostly Avery's beard. The persistent D.A. then showed Danny the mug shot of Jared taken the day he was arrested. After studying it carefully, the boy admitted that with a beard, Jared would also look similar.

Thinking he'd managed to focus the suspicion back on Jared, Bragg was all smiles when he finished. But the damage was done. It was obvious to all that Danny not only couldn't identify Jared's car, but even the most prosecution-minded juror would have to agree that the attacker fit the general description of half the male population in the county.

As far as Jared's case was concerned, Danny's testimony couldn't have gone much better. I should have been ecstatic, but I wasn't. While Bragg and McBean seemed to be suffering from a severe case of tunnel vision, I wasn't. I could no longer ignore the possibility that Avery could just as easily be the attacker as Jared. He not only matched the same general description, but he also had access to Jared's car. Plus, the thought that the Boonville boy had been abducted in a Blazer similar to Avery's kept eating at me. I hoped for Sarah's sake that my suspicions were wrong, but I couldn't bury my head any longer. I had to confront her father.

By the time I reached the farm, the rain was pelting my windshield with such force I almost missed the turnoff. Normally, I would have been able to see the lights in the main house as I approached. But except for a faint glow in the window of the guest house, everything appeared dark. There was no sign of either Sarah or her father—both the Lexus and Blazer were gone.

When I parked at the side of the guest house, I was startled by the howling wind as it pushed its way through the many pine trees. Trying to avoid as much of the rain as I could, I sprinted to the front door. I couldn't wait to get out of my wet suit and take a long hot bath. After that, Sarah and Avery would likely be back and the confrontation would begin.

As I opened the front door, I was surprised to see someone had turned the Lava lamp on. Knowing I hadn't, I cautiously pushed the door wider. The room appeared empty, the only movement the red globules in the lamp, undulating slowly to the top and then down again. As I stepped in, a figure jumped out of the shadowed darkness from the other side of the bed and ran directly at me.

"Mr. Dobbs!" the figure cried and stopped just short of me. It was the voice of a young man. He grabbed my arms, which I'd reflexively raised to protect myself. I could feel his hands trembling. "It's me, Bobby Miles."

I reached to my right and flipped on the overhead light. "What the hell are you doing here?"

"No! No! Turn it off!" he screamed and ran back to where he'd been hiding.

I rushed toward him to see what he was up to. He was huddled on the other side of the bed, head between his knees, shaking violently like a cornered animal. "Are you going to tell me what's going on?"

"Please," he cried out. "They'll kill me!"

"Who will?"

With the quickness of a cat he jumped over the bed, ran to the open front door, slammed it shut, and turned off the light.

"They can't know I'm here."

"Who's they?"

"Michael Victoria's gang." His voice cracked. "You have to help me."

"Help you?" I mocked and stepped toward him. "You're the last person I'd ever help."

He collapsed to the floor, whimpering something I couldn't understand. There was no doubt the kid was scared. And I had a good idea why. The Michael Victoria he was referring to was likely an ally of Salvador Martinez.

But I didn't care. The last time Bobby Miles had been scared and needed help, it had cost me my job.

"Not only won't I help you, I don't want you here. And just in case you've forgotten, you're the reason I stand a good chance of going to jail."

The kid's shoulders began to heave.

"Quit your damn crying." I grabbed him. "Don't you understand that you've accused me of a very serious crime? Not only my freedom, but my career is on the line because of your lies."

He sat up while wiping his eyes with the sleeve of his shirt. "I'm so sorry. You were the only one who seemed to care what happened to me."

"I did care, but I learned my lesson."

"You don't understand. They made me do it."

"Tell me something I don't already know," I snapped. "Now get out of here."

"I can't. He's trying to kill me." The glow from the lamp highlighted his young features. I was able to make out his tear-streaked face; there was terror in his eyes.

"All right, Bobby," I sighed, knowing I was sure to regret it. "Who exactly is Michael Victoria."

"The leader of the West Side Patrol."

"The gang Martinez belongs to?" I asked, trying to remember.

Bobby paused to wipe his runny nose with the back of his hand. "Yes," he said, "at least he used to."

"I believe I had a run-in with a couple of his buddies the day of my prelim."

"Then they're after you, too."

"I doubt it," I said. "What makes you think they're after you?"

"I don't think, I know. . . . I barely escaped."

"Escaped?"

"From my grandmother's. . . . God, I hope they didn't hurt her."

"When?"

"Last night," he stammered. "It all happened so fast. I heard my grandmother yelling at someone," he said, rambling. "They were inside. Victoria was one of them. I recognized his voice. That's when I ran out the back door."

"What about your grandmother?"

"I'm not sure," he sobbed and then rationalized why he hadn't stuck around to make sure she wasn't harmed. "When I ran down the street, I heard their car start and she was still yelling at them. That means she's all right, doesn't it?"

"Probably," I said, unsure of why I would want to ease his conscience. It sounded like the kid was nothing but trouble—not only for me, but for anyone he came in contact with.

"But why kill you?" I remembered the two punks in the rest room had said they would make sure Bobby wasn't around for my trial. However, I really didn't think they planned on killing him.

Bobby collapsed onto the bed and covered his eyes with his right forearm as if it would protect him. "He knows I can put him away for good."

"What are you talking about? Martinez has a double homicide to worry about. He's not concerned about you and a possible subornation of perjury charge."

"Not Martinez," he said, his voice rising. "I'm talking about Michael Victoria."

"How does he fit into all of this?"

"He's the one who forced me to lie about you."

I stood over the bed looking down at him. "Is it because Martinez's trial was about to start, and they knew he was going down in flames unless they came up with something fast? And you were that something."

Miles nodded his head.

"The problem was, I wouldn't go along with your cock-and-bull story, so I told him to forget it," I said.

"That must have pissed him off."

"I'm sure it did."

"Now he wants revenge?"

"I thought that once. But now I see revenge wasn't his real motive. Martinez and his buddies are too smart for that. He knew without your phony testimony he'd be dead meat if the trial started the next day as scheduled. So he thought of a way he could force me off the case, knowing he would get a new attorney."

"But what good would that do?"

"A new attorney would need several months to familiarize himself with the case and prepare for trial. That time would give Martinez the chance to come up with some other lie. One that a jury would more likely believe. Or," I added, knowing this was likely the real reason, "he thought his new attorney would be more willing than I was to help him shade the evidence in his favor."

Bobby had stopped crying. I don't think anything I said made him feel any better, but it seemed he felt safer just being with someone else. Even if it was unreasonable to assume I would be much help if those hoods really did show up.

"It makes sense now," I said, using the kid as a sounding board. "Martinez isn't the one who's afraid of you. Even if you ran to the cops and told them what happened, it would mean nothing to him. Because he's not the one who asked you to lie. Only the person who contacted you is at risk."

"And that's Michael Victoria."

But there was still something I was having a hard time buying.

"Assaulting me in the rest room and now trying to kill you. No way," I said, shaking my head. "Victoria would have too much to lose. Why would he do all that just because some kid, who no one would likely believe anyway, may say he committed some small-time felony. Even if he was convicted, all he would get would be a couple months in jail and probation."

"Not if he already has two strikes."

"Victoria has two strikes?"

Bobby nodded his head. "Now you see why he's so afraid of me?"

"I sure do," I said. In California another felony conviction, no matter how petty, would mean he would get twenty-five years to life.

Bobby was standing now, pacing back and forth like a caged lion. I knew he was probably right. Victoria did have too much to lose. He couldn't take a chance that Bobby would hold up during my trial. If the kid were to snitch him off, Victoria would be facing life in prison. That's why they wanted me to stop Sarah's cross-examination of Bobby at my prelim. They were afraid Bobby was close to breaking.

"Mr. Dobbs!" Bobby was at the window, holding the curtain slightly aside, looking in the direction of the highway. "I think it's him!"

The wind and rain had temporarily subsided. I could hear the familiar sound of the gravel driveway surrendering itself to Sarah's Lexus. I prided myself that it had taken me less than a month to tell by just the sound of the crunching gravel, the difference between her Lexus and Avery's Blazer.

"Calm down. It's Sarah Harris."

"Bullshit!"

I ran to the window to see for myself.

We both stood frozen as we watched an early 1960s model Chevrolet slowly drive past us. There were two men in front and two in the backseat. All four were looking straight ahead as they stopped in front of the main house and illuminated it with the high beams of the car's headlights.

"Do you recognize anyone?" I was whispering, even though I could see their windows were not only up, but the car was so far away they couldn't have heard the bark of a Saint Bernard.

"I'm sure it's Victoria."

The car backed up, turned around, and rolled back down the driveway. It was quiet. I could hear each of us taking short rapid breaths, inhaling and exhaling in unison.

"Don't move," I said, when suddenly the front passenger looked directly at our window.

"That's Victoria! He's gonna kill us!" Bobby screamed and let go of the curtain.

I heard the car come to a sudden, sliding stop, followed by footsteps in the gravel. They were approaching the front door.

"We have to get over there," I said to Bobby, pointing to the Christmas trees on the other side of the driveway.

We were crouched at the side of my car, hiding. The wind was howling again and the rain was so heavy it stung our faces. If we could get to the field, we'd find a place to hide. Between the darkness, the ferocity of the storm and thousands of trees as our cover, there was no way they could find us.

Squatting as low to the ground as we could, we waddled through the rain-soaked gravel to the back end of my car. I was grabbing the bumper to help propel me around the corner when I heard

Bobby crying. He was facedown with his knees buckled under his stomach, bawling like a baby. Standing over him was the man Bobby said was Michael Victoria. He had a gun. It was pointed directly at my face.

Admittedly, I was scared enough to lose all control over my bodily functions. But as afraid as I was, I was just as mad. Mad because of how helpless I felt at that very moment. Mad because some gun-toting punk had the power to decide whether I lived or died. I was mad enough to know that I wasn't going to let him kill me without putting up a fight.

I slowly raised both hands and placed them behind my head.

"Look at him, SA," Victoria said to me while waving his gun at Bobby. "I suppose you're going to cry, too?"

"Never!" Just then I threw a handful of gravel at Victoria's face and butted my head into the heart of his chest. Taken by surprise, he fell backward, slamming the back of his head against the steel rim of the tire.

Dazed, he lay on his back, moaning. I grabbed the gun, but he had too firm a grip on it.

"Let's go! Let's go!" Bobby cried. He'd replaced me at the rear of the car.

Still struggling, I heard male voices yelling something in Spanish, followed by several loud popping sounds. I looked to see if Bobby had been hit. He was gone.

More rapid gunfire.

Standing outside the front door were three men

with their arms outstretched. I could see bright silver flashes bursting from the tips of their hands, which were pointed at Bobby running across the driveway. With each popping sound the gravel exploded at his feet. He was an easy target.

Then I heard Bobby scream in pain. He was stumbling, staggering, using his hands to help him stay up. Finally, he collapsed into the first row of trees. I had no idea how badly he'd been hit.

One thing I was sure of—I'd be next if I didn't do something fast. Victoria was still on his back, vainly trying to focus. I pulled on the gun again, but it was as if his hands were cemented to it. I couldn't believe it. He was only half conscious.

Straddling each side of his stomach with my knees, I hit him on the cheek with everything I had. His body went limp and the gun dropped from his hand. When I grabbed it, I heard what sounded like an explosion. I covered my head as glass shattered all around me. Victoria's face was covered with it. I looked up; the back window of my car was gone.

Then the gunfire stopped. With the noise from the wind and rain, I couldn't hear what they were up to. I peeked over the trunk of the car. I saw them talking as they repeatedly pulled something from their pockets. They were out in the open, reloading.

I thought about picking them off one by one. But who did I think I was fooling? I had never even shot a gun before. I barely knew the barrel from the handle.

But I had to do something quick.

Still down, I held the gun firmly in both hands and reached over my head, making sure it was above the trunk of the car. I pulled the trigger repeatedly, firing indiscriminately into the air. I wasn't trying to hit anyone—that wasn't my plan.

At least a dozen bullets streaked into the darkness, and all three scattered for cover. By the time they realized I'd stopped shooting, I'd sprinted across the driveway and was several rows deep into the trees.

I paused behind a tree, out of breath. As I squatted there, I decided to go back and see if there was anything I could do for Bobby. I searched, frantically darting from tree to tree when I heard the sound of car doors closing, followed immediately by the starting of an engine. I didn't move. I was hoping they'd given up and were leaving.

Suddenly, the trees were awash in light. Then from behind me, "Dobbs," a man's voice shouted, and I was forced to the ground with someone on top of me. Instinctively, I cocked my arm to lash out at the attacker.

"They can see you," he said, wiping his face. It took me an instant to realize that under all the mud was Bobby.

"Are you OK?"

He was holding his right bicep, shaking violently. "It just grazed me."

I nodded toward the center of the field. "Can you keep going?"

Bobby's response was drowned out by the sudden roaring of the car's engine. It sounded like it was on the driveway only several yards away. We both froze, the rain pelting our heads.

"We have to make a run for it," I yelled.

Bobby took off running, serpentining in and out of trees. I followed, sprinting as fast as I could. We had a good start and could hopefully outrun them and stay beyond the reach of their bullets. But the trees were small. They could probably see our every move.

The roar of the car's engine got louder. It was coming straight at us, plowing its way through the field, knocking down trees as it went. Every time I made a turn in some direction, the car would imitate me.

Up ahead, off to my left, were the taller, more mature trees. There was no way a car could drive through them.

"Bobby," I yelled and pointed. "Over there."

We had no more than a hundred yards to go. But the car, with huge rooster tails of mud and debris gushing from its side, was no less than fifty feet behind us. And I was tiring fast. My legs were getting weaker with each stride. Out of breath, my heart was about to burst, each movement was labored, painful, but I wasn't going to let them catch me.

"Come on," I heard Bobby yell. He was at least twenty yards in front of me. I was chugging as fast as I could, but he was much younger and in much better shape.

Looking over my shoulder, I could see the car getting closer as it mowed its way toward us. Trees, branches, and mud were flying everywhere. Suddenly, the ground slammed against my face. My eyes covered with mud and pine needles, I could barely see. I'd tripped over a large rock.

I could hear the car getting closer. Wiping my eyes, I got up and staggered forward.

"Over here," Bobby shouted, and he ran into the first row of the taller trees.

I don't know how close the car was when I finally made it to the same spot where Bobby had disappeared. But a second or two later, the roaring of its engine stopped. I was in the middle of row upon row of eight-foot-tall Christmas trees, all mirror images of each other. The wind had stopped and the rain had been replaced by a light cool mist. I continued to push my way through. Except for the rustling of the branches, there was total silence.

I couldn't go any farther. My legs wouldn't let me. Stooped over, with my hands on my knees, I gasped for air, planning what I would do next. I remembered the main highway bordered these larger trees. If I could reach it before they found me, I was sure I could flag somebody down. That was my best hope, the highway.

As I forced myself to push on, I thought of Bobby and where he might be. He had to be safe if I was. Then I heard the roaring of the engine again. But this time it was different. Rather than a long continuous roar, these were shorter bursts. Each interrupted by a moment or two of silence. This went on for over a minute before I realized the car was stuck in the mud.

I plodded forward, knowing that as long as they continued to try to free their heap, we'd be safe.

A couple of minutes went by before I heard someone shouting from quite a distance behind. The now familiar sound of gunfire was followed by more shouting. This time the voices sounded closer.

But why the gunfire? Even if they gave up on their car and were now on foot, they were nowhere close to me. But what about Bobby? Where in the hell was Bobby?

It was too dangerous to go back and try to find him. I had to keep moving in the direction of the main highway.

I pushed through another hundred yards of wet branches when I heard a car come to a screeching stop ahead of me. Knowing I had to be almost there, I picked up the pace. After only a few more rows of trees, I reached a narrow clearing. On the other side, I could see the main highway and the red glow of a car's taillights.

That's when I saw Bobby. He was leaning inside the passenger door of Sarah's gold Lexus.

Chapter 24

"The two of you are lucky," Sarah said.

For the better part of an hour we'd been sitting in the waiting room of Mendocino County Hospital. We were expecting Bobby to come out of the emergency room any minute. An RN had already informed us that the bullet had only nicked his upper arm, and after they cleaned and bandaged it, he could leave.

Once Bobby and I were safely inside Sarah's car, she'd used her car phone to call the police. She'd pulled to the side of the road while we waited. It didn't take long for four black-and-whites with their sirens blasting to converge on the farm. They followed the destructive path the hoods had taken as they chased us through the field. But all they could find was their abandoned car, stuck in the mud. I was sure they'd heard the cops coming and had run into the hills, leaving their still unconscious leader, Michael Victoria, behind.

As if it wasn't enough that I was sore, dirty, wet, and physically exhausted, I also had to put up with McBean and his questions in the hospital. He finally left us alone when a nurse informed him

Victoria was conscious. He was grilling him right then, no doubt.

I sighed deeply. "If I had any luck at all, I never would have heard of Bobby Miles or his damn problems."

Sarah forced a smile, then lowered her head and stared at the floor as her foot outlined a figure-eight on the shiny linoleum. She had already been terribly worried about her father when this happened. When she had left the courtroom to make sure her father was all right, she'd found that he and his Blazer had disappeared. The rest of the afternoon and into the evening she'd been looking for him.

What had happened in court had raised all kinds of questions. I was sure Sarah had to be wondering whether or not I suspected him. But, more important, there was the possibility that she didn't know who her father was or what he might be capable of.

I tried a feeble attempt at a joke. "The bright side to all this is that your dad will have several hundred less trees to trim in the future."

"I don't even want to think about what his reaction will be," she said. "Assuming he ever shows up."

I placed my hand on her forearm to get her full attention. "Make sure he understands I'll pay for the damage."

For the first time that night she smiled. "With what? You're unemployed, remember?"

"Not for long. Mr. Bobby Miles will take care of that."

I knew that once Patterson talked to the kid, he'd have to dismiss the charges. I'd finally be out from underneath the cloud that had been darkening my life for the last month. "You and I are going to trot him into the D.A.'s office and tell them I want an apology."

She seemed distracted as she said, "I can't wait."

"I knew you were good. But a damn dismissal?" I nudged her side with my elbow. "You're not just good, you're great."

I chuckled, but her face went blank again. She glanced at her watch for the twentieth time since we'd been there.

"I wish they'd hurry up with Bobby."

"Me, too," I said, shifting in my seat. I was just as anxious as she was to get out of there. I needed to clean up and get a change of clothes. My underwear was soaked, and I was beginning to believe that maybe more than a few pine needles had found their way inside my shorts. I looked at the mud covering my clothes. "Once this stuff dries, I won't be able to move."

"How about me?" she said, inspecting the front of her new suit. Scattered randomly were splotches of dried mud and Bobby's blood from when she'd helped him into her car.

She looked at her watch again. "I wonder if I should call the house?"

"I'm sure your father's fine," I said. "He probably has some honey on the side you don't know about."

"I wish."

I leaned back and closed my eyes, wondering myself where he was.

"You suspect him, don't you?" she asked.

My eyes popped open; Sarah was looking directly at me. "Suspect who?" I stammered, not wanting to get into it. We were both exhausted. Plus, I wanted to talk to him first.

"Don't play games," she said impatiently. "We have to discuss it sometime."

I tried to defuse her grim mood. "I know that after what happened in court today, you must be concerned, but I'm sure there's nothing to it."

Her eyes flared. "You better not use my father as some kind of scapegoat."

I was chilled by her tone. "What the hell is that supposed to mean?"

"It means, you better not try to convince the jury—or anyone else, for that matter—that my father could just as easily be Danny's attacker as Jared." I tried to protest, but she added darkly, "It would be like you to try to confuse them just to get Jared off."

I was getting mad. "Do you honestly think I would do something like that?"

She wasn't backing down. "Most attorneys will do anything to get their clients off."

"Well, I'm not like most attorneys."

Sarah bowed her head. Her lower lip started quivering, and tears began to fill her eyes. She gently touched my hand. "I'm sure it's just a coincidence."

Seeing her so pained, I felt my anger begin to diffuse. "I am, too."

"I'm so afraid," she said, sniffling.

I brought my face to hers while taking both her hands in mine. Our noses were almost touching when from down the hall came a voice.

"Hey, haven't you love birds left yet?" It was McBean walking briskly toward us with a smirk on his face.

Sarah immediately pulled away, quickly wiping her cheeks with her fingers.

I stood and placed myself between the two of them to shield her from his view. "What's taking so long?"

McBean craned his neck, straining to get a glimpse of Sarah, who was still trying to compose herself. "That Victoria character is a clam," he said. "Won't say a damn thing except that he wants to talk to his shyster. Of course, he can't say much with all those wires anyway."

"Wires?"

"Yeah, wires," McBean said and laughed. "I guess I better be more careful about what I say to you." He turned to Sarah, who was now standing next to me. "Don't want to piss your boyfriend off. Seems as if one punch broke that gangbanger's jaw. Can you believe it?"

I shrugged, but I was as surprised as anyone by what McBean was saying. Must have caught him just right.

"What about the boy?"

"If you mean Miles, he's fine. They finished with him half an hour ago."

I was sure he knew we'd been waiting all this time for Bobby. But McBean no doubt figured if he had to be out this late, knowing he had to testify in the morning, he was going to make sure I was, too. "Half hour?" I growled. "Where is he?"

"He's gone. A deputy already left with him."

"But he was going to stay with us," Sarah said, looking at me to confirm it.

McBean smirked. "Nope, his lodging will be courtesy of Mendocino County for a while. It'll take at least a week to process the paperwork, then he'll be shipped to San Francisco."

"But why?" Sarah asked.

"Didn't make his court appearances like he should have."

"He has an outstanding warrant?" I asked.

"Drug case. Never showed up for his prelim."

I had a good idea of what must have happened. Bobby was afraid and never went back to court. That was something he had conveniently left out back at the guest house.

"He needs protection," I said. "Victoria and his buddies are after him."

"Victoria's in no position to do anything to anybody for a while. Just cool your heels and let me take care of it."

"But what about his gang?"

"Don't worry. I know how important he is to you, and you can bet I will do everything I can to make sure he gets to the big city in one piece."

Sarah and I both knew what that meant. Until Miles met with Patterson, I was still at risk.

McBean jammed his hands in his pockets and left. Halfway down the hall, he stopped and turned.

"Don't forget, Dobbs," he shouted, "the two of us have a date in court tomorrow."

"Right," I mumbled to Sarah. "And that's when I'll begin to expose you for the crooked cop you are."

Chapter 25

To my surprise Richard Stamps, the Sheriff's Department fingerprint expert, was the first witness Bragg called to the stand on the second day of testimony. However, once the D.A. was halfway through his direct, I realized why he'd saved McBean for last.

Just one year out of grad school, Stamps had very little on-the-job experience, and Jared's was only the second trial in which he'd testified. Stamps would answer each question only after pausing to look at his supervisor, who was seated in the front row behind the prosecution table. When Stamps said Danny's fingerprints were found on the Gummy Bear wrapper, his voice was so low, Priest had to ask him to talk louder. When he raised his voice for the judge, it changed from one octave to another as though he'd just begun puberty. Bragg finally completed his direct and turned his expert over to me. But not before he gave Stamps's supervisor a disgusted look on his way back to his seat.

Normally, a witness like Stamps would have been a defense attorney's dream. An inexperienced rookie was easy prey. But I felt sorry for the young man. It wasn't his fault his boss was an idiot for giving him such an important assignment. And if I pitied him, I was sure everyone on the jury did, too.

I was well aware that unless you have something to gain, the best cross-examination is no cross-examination. That way the jury will know whenever you do ask a question, it's because you feel it's important. They'll appreciate that and will tend to pay more attention. Besides, I'd had the same Gummy Bear wrapper examined by retired S.F.P.D. fingerprint expert, Robert Foltz, one of the most highly regarded experts in the state, and he was in total agreement with Stamps's analysis. I was contesting whether or not the wrapper was found in Jared's car, not whether Danny Barton's fingerprints were on it. Stamps wasn't my focus, McBean was.

"No questions."

Stamps gave the judge a confused look.

Amusement flickered in Priest's eyes. "You may step down," she said, "And you better hurry before Mr. Dobbs changes his mind."

"Yes, ma'am," Stamps said and scurried from the stand with relief written all over his face. Most of the male jurors snickered, while a couple of the women looked at me and smiled. I was sure I wouldn't regret that decision.

During his many interviews with the media, Bragg had boasted on more than one occasion that he would win his case with a "one-two-three-punch combination." Even though his first two punches, Danny and Stamps, had been a tad short of devastation, McBean would be a knockout punch if I couldn't come up with more to discredit him.

"Your next witness," Priest said to the D.A.

Bragg looked at McBean, who was seated next to him. "The people call Lieutenant William McBean to the stand."

McBean smiled throughout the first half hour of his direct, which dealt mostly with his training and experience. He knew how to play it. Make sure the jury liked him so there would be no way they could believe he'd do anything that wasn't by the book. Pausing after each question, he'd turn to look at the jury before he answered. His direct had been well rehearsed, but I never expected anything less.

"I moved from San Francisco to remove my teenage sons from the sex, drugs, and crime which pervaded the high school they were attending," McBean said, and at least two of the jurors nodded their heads. Of course, I knew the real reason McBean had left San Francisco and it had nothing to do with his sons.

Bragg scanned the jury. They were watching him intently. He turned back to McBean, who was ready to strike the deadly blow. "What was found inside of Mr. Reineer's 1956 Chevrolet after it was impounded?"

McBean made a disgusted face. "Filthy clothing, books, personal items," he said and blew air from his mouth, "a lot of junk."

"Junk?" Bragg queried. "Could you be any more specific?"

I knew where Bragg was going. He had to lay a foundation, not only for the discovery of the Gummy Bears but also to establish that there was so much stuff in the car that Jared probably wouldn't have noticed that Danny had dropped the candy there.

"Military records, photographs, various receipts, miscellaneous paperwork from the Veterans Administration, empty can of shaving cream, used rolls of toilet paper and," McBean said with a crooked half smile, "and a bottle of Obsession perfume."

"Women's perfume?" Bragg said in a mocking tone.

Bragg wanted the jury to think that Jared had some unusual sexual tendencies. That way it would be much easier for them to believe Jared preferred young boys.

"Objection," I said, rising from my chair. "How is listing every item found inside that car relevant?"

"Mr. Bragg, how much further are you going with this?" Priest asked.

"I believe the jury should understand the true condition of the interior of that car."

"But why is it necessary to go into such detail?"

"To show why an item of evidence that Lieutenant McBean has not yet discussed may have gone unnoticed by the defendant. It was because of—"

"Your Honor, if Mr. Bragg intends to argue any further, I believe we should approach sidebar."

All judges hate sidebar conferences and the time they take. By the frown on Priest's face I could see she was no different.

"Sit down, Mr. Dobbs," Priest said and turned to Bragg. "Proceed."

With a satisfied expression, the D.A. turned back to his witness. "I believe, Lieutenant," Bragg said, "we were discussing the perfume you found."

"Mr. Bragg, enough," Priest barked. "I'm sustaining Mr. Dobbs's objection."

"Then I would have to agree with Mr. Dobbs. Let's approach sidebar?"

"Stop right there," she growled. Priest then scooted her chair closer to the witness stand and leaned toward McBean. "Are you saying you found many miscellaneous items in that car?"

McBean hesitated, and I smiled. The judge wasn't in the script that he and Bragg had rehearsed.

"Yes," McBean finally replied.

"There was a lot of what I believe you referred to earlier as junk?"

"And trash," McBean added.

"So it would be fair to say that the interior of the car was, for lack of a better term," she said and paused, flickering a smile, "one hell of a big mess."

There was rustling and laughter from the area where the reporters were sitting. Priest spun on them and scowled. Without a word the courtroom silenced.

"Well, Lieutenant, did you hear my question?"

"Sure did," he answered eagerly, "the inside of that car was one hell of a big mess."

"Thank you," Priest said and turned to Bragg. "Now get to the point, Counselor."

Bragg walked closer, stopping a few feet in front of McBean. "Were you present when Danny Barton testified that he had a package of Gummy Bears with him the night he was abducted?"

"I was."

"Then tell me, Lieutenant," Bragg said, and paused to check the jury to make sure they were paying attention, "during your search of the defendant's 1956 Chevrolet, did you recover anything similar to the package of Gummy Bears that Danny Barton described?"

"Not similar," McBean scoffed. "We found exactly what that poor boy said he was in possession of. An unopened package of Gummy Bears on the passenger-side front seat."

Bragg hesitated, milking it for all it was worth. "You found an identical Gummy Bear package in the front seat of the defendant's car?"

"That's correct."

"And what did you do with that package?"

"Gave it to the scientific lab for fingerprint analysis."

"The same package that Mr. Stamps testified he found Danny Barton's fingerprints on?"

"The same."

"Your witness, Counsel," Bragg said to me. "I have nothing further."

Standing in front of the witness stand, I dug deep into my pant's pocket. After making a show of it, I pulled out a handful of change. One by one, I selected a coin and slapped it on the counter in front of McBean. "There," I said and thumb-flipped the last coin in the air, which he stabbed before it hit his face. "I believe that's one dollar and sixty-five cents."

McBean shrugged his shoulders. "So what?"

I slid the coins closer. "That's the exact amount you owe me."

"What are you talking about?"

The jury was on the edge of their seats waiting to see what I was up to.

"Isn't one dollar and sixty-five cents the exact amount that a package of Gummy Bears cost?"

McBean shifted nervously in his chair. The corner of his eye twitched.

"You did get an identical package of Gummy Bears from the cashier the day after Danny was attacked, didn't you?"

McBean's voice fell. "I'm not positive it was the following day."

"But you did get it, correct?"

McBean paused, studying me intently. He knew I wouldn't be asking this question if I couldn't prove it. "Yes," he finally said.

"And you obtained it before you sent a package of Gummy Bears to your scientific bureau for fingerprint analysis?"

"I'm not sure of the exact time."

"Do you want to refresh your memory by referring to the report?" I said, waving it in the air.

McBean's eyes flashed with impatience. "That's not necessary," he said. "I recall getting it from the cashier before I sent the wrapper to the lab."

From the corner of his eyes, McBean must have seen the jury studying him. He raised an eyebrow. "If you're implying the package I obtained from the cashier is the one I gave to the lab, then how do you explain the boy's fingerprints on it?"

"Why don't you tell us?"

McBean's face flushed with anger. He was grabbing the arms of his chair so tightly, I could see the whites of his knuckles. "I don't think you should be allowed to imply that the wrapper was planted without proof."

Priest slammed her gavel. "You know better than that, Lieutenant."

McBean shook his head violently. "Your Honor, it's just that he can't prove any of it. He shouldn't be allowed to accuse me like this."

"No one is accusing you," Priest said.

I had to put a stop to what the judge was doing. I had McBean where I wanted him. He was losing his cool. Who knew what he'd do or say next?

"That's not correct! I am accusing him."

"And I'll ask you again," McBean spat, "explain how the kid's fingerprints could have gotten on that package if it was planted."

"No more!" Priest slammed her gavel again. This time it hit to the side of her bench closest to the witness stand. McBean flinched as it missed his head by only a few inches. "I want to see both counsel and the lieutenant in my chambers."

Priest lectured the three of us through the lunch hour. Somehow the judge was aware that McBean and I had many past differences. She made it clear she wouldn't allow either of us to use her courtroom as a forum to slug it out. I walked out of her chambers sure she wouldn't hesitate to hold any of us in contempt—including Bragg, whether or not he was the county's head D.A.

When I returned to the courtroom, I noticed that Sarah and Avery's chairs were still empty. I was scanning the room to make sure there was no sign of either when my gaze was snagged by Otto Cosgrove's. He had been in the same seat ever since jury selection began—the one directly behind Bragg and next to Danny Barton's mother.

Cosgrove had always made it a point to give me a murderous look whenever our eyes met. But rather than upsetting me, I felt sorry for the man. He honestly believed Jared was responsible for his son's disappearance and this trial was his only hope that the person responsible would be punished. I could only hope by the time the trial was over, Cosgrove—like everyone else—would realize that Jared was a victim, too. The victim of a sly cop's unlawful act.

When Priest entered, I abruptly stood to resume my cross. Turning from the witness stand, I saw Sarah walking down the center aisle toward me. I could tell she wasn't happy.

"May I have a moment?" I said and the judge nodded.

"Still no word?" I whispered.

Sarah shook her head. "I'm really worried. I've called everyone."

I gently squeezed Sarah's shoulder. "I'm sure he's all right."

Priest tapped her watch. A signal for me to get moving.

Rapidly I switched gears. I walked to a spot directly in front of McBean. He appeared cool as he pulled his chair forward and adjusted the mike, waiting for me to begin.

"When we stopped, Lieutenant, I believe we were discussing the package of Gummy Bears you obtained from a clerk at Sav-on the day after Danny was attacked?"

"That's correct," he responded evenly.

"Do you recall the clerk's name?"

"I really don't," he said and pointed to his file located on the counter in front of him. "I better refresh my memory."

McBean thumbed through several pages before he settled on one. After reading it quickly, he closed the file. "Her name is Carol Sealy," he said. "I interviewed her to see if she remembered the boy."

I placed my hands on the counter in front of him. "Where is the package of Gummy Bears that she gave you?"

"I really can't answer that."

"You can't or you won't?"

McBean gave me a disgusted look, then waved his hand like I was some pesky fly. "It's nothing like that," he said. "It's just that I don't recall what I did with that package."

His confident and cavalier attitude was definitely getting to me. I halted to compose myself.

"You know those vultures in the detective bureau are always looking for something to munch on," he added as an afterthought. Chuckling, he turned to the jury. "Cops don't just eat donuts, you know."

There was the sound of suppressed laughter from the gallery. That's all I needed to set me off.

"You think all this is funny, Lieutenant."

"No, but your stupid questions are."

Not taking the time to grab her gavel, Priest

slammed her fist so hard in front of her that everybody in the courtroom jumped. "I already warned the two of you."

The judge had every reason to toss our butts in the can. And I wished she would have. Losing my cool was stupid. I had to remain calm, even if only outwardly.

I looked at Priest. "I apologize."

Glaring, she took a deep breath and slumped back into her chair. "Move on, Counselor."

"Lieutenant, have you tried to locate that package of Gummy Bears?"

"Until today, I had no reason to believe it was important."

I walked to the clerk and obtained a plastic bag which contained the alleged Gummy Bears found in Jared's car. I held the bag in front of McBean. "Are you sure that the Gummy Bear package in this bag is not the same one Carol Sealy gave you when you interviewed her at Sav-on?"

McBean grimaced and looked up at the judge, who was watching him closely. "I'm positive," he said, shaking his head.

"Then clear something up for me," I said, waving the plastic bag in front of him. "If Danny's fingerprints are on this wrapper, why weren't they found anywhere else inside the car?"

A smile returned to McBean's face. "That's simple. Your client wiped the car clean."

"Let me get this straight, Lieutenant," I scoffed, backing farther away to make sure everyone could see him. "You're saying that my client had the foresight to wipe the inside of his car clean?"

"That's correct."

"Yet," I said, scratching my head, "he left the Gummy Bears, which anybody with half a brain would know could connect him directly to Danny Barton, not only inside the car, but right in the middle of the front seat. Now, does that make sense to you?"

"Hey"—he chuckled—"if the damn crooks had any brains, we wouldn't catch half of 'em."

"But you already said he would have had to wipe the interior of the car clean, correct?"

He crossed his arms. "That's what I said."

"And did a heck of a good job of it, didn't he?"

"Except for the candy."

"Ah yes, the candy." I looked toward the heavens for an explanation. "Why would he be so dumb?"

McBean shrugged. "Like I said, the car was a mess. He probably never saw it."

"Could it be that the real reason my client never saw the candy was because it was never there to begin with?"

McBean's smile broadened. "Nonsense," he said like I was some kind of fool.

I was worried. McBean had managed to regroup and had his temper under control. I didn't know what the jury was thinking, but I couldn't take a chance they were buying what he was selling. No matter how much I feared Priest's wrath, I had to try to get under his skin again.

I walked slowly back to the witness stand and stopped directly in front of him. "My client never saw the wrapper, Lieutenant," I said and leaned my face so close to his that I could feel the warmth of his breath, "because you are the one who placed the wrapper on the front seat."

McBean thrust his head back. "That's ridiculous!"

"You put it there after he had been placed under arrest."

McBean paused to look at Bragg, who was closely watching his investigating officer.

"Didn't you?" I pushed.

McBean's chest began to heave. His face turned a darker shade of red. I could tell he was just about to blow when one of the jurors, a heavy-set, balding man closest to the witness box, sneezed. McBean turned to him with a startled look and blinked once. It was as if he had forgotten the jury was there. He slowly scanned the remaining members, and a certain calm came over him.

"All of this, Mr. Dobbs," he said in a controlled voice, "is nothing but a figment of your devious imagination. You defense attorneys are all alike. If you can't explain away the incriminating evidence, then you accuse the cops of planting it."

Out of the corner of my eye I could see the jury. Every eye was on me. McBean had managed to calm himself and in the process had turned the tables on me. Now I had nowhere else to go and he knew it. My only remaining hope was that Carol Sealy's testimony would, at the very least, create a reasonable doubt that Danny's fingerprints couldn't have been on the wrapper because he was wearing gloves. It was a long shot, but it was all I had.

"You're singing a very old song, Counselor," Mc-

Bean said, smirking. He knew he'd won this battle and was now rubbing my nose in it. "You just don't have any proof."

My cross couldn't end on such a sour note. If it did, I'd likely never recover. I had to make it at least appear as if there was nothing about what McBean said that wasn't expected.

"You don't think I have any proof?" I mocked, my voice rising with each word. "Stick around, Lieutenant, and we'll just see about that!"

Chapter 26

I gathered my file while the courtroom cleared. As soon as I'd finished with McBean, Bragg, with a broad smile and slight bow to the jury, rested his case. Priest then thanked the D.A. and advised the jury that with only an hour of court time left, the trial would be adjourned until the following morning at ten.

Jared leaned toward me. "What the hell did you say that for?"

Upset over my failed confrontation with Mc-Bean and surprised by the tone of his voice, I quickly faced him. "What did you say?"

Jared slumped in his chair without changing his look of disgust. "How are you ever going to live up to that promise?"

"What promise?"

"You're never going to be able to prove McBean planted that candy. How in the hell could you have ever said something like that?"

This was a side of Jared that was becoming more common, and I didn't like it. "Why don't you let me handle it?"

"You had McBean on the run and you let him get

away," he said. He pointed to the jury box as the last one walked off. "Then you compounded your mistake by inferring you can prove he's lying."

I wasn't about to sit there and listen to someone who had never been in a courtroom before critique me. I quickly gathered the rest of the papers and motioned for Sarah to get going. "We still have the cashier."

Jared gazed at the high ceiling and slowly shook his head. "All she'll say is that the boy was wearing gloves inside the store." He lowered his head to look me in the eye. "That doesn't prove he didn't take them off when he left, now, does it?"

"Well," I spat, "that's all we've got. If that isn't enough, then I guess you better get used to living in a six-by-ten cell."

When I motioned the bailiff to take Jared away, his expression changed to one of sadness. Better than anyone, I knew what had just happened. Jared was hoping I'd be able to pull off a Perry Mason and get McBean to break down. Like most defendants, he wasn't experienced enough to know that that happens only on TV. We were dealing with a real life—his life—and he was scared.

"Jared," I called out as the bailiff escorted him out the back door of the courtroom. He glanced over his shoulder with a blank look. "Everything's going to be all right," I said, unsure if I believed a word of it.

When Sarah and I reached the front doors of the courthouse, we could hear the press and TV crews out front waiting to attack. Since that first day when the mike had almost been shoved down my throat, I hadn't tried to force my way through them again. I might have snuck out the back once or twice, but for the most part, I'd tried to give them what they wanted.

But not this time. I was too emotionally drained and upset. After the previous night's romp through the Christmas trees, I'd managed only a couple hours' sleep. And since then I'd upset a judge, a D.A., a witness, and worst of all my client. I planned on going straight to the ranch, where Sarah and I would have to discuss her father's possible involvement.

"Ready to make a run for it?" I said to Sarah.

When I opened the front door, though, Otto Cosgrove was planted in the middle of the doorway. Behind him were shouting reporters trying to push their way past. Cosgrove folded his arms in front of him. It was his way of telling everybody he wasn't going to move until he was through with me.

"That jury better not buy any of your bullshit."

If he hadn't been ten times my size, I would have laughed in his face. First my client chews me out for doing such a lousy job, and then Cosgrove acts as if I actually did pull off a Perry Mason. I had to get out of there.

"I'm sure the jury will decide this case based upon their understanding of the evidence."

Cosgrove took a few steps closer. "But because of your bullshit they'll never hear that your client killed my son."

"What's that about Reineer killing your son?" a reporter shouted, and the feeding frenzy began.

Pushing and shoving, the media converged on Cosgrove, forcing the huge man to step back.

Sarah pushed from behind. "Let's go."

The reporters jumped on their tiptoes, trying to hold their mikes in front of Cosgrove's face. "I'm not finished with you," he yelled as we ran past.

We had entered the parking lot when Sarah came to a sudden stop. Mary Barton was standing in front of Sarah's Lexus with her head bowed.

"Are you all right?" Sarah asked.

The woman's eyes were red and puffy.

I didn't know what to say. I was afraid that like Cosgrove she wanted to tear my head off. I gestured to Sarah with a nod to get going.

"We have to leave," she said tentatively.

Mrs. Barton grabbed Sarah by the arm and nodded in the direction of the courthouse. "I was in there, you know."

"I was just doing my—" I said defensively, but she cut me off.

"Do you honestly believe Lieutenant McBean could have placed that candy in your client's car?"

Sarah spoke up. "We believe it's a strong possibility."

"My son's fingerprints are pretty damaging to your client, aren't they?"

"Very," Sarah replied.

"I want the man responsible to pay for what he did to my boy."

I stepped back and motioned to Sarah to do the same. I had the feeling the lady was a sleeping volcano about to explode.

"So do we," Sarah said, glaring at me for backing up. "But we don't think our client is that man."

Mrs. Barton buried her face in Sarah's chest. "Neither do I," she said, sobbing.

I was stunned. I was sure I must have misunderstood.

Sarah gently pushed her far enough away so she could look at Mrs. Barton's face. "What exactly are you saying?"

She raised her head, dabbing her eyes with her hankie. "I couldn't bear to know he went to prison for something he didn't do."

"Ms. Barton," I said, "do you know something we don't?"

She looked around as if she wanted to leave. I was afraid my question had spooked her.

"It's probably not important."

"Obviously you think it is or you wouldn't have approached us," I said. "Why not let us decide?"

"But what if your client is guilty and I tell you something that helps get him off?"

"I believe you know the answer to that," Sarah said softly.

The lady angled her head and fixed her eyes on Sarah's. "I know," she sighed. "What if I don't say anything and he's innocent?"

"Exactly."

Danny's mother took a deep breath and held it. "Phew," she said, exhaling, "this is really tough."

I motioned to Sarah's car. "Maybe if you sat down."

She touched my hand. "I'll be fine once I tell you."

"Tell me what?"

"If McBean did plant that package of candy . . ." she said, and paused to take another breath. "I know why my son's fingerprints are on it."

There was a sobering quiet as Sarah and I looked at one another, each wondering and hoping Mary could prove what she just said.

Sarah placed her arm around the woman's shoulders. "I know this isn't easy, but please help us."

With little additional prodding, Mary Barton told us she had been present at the police station when Danny was interviewed by McBean the day after the attack. The interview took place in a small room rimmed at the top of its walls by glass. McBean had her wait outside in a chair. Even though the door was closed and she couldn't hear what was being said, she could see everything.

"There was a package of Gummy Bears on the table directly in front of Danny during the whole interview. Then . . ." she said, and gave Sarah a pained expression, as if she didn't want to believe what she was about to tell us.

"Why don't we go somewhere more comfortable?" Sarah said, and I grimaced. Mrs. Barton was about to cough up what she knew, and Sarah had to be Miss Congeniality.

"I'm fine," she said. "If I don't tell you now . . ."

"Go ahead then," I pushed.

"Danny picked up the package and handled it while McBean stood right next to him."

There was a moment of silence as we considered the ramifications. What she said explained Danny's fingerprints, but why weren't McBean's on the wrapper, too?

"Did you notice whether or not Lieutenant Mc-Bean handled the package?" Sarah asked as if she'd read my mind.

Mrs. Barton was silent, gazing downward. She slowly lifted her head. "That's what bothers me so much," she said. "As soon as Danny placed the package back on the table, McBean picked it up with a pair of tweezers and placed it into a plastic bag."

"He didn't touch it with his hands?" I asked, almost before she'd finished.

"No, he didn't." She tilted her head upward and our eyes fixed on one another's. "Why didn't he want to get his fingerprints on it?" she asked.

But her expression told me she already knew the answer.

Chapter 27

In California each side must release to the other the names of witnesses and any statements they intend on introducing at trial. I was sitting in Priest's chambers and had just turned over my biggest break in the case—a summary of my interview with Mary Barton.

As soon as Bragg finished reading my report, he threw it on Priest's desk and announced he needed at least a week's continuance to investigate its accuracy.

"When did you obtain this information?" Priest asked.

"Last night." I turned to Bragg, who was seated to my left. "I could have a whole lot sooner, but neither the boy nor his mother were allowed to talk to me."

"That's not our fault," he said. "You have been known to rub people the wrong way."

"And you've been known to tell witnesses not to talk to the defense." My voice was elevated. "As a matter of fact, McBean ordered me off their property."

Bragg waved me off. "I heard about that. The mother requested McBean's assistance."

I didn't buy it. "Right."

Priest thumbed through the report. "What does her son have to say?"

Bragg stiffened. He was more anxious to hear my answer than Priest was. "Don't know yet," I said. "After all the notoriety this case has caused, the boy's father showed up with a court order giving him visitation rights. Danny's with him until tomorrow."

Priest nodded.

Bragg flipped his hand at the report, dismissing its importance. "I don't know what the big fuss is all about. So what if the lieutenant thought maybe sometime in the future the wrapper could be significant?"

Who was he kidding? "Only because he intended on planting it."

"I'm well aware of what you think, Counsel, and so is the jury." Bragg raised an eyebrow. "And it doesn't look like they're buying any of it, so why should I?"

He really was going to try to bluff it out. "Because then I didn't have any proof."

"You still don't. It's all pure speculation."

Priest turned to me. "Would you agree to a few days' continuance?"

I feigned thinking about it for a moment. I knew there was no way Jared would ever agree to waive time. He'd made that clear from the beginning. Plus, I didn't want to give Bragg the time to figure out a way to explain away McBean's suspicious actions.

"Danny Barton is the victim in this case. Both the police and the prosecution have expended hours, if not days, interviewing and questioning him and his mother. It's not like we're talking about a surprise witness who I just pulled out of a hat. All they have to do is talk to them. How much time could that take?"

Bragg had puffed himself up to his full importance. "I'll be the one to decide what and how I investigate. Not some damn defense attorney."

The judge slapped her hand on her desk. "Mr. Bragg, I will decide the course of this trial. Do I make myself clear?"

The D.A. offered only a casual nod, and the judge's eyes flared.

"Do you understand, Mr. Bragg?"

"Yes," he said grudgingly. "I understand perfectly."

She looked at me. "Then you won't stipulate to a continuance, no matter what the length?"

"It wouldn't be in my client's best interest."

A look of uncertainty crossed Priest's face. Then, without saying a word, she rushed out the door. What was going on now? Bragg and I looked at each other, but were hardly in a chatty mood. We sat silently until she returned a couple minutes later, followed by McBean.

"Have you seen this?" Priest asked as she handed my summary to the lieutenant.

McBean's face immediately filled with anger.

"Dobbs gave me a copy," he said. "And it's a big crock of shit!"

Bragg jumped up and grabbed the lieutenant's arm. He knew something his investigating officer didn't: Priest's patience was at an end.

"If I may have a second," the D.A. said, holding up his palm to Priest. He then pushed the startled lieutenant several steps back to the corner of the room.

"Just answer the question," Bragg whispered. "Can't you see she's breathing fire?"

McBean yanked his arm from Bragg's grasp and scowled at the D.A.

Priest was half smiling as she watched the two straighten their suits and square their ties. "Lieutenant?" she said. "I take it you've read all of it?"

McBean made a show of looking injured. "Yes, I have."

"Then how long would it take for you to conduct a full investigation as to its accuracy?"

"I don't see the need. There's nothing to investigate."

Bragg winced. He hadn't had time to inform his investigating officer that he'd already asked for a continuance. I was sure that was exactly why Priest had brought him in rather than sending the D.A.

"Why is that?" Priest asked.

"The way I see it, it's my word against hers."

"And possibly her son's," the judge added.

McBean smirked. "It doesn't matter. He'll only say what his mother tells him to. The jury will see that."

Priest's opinion of McBean was showing on her face. "You don't feel a continuance is necessary?"

Without looking at Bragg, McBean answered, "No reason for one."

"But you are disputing what the mother said to Mr. Dobbs?"

McBean hesitated as he watched Bragg walk to the window overlooking the entrance to the courthouse. Reporters had gathered on the steps, wondering why the trial hadn't resumed. "I sure am," he finally said.

"Mr. Dobbs?" Bragg said, with his back to us. "Why are you so sure that candy wrapper wasn't inside the car when it was searched? Or is that just one of your defense ploys?"

"It's no ploy." I went on to explain. "I arrived at the Harris farm less than an hour before Reineer was arrested. I'm a big fan of classic cars. When I saw one parked there, I had to look inside. And I agree," I said and nodded to McBean, "it was a mess. But for the life of me, I never did see anything on the front seat."

"So big deal," McBean scoffed. "At the time you weren't looking for anything in particular."

"Whatever," I said, feigning a lack of interest in anything McBean had to say.

"If you're so damn sure," McBean added, "why aren't you his witness rather than the scumbag's attorney?"

Considering the source, I let the "scumbag" remark pass. "Because who would believe someone who is not only a friend of the family that Reineer worked for, but is also, himself, represented by his employer's daughter? Plus," I said, looking at Bragg's back, "I'm sure you'd manage to get into evidence the fact that charges are pending against me in San Francisco. My credibility rating would be zero."

McBean bobbed his head. "And that's exactly why *we* shouldn't believe *you*."

"I couldn't care less what you believe. I was just answering your question."

McBean pointed a finger directly in my face. "That wrapper was there and you know it."

"All right, all right." Priest looked at Bragg, who was still studying the crowd below. "What exactly are you getting at?"

"Maybe we're going about this the wrong way," the D.A. said, with a hint of enthusiasm. "The way I see it, Mr. Dobbs has a cashier who will say the boy was wearing gloves."

"But she doesn't know whether or not he took them off when he left the store," McBean interrupted.

Bragg held his hand up for the lieutenant to be quiet. "Let's say, just for the sake of argument, that Mary Barton and possibly her son are unshakable about what they say you did with that candy wrapper. If we combine that testimony with the fact that the *only* item found inside the car with the boy's fingerprints on it is an *identical* wrapper, well," he said, shaking his head, "it appears as if we'd have a real dogfight on our hands."

McBean stomped up to the D.A. "What are you saying?"

"Instead of arguing about a continuance, maybe we should be discussing settlement."

"No way!" McBean roared. He grabbed the D.A.'s shoulders, spinning him around. "You know I'm within an eyelash of proving Reineer is also responsible for the disappearance of Gary Cosgrove," he said.

The D.A. scowled and shoved McBean's hand away. "*So what* if you have a couple of kids who saw the Cosgrove boy being driven off in a red Blazer? *So what* if Reineer has access to a similar car?" Bragg briskly shook his head. "We need a heck of a lot more than that."

"Give me time," McBean demanded. "I'll come up with more."

"You don't understand," Bragg said. "We're a heck of a long way from proving Reineer was the one who was driving that Blazer or, for that matter, that a Blazer was even used. We don't even know if any harm came to the child. There is nothing indicating foul play. We don't have a body. What," he said, throwing his hands in the air, "what the hell are you thinking?"

I had the feeling Bragg wasn't just telling McBean; he was trying to talk himself into whatever he was considering.

"We're out of time," Bragg added and walked back to stare out the window again. "If you ever do get enough, we'll file the appropriate charges. But as far as this trial is concerned, you can forget it."

"For the record," McBean fired back, "I don't agree with one damn thing you're saying."

"You don't have to." Bragg turned to me. "See if

your client will accept an assault, with a year in county and three years' probation."

Priest smiled. She had to be as surprised as I was by Bragg's sudden change of heart. For the first time since she'd been assigned the case, there was a chance of it settling.

"That's a damn joke!" McBean cried. "You can't be seriously considering—"

"Look," Bragg said, with his nose nearly touching the cop's, "you've blown smoke up my rear end for the last time."

McBean's eyes darted to Priest's, then to mine and back to Bragg. "What the hell are you talking about?"

"Because of what you did with that candy wrapper," Bragg said, shaking his head, "we no longer have a sure thing."

"Nothing has changed other than a ten-year-old boy and his mother are mistaken about what they think they saw. The jury will believe me."

"With your prior history, Dobbs would have you on your knees begging for mercy in ten seconds."

"What prior history?"

The D.A.'s voice was scathing. "You're a crooked cop, Bill. You were in San Francisco and you are now."

"Hey, I don't have to take this shit from someone who'd be crushing grapes if it wasn't for his old man's money."

Bragg just looked at him.

McBean must have realized that politicians like Bragg have to be thick-skinned. He wasn't going to get anywhere with a personal attack. He placed a hand on Bragg's shoulder as though they were old buddies. "We're both on the same team, aren't we, J. J.? We can still win this thing. I'm sure of it."

Bragg shrugged off McBean's hand, and stepped back to the window. "There's one big problem that you're overlooking." Bragg pointed out the window. "Once the Bartons take the stand, those sharks will investigate you with a fine-tooth comb. Every complaint or accusation that's been made against you since you graduated from the academy will be front page news. This jury isn't sequestered, and you know what that means," Bragg continued. "Even if your background was never brought up in court, the jury would find out."

"But they're not supposed to read the papers or listen to the news," McBean said, but his heart was no longer in it.

"You're living in a dream world." Bragg sneered at the lieutenant's fake naiveté. "The jury will have a hell of a lot more than just a defense attorney's unsupported allegations."

Frustrated, McBean let his hands fall to his sides.

"Agreed," Bragg said to me. "One year in county with a three years' informal tail."

I rose to my feet. "It's not my decision, but I'll relay it to Reineer and let you know."

On my way out the door, Bragg called after me. "Make sure you inform the guilty scumbag he better jump on it or I just might change my mind."

I didn't let the scumbag remark pass this time. I came to an immediate halt. "Guilty scumbag? A second ago you were acting like you thought he was framed."

Bragg wasn't conceding a thing. "Come on, Dobbs, I'm doing what I think is right. Everyone jumped the gun on this one. There should have been a more extensive investigation." He frowned at McBean, who was slumped in the D.A.'s chair with his head hanging. "One of my primary obligations as head district attorney is to make sure justice is served. Just because I question the police department's tactics doesn't mean I don't think your client isn't as guilty as sin."

"You know what, Bragg?" I shouted. "You're not interested in justice. You don't even have an inkling what justice is. All you're interested in is what's good for you. It's them, isn't it?" I said, pointing to the media below. "You're afraid of what a loss will do to your political career."

"Take that offer to your client, Mr. Dobbs," Priest interrupted, fearing any chance at settlement was quickly disappearing.

But I knew something the judge didn't. Bragg would never withdraw it. He was too afraid of losing.

I couldn't resist a parting shot. "That was a hell of a nice show you just put on, Bragg. But I think you believed from the beginning that the candy was planted and you filed charges anyway. Now it's damage-control time, and you're going to set McBean up as the scapegoat."

"You're entitled to your opinion," Bragg said nastily.

I looked at McBean, who had been listening carefully to what was being said. "You better start praying, Lieutenant. Because if Reineer does turn down this deal, get ready for a crucifixion. And I don't mean Bragg's. What he just said to you in here is nothing compared to what he'll say about you when he loses. He's not going to let you or anyone else ruin his trip to the governor's mansion."

Beads of sweat oozed from my forehead. It was hot. The nape of my neck was soaked. The heater must have been broken—locked on full blast. Or maybe it was just me. I'd had a severe case of nerves ever since I'd walked out of Priest's chambers. My internal thermostat was all out of whack.

Bragg's offer wasn't what was bothering me. It was much more than that. I wanted the trial to end. Even though I was convinced Jared was innocent, I wasn't so sure about Avery. Where was he? Why had he disappeared right after Danny pointed at him? Was pedophilia what had caused him to resign from the bench?

If Jared didn't take the deal, I was afraid McBean would talk Bragg into trying to connect Jared to Gary Cosgrove's disappearance. And if that should ever happen, I'd have to fully develop the possibility that Avery could have done it. That was the real reason I felt as if I'd been sitting in a sauna all morning.

Jared flipped the report of my interview with Mary Barton across the table. "You go back in there and tell Bragg to quit wasting my time. This trial is almost over, and the sooner that happens, the sooner I'll be out of here."

"Think about it," I said. "With good behavior

and work time, you'll be out of here in three or four months."

Jared was not impressed. "When I'm found innocent, I'll be out in a couple hours."

"But you're rolling the dice. If you're found guilty of assault and kidnapping, you're looking at eight years to life."

"So what," he muttered. "A few more months in here will be as good as the death penalty to me, anyway."

I had no idea what he meant. "Could you explain that?"

His eyes cleared, and he looked as though he'd almost made a mistake. "It's just that I don't want to spend any more time in here than I have to," he said. "And as long as the kid's mom sticks to her story, I'm sure the jury won't let that happen."

"Then you have a lot more faith in them than I do."

"Hey," he said, smiling, "faith's all I've got."

I wanted to push harder, but his confident attitude strengthened my belief in his innocence.

He leaned back in his chair, studying me. "You think I'm guilty, don't you?"

I sighed in exasperation. "Why is it that every time I present an offer to a client and explain to them the risks of not accepting it, they think it's because I don't believe them?"

"I don't know about the others, but I can't believe you feel there is any risk now that we have the so-called victim's mother on our side."

I had to rein in his optimism. "She's not on our side. And as far as the jury is concerned, she *is* the victim's mother, whether you did it or not. And the jury will want to blame someone. In emotional cases such as this, half the time they'll decide guilt or innocence based on emotions only. Very often reason gets tossed out the window."

Jared didn't want to hear this, and he scowled. "It's not like the kid was brutally raped or something."

"He doesn't have to be. The jury wants to make sure it doesn't happen to anyone else. Call it conscience or whatever you want, but I tell you they don't want to live with the possibility they let someone who may do it again go free."

Jared grinned like I wasn't telling him anything he didn't already know. I was aware he was a bit off center—but he wasn't stupid. He was as intelligent a client as I'd ever represented. So much so that I wanted to get his opinion about what was bothering me.

"Tell me, Jared, do you think Avery could have had something to do with the attack?"

Reineer lurched forward in surprise. "Give me a break," he said. "You're not thinking about that damn red Blazer and that kid in Boonville again."

I didn't respond.

"Why would you even intimate something like that? You have all the proof anyone would ever need that McBean planted that damn wrapper and now you want to pin it on a friend."

The two of them were closer than I'd thought. I stood to leave, regretting I'd even brought it up. "So you want me to tell Bragg to stick it in his ear?"

Jared's lip curled. "Or anywhere else it fits."

I knocked on the steel door.

"I hear there's a kid in here who's accusing you of perjury," Jared said as I waited to be escorted out.

"His name is Bobby Miles."

"It's pretty rough on a young kid like that in here. But since he's snitching you off, I'll bet that doesn't bother you much."

"As a matter of fact, it does," I said as the cell door opened. "Keep an eye on him for me, will you? Someone is out to get him, and I want to make sure that doesn't happen."

"As good as taken care of," I heard him say before the door slammed shut.

Chapter 28

When I informed Priest that Jared wouldn't accept the offer, Bragg stomped out of the judge's chambers without saying a word. He'd thought for sure Jared wouldn't refuse. My reading was that Bragg felt the same as I did; with what Mary Barton and possibly Danny had to say, a once sure victory for the prosecution was now, at best, a coin flip.

The trial was to resume only long enough for my opening statement. The proceedings would then be adjourned until Monday morning, when I'd call my first witness. As we waited for the jury to settle in, I mentally prepared myself for what I was about to say. My opening would be brief. I'd summarize the testimony of my only witnesses.

"You may begin, Mr. Dobbs," Priest said.

I walked to within a few feet of the jury box. "Ladies and gentlemen, I will be giving you a brief overview of what the defense intends to establish, but before I do, you must understand that the defense doesn't have to produce any evidence. We can rely totally on the evidence already presented to you by the prosecution. Why is that? you might ask yourselves."

I paused briefly to underscore the importance of what I was about to say. "Because a defendant is presumed innocent, and that presumption remains until the prosecution proves beyond a reasonable doubt every element of the crime. Now, some of you may look upon reasonable doubt like it's some mythical curtain all defendants hide behind. But it isn't. It's the foundation of our judicial system which you are sworn to uphold."

I stopped in front of Bragg; as usual he was writing something on his legal pad while slouched in his chair, acting unconcerned. "You must not look to the defense to clear up any doubts you may have," I said, raising my voice as I pointed at the D.A.'s face. "Because that's his job. If you have any doubts that every element of the crime was committed by my client, then that's all you need. You don't have to look any further. Why? Because that means the prosecution hasn't met their burden."

I looked down at Bragg and shook my head. "Mr. Prosecutor, you seem to have forgotten what a trial is all about. I say forgotten because I know it's taught in all the law schools. It's rudimentary." I squatted in front of Bragg until we were eye to eye. "Where is your proof? We've all been waiting patiently for it. Could it be you never had any to begin with? That my client has been sitting beside me for the last several days because you needed a scapegoat? You arrested and charged Mr. Jared Reineer because you had to take the heat off your office. Was the pressure that bad, Mr. Bragg? So bad that you are prosecuting my client based on the paltry bits of proof we've been forced to sit here and listen to?"

Bragg looked up at Priest. I expected an objection at any moment. I was beyond the parameters of making an opening statement. I was arguing the case. I decided I'd made my point and it was time to discuss the witnesses I intended to call.

"The defense will be calling two, maybe three witnesses to the stand. Two you haven't heard from, the other you have. My first witness will be Carol Sealy, the cashier at Sav-on drugstore. She will explain that she not only recalls Danny Barton purchasing a package of Gummy Bears on the night he was attacked, but also remembers he was wearing a pair of gloves from the time he entered until he left."

Suddenly, every juror's head turned toward the back of the courtroom. A uniformed officer rushed to the counsel table, where he whispered something to McBean, who then immediately followed the officer out of the courtroom. Like everyone, I had no idea what it was about.

I paused to give the jury time to refocus. "My remaining two witnesses will be Danny Barton's mother and possibly Danny himself." I hesitated when two female jurors looked at one another. It was obvious they didn't like the thought of putting the poor boy through any further trauma.

"I'll be calling one or both because you need an answer to one very important question. A question that was posed by Lieutenant McBean himself. If you recall the lieutenant asked me—no, dared me—to explain how Danny's fingerprints could be on that candy wrapper if it wasn't the same package the boy had lost that night. Remember that?" A few of the jurors' heads bobbed, and I continued. "They will answer McBean's question. And after you hear what they have to say, you will be convinced that the only evidence directly linking my client to the attack was planted by law enforcement." I pointed to McBean's now empty chair. "Two, maybe three witnesses will convince you that my client, Mr. Jared Reineer, was set up by Lieutenant William McBean."

Just as Priest promised, the jury was excused until Monday. Jared and I waited for the courtroom to clear. He had something he wanted to say.

"What about me? Aren't you going to put me on the stand?"

"No reason to. A defendant should only testify if he absolutely has to."

Jared looked to Sarah, hoping she'd agree with him. "But they'll want to hear what I have to say."

"It's not crucial," she said and placed her hand on his arm. "You have to trust Hunter."

Jared shook his head obstinately.

"Unlike other witnesses, if they think *you* lied to them about anything," I added, "they'll vote against you no matter how weak the prosecution's case is."

"But they won't think I'm lying—" he said, but was interrupted when the back doors burst open. McBean and the officer he'd followed out earlier marched straight toward us.

"He's dead!" McBean yelled as he came to an abrupt halt.

My first thought was that he was referring to Sarah's father. "Avery?" I blurted.

"Avery?" McBean gave me a confused expression. "I'm talking about Miles."

"Bobby Miles?" I felt my stomach sink. "How?"

"His throat was sliced from ear to ear."

I jumped up, my sorrow laced with anger. "Damn it, I told you they were after him."

"I protected him the best I could."

"It doesn't sound that way to me," I shouted.

"Get off my case," McBean yelled back. "It's not some damn country club in there. Shit like this happens."

I planted my hands on my hips, and squared off with him. "And I suppose you don't have any idea who was responsible?"

"None," he said flatly. "But whoever it was, must have had to prove to someone else he did it."

"What are you talking about?"

McBean made a face that showed even he was disturbed by the brutality. "Ripped the kid's earring right off. Took the whole lobe with it." His expression hardened. "We find out who has that earring, and we've got the killer."

Chapter 29

For the last half hour Sarah and I had been in Danny's bedroom. His mother was downstairs preparing the store for what she hoped would be a busy weekend. We were on the edge of his bed, trying to draw his attention away from the TV. He was watching a rerun of *The Simpsons*.

The thought of whether I should have done more to ensure Bobby's safety haunted me. But what could I have done? I wondered if warning McBean was where I had screwed up. He must have known Bobby's changed story would clear me of all charges. I wouldn't have been surprised if McBean intentionally placed Bobby in a vulnerable position just to spite me.

Oblivious to the importance of why we were there, Danny watched a young, yellow-faced cartoon character being chased around a house by one much older and fatter. From what I could make of it, they were father and son. "Bart's so funny," Danny said, and looked over his shoulder to see if we agreed.

Sarah gave him a perfunctory smile. "Isn't he, though?"

Danny had already informed us that he was sure he had never taken his gloves off that night and didn't understand how his fingerprints could be on the wrapper he lost. We were now discussing his interview at the station. If the boy confirmed what his mother had told us, Jared's freedom would be guaranteed.

"Was that the first time McBean interviewed you?"

"Second," Danny said. "The first was the night I was attacked. He sat right where you guys are. My mom wouldn't let him stay very long. She thought I was too upset." Danny turned, though his eyes remained glued to the set. "She was really the one who was upset though. I was fine."

"I'm sure you were." Sarah winked at me. "I'll bet he was scared to death," she whispered.

I was forced to talk to the back of his blond head. "During the interview at the station, did Lieutenant McBean ever show you a package of Gummy Bears?"

"Yep. Just like the ones I'd lost."

"What did he say?"

"It was no big deal, really," he said and laughed when the older bald-headed guy started choking the squiggly haired kid.

Sarah could probably tell I was about to yank the damn plug out of the wall. "What were you saying?" she asked.

"He put a package of Gummy Bears on the table and asked if it looked like the one I lost."

"Then what happened?"

"I told him I thought it was, but that wasn't good enough." Danny grimaced. "He's sort of pushy."

"Why do you feel that way?"

"Because he told me to pick the package up and look at it, to be sure. I really didn't have to. I knew it was the same. Oh, boy!" Danny said as a mouse shoved a stick of dynamite into a black cat's mouth. The boy slapped his hands when the cat's head exploded all over the wall. "Itchy and Scratchy are my favorite part."

Sarah and I watched as the cat's blood and eyeballs flowed freely down the wall. "Cartoons have sure changed since I was a boy," I said.

"What hasn't?" she deadpanned and her mouth dropped as the mouse kicked the cat's eyeballs out the door.

I placed my hands on Danny's shoulder. "This is really important. Do you think you can turn the TV off for a while?"

"Oh, sure." He flipped it off. "I've already seen it five or six times anyway." He glanced at the forty-niners clock above his dresser. "Better hurry, though, *Beavis and Butthead* will be on pretty soon."

"Beavis and Butthead?" I said to Sarah.

She shrugged her shoulders. "Can't wait."

Danny jumped on the bed next to Sarah. The subsequent quake caused her purse to fall to the floor, spilling most of what was inside next to our feet. He started to scoot off the bed to help pick up the mess, but Sarah stopped him. We finally had his attention, and she wasn't going to let a spilled purse interfere.

"Don't worry," she said. "Tell us what happened next."

"I picked up the Gummy Bears and looked at them, just like he asked."

"And?"

"I told him they looked the same and put them back on the table."

"Then what happened?"

"I got up to leave because I was worried about my mom. She'd been waiting a long time."

My next question was crucial. "Before you left, did you see what McBean did with the package?"

"He put it in a plastic bag." Danny was whispering like he was telling a secret. "He used a . . . what do you call it?"

I took a deep breath. I wanted to help him out, but I couldn't put words in his mouth. "Try to remember."

He stared at the floor, thinking, and his eyes became as big as saucers. "That's what he used." Danny dropped to the carpet and picked up something that had fallen out of Sarah's purse. "What's this called?"

"Tweezers," Sarah said.

I had to be sure there was no misunderstanding. "McBean used tweezers to put the package of Gummy Bears into the plastic bag?"

"I'm sure of it," he said and handed them to Sarah, who was kneeling next to him.

I paused to control my enthusiasm and considered whether I should call both Danny and his mother to the stand or just one. If one, Danny would be my choice. He could testify not only to what happened at the station, but also that he didn't recall ever taking off his gloves. I couldn't think of anything better than the victim testifying for the defense. Especially when that victim was so likable and convincing.

"It looks like you'll get to see . . ." I said, glancing at my watch. "What did you call it? Clevis and Buttface?"

Danny shook his head as if he couldn't believe anyone could be so stupid. "It's *Beavis and Butthead.*"

Sarah looked around to make sure they'd picked up everything.

"I think there's something still under here," Danny said as he reached underneath the bed and felt around. After a second or two, he pulled out a yellow canister about the size of a large tube of lipstick.

He handed it to Sarah. "This is the same perfume my mom uses."

"Really?" she said, taking it from him. With a concerned look, Sarah slowly placed it in her purse. I reached for her hand to help her up, and she stared at it like it wasn't there. Still on the floor, she reopened her purse and withdrew the canister of perfume. "Is Obsession your mother's favorite perfume?"

Danny looked at the canister and then at Sarah's bewildered face. He dropped to a prone position and lifted the bedspread. "Maybe there's something else under here," he said, and crawled far enough under the bed so that his head and shoulders were hidden.

Sarah grabbed him by the ankles before he went any farther. "Danny," she said, holding onto him, "was Obsession the perfume you were going to buy for your mother that night?"

The boy didn't respond. He'd gone perfectly still.

I didn't know what Sarah was up to. But by his evasive actions and now his silence, I had a feeling the boy did.

"Danny," she persisted, "I have everything. You can come out now."

I patted her shoulder. "What's up ?"

Sarah didn't respond. Instead she pulled on Danny's legs. "You better talk to me," she said sternly. "Or your mother will hear about it."

I was shocked. Danny was going to save Jared's bacon, and Sarah decided to threaten him. I grabbed her by the arm. "What are you doing?" It was too late. She'd already dragged him out.

He was on his back, looking up at her. "I think we better talk," she said.

The boy sighed as he sat on the bed and hung his head.

Sarah got straight to the point. "You left Sav-on with more than the Gummy Bears, didn't you?"

Danny screwed up his face. He appeared as if he was about to cry. "I'm sorry. I never did anything like that before."

Sarah gently ran her hand up and down the boy's forearm. "You wanted to make sure your mother had at least one present to open, didn't you?"

Danny nodded.

"Since you didn't have enough money at the time, you decided to borrow some perfume?"

"I was going to pay them back . . . I promise."

"I know," she said and angled her head as she studied the boy's face. "Why don't you tell us exactly what happened."

Danny shook his head, and a tear fell from his cheek. "When I walked into the store, I went straight to the candy section," he said. "I grabbed a bag of Gummy Bears and went to where the perfume was."

Danny then lowered his head. "Obsession has always been her favorite. But when I checked out the price, I knew that even if I put the Gummy Bears back, I couldn't afford even the smallest bottle." Danny frowned.

"So you stole it?" I pushed.

Sarah made a show of glaring at me, then turned back to the boy. "You're doing fine," she said. "What happened next?"

"When I saw no one was watching, I picked up a small box of Obsession and walked to the magazine rack and looked at a copy of *Beckett's* baseball-card price guide. I wanted to make it look as if I was reading it. I felt so guilty about what I was doing," he whimpered. "When I'd saved enough, I was going to go back to the store and leave the money for what I took. Then, I figured everything would be all right.

"We understand," Sarah said in a soothing tone. "Go on."

Danny stared at the floor as he told us what happened next. "I looked around one last time, then I slowly moved the small yellow box to my side and let it fall into my coat pocket," he said. "Then I paid for the Gummy Bears and left"

"What happened to the perfume?" Sarah asked.

"When I ran into the man, I thought he was the store's security guard, so I handed it to him."

I bent on one knee so I could look Danny in the face. "Are you saying you gave the bottle of Obsession to the man who attacked you?"

"You won't tell my mom, will you?" he said and began to cry.

I finally understood the ramifications of what Danny was telling her. The item of women's toiletry that had been found in Jared's car was a box containing a canister of Obsession perfume.

I pulled Sarah to the corner of the room. "Do you know what this means?"

She placed her index finger over her lips to shush me.

"But a box of the same perfume was found in Jared's car," I said, as if it was news to her.

She fixed her gaze on me. "And if anyone else finds out that Danny had that perfume with him . . . Don't you understand what this means?"

"Of course I do. I may be a little slow, but I'm not stupid. If that's the same perfume, then there's no doubt Danny was in Jared's car."

Tears began to well in Sarah's eyes.

"If you're crying for Jared, I wouldn't. It looks like he's been lying to us all along."

A very uneasy silence ensued. I knew what was

bothering her. The Obsession proved only that Danny had been in Jared's car. It didn't prove that Jared was the person driving it.

Sarah looked up at me. A tear ran down her cheek. "Where in the hell is my father?"

Chapter 30

Sarah left the Bartons' without saying a word. I'd hoped she'd go straight to the farm to look for Avery, but by the time I'd arrived, there was no sign of either. During the remainder of the night and the following morning, I telephoned her apartment—but not even her answering machine responded. I knew there was no escaping the fact that her father was a prime suspect. After her reaction in Danny's bedroom, I was sure she'd reached the same conclusion. Also, she knew something I didn't—the reason her father had been forced to retire from the bench.

For most of the afternoon I drove back and forth between her apartment and office, hoping she'd show up. It was after four o'clock when I finally gave up and drove back to the farm. When I pulled in front of the guest house, I was so focused on looking for Sarah's Lexus that I almost didn't notice Avery's Blazer parked in front of the main house.

Knocking several times on both the front and back door, I walked to the field, thinking he was probably surveying the damage to his trees. I wasn't sure what I'd do or say once I found him. There was always the direct approach. I could walk right up and ask, "Hey, Judge, I can get Jared off by proving *you're* the child molester. Want to help?"

Before I made it across the driveway, the guest house door slammed shut. Avery was heading for the main house with a large plastic bag slung over his shoulder.

"Avery," I called out. He stopped like a deer frozen by oncoming headlights. "We need to talk."

He ran to the main house.

I rushed up behind him as he repeatedly stabbed his key into the door lock. "Please, Avery."

"I'll be right out," he said and closed the door.

His evasive actions didn't do much to relieve my suspicions. I had to see what he was carrying. I flew through the front door and stopped immediately. Avery was walking toward me, empty-handed.

"I said I'd be right out." He walked past me to close the door.

"I thought you said 'come in,' " I lied.

He hesitated, as if searching for the right thing to say. "It was just some of Jared's stuff that I figured had to be in your way."

"What kind of stuff?"

"Personal things," he said and walked into the kitchen, where he rummaged through the refrigerator. "Want something cold?"

"Not now."

"A beer? A coke? Which is it?"

With what I had to say, I didn't want to give him the impression that I was there to shoot the bull. "No, thanks."

"Where's Sarah?"

"Looking for you, I imagine. You've had her pretty worried."

"That sounds like her," he said and paused. "I really didn't think you'd mind."

"About what?"

He popped open a can of beer. "For being in your room without asking." He held the can out to me. "Are you sure?"

I waved it off. "I'm fine."

He walked to the kitchen window. "What the hell happened out there?" he mumbled, looking out at the field.

I could tell, like me, he had something else on his mind. "That's a long story," I said. "I'd like to discuss something else before we get into it."

He sat at the kitchen table and took a swig. "Go ahead."

I was having a difficult time deciding on a way to begin.

"Hunter, I know what you must be thinking. What everyone must be thinking." He took a long pull from his beer. "There are just too many coincidences."

"At first I tried to shrug it off. But when the boy pointed to you, I couldn't ignore the possibility any longer."

Avery drained the rest of his beer, and made a show of slamming the empty can on top of the table. "I understand."

"It has to be either you or Jared."

He folded his arms across his chest. "Go ahead. I'm listening."

I paced the kitchen and explained that Danny told us about the stolen bottle of perfume, which he eventually handed to the man who attacked him.

Expressionless, Avery pondered what I'd said. "And Sarah heard everything?"

I wasn't sure how to interpret his aloofness. "She's the one who suspected the boy was hiding something. If it wasn't for her, I never would have found out."

"Where's the box of perfume?"

"With the rest of the items McBean took from Jared's car and released to Sarah," I reminded him. "It should be in the bag you were carrying."

Avery raised an eyebrow at that. "It's not."

My voice became cold and accusatory. "Then it's because you got rid of it."

He shook his head.

"Tell me this: Why did you retire from the bench?"

Judge Harris was not to be browbeaten. "What exactly is in that petty mind of yours?"

"Just tell me what happened," I said. "There are other ways I can find out."

He was quiet for a time, stroking his beard. Finally he exclaimed, "How could I have been so wrong about Jared?"

"Jared!" I shouted. "We're talking about you."

"You are, but I'm not." His chair screeched as he pushed it out from the table and stood. "I'll be right back."

"You're not going anywhere," I said. I was reaching for him when Sarah appeared; neither of us had heard her come in the house.

"Hey, what's going on?" she snapped. Sarah yanked me by the arm, jerking me around. "What do you think you're doing to my father?" She turned to where he'd been standing, but he was gone.

I pulled my arm from her grasp, and she marched to the other side of the table. Clutching the top of one of the chairs with both hands, she scowled at me as though she wanted to crush my head with it.

Then her face went blank. "Jared did it."

"Come on," I said and walked as close as I dared. "How can you say that? Don't you see that you are totally ignoring—"

Sarah cut me off. "Jared's fingerprints are all over the box of perfume."

"Who says?"

She gave me a quick, edgy smile. "It was with the stuff McBean gave me." She reached for my hand. "I've been with Robert Foltz all day."

"The fingerprinting expert?"

"There were other prints, but Jared's were the only ones he could identify."

"Including your father's?"

Sarah smiled. "Not even a smudge . . . and the same goes for Danny's."

The thought of what this could mean made me feel light-headed. If what she was saying was true, I was representing a guilty man after all.

Sarah placed her hands around my waist and hugged me. I started to push her away, but she pulled my face to hers. "I was so afraid it was my father," she said as our lips parted and she looked at me with her deep blue, tear-soaked eyes.

Avery appeared behind us with a manila envelope tucked under his arm. "It's time we all had a long talk."

Without saying anything more, he led us into the living room, where he sat on the sofa next to me. Sarah sat cross-legged on the floor in front of us. "It looks like Jared fooled us," Avery said, a low rumble of anger in his words.

Maybe he was right. But before I made up my mind, there were a couple of things still bothering me. "There is another possible explanation for Jared's prints being on that box."

Sarah's eyes narrowed. "Why are you pressing so hard to implicate my father?"

"I'm only saying Jared could have handled the box sometime later—after someone else left it in the car."

Avery held his hand out for the two of us to stop. "There's something else, isn't there, Hunter?"

"It's just that Jared doesn't have any prior history of doing anything close to what he's being accused of."

"And I suppose my father does?"

"Judge," I said, ignoring Sarah, "you still haven't told me why you resigned from the bench."

Sarah's voice filled with venom. "What the hell does that have to do with anything?"

I never moved my gaze from his face. "I must know."

Avery took a deep breath and slowly let it out. "It was just a big misunderstanding."

"It was no such thing," Sarah said. "You had no other choice."

"But why?" I asked.

"Because she's a bitch!" Sarah said.

Her father stopped her from going on. He then explained that approximately eight years ago he had been in the throes of a bitter divorce. Some of what he was saying I already knew, but what I didn't know was that his first wife—Sarah's mother—had died of breast cancer when Sarah was only seven; Avery had raised Sarah as a single parent. As soon as she enrolled in college, he fell in love with a probation officer half his age. Within a matter of weeks they married.

A month after their first anniversary she gave birth to a boy, who became the center of Avery's world. However, less than a year later, it became obvious to everyone, including Avery, that his beautiful wife was having an affair with a fellow probation officer. Avery filed for divorce and sought custody of their one-year-old son; his wife bitterly contested.

Two weeks prior to their divorce trial, Avery received a telephone call that his son had been taken to the emergency room with several broken ribs. He rushed to the hospital and was immediately met by two uniformed officers who suspected the boy had suffered his injuries at the hands of another. A few days later his wife threatened to tell the police she saw Avery strike the child on several occasions when the boy wouldn't stop crying. If he agreed to drop the custody battle, she wouldn't contact them. When he wouldn't give in to her blackmail, she did exactly as she'd threatened, and a full-blown investigation was conducted by not only the D.A.'s office, but the Judicial Council as well.

"And that's when you screwed up," Sarah said quietly.

"What could I do? When I wasn't being hounded by the police, the damn Judicial Council was all over me. I couldn't take it. Plus," he said, and his face turned from one of anger to that of sadness, "after what they put me through, I had a new perspective on what the judicial process was all about. The bit about being innocent until proven guilty took on a whole new meaning. I could see that what I'd believed in most of my life was bunk. I'd lost faith in something I'd been an integral part of. A judge has to believe in the system, and I no longer did."

"Do you think she intentionally injured your boy?" I asked.

"I never thought that for a second. He must have fallen from either the crib, the stairs, a chair or . . . who knows. . . ." He hesitated to compose himself. "What I do know is she saw an opportunity and went for it. No matter how much it hurt me."

"Were charges ever filed?"

"They had nothing but her vague statements, which even the police had problems with," he said. "They couldn't corroborate a word of it."

"And after he resigned, the Judicial Council lost interest," Sarah added.

I sank deeper into the sofa, feeling sorry for him. Even if he was fudging the truth, it didn't matter. Child abuse and child molestation required entirely different mental states. Nothing Avery had been accused of came close to what had happened to Danny.

"All right," he said, wiping his eyes with the back of his hand. "Now can we discuss what *I* found out?"

I felt guilty I'd even suspected him. "If you still feel like going on after my inquisition."

Avery wasn't offended. Instead, he stated firmly, "I have definitive proof that Jared drove my Blazer the day the Boonville boy was kidnapped."

That caught my attention. "Jared was in Boonville?"

"Only a few miles from where the boy was abducted." Avery took a yellow piece of paper out of the envelope he'd been holding and handed me an invoice from a company called Greener Garden Nursery. "The signature at the bottom is Jared's."

After studying it, I handed it to Sarah. "It sure looks that way."

"Greener Gardens is where I buy all my supplies, including seedlings," he said. "As you can see, Jared picked up over two thousand of them that day."

"But how do you know he was using the Blazer?"

"All of that," he said, pointing to the invoice, "would never have fit in his car. That's why I let him use the Blazer."

"Is that where you've been all this time?" Sarah asked. "Boonville?"

"Don't you think I knew what everyone was thinking when that boy pointed at me in court?" Avery paused. "It was happening to me all over again. All I could think was that I was being suspected of a crime I didn't commit. I already knew about that poor boy being kidnapped in a Blazer just like mine. I had to investigate."

Sarah hugged him. "You were gone so long. I didn't know what to think."

There was silence as they held one another tightly in their arms.

"The box of perfume proves Jared attacked Danny," I said thinking out loud. "And that invoice shows he was in Boonville the same day that other boy was kidnapped. I can't believe what this means." Avery started to say something, but I cut him off.

"It means the boy is most likely dead, and Jared is responsible."

"I'm afraid so," Avery said.

I walked to Avery's liquor cabinet and poured myself a scotch to the top of the glass. "Jared's not just a damn child molester, he's likely a murderer, too." I took a gulp and turned to Avery, holding up the half full glass.

"Go ahead," he said. "Have all you want."

I drained the rest of it. "This is just great. I'm going to get a murderer off."

"There's something else," Avery said, and nodded at my empty glass. "Have some more. You're going to need it."

I promptly poured myself another. "I'm listening. It can't get much worse."

"It may not stop with the Boonville boy."

I suddenly felt sick. I had a horrible feeling about what he was going to tell me.

"Jared was in Fresno for at least a year before he arrived here. After the invoice confirmed what I'd suspected, I drove straight to Fresno."

I hung my head. "Please don't tell me there have been others."

"I'm sorry, Hunter, but it took me less than an hour at the Fresno library to find out that two children had turned up missing the same year Jared lived there."

I started to sway; my legs felt weak and rubbery.

Avery shook his head. "The two children were boys. I'm afraid Jared is a very sick person."

"But he can't be. . . . I'm not buying any of it."

Sarah walked behind me and began kneading my shoulders.

"There's no way," I said. I grabbed at a straw. One thing I was sure of. I spun on Avery. "McBean planted that damn candy. I'm sure of it."

"He probably did. But that doesn't mean Jared's innocent," Sarah said softly. "McBean had a hunch, but knew he had a weak case. He had to make sure his prime suspect wouldn't get away with it."

I didn't want to hear any more. I gulped the rest of the scotch in one breath. Alcohol was flooding my system. My shoulders seemed to melt as the fiery liquid made its way through my bloodstream. I was hoping I'd pass out. Maybe when I awoke, everything Avery had said would be nothing more than a bad dream.

"And I suppose," I mumbled disconsolately, "that those boys were around ten years of age?"

"One was only seven."

I made a beeline for the toilet. The scotch didn't

taste nearly as good coming up as it had going down.

Half conscious, I was slumped on the cold linoleum floor when Sarah walked in, followed by her father. Dazed, I held my hand out. As they pulled me up, everything began to spin violently. I quickly jerked away and dove for the toilet again.

When I was done retching, Sarah placed a cold, wet towel behind my neck, and I laid back on the cool floor and closed my eyes.

"I know somebody who might be able to help," I heard Avery say. "I'll try and set something up."

"I'm so sorry for getting you involved in this, Hunter." Sarah gently wiped my forehead. "You sure got the short end of the stick on our deal. Bobby Miles is an angel compared to Jared."

With everything that had happened I'd almost forgotten. Bobby Miles was dead.

"*Was* an angel," I mumbled.

Chapter 31

San Luis Obispo Correctional Facility is nestled between miles upon miles of grazing pasture off Highway 227 between San Luis Obispo and Morro Bay. From the highway it looks more like a country club than a place where some of California's most violent offenders will be housed for the remainder of their lives.

Avery and I sat in a ten-by-ten room, surrounded on three sides by floor-to-ceiling bars. The late-afternoon sun was shining through a small, wire-mesh window located halfway up the only concrete wall, creating a checkered effect throughout the room. The pungent smell of manure from cattle grazing beyond the prison walls pervaded the air.

"The Colony," as it's referred to, is segmented according to the security classification of each inmate. We were in G Section, where an exclusive group of offenders were segregated from the general population, not because of the risk to other inmates' safety, but their own. It housed most of the convicted government, judicial, and law enforcement officials, along with a smattering of high-profile murderers that the general population of inmates would love to get at.

We'd been waiting more than twenty minutes for a half-hour interview with an inmate named Roger Ruby, who for more than ten years had been the West Coast's head of the FBI's Serial Killer Crime Unit. The last five he'd been eating, sleeping, and showering within a few feet of the scum he'd devoted his career to locking up.

According to Avery, for more than three years, Ruby and his unit had been investigating the rape and partial dismemberment of coeds up and down northern California. During that time, twenty-eight young women fell victim to the massacre. Frustrated that he couldn't figure out who was responsible before more were killed, every time a new victim was found, Ruby would blame himself.

In 1989, Cynthia Ellington—number twenty-nine—was murdered. This time the killer—a white male, medium build, in his late twenties—was caught in the act by a passerby and fled before he could dismember any of Ellington's body. At her funeral, just before the casket was closed for the last time, the mortician noticed that a locket which her mother had lovingly placed around her daughter's neck was missing. He scanned the mortuary's video security system and caught on tape, removing the locket, a young male matching the exact description of Ellington's murderer. Ruby's unit was notified and within an hour the person on the tape was identified as William Conners. The FBI obtained not only an arrest warrant for Conners, but also a warrant to search his house. In a freezer in the garage were over fifty body parts—hands, feet, breasts, and one head. In Conners's bedroom, Ruby found a shoe box full of souvenirs he'd taken from each of his victims, including Ellington's locket. When Ruby placed Conners under arrest, the young man wouldn't stop laughing and Ruby snapped. He shot Conners once through the head.

Even with the Bureau standing behind their number one man, Ruby was charged with murder. Judge Avery Harris had presided over the three-week trial, which eventually resulted in Ruby's manslaughter conviction.

Both Avery and I were standing in front of the window when the large metal door swung open. A man in his fifties walked in.

"You've got thirty minutes," the guard said and shut the door with a loud bang.

The man stood just inside the door, glancing back and forth between the two of us.

Avery walked toward him. "Hello, Roger."

The man stood for a moment, eyeing Avery's extended hand. A smile slowly crossed his face, and they embraced like best of friends. "It's been, what, a year?" Ruby said as they parted. "Why so long?"

"Sorry, but with the farm and all . . ."

"I've been pretty busy, too," he said, and they smiled.

Ruby turned to me. "Who's he?"

"Hunter Dobbs," I said, and he walked past me like I wasn't even there.

"He's an attorney," Avery said.

Ruby grunted something unintelligible as he stared out the window.

"I need to discuss a case I'm handling."

Another grunt.

"Hunter could really use your help."

Ruby shook his head as he gazed outside the window. "Would you look at that guy?"

We stepped next to Ruby and looked out at dozens of small green buildings, each surrounded by a ten-foot, chain-link fence with accordion barbed wire running along the top. The only movement was that of a bearded, middle-aged man walking inside the nearest enclosure. He wasn't taller than Ruby. But rather than Ruby's overgrown, military-style buzz cut, the guy's hair was long and straggly. An ex-hippie for sure.

"It's really ironic," Ruby said as the man paced nervously. "Who'd have thought I'd have to live close to someone like that."

"Who is he?" I asked, not having the foggiest.

Avery gave me a you-should-know-better look.

"Charles Manson," Ruby said flatly.

"That's Manson?" I said, like a teen at a rock concert.

Manson jerked his head to see who'd screamed. Seeing no one, he walked to the other side of the building out of sight.

"Charlie to me." Ruby chuckled and winked at Avery. "After all, we're neighbors." He then placed his arm around Avery's shoulder. "So you need my help?"

Avery grinned sheepishly.

"I believe I needed yours at one time," Ruby said in a serious tone. "Just in case you've forgotten."

"There was nothing I could have done."

"Take it easy," he said. "Let me have a little fun. It's not often I get the chance to give someone a hard time."

"Will you help?" I pushed, knowing we only had a few minutes.

"As long as it's for the judge," Ruby said and walked to a table standing in the middle of the room. "Pull up a chair and tell me what's so important."

We both sat across from Ruby as Avery explained everything we knew about Reineer and the dead or missing children.

"The first thing I need to understand," he said, as soon as Avery finished, "is why a defense attorney should care."

I paused for a moment, not sure I understood myself. "I have to know what kind of person I represent."

Ruby gave me a quizzical look.

"Maybe," I went on, "if I know he's responsible for what we suspect, I'll be able to talk him into taking some kind of deal. That way he'll be off the streets for a while. Or maybe I'll be able to talk him into getting some help."

"If he is a true serial killer, you won't talk him into any damn deal. And as far as getting him some help . . ." Ruby said, and laughed at just the thought of it. "Christ, you're not dealing with someone who is strung out on speed and just needs some counseling to kick a bad habit. Look," he said, leaning toward me, "I'm not buying whatever it is you're selling."

I looked to Avery for help.

"Just answer a few questions, Roger." Avery nodded at me. "He won't use any of it to help get his client off."

Ruby slumped back in his chair and gazed at the shiny enamel ceiling. He was obviously battling with the thought that he could be helping a defense attorney set some maniac free.

"All right," he finally said, sitting up straight. "But I might not be able to give you anything useful."

"I'm willing to take that chance."

He smiled at me for the first time, then his expression turned thoughtful. "The only thing you really know about this character's M.O. is that he stalks his intended victim beforehand?"

"And then somehow entices or forces them into his vehicle."

"And you were with him in 'Nam?" he said, turning to Avery.

"For six months. I was his platoon leader."

"Do you know anything at all about his family?"

"He's an only child, and his father was either killed, or left when he was very young. I'm not sure Reineer even knew him."

"Does that mean something?" I asked. "Because both the boy from Boonville and Danny Barton have only one parent that cares for them."

Ruby paused, thinking. "Nah," he said, "half the kids nowadays have only one parent at home.

That's probably just a coincidence. But tell me more about Reineer's childhood—school, friends, relatives, etc."

Avery stroked his beard as he tried to remember. "He had a lot of problems with his mother. She was very domineering—controlled everything he did. I remember he hated her but other than that . . ."

"Is she alive?" Ruby asked.

Avery hesitated. "He did tell me he hadn't seen her for over ten years. Something about her disappearing late one night and he hadn't heard from her since."

"Another missing person," I remarked. "I wonder how much he had to do with that."

"Probably his first victim," Avery added.

"I doubt it," Ruby said. "He would have killed others before he ever got up enough courage to do her in. But I wouldn't be surprised if she was the reason he went off the deep end in the first place."

"Then you think he may be a serial killer?" I asked.

Ruby saw how concerned we were. "You have to understand that I normally don't know who the suspect is. That's what I have to find out from all the clues I'm given. I almost always have a body, a crime scene, and everything I need to know about the victim's habits. After carefully studying each, I can usually come pretty close to formulating an accurate profile of the killer. But that process sometimes takes weeks, months, even years."

"We don't have that kind of time," I remarked. "The trial will be over in a few days."

Ruby frowned. "I want to help, but except for an

unsuccessful attack somewhere in a forest and some kid who, after he played marbles, jumps into a Blazer, you can't provide me with anything. No method of killing, no body, no weapon, no souvenirs from a victim, nothing."

It was unlikely that even with additional time there would be much more I could give him. There were no bodies, no weapons. . . . Then it hit me. "What were you saying about souvenirs?"

Ruby gave me a confused look.

"You said if there were souvenirs, it would help. What did you mean by that?"

"Only that it's very common for serial killers to take something from their victims."

"But why?"

"So they have something to remind them of the excitement and stimulation they receive during the kill. It helps them relive the event and gives them the courage to do it again."

Avery looked as horrified as I must have.

"It appears there's something we failed to mention that may be significant," I said. "Reineer has a necklace with what I thought was just a bunch of his personal junk attached to it. Stuff I assumed he'd collected since he was a kid."

Ruby looked at me with dawning interest. "There's a good chance each item on that necklace belonged to one of his victims."

"But there are at least a dozen. Does that mean he may have killed that many?"

"I'd bet on it."

My mind was spinning so fast I could hardly talk. "But why would he risk wearing something around his neck that could directly connect him to his victims?" Avery asked.

Ruby chuckled. "I've asked that and similar questions of some of the worst killers ever known to man." He shook his head. "All I can say is that without every one of their souvenirs, they'd just as soon be dead themselves."

I perked up. "Every souvenir?"

"Like a link in a chain. If one's missing, they might as well be missing all of them."

"It doesn't make any sense," I said, shaking my head.

Ruby looked at me as if I should know better. "There's one thing you better understand," he said. "They all have different reasons for their behavior, and I haven't found a one yet that makes any sense. They're nuts. And you'll go crazy, like I did, if you try to make sense of anything they do."

Chapter 32

I had been waiting nearly twenty minutes for Reineer. I'd requested the small attorney interview room with the concrete-and-glass partition separating the two sides. I wasn't sure what either of us would do once I confronted him.

My stomach hadn't stopped churning ever since Avery and I'd left the prison. Along with Sarah, we'd worked all of Saturday night and most of the next morning piecing together years of Jared's reign of terror across the western United States. Including Ukiah, he'd lived in four cities during the previous eight years. In all, a total of nine boys, ranging from seven to eleven years old, had disappeared under circumstances similar to what had happened to Danny and the Cosgrove boy.

The door opened and Reineer, with his feet shackled, shuffled in. "Who in the hell did you piss off to get stuck in this tiny place?" he asked.

He'd no idea what I'd found out since we last met. I also knew it wouldn't take me long to tell him.

"Give any more thought to Bragg's offer?"

Reineer rolled his eyes. "Are you kidding me? Is

that what you got me out of a nice warm bunk for?"

"I'd take the deal if I were you."

"But I thought you agreed with that decision."

"Only because I believed then you were innocent."

Reineer's eyebrows rose only slightly. It was as if he'd been expecting this announcement.

I rose from my seat and leaned into the glass. My hot breath fogged the window. "You're going down, Reineer."

Something cold ran through me as his eyes narrowed. The haunting depth of his stare seemed to pull me in.

"Hunter," he said in a near whisper, "sit down."

I lowered myself to my seat.

Carefully, he said, "There could be an innocent explanation for why my fingerprints are on that box."

"How did you know?"

"I was sure you'd get it analyzed. I would have expected nothing less."

Our eyes were locked. I wanted to turn away, but I couldn't.

"Then you admit you attacked Danny Barton?"

He looked around to make sure there was no way anyone could be listening. "And loved every minute of it."

I should have been outraged. I had come in ready to tear his head off. Yet there he was admitting it, and for some reason I was calmer than when I'd first walked in.

"You're not going to get away with it."

"Oh, won't I?" he said with a satisfied grin. "We

both know that kid will never mention the box of perfume and the cops won't ever know."

"Maybe not, but I do."

He hesitated for a moment, then shrugged. "I admire your high ideals, but they really don't matter."

"They matter to me."

"Good." His voice hardened. "But you're not my priest. You're my attorney. Start acting like it."

"And as your attorney I have to know about the others."

"What others?"

I reached into a manila envelope I'd brought into the room. Inside were some of his personal belongings taken the day he was arrested. "Remember this?" I pulled out his necklace, twirling it around my index finger.

Reineer's gaze fastened on the necklace. The pull it exerted on him sickened me.

"You pissed all over yourself just because they wouldn't let you keep it."

I placed the necklace on the counter and fingered several of the items attached to the strand of old leather. "So who's was this?" I asked as I rotated an agate marble between my thumb and forefinger. "Which one of your victims did this belong to?"

Like a dog watching his master hold a treat, Reineer didn't take his eyes off the marble.

"Whose is it?" I yelled.

Slowly a contented expression appeared on his face. "Boonville," was all he said.

My stomach began to feel nauseous. I wanted to leave, but I wasn't about to let him off that easy.

"And what about this one?" I pressed, showing him a rabbit's foot. "Which poor boy had this with him when you killed him?"

With his eyes still fixed on the necklace, he asked, "What is it you want?"

I slowly ran my finger along each item. "I wonder which one of the twelve is the oldest? Who was your first?"

Moisture begin to form in Reineer's eyes. It was as if I were holding my finger on the switch at his electrocution. That was when I noticed that a strand of braided hair tied in a circle had several threads of gray in it.

"Could it be," I said, stroking the hair, "that this is all that's left of your poor mother?"

Reineer's look changed to one of anger. His face reddened as he leaned into the glass to get as close as he could. "Are you done playing your games?"

The sound of his voice made the skin on the back of my neck prickle. I stuffed the necklace back into the envelope. "Yeah, I'm done."

Reineer slapped his palm on the counter. "You can't breathe a word of what you think you know to anyone."

"Think? I'm sure of it."

"And I'm sure you also know you have an ethical duty to keep your mouth shut."

Hearing him spout the law filled me with loathing. "I'm aware of my ethical obligations."

"Especially the Fifth Canon," he said.

"The Fifth Canon?" I smirked. "You're not half as smart as you think. If you were, you'd know attorneys are no longer governed by Canons of Ethics."

"And if you knew half as much as you think you do, you'd know that the Fifth Canon is the foundation of all federal and state rules governing the manner in which an attorney should represent his client." A slight smile returned to his face. "Even if that client is guilty."

I knew he was right, and that's what had been eating at me. But I wasn't about to let him know that.

"All the information you have about me, including my necklace, is privileged. You can't mention it in court. If you ever did, any conviction would be overturned on appeal."

"I'm not sure what I'll do," I said. "You'll just have to lie awake all night wondering."

Reineer grinned, and a feral light came into his eyes. "Go ahead and tell them," he said. "Tell everyone. Because if you do, any conviction would be easily overturned on appeal."

I paused for a moment, thinking about all the time Reineer must have spent in the jail's library to learn all that stuff. I wasn't done though. "There's one thing you haven't considered," I said and held up the envelope. "If I do open my mouth and you are tried for the murders this necklace will connect you to . . ." I paused. "Hell, with all those trials and appeals, you'll be without this necklace for years."

Reineer's eyes darted back to mine. I could tell he hadn't considered the possibility.

"How much longer can you live without it?" I

waved the envelope in front of him. "You already look like hell. You've lost weight, your eyes look like death, and it's only been a little more than six weeks. If I were to tell everything I know, you won't live long enough for one of those trials, let alone all of them."

Reineer was silent. I'd struck a nerve, and I was enjoying the hell out of it.

"You'll die if you don't get your little souvenirs back, won't you?" I said. "How long would that take, exactly? Months, weeks, or maybe just a few days?"

I pulled out the necklace again and handled the rabbit's foot. "I've always wanted one of these," I said. "You wouldn't care if I keep it. Good luck charm, right?"

Reineer jerked his head violently. A vein pulsed in the middle of his forehead.

"Oh, I forgot," I said, as if talking to a child. "You need all of them, don't you?"

I grabbed the rabbit's foot firmly like I was going to rip it from the necklace.

"No!" he screamed.

I continued to hold a firm grip on the rabbit's foot. Reineer's eyes narrowed. "You know what I can do."

I shook my head. "You don't scare me, asshole."

"Don't cross me," he said savagely.

"Look," I said, enjoying seeing him in pain, "stop threatening me. It won't do you a damn bit of good."

We both sat silently glaring at the other. Then, like a light switch, Reineer's expression changed.

His eyes crinkled with joy. "Do you remember that young man you asked me to watch for you?"

I was thrown by his change in topics. "His name was Bobby Miles."

"I know," Reineer said as a big smile crossed his face, fully exposing his front teeth. A strand of gold metal was wrapped around two of his upper teeth. It was Bobby's gold earring.

Bile rose in my throat. "You sick piece of shit." I wanted to claw my way through the glass. "Why . . . ? Why? What the hell did he ever do to you?"

"It was my pleasure," he said as if he were proud of it. "He was accusing you of a crime you didn't commit, wasn't he? I could never let something like that happen to *my* attorney."

My stomach was still heaving. "I can't believe how sick you are."

Reineer grinned. He knew I was shaken. His cockiness was back. "Now that you fully understand what I'm capable of, even from in here . . . you better keep your mouth shut."

I stood to leave. I couldn't let him know how much he was frightening me. I tried to maintain some semblance of calm, if only outwardly. "Is that a threat?"

"Fact!" he said defiantly. "Don't ever test me again."

When I opened the door, our eyes locked again. It was as if a fog had lifted and I'd seen Reineer clearly for the first time. There was no emotion in those dark green eyes of his. No fear, no anger, nothing. Just a chilling coldness. I'd looked into the eyes of every kind of vile, despicable criminal imaginable, but I'd never seen a pair like his. They were the eyes of a man without a soul.

Chapter 33

I shouldered up to the bar at Snooky's, a cocktail lounge across the street from the courthouse. The inside was dark and smoky, so my eyes needed a moment or two to adjust. It was crowded for a Sunday afternoon. Three noisy bar lumps to my right whooped and hollered as they watched the Forty-niners on one of the half dozen TVs. I decided to try one of the booths in the rear where it was quieter.

As I walked through the darkened haze, I noticed a waitress bent over a table—her short skirt hiked up—taking an order. Except for the string-like thong of her bikini panties, her rear was bare. I slowed my pace to take in the sight and chuckled to myself. Why was it that whenever I got this depressed I'd end up on the prowl? Maybe because whenever I felt that way, I always ended up in a place like this.

The young lady must have sensed me gawking. She quickly straightened. My eyes shifted to hers, and I mouthed the words, "Double Chivas," and plopped into a booth.

Only moments had passed since my confrontation with Reineer. I knew Sarah and Avery were anxiously awaiting my return, but I needed some time alone. Time to digest all the information I'd learned in the last forty-eight hours. I felt so foolish. A fool to have been so totally duped by a client. A fool for not pushing McBean to make sure Bobby was sent back to San Francisco immediately. A fool for drooling over a waitress who was walking toward me with a double Chivas. But most of all a fool for thinking that either the scotch or the waitress would help alleviate the pain.

"Here you go," she said, placing a napkin and then my drink in front of me. "Want to run a tab?"

"I probably should. I have a feeling this won't be the last," I said and quickly gulped it down.

She put her hands on the table and leaned over me. I could see the three bar lumps eyeing her from behind like I had. Watching them giggle like pubescent boys, I realized the football game wasn't the only reason this bar was so crowded.

"I've never seen you around here before."

"Business. I'll be leaving in just a few days."

"Is that so," she said.

I looked into her big brown eyes.

She stood there, inviting me to say more. Just then the front door opened and the light from the sunset flooded the room. Every head turned and watched as Sarah, in a soft, off-white sheer dress, stood in the open doorway, her shapely body silhouetted by the light outside.

"Damn," I mouthed as she peered about the bar.

She must have seen my car out front. "Sarah," I called out and she headed toward my voice.

The waitress scowled. "Who's that?"

"My attorney."

"I'll bet," she said, and straightened as Sarah took a seat across from me. She flipped a napkin in front of Sarah. "What'll it be?"

Sarah was put off not only by the napkin toss, but also the tone of voice. "Coke," she said sourly. She eyed the empty cocktail glass I was holding. "And he'll have the same."

"Forget it. Carbonation gives me gas," I said and handed over the glass. "Give me another double."

When the waitress walked away, it occurred to me that maybe it wasn't the scotch that was bothering Sarah, but the fact that the waitress had been flaunting her stuff for me.

"Did I interrupt something?"

"Nah," I lied, watching the waitress as she walked away.

"I thought the booze was what made you so sick the other night."

I wasn't going to be scolded like a child. "I got sick because your father broke the news that my client is a serial killer. The booze had nothing to do with it. And," I added, "why are you being so damn pissy with me?"

"I'm not," she said, though the stridency in her voice didn't lessen. "If you keep this up, you won't be in any shape to proceed tomorrow."

I chuckled. "Do you think I'd jeopardize that crazy S.O.B.'s chance for being found *not guilty*?"

Sarah took a deep audible breath, and I kept going.

"Wouldn't it be a shame?" I slapped my hand on the table. "Thanks to a hangover, a serial killer might get convicted of assault and kidnapping. Now, wouldn't that just break your heart?"

We were both silent as the waitress reappeared with our drinks. I immediately drank mine.

Sarah watched, her face grim. "I understand how you must feel. But don't you think you've had enough?"

"Nope."

"Well I think you have," she said in a stern tone.

I started laughing, but in an instant her hand clamped tightly on my wrist. Strangely enough, it didn't upset me. She wanted me to stop because she cared. I tried to straighten myself, but my other hand kept noticeably slipping off the seat of the booth.

"Maybe you should eat something," she said, nodding to a spot behind me where two lone players were shooting darts. Farther back there was a cook-your-own grill where someone's steak was charring.

"I just might do that," I announced loudly enough for everyone to hear. I held up my glass for the waitress to see. "As soon as I have one more."

"You're already drunk," Sarah declared. "You better stop."

"Oh no, I'm not," I said, but my head began to weave. "Don't you understand, Sarah? I just left Reineer and he not only admitted everything, but he also threatened me. How can you get on me for having a couple lousy drinks to help calm my nerves?"

"You have more on your mind than just calming your nerves." She nodded at the waitress, who was waiting for the bartender to pour me my third double. "I suppose that young girl was giving you what? A massage?"

I smiled. Sarah was jealous and I liked it. But I had to wait for the waitress to place my drink on the table before I could say anything.

"Will there be anything else?" she asked.

I lifted my glass in one hand and pointed to a spot halfway up the glass with the other. "When it gets this far down," I said, feeling my tongue thickening, "get me another."

"I keep telling you that's not going to help," Sarah said. The longer I looked at her, the more I understood why everyone in Kellogg's courtroom that first day had acted like the current month's *Playboy* centerfold had just walked in.

The three bar lumps cheering a Forty-niner touchdown broke the silence.

"You sure look beautiful when you're upset," I heard someone say. But my lips seemed to be the only ones moving. For weeks I'd intentionally tried everything possible to make sure I didn't put a move like that on Sarah. Yet there I sat plotting how nice it would be to be with her on something other than a professional basis. I wanted to get her into bed. That's when I realized I had way too much to drink—I was a goner.

"I'm not upset."

"Whatever," I said, and propped my elbows on

the table, enjoying her face. "Have I ever told you how beautiful you are?"

"That's twice," she said, running her finger around the rim of her glass. "But that's the booze talking."

"It is not!" I bellowed.

"You'd never say anything like that if you were sober. It's obvious that once you've had enough to drink," she said nodding in the waitress's direction, "anybody would look good to you."

I leaned into Sarah and pointed at the waitress. "She isn't that bad looking, is she?"

"Not for what you had in mind."

"Phew," I said, blowing air between my lips. "I thought for a second I'd had too much to drink."

That finally brought a smile to Sarah. "You're impossible."

I tried to focus on Sarah's face, but my head was bobbing. I rested it on the cushioned seat behind me. Then my attention was drawn to two boys about Danny's age as they zipped past the front window on their skateboards.

"What the hell am I going to do?" I said as they zigzagged down the sidewalk. "There's almost a dozen pieces on that damn necklace. Do you know what that means?"

"Father told me what you suspect."

"Well I don't suspect it anymore. Reineer admitted it."

"I wish there was something I could do."

"There is," I said as I tried to sit upright. "You can help me get him convicted."

Sarah gently placed her hand on my arm. "Dad and I talked about it at length and—"

"And there's nothing I can do except present every defense that the law permits regardless of my personal opinion as to his guilt or innocence," I finished for her.

"You're stuck," she said.

"But if he gets off, he'll just continue his murderous rampage. There has to be a way we can make sure he won't be set free." I lowered my voice. "Maybe we could leak some of what I know to McBean. Like maybe that his fingerprints are on the box of perfume."

Sarah squeezed my hand. "Ethically you can't."

"Screw my ethics. We have to stop him."

"Neither you, me, nor my father," she said, her concern rising with each word, "nor anyone who has worked with the defense can do anything even close to what you're suggesting. All we can do is pray that somehow, someday, he'll get caught."

"Tell that to all the kids he's going to rape and kill," I said, my voice catching in the bottom of my throat.

Sarah was right. I was just hoping against hope she'd had an idea. But we both knew there was no way I could ever use anything I knew about Danny, or any of Reineer's other victims, against him. My hands were tied. And no one knew that better than Reineer himself.

Sarah stood and firmly gripped my arm. "I think it's time I put you to bed."

That perked me up. I looked up at her, barely able to focus. "Only if you agree to tuck me in?"

Sarah smiled as she pulled me up. "We'll see, lover boy."

Thanks to the strength of Mr. Chivas, that was the last thing I remember either of us saying that night.

Chapter 34

The courtroom was packed. Every seat not occupied by court regulars and media was filled with members of law enforcement. Some in uniform, some plainclothes, they were waiting to see if the big-mouthed attorney from San Francisco would make good on his claim that he'd prove their chief of detectives had planted damaging evidence.

Priest gaveled the room quiet. Two bailiffs held the doors open as Carol Sealy paused to pat down her newly permed hair. Dressed in a pink work dress with a Sav-on badge pinned to her chest, she squared her shoulders and walked down the center aisle with a self-conscious smile. She was uncomfortable being the center of attention and was likely wishing she was still outside, sneaking a smoke. When she walked past me, I could tell by the carcinogenic waft enveloping her that she'd had one only seconds before.

I glanced past Reineer at Sarah's empty chair. When I finally did manage to get out of bed, I found a note on my dresser from Sarah. It said she was driving to San Francisco to meet personally with Patterson. She wanted to make sure they'd be dropping the charges against me now that Bobby Miles was dead.

I couldn't help but think about what may have happened between the two of us the night before. Something awakened me about four in the morning. I could have sworn it was the front door clicking shut. When I turned on the light, I found the blankets on the double bed pulled aside like someone may have been lying next to me.

I jerked as the sound of the clerk's loud voice reverberated throughout my skull. "Do you solemnly swear to tell the truth, the whole truth, and nothing but the truth?" the clerk bellowed as he administered the oath.

My head was so sensitive to sound, I could hear Reineer breathe. God, what I would have given at that very moment to make sure that breath was one of his last. All I could think of was there had to be a way I could be sure he was voted guilty. But between my certain disbarment and Reineer's conviction being overturned on appeal, there was nothing I could do. I had to ask every question and raise as much doubt in the jurors' minds as possible.

With little enthusiasm, I systematically led Sealy through her contact with Danny that night. She specifically recalled the boy and smiled every time she mentioned his name. Like the rest of us, she was obviously smitten by him.

"I watched him from the moment he walked in." She went on to explain that she recalled he was wearing gloves from the moment he had entered until he left.

I moved on to her meeting with McBean the following day.

"He asked me to get him a package of Gummy Bears," she said. "The same kind the boy bought."

"Then what happened?"

"He told me to put it in a bag for him."

I paused, knowing the next answer could be the most damaging to McBean's credibility. It would lay the foundation for Danny's testimony later.

"Did you ever see him touch the package of Gummy Bears with his bare hands?"

She hesitated. Like everyone else, she knew the point I was trying to make and even though she was my witness, her sympathies were with the prosecution. But to her credit, she testified as she remembered it.

"I can't say I ever did see the lieutenant touch the wrapper with his hands."

I knew Bragg would likely object to my next and last question, but I also knew that many times the question was more important than the answer. The question itself would leave the jury wondering.

"Why didn't Lieutenant McBean touch that candy wrapper with his bare hands?"

Sealy paused for a moment to consider it. I was wondering why Bragg hadn't jumped to his feet screaming out an objection. Finally Sealy's hesitation caught Bragg's attention. He lifted his head as if a light had been flipped on.

"Objection," he shouted. "This witness has no idea what Lieutenant McBean was thinking or what he would or wouldn't do."

"Sustained," Priest said and waved at me to proceed.

"Nothing further," I said and turned to Bragg. "Your witness."

Bragg questioned the elderly lady for thirty minutes before he realized he couldn't put a dent in her story. When he finally did give up, Priest recessed for lunch. As usual, I had to remain seated next to Reineer while the jurors were escorted from the courtroom.

"Have you heard from Sarah?" I mouthed to Avery who was back in his old seat.

"Not yet," he whispered.

Reineer leaned over as I gathered the files strewn across the table. "I must talk to you," he said sternly. They were the first words either of us had said to the other all morning.

I shoveled the rest of the files into my briefcase. "I'm busy."

"You didn't spend enough time examining that old witch," he said. "Why didn't you emphasize that McBean didn't want to touch that package because he'd get his fingerprints all over it?"

"Didn't you hear Bragg object?"

"So what? You should have kept it up until you were sure every one of those twelve idiots knew exactly what you were driving at."

I didn't have to put up with his shit. "Are you finished?"

"I'll tell you when I'm finished."

I edged away from the table. I didn't want to be next to that maniac any longer than I had to. Before I had a chance to push away, Reineer reached for my leg and squeezed so hard that it felt like a metal prod was driven through my kneecap.

"That hurts," I yelled.

The bailiff catapulted toward us. "What the hell's going on?"

Reineer released me as the bailiff pulled on the back of Reineer's chair. "Let's go."

Reineer wouldn't budge. "I'm talking to my lawyer," he said.

"It doesn't look like he wants to talk to you."

Reineer looked at me. "It's about Sarah," he said solemnly. "You better listen."

More threats, no doubt. It was better to have him make them now while an armed deputy was present.

I looked at the bailiff. "Could you give us a couple?"

"No way."

"Please," Reineer said, "it won't take but a minute."

I nodded that everything was all right.

"Only a couple minutes," he said. "And you better behave, Reineer."

Without taking his eyes off us, the bailiff stepped far enough back so we could talk in private. From behind us someone firmly placed his hand on my shoulder. It was Avery.

"Do you need me?"

Reineer narrowed his eyes. They appeared so much darker than at any time in the past. But that's how I saw Reineer now. Everything about him was dark. He was the Grim Reaper and I was his helper.

"Get out of here, old man," he said. "I want to talk to Dobbs. Alone."

I assured Avery everything was fine and I'd be right out. But before he left, he made a show of scowling at his long-time friend.

"You like Sarah, don't you?"

Reineer's question caught me off guard. "If that's what you want to talk about, I'm leaving." I placed my hands on top of the table to help push myself up.

"Don't move," he ordered. "I'm not done with you."

"You're not done with me?" I said in a mocking voice. "Well, I'm done with you."

Reineer grinned. "You know you'll never marry her."

I did a double take. "What was that . . . ? What did you just say?"

His face went blank. "You're afraid you'll hurt her the same way your father hurt your poor sweet mother."

I was speechless. How did this sicko know so much about me?

"Too much liquor can make a person irrational," he added.

"You're probably right," I said. "Booze was my father's excuse. What's yours?"

Reineer blew air from his mouth. "That's simple," he said. "I'm just plain old crazy."

"You've got my vote."

He grabbed my arm. "You better do a better job."

"Or what?" I pulled away from him. "You'll kill me, too?"

Reineer didn't respond. He was too busy grinning at the deputy.

"If you ever were to harm me, you'd need a new attorney. You know what?" I leaned into him, so close that I could feel the warmth of his stinking breath. "That would mean the judge would have to declare a mistrial, and it would have to start over. You'd be separated from your precious necklace the whole time."

Reineer gave me a look as though I was someone he was being forced to put up with. "Let me know when you've finished with your irrelevant bullshit."

"Cut the tough guy act. You won't do shit to me and you know it."

A look of amusement flickered across his face. "Maybe not to you," he said and flashed an evil smile. "But Sarah, now she's a different story."

Chapter 35

Priest was ten minutes late returning from lunch. Hurrying to her chair, she asked me to call my next witness. The bailiffs at the back of the courtroom escorted in Danny Barton, who'd been waiting outside with his mother. Bragg did everything he could by way of body language and facial expression to make sure everyone was aware he didn't like Danny being subjected to the trauma of a further examination.

But as before, Danny appeared at ease as he made his way up the center aisle. He stopped in front of the witness stand and turned to the clerk with his hand in the air.

Priest smiled. "That's all right, son. You don't have to do that again."

"No kidding," the boy said, as if he'd been looking forward to it. He shrugged, jumped the step to the witness chair, and plopped into it.

"But I do have to remind you that you're still under oath," she said in a motherly tone.

"Oh, I won't lie." Danny reached for the microphone, pulling it down to his mouth. He then looked at Bragg, waiting for the D.A. to begin.

I slowly rose from my chair. "This time I get to go first."

Danny's face reddened as he turned to the sound of my voice. "I knew that."

Pausing for the faint ripple of laughter to subside, I glanced at the jury. Each one was sitting straight, their faces tensed with anticipation, their eyes glued to the witness. The boy's testimony was what they'd been waiting for ever since I'd made my opening statement.

Except for confirming Danny didn't recall taking his gloves off, I intentionally bypassed anything that dealt with the night of the attack. My focus was on the interview the following day.

Danny had little trouble explaining how McBean asked him to inspect a package of Gummy Bears that was later placed into a plastic bag using tweezers. The foundation had been laid. But my most difficult task remained—making sure the jury understood that the package of Gummy Bears that McBean testified he had retrieved from inside Reineer's car was the same package Danny had inspected at the station.

I placed People's Exhibit Number Five, the plastic bag which held the package that McBean had testified was retrieved from Reineer's car, on the counter in front of the boy. "Have you ever seen this before?"

Danny lowered his head closer to make sure. "Looks like a package of Gummy Bears inside the bag."

There was no way Danny would be able to tell one package of Gummy Bears from the next. But I had to ask the question to underscore the possibilities Danny's anticipated answer would raise.

I nudged the plastic bag with my finger. "Does that look like the package of Gummy Bears that Lieutenant McBean gave you to inspect?"

Danny angled his head, studying it. "Can't tell because of the plastic bag it's in."

"Then let's take it out." I opened the bag and withdrew the candy wrapper. "Now will you tell me if that's the same package Lieutenant McBean had you look at the day after you were attacked."

Danny held the small package daintily between his thumb and forefinger, inspecting it. "I don't remember all this gray stuff."

"I believe that's the powder they use to locate fingerprints."

"Oh," he said and cheerfully placed the package on the counter. Without any further prodding, he said, "It could be the same package the lieutenant showed me."

I was finished and about to turn Danny over for cross when I noticed a smug smile on Bragg's face. And I had a good idea why. He was planning on turning my last question around by asking the boy if he could say that the package sitting in front of him was definitely not the package he'd lost that night. But what Bragg failed to realize was I really didn't care. All I'd set out to do was leave the jury questioning either possibility, hoping they'd consider that in conjunction with the suspicious way McBean had handled the package. Once that happened, it wouldn't take much more for them to conclude McBean had planted it.

Then it occurred to me that I'd be better off asking Danny the same question Bragg was likely planning. That way it wouldn't look like I was afraid of the answer.

I approached the witness stand. "Would it be fair to say, Danny, that there is no way by just looking at this package," I said and nodded to the exhibit that was still in front of him, "that you can tell if it's the same one you lost that night?"

Danny reached for the wrapper and held it in front of his face. He then fingered the ridges on both the top and bottom.

"It's not," he said in a matter-of-fact tone.

Bragg and McBean had the same surprised look that I was doing my best to hide. The courtroom was totally silent, everyone wondering, trying to digest exactly what Danny meant. Bragg placed his hands on the table and started to get up as though he was going to object, but must have reconsidered it. There were no grounds and he knew it. But that didn't stop him from scowling at me. I was sure he thought I'd carefully planned this for its dramatic effect. In fact, I was more upset than he was. All I could think of was that the boy must have misunderstood my question.

"Are you saying the package sitting in front of you *isn't* the same package you bought at Sav-on the night you were attacked?"

"I'm positive."

"How can you be so sure?"

"Simple," he said. "As soon as I left the store, I tried to open it but couldn't." Danny looked at his mother and gave her a half smile. He then turned back to me. "I had my gloves on, so I had to use my teeth."

Danny had no idea of the importance of what he was saying. "Are you sure? You have to be sure."

"I remember," he said, fear flickering in his eyes, "because when I ran into the guy, the piece I ripped off got stuck in my throat. It hurt."

The bit about it getting caught in his throat clinched his believability.

McBean was staring daggers. I was sure he knew as well as anyone Danny's answer to my next question. I knew because I could see the package on the counter. McBean knew because he was the one who'd planted it in Reineer's car.

"Would you please look at People's Number Five and tell us if you can see on any part of that package where you may have ripped a piece off with your teeth?"

"There isn't because that's not the same package I had with me that night."

The courtroom erupted. Reporters were scrambling out the door to be the first to call it in. The jurors were talking to one another. And even with Priest continuously rapping her gavel, two full minutes passed before calm was finally restored.

"One more outburst like that," Priest eventually bellowed, "and this courtroom will be closed to the public for the remainder of the trial. And that goes for the media, too." She eyed their seats. But except for two older types who were furiously writing something in their steno pads, the chairs were empty. The rest were somewhere outside preparing that night's top story.

Priest looked at me. I stood at the far end of the jury box, leaning up against the wall. I would have returned to my seat, but the last thing I wanted was to sit next to Reineer, who was smiling from ear to ear.

"Nothing further," I said.

Bragg slowly rose from his chair, shaking his head like he'd just heard the whopper of all tales. "Tell me, son," he began, and the boy stiffened. He could tell by the tone of the D.A.'s voice and the look on McBean's face that they weren't happy. "When you inspected the package at the station, did you ever inform the lieutenant that it wasn't the same package you had with you that night?"

"I don't think so."

"Why not?"

Danny hesitated and scrunched his face. "Because all he did was ask me if it looked like the package I lost."

"And if the lieutenant were to have asked you if it was the same exact package, you would have told him it wasn't."

"If he'd asked."

"Because that package had a tear or a piece ripped from it, is that what you're saying?"

Danny rolled his eyes at having to repeat himself. "Yeah," he answered. "It had a piece torn from it."

Bragg paced in front of the boy, with his hand cupping his chin. "How many times have you discussed what happened that night with either Lieutenant McBean or myself?"

"A lot."

"And you never once said anything about tearing the wrapper with your teeth."

Danny gave him a quick, edgy smile, but said nothing.

"Why is that?" Bragg pushed.

Danny shrugged. "I didn't know it was important, and you never asked."

"But Mr. Dobbs asked you about it when the two of you had a discussion at your house the other night. Isn't that correct?"

Danny's eyes shifted to mine. He didn't know I'd informed Bragg about our talk. He had to be concerned about whether or not I'd also mentioned the bottle of perfume he stole.

"Well," Bragg said impatiently.

Danny turned back to the D.A. and scowled. "Are you saying Mr. Dobbs told me to lie?"

"Not exactly," Bragg said, "but that will do."

"No way," Danny said without hesitating. "He wouldn't do that."

Bragg raised an eyebrow. "Oh, really?"

"And even if he did, I wouldn't." Danny's face reddened with anger. "Didn't you hear me promise the judge I'd tell the truth?"

Question after question, Bragg tried to get the boy to admit he'd never told anyone that he'd ripped the package because it either never happened or he was mistaking it for some other occasion when he may have used his teeth. But Danny never wavered, and the more Bragg tried to trip him up, the more apparent it became that the boy was telling it exactly as it happened.

Before Bragg finished trying to find a chink in

the youngster's armor, my legs began to weaken. I felt woozy. It could have been nerves, my hangover, or a combination of both. I had to sit down, but my regular seat—the one next to Reineer—was the only one vacant.

As I pulled my chair out, I noticed a suspicious movement coming from underneath the table in the area of Reineer's upper thigh. Taking my time to be seated, I watched as he methodically moved his hand over his pants across an erection.

My client was stroking himself in the presence of the very people who would soon be deciding his fate. I was stunned. It was not only revolting, but shockingly risky.

I leaned over to tell him to stop, but Reineer was the first to speak. "That boy sure is cute."

I'd represented a lot of perverts throughout the years, but few had repulsed me like he did at that very moment. As he continued to stroke himself, I got an idea.

Stationed along the wall to my left, the jury box ran perpendicular to the counsel table. Half the jury members were positioned across from or in front of the table, while the others were positioned to the rear of it. With Bragg still at the witness stand and McBean pushed up snug to the table, if I wasn't in the way, some of the jurors would have a clear view of Reineer. He'd be caught in the act and exposed for what he was. Maybe then, even if they believed the Gummy Bears were planted, they'd convict him anyway.

Nonchalantly, I pushed my chair away from the table and folded my hands behind my head like

I was bored with Bragg's repetitive questions. I turned to my left to see how many of the jurors were looking. But, as I should have expected, each was raptly listening to the young boy's testimony.

The thought of causing some type of distraction occurred to me. Maybe then at least one or two of them might notice. But I couldn't be too obvious or Reineer would be alerted. I frantically searched my mind, trying to think of something when Reineer folded both hands in his lap—secreting his erection.

He slowly turned. "Nice try," he whispered. "You'll regret *that* stunt."

Chapter 36

I was sitting in the same booth in the same bar with my familiar double Chivas. Avery sat across from me, drinking his fifth beer. Originally, he was supposed to drop me off to pick up my car. But as soon as we pulled in, we decided there wouldn't be any harm downing a quick one before our drive home. Hopefully by then Sarah would have returned from San Francisco.

The complexion of the trial had changed dramatically since I'd called Danny back to the stand. Reineer was no longer the focus of the trial—McBean was. The sudden shift wasn't that different from other trials I'd handled where law enforcement's credibility had been successfully attacked. Once a jury becomes convinced an officer of the law has lied about a critical issue, they will normally rule in favor of the defendant. Not that they necessarily believe he's innocent, but because they don't know what else about the prosecution's case is tainted.

Avery and I stared out the window and watched a heavy rain pelt the cars as they passed the bar. Directly in front of us, stopped at the corner light, was a Jeep Cherokee driven by a man in his mid-thirties. Sitting next to him, a boy about eleven or twelve repeatedly flipped a basketball into the air. The two reminded me of Otto Cosgrove and Reineer's most recent victim, his son, Gary.

"Can you imagine how terrible it must be for Cosgrove not to know whether his son is dead or alive?" I watched the father reach for the ball and quickly toss it back to the boy. "Every time his phone or doorbell rings, he'll think it could be news about his son. It won't matter how many years pass."

The light turned green, and the Cherokee took off down the street. "He'll go to his grave wondering whether his boy is dead or alive."

Avery shook his head as we watched the car disappear from view. "You're right," he said and took a sip of his beer. "It'll never be over until the boy's body is found."

"And there's not a damn thing we can do," I said, mostly to myself. "So many children murdered and I can't say a thing."

"You have to accept it."

"But it's not right."

"What's the alternative? How can any client ever trust his attorney and talk to him in confidence if that attorney can run to the authorities about what he was told? Attorneys are hired to defend—not to help the prosecution convict. And they can't bail out just because they think their client is guilty."

"I don't *think*—I *know* Reineer's guilty."

"Hello."

We looked up and saw Sarah looking down at the two of us. The waitress was next to her, placing Avery's next beer on the table.

"Coke, right?" I asked Sarah and shifted to the side to make room.

"I'm fine." She eyed my full glass of scotch. "I thought the trial was concluding tomorrow."

"It is." I patted the seat I'd vacated. "Sit down and tell us what Patterson said. When is he going to dismiss the charges?"

Sarah folded her arms across her chest. She looked like a sixth-grade teacher after she'd caught one of her students tossing a spit wad past her head. "I'm not going to talk about it here." She faced her father. "How many has he had this time?"

Sarah obviously wanted to pick a fight about my drinking, and I didn't blame her. She'd been more than understanding the night before. But her patience seemed to be at an end. *Her* problem was she'd picked the wrong time to take a stand.

"*He* . . . has a name," I jumped in before Avery could answer. "And *he* . . . will decide how many *he* . . . has."

"Who appointed you his guardian anyway?" Avery said. "Lighten up."

"If it happened only now and then, it wouldn't bother me," she said. "Last night I gave him the benefit of the doubt."

I looked at her stern face and smiled, wondering if the benefit of the doubt was the only thing she gave me last night.

"This is ridiculous," she went on. "He's finishing a very important trial first thing in the morning."

Avery was trying his best to suppress a smile, but couldn't hold it. He burst out laughing.

"What's so funny?" Sarah growled.

I held up my glass. "I ordered this over an hour ago."

Sarah gave me a look as if to say I was playing her for some kind of idiot.

"Really," I said, holding it up again. "There's no cubes, because they melted long ago."

"Honestly," Avery said, chuckling. He held the palm of his hand in front of his chest as if he was taking an oath. "He hasn't taken a sip since we've been here."

Sarah gave me a quick apologetic smile before she jerked her head at her father. "But it doesn't look like you can say the same, does it?"

"Ah, a few beers once in a blue moon shouldn't be a big deal."

Sarah patted her father on the shoulder. "Don't worry about it," she said and sat next to me.

"So what happened?" I asked. "When do I go back to work?"

Sarah's eyes dropped as she nervously fidgeted with the salt and pepper shakers to the left of her. That's when I knew she didn't have good news.

"Patterson refuses to drop the charges."

"But why? Miles changed his story."

Avery started to say something, but Sarah put her hand on his arm to stop him. "They never got a chance to talk to Bobby before he was killed," she said. "All they have is your word."

"And we know what that's worth," I scoffed.

"So what's Patterson going to do at trial? Read the kid's preliminary hearing transcript to the jury?"

"I'm afraid so."

If I'd detested Reineer before, I loathed him now. Without Bobby to say he'd lied at the prelim, I stood a good chance of being convicted.

I was tempted to drink the Chivas, with or without the ice. "Let's get the hell out of here."

"My Blazer or one of your cars?" Avery said with a grin. "Who gets to take me home?"

I smiled at Sarah. "Looks like it's my turn."

Sarah reached for her father's hand to help him up. "We'll leave your Blazer here."

"Let's take his," I said. "Mine's already been here this long anyway. . . ."

"Fine," Sarah said, and as Avery walked past, she gave him a friendly scowl. "Although we should make you walk."

When I stood to follow them out the door, Sarah's eyes met mine. We both looked at one another, waiting for the other to say something. I was at a total loss. She had no idea I didn't remember anything about the night before. I didn't know what to do.

Thankfully, Avery broke the awkward moment. "Are you guys coming?" he shouted as he held the front door open.

As our eyes parted, Sarah gently placed her hand in mine. "I think we better talk," she said. "I'm sure you know what it's about."

"I sure do," I lied.

* * *

Avery sat beside me as I followed Sarah's tail-lights onto the main highway. He was just drunk enough to moan at every bump in the road. As we left the traffic of the city behind, he craned his neck to look at the speedometer.

"She's sure going awful fast with the rain and all."

I couldn't resist. "Only forty-five," I said and grinned. "But I'm sure after six beers, it must seem like we're both going about ninety."

"Very funny," he said and rested his head back. But his eyes remained fixed on Sarah's Lexus in front of us.

"About your closing argument?" he mumbled. "What's the plan?"

"An Al Pacino would be fun." I glanced to see what his reaction would be. "I'll eloquently inform the jury that my client is guilty."

"Isn't that the one where Pacino represents a judge accused of rape?"

I made a sharp turn around a curve. "*Justice for All.*"

"I think I had too much to drink," Avery said, his face ashen. "And all these damn curves sure don't help."

He covered his mouth with his hand, and I panicked. "Do you want me to stop?"

Avery took a deep breath and exhaled. "No, I'm all right." Removing his hand from his mouth, he gestured to the roadway in front of us. "After the next curve the road straightens out."

When I glanced to make sure Avery was fine, he lurched forward, squinting at the roadway. I jerked my head and saw Sarah's brake lights veiled in a cloud of smoke. The Lexus was in a four-wheel skid, heading directly at a sharp curve.

"What the hell's happening?" Avery screamed as the taillights sailed over the shoulder into the darkness.

I slammed the brakes, and the Blazer came to a sliding, screeching halt. We ran to the edge of the cliff and froze—watching metal and glass explode off Sarah's Lexus as it bounced from tree to tree and toward the riverbed far below.

Chapter 37

It was after midnight. We had already paced every inch of Sarah's recovery room at Mendocino County Hospital. The loud clacking of Avery's steel-toed shoes sounded strange in a place where everyone's foam-cushioned soles squeaked.

Three rescue teams had worked for more than an hour to free Sarah from the wreckage, which ended up headfirst against the last tree before a hundred-foot plunge to the river below. She was lucky to be alive.

We met with the portly Dr. Jonathan Slocum immediately after Sarah's surgery. He'd informed us that even though she was still unconscious, he didn't feel any of her injuries were life threatening.

"Seven broken ribs, a pierced lung, and a broken arm was all we found," Slocum said, as though she'd only skinned her knee. "In a few months she'll be just fine . . . as long as she comes out of that coma."

I was on the edge of a chair, holding her hand, sickened by the sight of all the tubes and wires coming out of every part of her. As she fought for her life, I couldn't help but wonder how she could have accidentally lost control on a road she'd driven thousands of times before. Or maybe it wasn't an accident after all. I reflected back on the threat Reineer had made. He said I'd regret what I did to him in court just hours before she ran off the road. Was Sarah his revenge?

I wondered how he could have managed it from inside his cell. But the answer was simple. I'd been around long enough to know how easy an inmate can control what goes on outside. All Reineer would need is a recently released inmate or one of their friends to do the dirty work.

The sound of Avery's boots approached from down the hall. He was concerned that Sarah had been out of surgery for over two hours and still hadn't regained consciousness. He'd left ten minutes earlier to locate Dr. Slocum to find out why.

He walked past me without saying a word and gripped the bed's side rail as he bent over to give his daughter a kiss on the cheek. "The doctor doesn't seem that concerned," he said.

"Then why hasn't she come out of it?"

Avery reached for Sarah's hand and gently cradled it in his as he sat in the chair next to me. "Probably just the shock to her system." A look of concern crossed his face. "But it could also be the buildup of pressure inside her cranium."

"Meaning what?"

"Bleeding inside the skull," he said. "If that happens, they'll have to relieve the pressure."

"How?"

The retired judge slumped back into the chair. His face was pale, his eyes droopy and red—the same color as the blood smeared on the front of his shirt from when he'd held Sarah in the ambulance.

"They'll have to drain the fluid."

The sheet over Sarah's chest rose and fell every time she took a breath. "She has to be all right," I said. "There's so much I have to say to her."

"She will be. . . . And there will be plenty of time to tell her how you feel."

"When I saw her fly off that embankment, I thought I'd lost her forever," I said and hesitated. "It's happened to me before."

Avery gave me a concerned look.

"The same thing happened to my father. . . . He didn't survive."

We both looked at Sarah. Her breathing was noticeably louder.

"Maybe we should get someone." I reached for the bed rail to propel myself upward.

Avery grabbed my arm. "Her respiration, heartbeat, everything is being monitored at the nurses' station. They'll know way before we do if something's wrong," he said as her breathing became less labored. "Tell me what happened to your father."

Watching Sarah's every movement, we both sat back in our chairs.

"I was ten years old and asleep when my mother's screams had awakened me," I said, remembering. "My father was drunk, beating her unmercifully. I ran downstairs, and like I had many times before, yelled, cried, and pounded on his chest begging him to stop hurting her. Normally, that's all it would have taken. But this time was different. He was out of control. He wouldn't stop no matter how much I pleaded. I was sure he was going to kill her.

"He pushed me aside and lifted my mom by her hair and slammed her face into the wall. He laughed as he let go of her semiconscious body, which fell limply to the floor. When I saw her lying there with that unforgettable look of fear on her swollen and bloodied face, something in me snapped.

"I ran to my bedroom and grabbed my Louisville slugger. I had to stop him. By the time I got back, he was kicking at her stomach, daring her to get up. I walked behind him and raised the bat over my head. Then with every ounce of muscle I could muster, I exploded it on the back of his skull. His knees buckled and he dropped to the floor.

"But either I was too small or he was too big, because in a matter of seconds he staggered to his feet and turned to me, blurry eyed while reaching out for me to hand him the bat. I was petrified when the bat fell from my hands onto the floor. We both watched as it slowly rolled to his feet. Still woozy, he leaned over to pick it up, but almost fell. Righting himself, he focused on me and then the bat as he slowly lifted it over his head. I cowered, covering my head with my arms, waiting. My mother jumped on his back, hitting and scratching while yelling at me to leave.

"The next thing I remember, I was out the front door, running as fast as I could. I'd no idea where I was going, only that I had to keep running. If he ever caught me, he'd kill me for sure.

"I was on the main highway when I heard his

car start, followed by the sound of tires spinning on the dirt road in front of our house.

"He was coming after me.

"I ran and ran, hoping he was too drunk to get very far. Then from behind, I heard the screeching of tires as the car fishtailed onto the asphalt. The car was directly behind me.

"I had to get off the road. To my left was a ledge with at least a hundred-foot drop into a rocky ravine. To my right, a sheer cliff face. I knew I couldn't outrun him, but there was no place to go. Just maybe, he'd calmed down, I thought. I stopped and waved my arms for him to stop. But the engine got louder and the headlights brighter. The car was picking up speed. I stood paralyzed in the middle of the road.

"When the lights were on top of me, the car veered onto the dirt shoulder. The back end slid around in the loose dirt until the car sailed over the edge.

"His car never touched anything but air until it hit the bottom of the ravine, where it exploded on impact.

"I never knew if my father wanted to kill himself that night. But, I did know one thing for sure as I watched it burn—he would never hurt my mother again."

Avery reached for my hand, a gesture I found uncomfortably touching. So much so that I had to pull away or risk a flood of tears. Why was I telling him this now? I'd never told anyone but Uncle Joe, and the painful truth of it had been bottled up inside me for so long it almost felt at home there. But now—looking at Sarah, so silent in that hospital bed—I felt if I didn't tell Avery, the secret would explode, leaving me hopelessly poisoned, contaminated, maybe dead. Perhaps I had to tell him so my behavior over the past few weeks would make some sense to him—and by proxy to Sarah. Or maybe I just needed it to make sense to me.

"I ran into the house and my mother was lying on the floor. If it wasn't for the clothes I wouldn't have recognized her. Her face was . . . He'd crushed it with my baseball bat."

Avery shook his head as I tried to compose myself.

"He was always drunk," I said. "And it looks like I'm no better. The going gets tough and the first thing I do is turn to the bottle."

"Damn it, Hunter," he said. "Quit comparing yourself to your old man. You can choose not to be like him. You already have."

I had to smile for the first time in hours. That was the Avery Harris I remembered—no robe and a little heavier around the midsection, but the same old bark.

"She's always been fond of you, you know." He was whispering as if Sarah could hear him.

"What do you mean by always?" I asked. "We never really knew one another until just recently."

"She would come into my court and watch you. She admired and respected your ability. She always said she wanted to be as good as you in court." He then chuckled. "Actually, I think she admired you so much because you were one of the few who would stand up to me. I couldn't intimidate you."

"Oh yes, you did," I said. "If you only knew how much."

Avery smiled and placed his hand on mine. "Tell her how you feel and see where it takes you."

"But I'm afraid. I mean she deserves a whole lot better."

"Let her decide. What happend to you and your parents was horrible, but maybe Sarah can help you lick it."

The conversation had become familiar somehow.

"This is the second time today my parents have come up in a conversation," I told him.

He gave me a puzzled look.

"Reineer," I said. "And for the life of me, I can't figure out how he knows so much about me and my past."

Avery inhaled deeply and slowly let it out. "I'm sorry," he said and placed his hand on my knee. "I'm to blame."

"What do you mean?"

"I may have mentioned a few things about your troubled past to Jared."

"When would you have done anything like that and . . . why?"

He leaned toward Sarah and gently placed his hand on hers. "It was before it happened," he said referring to Reineer's arrest. "Jared and I would get awful bored hacking away at trees all day. So, we'd talk."

"But why about me?" I asked. "And why about what happened to my family?"

"I've known about your mom and dad all along," he admitted. "I recall when it happened. You were front-page news for days."

"I sure was," I said, remembering it only too well. "I was all over the TV, too. For weeks . . . But why was it brought up in front of Reineer?"

"Jared was in the field when Sarah told me you were on your way. He must have picked up on how excited Sarah was about you."

"So." I wanted him to keep going.

"That's when I told him everything I knew."

"But my whole life . . . ? Good Lord, Avery, you two tree-trimmers did quite a bit of gossiping, wouldn't you say?"

"I never imagined it would come to this. We were just two ex-army buddies shooting the bull."

I looked at him with a crooked smile. "So Reineer is just a good listener and not some psychic evil wacko after all."

"Evil wacko, yes. But psychic," he said, sighing, "not hardly."

But something still nagged at me.

"When Reineer was telling me about my mother and father, it wasn't polite conversation. He was doing it for a reason."

"What reason could he possibly have?"

"To scare me enough to make sure his threats against Sarah had some bite."

Avery quickly sat up and gripped my forearm tightly. "What threats?"

"He told me if I ever did anything to jeopardize his acquittal, Sarah would be the one who'd suffer."

"I see," he said, musing over it.

"That's why you're going to let me borrow one of your handguns."

"For what?"

"If what happened to Sarah wasn't an accident, then who knows what he'll try? Especially when he gets out."

"You mean *if*."

"No, I mean when. And so do you."

"It had to be an accident," he said, shaking his head. "We were right behind her when she ran off the road. It wasn't like someone forced her off."

Avery began to pace, the same way he had when Sarah was wheeled in from surgery. "Jared has you shaken. He's got you overreacting."

"What about the gun?" I pushed.

Avery offered me a smile. "I heard what happened the last time you tried to use one. Something about hitting a couple of crows when you were aiming at those gangbangers who were after you and that kid."

"I wasn't trying to hit anyone," I said. "I just wanted to scare them."

"Who? The gangbangers or the crows?" Then he turned serious. "I'll give you one tomorrow."

"Before court?"

"You're not appearing tomorrow. You're exhausted."

"I'll be fine. Plus, I'm no good here, " I said. "I

want to get it over with. The sooner that nut is out of our lives the better."

"But that also means," Avery said, then hesitated. "The sooner he'll be free to hurt someone else."

"No," I said. "I'm going to do everything I can to make sure that never happens again."

Chapter 38

The jury would begin their deliberations sometime in the afternoon. Bragg had nearly finished with McBean, his only rebuttal witness. Then we'd make our closing arguments and Priest would instruct the jury and send them off to deliberate. Their most difficult task would be selecting a foreman. The verdict could be phoned in—not guilty.

To Bragg's credit, though, he never gave up. For more than an hour, he tried everything possible to rehabilitate his investigating officer. But with all his huffing and puffing, all he managed was to blow a little smoke—that somehow, some way, I'd convinced Danny to say the Gummy Bear package was torn. Otherwise, the boy would have mentioned it sooner.

But I had the advantage. There were other witnesses to support my position, while all the D.A. had was McBean: McBean to deny he planted the wrapper; McBean to deny that after he interviewed Danny, he handled the wrapper with a tweezers; and McBean to deny that Danny ever mentioned the wrapper was torn. My job for McBean's cross was to make sure the jury understood that Bragg's smoke screen had a major flaw.

"Lieutenant," I asked as soon as Bragg took his seat, "you testified that when you met with Danny Barton, you asked him to inspect a package of Gummy Bears?"

"That's correct," he said, then added, "it was the same package I'd obtained from Ms. Sealy. I wanted to see if it was similar to the candy he'd purchased the night he was attacked."

"But why did you feel it was important if you hadn't found the package in my client's car yet?"

"The boy had already told me he'd lost it during his abduction. I wanted to make sure I knew what to look for."

My head bowed as if I couldn't grasp what McBean was trying to get everyone to swallow. "When you gave him that package, what exactly did you say?" I asked.

"I'm not sure what my exact words were."

"Then why do you feel Danny should have told you it wasn't the candy he'd lost because the package didn't have a tear in it?"

"I sure would have. Wouldn't you?"

"But neither of us is ten years old, are we?"

McBean sighed deeply, like he was dealing with an idiot. I didn't care. I'd made my point and he knew it.

"Tell me why a ten-year-old, or even a thirty-year-old, for that matter, would have any inkling that a tear in the package he'd lost was important?"

"Sounds reasonable to me."

"But when you interviewed Danny you hadn't searched my client's car yet, correct?"

McBean hesitated. He'd testified too many times not to realize where I was headed. "Well—" he started to say and I cut him off.

"You had no reason to ask Danny whether or not it was the candy he'd lost because you hadn't searched my client's car yet," I said, my voice rising with each word. "Am I correct?"

McBean shrugged.

"You asked Danny if the package was similar to the one he purchased and that's all you asked him, isn't that correct, Lieutenant?"

"I already told you I don't recall my exact words."

"So you did," I said, and stepped to within inches of his face. "But correct me if I'm wrong, there would have been only one reason you would have asked Danny Barton whether or not the package you obtained from Ms. Sealy was the exact one he'd lost that night. That would be if you already planned on it being the same package you'd find in my client's car the next day."

McBean jumped to his feet. "I keep telling you I didn't plant that package." He turned to the jury. "There's just no proof that I did anything like that."

I gazed up at McBean, looking annoyed as I folded my arms across my chest, readying myself for one last parting shot. "Lieutenant," I said in a strong but controlled voice, "do you have any proof that you didn't?"

Bragg and I completed our closing argument in less than two hours. A record, I was sure, for such a notorious case. But we both knew the outcome was certain, and a quick summary of our positions was all that was required. I emphasized whenever possible that without the package of Gummy Bears, the prosecution had nothing. It did take me longer than I'd anticipated, but only because I had to pause now and then to compose myself. I ached for the opportunity to stand in front of Reineer, point my finger directly in his face, and tell the jury they couldn't let him go free because he'd kill again.

Then, with painstaking slowness, Priest read the lengthy boilerplate jury instructions. It was a little past four when court was adjourned and the six-man and six-woman jury retired to begin their deliberations.

"You surprised me, Counselor," Reineer said.

Ignoring him, I closed my briefcase and snapped it shut.

"Thanks to you, I should be out of here real soon."

"Thanks to me," I scoffed. "If it were up to me, you'd be burning in hell at this very moment."

"Now, now, now," he said glibly. "If you get this pissed when you're staring victory in the face, what are you like when you're losing?"

"You'll find out if I ever get the opportunity to represent you for murdering any of the dozen children you've killed."

"Nah," he said and chuckled. "If they haven't connected me to any of them by now, they never will. But you never know about number thirteen. I could screw up again."

Before court Avery had given me the gun I'd

asked for. At that moment I was thankful it was sitting in the trunk of my car.

"And when number thirteen does happen," he added as he winked at me, "you'll be the first person I call."

Chapter 39

I knew there was no escaping them, so I didn't even try. As soon as I opened the courtroom doors, I found reporters with notepads and pens ready, radio and televison newscasters with microphones, cameramen with cameras and minicams, electricians pulling cable—each positioned in front of me, walking backward, shouting questions. I finally stopped at the top of the courthouse steps.

"Please," I said as loudly as I could. But I failed to make a dent in the clamor.

"People, please," I yelled several more times, waving my arms over my head to let them know I had something to say.

Slowly the din subsided.

"I'm sorry, but I have to be somewhere and I don't have much time." They exploded again, each shouting similar questions.

I decided to try a different approach. I stood with my hands folded across my chest like a pouting five-year-old. It worked.

"At this time I will not speculate as to how long the jury will deliberate or what I feel their verdict will be."

A young freckle-faced man with pen poised was standing directly in front of me. "Is your client going to sue the county for false arrest?"

I wanted to tell him that I wished Reineer was dumb enough to do exactly that. Whoever the county hired to represent them would do a heck of a lot better job investigating Reineer's background than McBean had.

"Isn't that question a bit premature?" I said.

The crowd jostled forward, pushing me back to the edge of the steps. They were out of control, and I'd had enough aggravation for one day. I bulldozed my way down the steps, yelling the old standby, "No comment."

As I neared my car, I could hear the footsteps of someone running faster behind me. I came to an immediate halt and spun around to confront whoever it was. The freckle-faced reporter didn't stop in time, and we collided head-on.

On my butt with my briefcase and Reineer's file spread all around me, I looked up at the kid, who hardly seemed affected by the collision. "Didn't you hear me say I have no further comment?"

"I'm sorry," he said and squatted to help me pick up the papers. "But they're looking for you." He nodded toward the courthouse. "They want you right away. The jury's already back."

News that the verdict was in spread like wildfire. By the time Reineer changed out of his jailhouse blues back into his trial suit, the courtroom was already bursting at the seams. Out of the corner of my eye, I could see that both Danny's mother and Otto Cosgrove were sitting in their assigned seats. Behind me, where Avery normally was, a middle-aged man with buck teeth and dirty overalls sat smiling, seemingly excited that he was lucky enough to have a front-row seat.

The reading of the verdict was that part of a jury trial I'd always found the most troublesome. Days, weeks, sometimes even months of devoting myself to a certain position always came down to that one moment. A moment when a person's freedom would be either taken or restored—or worse—a moment when a human being would be told whether he lives or dies.

I could sense Reineer to my right, staring at the jury, hoping to read something in their eyes, facial expressions, or shifting positions. I chuckled to myself, knowing full well he was wasting his time. After my first murder trial, which I'd felt I'd won easily, the jury had deliberated for more than a week. When they finally took their seats to announce the verdict, they were all smiles. I knew for sure I'd won. I was ecstatic. Then the clerk read the verdict: guilty as charged. In a state of shock, I sat expressionless as the jury filed out of the courtroom. Without exception, each one stopped to congratulate me for doing such a fine job. But my client, the newest addition to death row, sure didn't think so.

"Mr. Carbajal?" Priest said as she buttoned her robe. "I understand the jury has reached a verdict."

"We have, Your Honor," the elderly gas station owner and elected foreman said.

There was dead silence as the foreman handed the

verdict forms to the bailiff, who in turn handed them to the judge.

Priest studied each form, glanced at Reineer, and then handed them to Billy Danks to read. "Would the clerk please read the verdict?" she announced as if her clerk were across the room rather than standing only a few feet away.

"We the jury in the above entitled court," Danks said in his booming gruff voice, "find the defendant, Jared M. Reineer, not guilty."

Except for a few reporters exploding out the back door to call it in, there was an eerie silence throughout the courtroom, similar to when death finally befalls a loved one who has been suffering horribly from a terminal disease. Even though everyone expected it and sometimes even wanted it to happen, once it does, you're not sure it was best or what you really wanted all along. Maybe, just maybe, the gallery suspected what I knew. Reineer was guilty, but because of what McBean did, no one could ever be sure. That was what "reasonable doubt" was all about. To my dismay, the system worked.

The only bright side—dim at that—was it was finally over. Reineer's hadn't taken as long as most trials, but sitting next to him, I felt like I'd been there a lifetime. Everything I'd believed and fought for, including my duty to represent with indifference the guilty as well as the innocent, seemed a farce. Maybe I'd been on the wrong side my whole legal career. Maybe it was better that sometimes the innocent be convicted at the expense of the guilty going free. Maybe that was the price we all had to pay. At least that way the future Danny Bartons and Gary Cosgroves would stand a chance.

As soon as Priest discharged the jury, there was a race between Bragg and McBean to the back door. Bragg would likely devote the rest of the day preparing a statement for the media, while McBean would continue as before. He would gain nothing from the experience.

But I had. I wasn't about to let Reineer add more trophies to his collection.

"It's not over," I said. We were waiting for the bailiffs to clear the courtroom so they could take him to lockup. He'd change, sign some paperwork, his personal belongings would be returned—then they'd cut him loose. He had been looking straight ahead, expressionless, ever since the verdict was read.

"Did you hear me?"

With a chilling leer Reineer's eyes slowly shifted to mine. "It is over, Counselor, and I have you to thank for it."

I rose from my chair and placed my hand firmly on his shoulder. "No, it's not. Not by a long shot."

Chapter 40

It was a little before five; the way I'd figured it, Reineer would be released in less than an hour and he'd have to come here to retrieve his necklace.

"I'm here for Reineer's property," I told the desk sergeant, who'd hung up the phone as soon as he saw me walk in. He stretched back in his swivel chair, glaring at me. He'd obviously heard about the verdict.

"The property room closes at five," the sergeant said as he chewed on the mustache which had overgrown his upper lip. "You'll have to wait until tomorrow."

I tapped the face of my watch with my finger. "I'm his attorney and unless you're operating by Central Mountain Time, there's still ten minutes before it closes."

He nodded at the door behind him. "Most everybody around here was at the trial. They went straight to Snooky's from there. It's just across the street."

I cut him off. "I know where it is."

"The property deputy is Carter, Jimmy Carter. He'll be the one eating all the peanuts," he joked.

I didn't laugh.

"Of course, I'm not sure it's wise for you to go there right now." His face went blank. "You're not the most popular guy in town, if you know what I mean."

My patience was at an end. "Who's in charge?"

The sergeant scowled. "Do yourself a favor and leave before I—" he said, but was interrupted when the security buzzer on the door sounded. It burst open and McBean appeared breathing fire. He slammed the door shut and charged straight at me. "What the hell do you want, Dobbs?"

"I'm here for my client's things."

"He'll get them when he's released."

"Not according to him," I said and nodded at the heavy-set cop. "He says the property room's closed."

Even though our eyes were locked, I could see McBean tightening his hand, forming a fist. "Are you calling the sergeant a liar, too?"

"Why don't you just give me his stuff and I'll be on my way?"

"Tomorrow."

"If you give them to me now, he'll be out of town before midnight and out of your hair forever."

I paused to give him time to think about it before I continued. "So far I've been able to avoid the press. But I'm sure that will be impossible if we both have to come back."

McBean silently pondered it. After a moment, he turned to the sergeant. "Go get it."

"But, Lieutenant," the lower-ranking cop said, "Carter's gone for the day."

"Now!" he shouted.

The sergeant took a deep breath, lifted the waist of his pants, and reluctantly walked off.

"Both of you," McBean said.

I'd no idea what he meant, but was sure it had to be something with a bite to it. "What about the both of us?"

"I want you out of town by midnight, too."

I had to smile. Our little confrontation had all the earmarks of a second-rate western. "Is that right?"

"Everything is a big joke to you, isn't it?" McBean stepped closer. "I hope you burn in hell for getting that scumbag off."

"I'll probably burn in hell, but it won't be for doing my job."

"Job," he scoffed. "You damn defense attorneys are a hoot. Always spouting the Constitution, pretending you're its guardian. But I know all you care about is winning. No matter what the consequences."

"You're right about the Constitution," I shot back. "Screw it! Screw the judges! Screw the juries! Who needs any of them? We'll just leave everything to crooked cops like you."

McBean's face turned a brighter red. He glanced around the room to make sure no one was looking. Then he grabbed the lapels of my coat and slammed me against the wall. "You piece of shit," he yelled as he lifted me.

The neck of my shirt was choking me. The tips of my shoes were the only things touching the floor. "You don't understand."

"What I *do* understand," he said, pushing me

farther up, "is that you're not here to get any of Reineer's personal shit. You won the big one, and now you're here to rub it in."

I grabbed McBean directly under his armpits. My right hand found the holster of his gun. He stiffened.

"Just try it," he dared and slowly lowered me to the floor.

When he finally let go, McBean reached for the handcuffs which were hanging from his belt. I knew he was bluffing. He wasn't about to arrest me. The media would be all over him, and with the beating they'd been giving him, I was sure he wanted to lay low for a while.

"I hope you understand that by planting that candy you guaranteed Reineer's acquittal," I said.

"Don't put that guilt trip on me." McBean stepped closer. Our noses were almost touching. "You're the one who got that psycho off."

"Tell it to someone who doesn't know better."

It was obvious I was getting nowhere going toe to toe with him, so I backed up a few steps to ease the tension.

"It's just that I'm afraid," I said.

McBean smirked as though he thought I was afraid of him.

"What I mean is, I'm afraid the next Danny Barton won't live to tell about it."

McBean looked confused. "What the hell are you saying, Dobbs?"

"Don't let Reineer out of your sight until he's out of the county." I lowered my voice, conspiratorially. "He's going after someone tonight."

McBean's interest was piqued. "What exactly did he tell you?"

I shrugged. "Attorney-client privilege."

McBean smiled as though he thought I'd already told him more than I should have. "Do you really think he'd try something like that right after he's released? It doesn't make any sense."

"Nothing about Reineer makes sense. He's nuts." I tapped my finger on McBean's chest. "If anything should happen to some other innocent child tonight and you did nothing . . ."

McBean stared at me for a moment, then glanced at the sergeant, who'd returned with Reineer's belongings. McBean grabbed the envelope.

I kept pushing. "Think what it will do for your public image," I said. "Catch him in the act and everyone will forget about what happened today. What do you have to lose but a little time?"

"But if that scumbag knows I'm following him, he won't try anything until he's out of the county." McBean was almost mumbling to himself. "If that happens . . . no one will be there to stop him. . . ."

I was silent, letting him think it through. It had to be his idea or he'd never do it.

"But if he doesn't know I'm watching . . ." he said and stopped. A few seconds passed and McBean's eyes widened as if he could see clearly for the first time. "You don't fool me, Dobbs. You're sending me on some wild goose chase."

"You're wrong," I said.

McBean shoved the envelope into my chest. "You have what you supposedly came for. Now get the hell out of here."

"What's the big deal?" I said. "If you follow him and I am wrong, at least you'll know he's left the county and is out of your life forever."

"Yeah, yeah," he said as he pushed me out the door. "You can bet if I do follow him, it's because I planned it all along. It wouldn't have anything to do with something you told me."

I wanted to tell him he never would have thought of it on his own. But there was no reason to push it. I was sure McBean would follow Reineer. I had gotten what I was after.

Chapter 41

Avery was in the same chair that I'd left him in the night before. I gently placed my hand on his shoulder. "How is she?" I asked, but he didn't move a muscle. He was asleep—out cold.

"Why don't you ask her yourself?" a frail voice said from behind.

It was Sarah—her eyes barely open—trying to muster a smile. "Let him sleep." She slowly raised her hand for me to hold. The weakness of life in her momentarily numbed me.

"My car?" she said and paused to catch her breath.

I softly placed my fingertips to her lips to hush her. "Please don't talk."

She tried to look at me, but her eyes seemed to wander—too weak to focus.

"Did I hit it?"

"Hit what?"

"The deer," she said. "You must have seen it."

"Of course I did," I lied. "It's fine."

She gently squeezed my hand. "What about the trial?"

"It's over . . . not guilty."

Sarah slowly shook her head and her eyes closed. When she opened them, a tear ran down her temple, curling around her ear. Except for the rhythmic beat of her heart monitor and Avery's heavy breathing, there was total silence.

I leaned over and gently kissed her lips. "I love you."

"I love you, too," she said, our lips still touching.

I gently slid off the edge of the bed.

"Stay with me?" she whispered.

"You need your rest."

"Please," she said, and her eyes widened. "Please don't go."

"I'm sorry," I said and kissed her one last time. "There's something I have to do."

Chapter 42

In a dark corner of the guest house, I waited for Reineer to come through the front door. I was sure he wouldn't be much longer. Once McBean informed him that I had his necklace, he'd get to me as soon as possible.

Avery's gun was in my right hand.

My body tightened when I heard the sound of gravel crunching—someone was heading up the driveway. Within seconds a car door closed, followed by the sound of footsteps quickly approaching. The front door burst open, and Reineer appeared, looking around the darkened room like a nervous sparrow.

Slipping the gun into my back waistband, I stepped out of the shadows and flipped on the light so we could get a better look at one another.

"What took you so long?"

"I had something to take care of," he said, then his eyes became fixed on his necklace; it hung down on my chest.

"Give me that!" he shouted.

"I don't think so. . . . It's stolen property."

"Stolen from me," he said. "And I want it back."

"Why don't we take it down to the police station and you can tell the cops all about it?"

He looked at me for a while, figuring it all out before he spoke.

"How about it?" I said evenly.

Reineer's concerned look changed to a wide grin. "You may be a hell of an attorney, Dobbs, but you're a piss-poor bluffer."

"Bluffer!" I paused to let the word rumble about in his head. "Just try me."

Reineer reached over the dresser and pulled aside the curtain and looked outside. He had to be sure no one else was around.

"Enough of your bullshit!" he shouted as he let go of the curtain. "I only went along with you this long because I figure I owe you."

"You don't owe me shit. I wanted you to rot in that place for the rest of your life."

Reineer took another step back, but came to an immediate halt when I clutched his neckalce with both hands.

"You've made your point and I hope your conscience feels better for it," he said. "But why don't you just give it to me and I'll be on my way?"

I dismissed him with a wave of my hand. "Go to hell."

His face reddened. He lifted his hand over his head and slammed it on the top of the dresser. "You of all people should know what I'm capable of."

"I'm well aware. But I'm a lot bigger than the fifty- or sixty-pound children you're used to."

Reineer turned abruptly to his left, opened the

closet door, and pulled out the machete he'd used to trim Christmas trees.

"And the bigger they are, the more they bleed," he said and lifted the huge blade over his head.

"If you really want it that bad." I held the necklace out to him. "But first put the machete down."

His eyes glued to the necklace, Reineer lowered the blade and rested it against the wall, sharp tip down. That way he had quick access in case I changed my mind.

I walked forward, but stopped when I was within a few feet of him. "Here," I said and tossed him the necklace. "For whatever good it will do you."

Reineer closed his eyes and took a deep breath, clutching the necklace tightly with both hands against his chest. It was as if he was receiving some kind of power from it. After a moment his eyes jerked open.

"Where the hell is it?"

I shrugged. "I don't know what you're talking about."

He grabbed the machete and advanced on me. "You're a damn liar!"

I reached for the gun. "Drop it!"

Reineer stopped short. His gaze darted about the room as if he were unsure what to do next. Finally he let the machete fall to the floor with a loud clang.

"Kick it under the bed."

Reineer slowly slid his foot to the side and with one swipe kicked the machete. It slid across the wooden floor under the bed. It clinked as it collided against the wall.

"Now tell me what you did with it," he said.

I lowered the barrel and pointed it toward the head of the bed. "Is that what you're referring to?"

Resting in the middle of a pillow, like an egg on a satin cushion, was the small agate marble I'd taken from his necklace. Gary Cosgrove's marble.

As he stepped toward it, my grip tightened. "Don't move."

Reineer's stare remained fixed on the marble. "You know I'll never leave without it."

I raised the gun and stepped closer until the end of the barrel was no more than a foot from his face. "I know you won't."

"Please," he said and dropped to his knees. I shoved the gun to his forehead. His hands, then arms began to tremble. Within seconds his whole body was shaking violently, nearly convulsing.

"Did those children have to beg?" I said. Just at the thought of it I could feel nausea pushing against my throat. "Did you make them beg for their lives just like you're begging now?"

I slowly pushed the gun forward. The pressure of the barrel caused the top of his head to tilt upward. I could see his eyes. I cocked the hammer—a loud click. He flinched.

"You should be so lucky." I backed up toward the head of the bed and placed the tip of the barrel against the marble.

With a panicked look, Reineer screamed, "What are you going to do?"

"Destroy something you fear losing more than your own life."

I pulled the trigger. The marble exploded into a cloud of fine dust, except for a small fleck that hit the corner of my eye. When I reflexively reached for my face, Reineer vaulted head first into my stomach. I fell backward onto the floor, where we struggled as he tried to grab the gun from my hand. A loud popping sound was immediately followed by a horrific burning sensation in my left bicep. My whole upper arm felt as if it was on fire—the muscles went limp. The gun fell from my grasp.

I tried to stand, but could only get as far as my knees. When I looked up, I saw Reineer standing over me. With the gun in his hand. He had a bead on my head.

"You have no idea what you just did," he said and glanced at the agate dust all over the bed. "You have no idea."

As quickly as the pain had shot through my arm, it just as quickly diminished. It felt like a heavy brick was dangling from my shoulder.

I tried to push myself into Reineer's gut the same way he had to me. But my legs were too rubbery. I ended up on the cold wooden floor, facedown in a pool of my own blood. When I sat up, I could barely make out Reineer's hand—with the shiny gun in it—smashing into the side my head.

Chapter 43

My eyes opened to blackness. I was entombed in a thick gritty liquid. I tried to breathe, but the mixture filled my mouth, then my lungs. My whole body began to heave. I was disoriented, unable to tell top from bottom. I frantically flailed and thrashed about, searching for air. Suddenly, I felt lightheaded, every limb too heavy to move. Before I faded into unconsciousness, a last thought bubbled to the surface: That maniac Reineer got away with it, after all.

I was lying on my side, gasping for air. A heavy rain pelted my face, clearing the mud from my eyes. That's when I saw Reineer standing directly above me. Behind him—resting on a large flat rock—was Avery's gun.

"I'll bet that scared the living shit out of you," he said, looking at the hole he'd pulled me from. "Would have left you there, but you were in the way."

Confused, not knowing what he meant, I strained to see where we were. Except for the headlights of his car, shining directly on us, there was total darkness.

"Don't get any ideas," he said, seeing me eye the gun again. He grabbed the handle of a shovel, stuck blade first in the wet dirt, and jumped into the hole.

He looked at the swampy hole, which was halfway between his knees and waist. "Bet you really feel stupid," he said. "You almost drowned in a couple feet of water."

Reineer poked around the mire with his shovel. I tried to ask him where we were, but I only managed a gurgle and then coughed up black gunk. After several more jabs, he set his feet and began to dig—always making sure he threw the excess mud in my direction.

As I floundered in the mud he was tossing at me, I couldn't help but think about how my plan hadn't worked. It seemed simple enough. I'd get Reineer's necklace, remove Gary Cosgrove's marble from it, then give it back to Reineer minus the marble. I was sure that before he left the county, he'd go to wherever the poor boy was hidden or buried. If someone like McBean, or one of his cohorts, followed Reineer, they'd catch him red-handed.

With a bullet hole in my arm, it was painfully obvious that the plan had one major flaw. Me. Why did I have to overplay my hand and dramatize the fact that Reineer needed to replace the damn marble? How could I have been so stupid? Why didn't I just toss Reineer the necklace and order him to leave? McBean could have taken it from there. That's when it occurred to me. Where in the hell was McBean? My only hope was that he was out there somewhere in the darkness just waiting for the right moment.

But I couldn't take that chance. Even though I was weak and groggy, I had to try to make a run for it.

"Not such a bad place to spend the rest of eternity," Reineer said and rested his chin on the handle of the shovel. "But it's too bad you'll have to share it with somebody."

He resumed his digging.

It was now or never.

Though my left arm was useless, I awkwardly struggled to my feet. When I pushed off, my pivot foot slipped and I ended up flat in the mud. Unsure if Reineer had noticed, I tried it again. Halfway up, a powerful whack to the side of my head spun me to the ground.

Dazed, trying to focus, I could barely see his face next to mine. Reineer had swung the shovel so hard, he'd lost his balance.

"I wouldn't try that again," he said as he rose, wiping the mud from his face.

"Or what? You'll kill me?"

"That's the attitude, Dobbs," he chuckled. "A soldier to the end."

That was the first time I'd ever heard him laugh. It didn't suit him. But Reineer was in his glory. He was free and had his good-luck charms around his neck which, I was afraid, he'd planned on adding to before the night was over. He was one happy psycho.

"But why out here? Why didn't you kill me back at the house?"

"Couldn't leave any evidence." He jumped back into the hole. "Have to make sure there's no corpus delecti."

I knew full well what he meant. Without a body—or any direct evidence of death—it was difficult if not impossible to arrest a suspect, let alone convict one.

"How do you think I've been getting away with it all these years?"

"Your luck will run out."

Reineer laughed in between tosses of mud. "There's no luck to it. . . . I'm immune."

"Because of that necklace?"

His face went blank. "What about my necklace?"

"Just that you're nothing without those souvenirs," I said. "You think if you were to die without every one of them, you'd rot in hell."

Reineer smiled. "I'm going to rot in hell no matter what."

He poked the shovel several times next to where he'd been digging and dropped to his knees. With the mud above his waist, he reached down, clawing like a dog searching for a lost bone.

"Gotcha, you little bugger," he said and slowly lifted a partially decomposed human head. I was sure it was Gary Cosgrove's.

I watched as he slowly rotated the head in front of his face. I almost gagged as the hair and scalp slipped from the rotting skull, dropping into the muddy water below.

"Say hello to the Boonville boy."

"You're insane," I said as he revered his prize a few moments longer.

Reineer tossed it back into the hole. "He's sure not as cute as he used to be."

I looked around for some sign of McBean. He had to be out there somewhere. Knowing him, he was probably enjoying watching me squirm.

Reineer reached down and feverishly searched the boy's pants as he straddled the rest of his remains. "Here it is." He held up a small pouch for me to see. He then loosened the drawstring, opened it, and withdrew a marble—similar to the one I'd blasted. He put it in his pocket and was about to drop the pouch back into the hole, when he gripped it tightly. "Better not take any chances," he said and jammed the pouch of marbles into his coat pocket. "I don't want to ever have to do this again."

Reineer climbed out of the hole. "Now it's your turn," he said, fingering the necklace. "But first tell me what *you* have for me."

"I thought you only took souvenirs from little kids?"

"Of course not," he said like I should know better. "I'm responsible for everyone's souls. And everyone's responsible for mine." A devil-like grin crossed his face. "Like my mother, it doesn't matter how old they are."

"And like Bobby Miles?"

"Exactly," he said and rubbed Bobby's gold band, which he'd already removed from his teeth and attached to the leather strap. "Although, killing him did bother me."

I found it hard to believe that killing anybody or anything would ever faze him—he was so clearly, so dangerously, insane. "Why would killing a man bother you more than killing a child?"

Reineer chuckled. "No, no, no, you're misunderstanding me," he said and walked to his car. "It only bothered me because I couldn't hide his body."

He opened the car door and leaned inside, searching. "I killed him because he ratted. Remember? He was my gift to you."

"You're full of shit," I shouted as he walked back carrying something shiny. "You killed him because you knew he never had a chance to tell anyone that he'd been lying about me all along. He was going to clear me."

"Doesn't matter anymore," Reineer said and stopped next to me. He lifted the shiny object he'd just taken from the car—a large buck knife.

Standing above me, Reineer grabbed my hair with his free hand. He was going to take my scalp just like his mother's.

If McBean waited another second, I'd be a goner.

"You won't get away with this," I said, trying to buy more time. "The cops are watching you right now."

"Cops?" he said as though he was going to humor me this one last time.

"McBean," I said. "He followed you out here."

Reineer let go of my hair and laughed all the way back to his car. He opened the trunk and reached inside. "I'll bet you thought he was going to save you," he said and pulled something up from the trunk. It was McBean's head.

"Sorry, Counselor, but it looks like he's in worse

shape than you are. . . . He's not going to be much help."

Reineer pulled McBean from the trunk and dropped him headfirst into the mud. I heard a faint moan. He was alive. But barely—like me—and not for long.

Reineer walked toward me. His crazed look sent ripples of fear throughout my body.

"A bone from your body would look good on my necklace," he said nonchalantly. Then, with a sudden fury, Reineer jumped on me. As we wrestled in the mud, he grabbed my injured arm's hand by the index finger. I struggled to pull away as he lifted the knife over his head. I felt the whoosh of air beside my cheek when he swiped at my hand with the knife—his grip broke loose along with my finger.

In the mud, I convulsed in pain. My hand was burning as though it was submerged in boiling water. The pain was screaming up the same arm which only moments before had had no feeling at all.

"You won't be needing this," he said and dropped my finger into the pouch, along with the boy's marbles. He then grabbed my hair and dragged me to the edge of the hole where he held my face in front of his.

"Anything you want to say?" he asked and forced me into a kneeling position. I looked down into the hole to see where I'd end up. Floating beneath me was what was left of the boy's head, the brown leathery skin glistening from the falling rain, his hair and scalp floating next to it.

"Rot in hell!" I yelled. Reineer grinned as he

jerked my head back by the hair and shoved the barrel of the gun against it. Our eyes locked for the last time.

He cocked the firing pin. I instinctively flinched at the sound of the loud, deafening blast. Suddenly, I was covered by a warm liquid. Then I felt him let go. I opened my eyes. Lying next to me was what was left of Reineer. His head was gone. Nothing remained but the bloody stump of his neck.

The crazy bastard was dead.

I looked up, wiping Reineer's blood from my eyes. Standing above him was Otto Cosgrove cradling a shotgun in his arms. He was starring blankly into the hole where his son's jaw was still jutting upward.

"That's my boy in there," was all the big man said before he dropped to his knees and sobbed like a baby.

Chapter 44

"It's just like Patterson to keep me waiting for my own hanging."

Sarah looked stunning, dressed in a mauve suede suit. Except for a small scar under her left ear, there was no way to detect she'd been in a horrific accident less than a month before.

"Any feeling yet?" She'd noticed me massaging what was left of my finger.

I waffled my hand. "Now and then," I said, looking at it.

With my arm in a sling, I'd helped Avery prepare his trees for Christmas harvest. One-handed, I'd attacked his trees like an old hired hand. Surprisingly, I'd actually enjoyed the physical labor. Or maybe it was the company of Sarah and her father I liked so much. Avery and I had become friends, best of friends. Sarah and I became lovers. Etched in my memory forever is each and every moment I've been fortunate enough to spend with her—except for the "Chivas night," as I think of it. Although, I never did admit to her that I don't remember what happened that night, I think she knows.

We were in Department D of the San Francisco Superior Courthouse, waiting for my trial to begin. Avery was seated directly behind us, looking worried. Our biggest concern was that I was our only witness. It was actually more than a concern—it was a problem. There wasn't a juror in the state who felt a defense attorney's word was worth a hoot. My only consolation was that Patterson wasn't in much better shape. All he had was the preliminary hearing transcript of a scared-to-death drug dealer. It would have been fun if it wasn't my ass on the line.

The back doors were opened, and Sarah and I looked over our shoulders to see if Patterson had finally decided to show up. But it was Steve Ogden, my boss. He walked straight up to Avery and they shook hands, exchanging greetings like old buds.

All of us came to attention as the bailiff announced that Judge William McConnell was taking the bench. As soon as he sat in his huge leather chair, the judge's eyes shifted about the courtroom and finally settled on the seat normally occupied by the district attorney. "Where's Patterson?" he barked at his clerk.

The young lady shrugged and the judge scowled. She must have known what that look meant because she picked up the phone and started punching in the D.A.'s telephone number. Before she finished, her head quickly turned to the rear of the courtroom. She slammed the receiver into its cradle as she watched Patterson rush down the center aisle.

"Mr. Patterson," the judged snarled, "I'm happy

to see you finally decided to grace us with your presence. If this is any indication of—" McConnell stopped short when Patterson held up his hand to indicate he had something to say.

The judge grimaced. If Patterson had tried a case in the last ten years, he would've known judges didn't like to be interrupted.

"If I may, Your Honor," he said in a conciliatory voice, "I apologize for being late, but I've been interviewing a witness who has just come forward with new information. It may have a critical impact on the outcome of this case."

Sarah jumped to her feet. "I've not been told about any new information," she said. "The trial is scheduled to begin today, and my client will not waive time just so Mr. Patterson can piece together a case he should have prepared for weeks ago."

McConnell nodded his head. "I agree with Miss Harris," he said to Patterson. "Unless you have a strong offer of proof as to why you are coming forward with new information at the start of trial, I may not allow it."

The D.A. paused to glance at the back doors. "I'm afraid there's a misunderstanding."

"There's no misunderstanding. The defense is ready—" Sarah stopped in midsentence when the back doors burst open.

It was McBean.

His jaw had been shattered when Reineer took a tire iron to it. Like me, McBean was lucky to be alive.

"What's he doing here?" Sarah mouthed as he

and Patterson stepped toward one another. They met in the middle of the aisle and began to whisper.

I shrugged. His presence was as much a surprise to me as it was to her. But knowing McBean, he was up to something.

"Mr. Patterson," the judged coaxed.

The D.A. held up his hand for the second time. "One moment."

Patterson and McBean spent the next few minutes engrossed in a conversation. Every so often one of them would glance at me. I could tell by the way McBean's mouth barely moved that it was still wired shut. Finally, they separated and McBean took a seat in the gallery behind Patterson. He was ready to address the court.

McConnell's eyes fixed on McBean, then Patterson. "Is he your new evidence?" the judge asked, nodding at McBean.

"Actually, he is," Patterson said. The judge grimaced. McConnell had been sitting on the superior court bench for more than twenty years, and he was well aware of McBean's reputation.

"Is Mr. McBean still involved in law enforcement?"

"He's a detective lieutenant in Mendocino County."

McConnell nodded; his expression said, "I was afraid of that."

"Lieutenant McBean has supplied me with new information which goes to the heart of this case." Patterson turned to me and either sneered or smiled. I couldn't tell which.

"It appears," he continued, "that Lieutenant

McBean interviewed Bobby Miles just prior to his death."

"That's bullshit," I said to Sarah and she jumped to her feet again.

"That would have had to occur more than a month ago," she snapped. "Even if the lieutenant did talk to Mr. Miles, it's a little late to be coming into court with whatever that young man may or may not have said."

"Counsel!" Patterson glared at Sarah. "If you'd just let me finish."

I glared at McBean and he answered with the same expression Patterson had given me earlier. And I was still confused by it.

"Go ahead," McConnell said, waving the D.A. on.

"Mr. Bobby Miles informed Lieutenant McBean that the accusations he'd made against Mr. Dobbs, including his testimony at the preliminary hearing, were entirely false."

I stiffened as Sarah grabbed my arm, digging her fingernails into my skin.

"Mr. Miles informed the lieutenant that he'd lied because of the threats made against his life by members of Salvador Martinez's gang. Who, I might add," Patterson said for my benefit, "was just last week convicted of a double homicide."

Patterson turned to me and offered up a smile; I was sure this time. "There is a People's motion to dismiss all charges against Mr. Hunter Dobbs."

McConnell didn't hesitate. "Granted," he said, rapping his gavel once for effect. "Case dismissed." The judge looked at me with a broad grin. "Mr. Dobbs, you're free to go."

Sarah and I embraced. "Can you believe it?" she said.

Avery grabbed my shoulder from behind. "Congratulations," he said. I extended my hand, which he promptly pushed aside. He wrapped his arms around the two of us and gave what could best be described as a bear hug.

"Thank you, Avery," I said as we parted. "I don't know what I would have done without the two of you."

I looked for McBean, but he was gone.

Ogden, who'd been standing a few feet away approached us with a timid grin. "It looks like I'll have to reschedule the office's case load. Have to make room for my number one trial attorney."

The dismissal had come as a surprise. I hadn't given much thought to what I'd do once the trial was over.

"As a matter of fact," Ogden added, "there's a murder trial beginning in a couple weeks that I think you're perfect for."

There was an awkward silence as I pondered what Ogden was saying. Both Sarah and Avery looked at me.

"I don't think so," I finally said.

Ogden's mouth dropped. He looked blankly at Avery. He offered no help.

"The Christmas tree harvest is in full swing," I continued. "I'm too busy to handle a murder case."

Ogden nodded. "Well," he said, "I guess I can live with that. I'll just hold your slot open until after the first of the year."

I placed my arm around Sarah's waist and we

gave each other a knowing glance. "No need," I said. "There's a one-person law firm in Ukiah that won't be handling any more criminal law. . . . I'll be applying there."